PERFECTIONS

KIRSTYN McDERMOTT

Second edition published in Australia in May 2014
by Twelfth Planet Press

www.twelfthplanetpress.com

This novel © 2014 Kirstyn McDermott

Design and layout by Amanda Rainey
Typeset in Sabon MT Pro

National Library of Australia Cataloguing-in-Publication entry (pbk)

Author: McDermott, Kirstyn, author.

Title: Perfections / Kirstyn McDermott.

Edition: Second edition.

ISBN: 9781922101174 (paperback)

Subjects: Fantasy fiction.

Dewey Number: A823.4

For my own dear sisters,
Emmelene and Danielle,
with all my love
and absolutely no subtext.

xxx

1

Antoinette watches her sister swing the suitcase from the back seat, almost expecting that slim, white wrist to flex and snap beneath the weight. *Two Minute Passenger Drop Off Zone*, the sign beside them declares, and even this early in the morning there's a line of cars impatient for their turn.

'He knows how to pick his moments,' Jacqueline mutters, smoothing her skirt as she straightens. Then, almost an afterthought: 'Bastard.'

Antoinette smiles, or tries to, tries to force the corners of her mouth to lift despite the grief still lodged in her throat. Because if she doesn't smile, she's going to cry, and she's done far too much of that already. No, she needs to keep it together. The drive back from the airport will be long and lonely enough; if the tears start again now they might never stop.

'Ant, I'm sorry about this.' Jacqueline pushes a stray curl back behind Antoinette's ear. 'If I could cancel the trip, even delay it a week or two...'

'No, it's okay, I'll be okay.' But it isn't, and she won't be.

'Tell me,' Jacqueline says. 'Tell me what you need.'

What she needs? What she *needs* is for her sister to stay right here in Melbourne. To sit with her and rub her back in slow, soothing circles. To tell her not only that everything will be fine, but exactly how it will be so, and when. Just like she always has, since forever. No matter the crisis—broken doll or skinned knee, failed exam or disastrous haircut—Jacqueline always knows how to fix it, always knows exactly what to say to make Antoinette feel better.

Except this time she's leaving.

Off to Brisbane to mollycoddle some artist on behalf of the stupid gallery she works for—on a *Saturday* for crying out loud—and god knows how long she'll be away. Antoinette has known about it for days, of course she has, but with everything that happened last night, with Paul's final words looping on constant rotation through her head—

And here it is again, the bitter-sharp edge of tears.

'Well.' Jacqueline smiles, brief and sardonic. 'If it gets too lonely at my place, you can always go stay with our mother for a while.'

'Yeah, there's always that.' Antoinette smiles too, because it really is laughable, the idea of running back home to their mother with her unvoiced I-told-you-so's and weak herbal teas, her pity-soaked looks and the inevitable list of chores and time-sapping suggestions which would be drawn up and stuck to the fridge. *Stay busy*, their mother's timeworn motto. *Keep your hands working and your mind distracted and soon you won't even remember why you were so upset in the first place.*

Self-imposed amnesia: Sally Paige's solution to all manner of ills.

'It'll be okay,' Antoinette says again. 'I should probably start looking for some place to live, anyway.'

Jacqueline frowns. 'Don't feel rushed into anything; you know you're welcome to stay as long as you need. You still have the spare key?'

Antoinette nods. 'Don't worry about me.'

Please worry about me.

Behind them, a car horn bleats and Jacqueline glances at her watch, sunlight glinting off classic marquisette, and she's really sorry, she says, but she can't miss her plane. Time for one last hug, and Antoinette holds on tight, presses her face into the thick, silk-dark swathe of her sister's hair, not wanting to ever let go, to ever *be* let go. But Jacqueline's already pulling away, walking away, navy blue trolley case nipping at her heels, and just as those huge glass doors slide open to swallow her, she turns, one hand lifting.

'Call me if you need anything, Ant.'

I need you to stay.

A wish too impossible to voice, so instead she just waves, waves as Jacqueline strides into the airport and out of sight, waves as the driver behind her leans on his horn yet again, waves until her arm aches to be lowered.

And waving still, deep down inside where the hurt blooms boldest, as she slides into her empty car and reaches for the key left waiting in the ignition.

Please. I need someone to stay.

Jacqueline tugs her seatbelt tighter. Stares out of the window at the tarmac too far below. Her fingers dig reflexively into the armrests.

'Are you scared of planes?' The little boy next to her is four or five years old. There are two teeth missing from his grin. 'I'm not scared of nothing!'

'Really?' Jacqueline says. 'Not of anything?'

The woman in the aisle seat sighs and pats him on the knee. 'Don't be making a nuisance of yourself, Caleb. Leave the nice lady alone.' She's much older than Jacqueline, perhaps in her late forties. Mother or grandmother; it's difficult to tell.

'It's all right,' Jacqueline says. 'He isn't bothering me.'

'You want him then?' the woman replies, deadpan. 'Free to good home.'

'Oh, ah…'

'Mum-mee!' the boy wails. He tugs at the woman's sleeve. 'Stop it!'

'Caleb, if you promise to sit very still and not say another word for ten whole minutes, you can have a lolly.' The boy's eyes light up. He starts to open his mouth but his mother shakes her head. 'Not. Another. Word.'

He presses his lips together. Zips a pinched finger and thumb across them.

'I take it back.' His mother winks. 'Free to *any* home.'

Jacqueline isn't sure whether she's supposed to laugh or not. She wishes Ant was here. Her sister knows how to make small talk. To banter easily with strangers she'll never see again. Jacqueline can never think of the right words to say or even see a reason for saying them. Perhaps she should have asked Ant to come along. Perhaps a few days in Brisbane would have been good for her. It might have helped take her mind off that idiot, Paul. Or at least made sure she didn't go running back to him at the first hint of an excuse.

Caleb tugs his mother's sleeve again. She rolls her eyes. 'What?'

'How-do-I-know-when-is-ten-minutes?' he whispers, running the words together in a single anxious breath.

'Look.' She shows him her wristwatch. 'When that big hand is on the number seven, okay? That will be ten minutes. Now, shush.'

The boy zips his mouth again.

'Don't worry,' his mother says to Jacqueline. 'He's a pretty good flier.'

Jacqueline smiles.

'It was always the thing I dreaded most about flying, being stuck near some screaming kid. Used to put my teeth on edge. Funny thing, it doesn't seem to bother me so much, now I got one of my own.'

'It's fine, honestly.' She grabs the inflight magazine from her seat pocket. Pretends to find something of interest within its glossy pages. It's not the flying part she hates so much as the feeling of being trapped. Surrounded by people she doesn't know how to read or relate to. It's exhausting, the need to be always on her guard. To be constantly on show. Not for the first time, she wishes Dante had decided to go to Brisbane himself. Not that her boss would ever deign to do his own grovelling.

Better you than me, babe. Catch more flies with honey, and I don't think my sweet arse will likely interest the dude.

The dude. Ryan Jellicoe. Dante's latest Great Undiscovered, or near enough, with his first solo show—his first show outside of Brisbane at all—due to open in less than six weeks. Only there hasn't been a single progress report since the contracts were signed. Not a sketch or a photograph or even a synopsis of what the artist is actually planning to put together. His phone has been off for weeks and the daily volley of emails Dante insists she send remains unanswered. And so, this rescue mission. Carrots and sticks and Jacqueline on orders to flush Ryan Jellicoe from his hidey-hole no matter what.

Get up there, Jacks. Get your face in his face and make sure those paintings are damn well done.

Jacks. She grinds her teeth on the nickname. It's what you would call a dog, or the latest whizz-bang antibacterial home cleaning product.

Beside her, Caleb is kicking the back of the seat in front of him. Light taps, born less of malice than boredom, but his mother leans over and stills them. She frowns and shakes her head. Lifts a finger to her lips. The boy sighs loudly and crosses his arms. Puffs air into his cheeks like a bullfrog.

Jacqueline smiles, half to the boy, half to herself. She turns back to the window as the plane accelerates down the runway. They lift into the air and the outer suburbs of Melbourne fall further and further away. This far from the city, it's all housing estates. Two-storey dollhouses cluster around fresh new cul-de-sacs. Satellite dishes mushroom on every rooftop. Matchbox cars dot the driveways. *Cookie-cutter lives*, Ant calls them, and Jacqueline can see her point. But still. She tries to picture herself in such a world. House, husband, children—children like Caleb, still kicking his feet beside her—the whole perfect, prefabricated package. Rules to follow. Patterns to keep. An order to be maintained. How easy it would be to lose herself in that.

Jacqueline swallows. Closes her eyes.

And then what? People around her all day, every day. Watching with their sharp, assessing eyes. Judging what kind of a mother she was. How well-behaved the children, how well they were dressed and schooled and fed. Honestly, how long would she last before the cracks began to widen and split? How long before she—

Her stomach cramps. Pain stabs beneath her ribs.

She gasps, doubling over as much as the economy seating will allow, the taste of metal rising in the back of her throat. She'd hoped they were done with, these spasms which have plagued her for the past couple of months, but apparently not. Dry mouthed, fingers pressed to her temples, she takes slow, deep breaths, bracing herself for the familiar swell of nausea. Everything is pressing too close, stifling and claustrophobic. The roar of the plane's engine is too loud. It's too much to bear; any second now she will fly apart, fall apart and—

be calm be quiet be still

The voice doesn't belong to her, isn't anything like the voice she sometimes uses to talk to herself inside her head, but she feels like she knows it. Has always known it, right from the very first time she heard it, *felt* it echoing up from the back of her skull. All those weeks ago, lying curled on the kitchen tiles that seemed to slope beneath her grasping hands. Nothing in her head but that voice. *This* voice.

be calm be quiet be still

Strong words, commanding words, and Jacqueline tries to focus on them. Tries to use them as anchors to keep her here. To keep her now. She doesn't realise how hard she's been chewing on the inside of her cheek until she tastes blood. At last, the pain eases and her breathing slows.

Control, she tells herself. *Control.*

'Are you okay?'

Caleb's mother is leaning over, her brow creased with concern. Her son is staring at Jacqueline with wide, dark eyes. One little fist is bunched into his mouth. Saliva glistens on his skin.

Jacqueline makes herself sit up. 'I'm fine.' She straightens her skirt. Tucks her hair behind her ears. 'Just a ... a headache. All of a sudden.'

'Do you need anything? Should I call someone?'

'No, I'm fine.' She swallows. Knots her hands together to keep them from trembling.

'I have some Panadol in my bag,' the woman says.

'Thank you, but I really am fine.' She forces herself to smile. To make it seem warm, grateful for the offer. 'I just need to rest my eyes for a while.'

'Mummy,' Caleb whispers. 'Is the lady sick?'

'No, honey, she just needs to have a nap.'

'Is it ten minutes yet?'

'Oh, Caleb. Here.' She digs into her jacket pocket. Pulls out a packet of brightly coloured jelly snakes and holds it out to her son. 'Just one now.' Her eyes don't move from Jacqueline's face. 'You're sure you're okay?'

'I'll be fine.' Jacqueline leans back in her seat. Even with her eyes closed she can feel the woman staring at her. Can feel the boy fidgeting in his seat as he sucks on his lolly. She tries not to move. Tries to keep her breathing even and regular, as though it's a test she needs to pass.

Stop looking at me. I'm normal. I'm fine. Stop looking at me.

She's exhausted. Worn and frayed and close to falling apart. She should see someone, she knows that. Push past the paranoia she shares with her mother when it comes to doctors and hospitals, and find out what's wrong. When she gets back perhaps. If she has time. If she isn't feeling better by then. If the ... *episodes* haven't stopped of their own accord. She could tell Ant about it.

Leave it to her sister to make the requisite appointments. Perhaps with Ant at her side, she'll be able to force herself to walk into a waiting room. Perhaps—

Stop it. Running in circles won't get you there any sooner.

Jacqueline presses her cheek to the window pane. The surface is cool against her skin. She tries to think about nothing at all until they land.

Antoinette swears and pulls over to the side of the road, slaps the steering wheel hard. 'Idiot,' she tells herself. Too busy thinking about Paul—trying *not* to think about Paul—driving on autopilot since the airport and now she's here, less than fifteen minutes from home without even realising it. Home; hardly. Paul made that only too clear, and now she'll have to fight cross-town traffic to get back over to Jacqueline's.

'Idiot,' she repeats, softer this time.

Again, wishing her sister was here to keep her company, to keep her mind off the Paul-shaped hole that yawns in her guts. Tonight will be okay, she's working the dinner shift at Simpatico, six until one or even later, and the trendy South Melbourne restaurant will be packed to its usual Saturday night capacity. No chance to worry about anything apart from how rare Table 14 are wanting their steak, or why Table 3 haven't yet received their mains when they'd been ordered several lifetimes ago, honeydoll, and does she think she can manage to hustle her pretty arse back to the kitchen and bring them something to eat before Christmas?

Until then the day stretches ahead of her, blank and unbearable.

If yesterday hadn't happened, she and Paul would probably be having brunch right now, maybe planning to watch a movie later that afternoon, *Casablanca* or *Dracula* or *Whatever Happened to Baby Jane*, some old monochromatic favourite they could laugh and quote their way through. Or maybe Jai would drop by to read them some of his pretentious uber-emo poetry and moan about how he still couldn't get anything published, and *thank god* they'd laugh after he left; the world wasn't ready for Jai. Then Paul would ask if she *really* had to work that night, and she'd sigh and tell him yes, she'd already promised, careful not to mention how she'd asked for the shift specially because Simpatico pays excellent weekend wages and their money situation was a little tight this month.

And what will he do about such tawdry matters now?

Antoinette shakes her head. Why should she care? He's the one who ended it, he's the bad guy here. Paul, with that ugly sneer curling his lip as he leaned against their bedroom door, watching her stuff things at random into her overnight bag, sobs caught silent in her throat.

Might as well take it all, Ant, don't think you're coming back.

She wants to hate him, *needs* to hate him. Needs something more than anger and betrayal and the hollow scrape of loss, something that will cut through the love that sits stubborn in her heart. Four years worth of love, after all, four years of curling her arms about his waist, feeling his lips pressed against her throat—can she really expect that to vanish in a breath?

Can she expect it to vanish ever?

Never should have trusted you, Ant. You've always been so fucking resentful.

Maybe just a little. All those long nights waiting tables, her feet red and aching from hours spent in heels too cheap for the wear she puts them through, because the bills had to be paid somehow. By someone. Paul at home with his laptop, expensive cigarettes and fresh-ground coffee from the boutique café around the corner—*necessary evils, Ant, can't think without them*—with the odd payment that came in for reviews or articles slipping straight back out again. A new CD, a couple of books, the leather coat he refused to return.

So, yes, maybe a little resentful.

But what of it? She isn't a saint, and martyrdom was never part of their deal. Isn't it enough that she put her whole bloody life on hold for him, that it was her dumb idea in the first place? Such naive, besotted notions of self-sacrifice; everyone tried to tell her so. Even Paul gave her a chance to back out.

You sure about this, Ant? It might take me a year or two.

But she never doubted his talent. Not from the very first time she heard him read—a spoken word night in the little Belgrave café where she worked at the time—his story a kind of urban fairytale, reworked and jagged, catching right at her core. She put down her pad and clapped along with everyone else at the end, but hers were the eyes he looked into, hers the smile he mirrored. And when her shift was over, he was waiting by the bar, all soft hands and eyeliner, wanting to buy her a drink.

Falling in love was *that* easy.

And it made everything else seem easy as well. In less than two months—dizzying, heart-in-mouth months—she had moved in with Paul, counting the sudden departure of his flatmate as a portent, despite the furious protests of her mother. Because she loved him. And it was because she loved him, because she couldn't bear to see him slumped over his laptop each night, exhausted and demoralised after selling mobile phones to idiots all day, that she offered.

Quit your stupid job. Concentrate on your book.

Because she loved him. Because she believed in him. Never doubting that his novel-in-progress would be magnificent, a masterpiece, if only he was given the time and space to finish it. Not a single doubt. Not once. Not ever.

Until three months ago, when she snuck her first peek at his manuscript.

If only she hadn't. If only—

Antoinette clenches her jaw. Enough. It's over, *they* are over. Four years shredded to ruin overnight, and why can't she hate him for it? Even the tiniest spark of loathing would do.

'I hate him,' she whispers. 'I hate you, Paul.'

The words even *taste* empty.

'Oh, for godsake.' Do something, girlie-girl, do anything.

Antoinette tugs her mobile from her jeans pocket and calls her home number, her *old* home number. The sound of ringing is distant in her ear and she taps the steering wheel, come on, come on, pick up the bloody phone.

'Hey.'

'Paul, it's—'

'This is Paul, leave a message or whatever and I'll call you when I can.'

A pause, then that familiar mechanised beep which throws Antoinette so completely off kilter that she can't speak, can only gasp mutely into the handset for what seems like minutes until finally, *finally*, her tongue finds the words.

'Paul, um, hi. It's me, it's Ant. Look I … I'm going to come over, okay? I need to pick up some more stuff, so if you're there, um, if you get this before … look, I'm coming over. Do what you want.'

Blood rushes to her cheeks as she flips the phone shut.

He changed the message. Paul, who will wade waist-high through rubbish rather than empty the garbage bin, who will happily wear the same rancid boxer shorts for a week if the alternative means putting on a washload, who constantly litters the place with half-read books because he can't be bothered returning them to the shelves. This very same Paul has gone to the trouble of recording a brand new message onto their answering machine.

Has deleted her voice, her name, her existence.

In less than twenty-four hours.

Antoinette rubs at her eyes. Sags back into the seat as tears spill fresh down her cheeks. She's tired, so utterly tired of the whole bloody thing. God, how she wishes Jacqueline were here. She'd know what to do, she *always* knows. Jacqueline, princess of poise, queen of control. *She* certainly wouldn't be sitting here, blubbering all over the place like a big fat baby.

A giggle catches in Antoinette's throat, escapes as a hiccup. The very idea of her sister in such a state is ludicrous; if Jacqueline has let slip even a single, solitary tear since the age of about eight, Antoinette hasn't seen it. As for heartbreak, well. There has never been anyone romantic in Jacqueline's life. At least not anyone serious enough to merit more than a fleeting mention over lunch.

Do I get to meet him?

He's no one special.

Their standard sisterly call and response.

Jacqueline, have you ever been in love? Antoinette asked once, not long after meeting Paul, not long before she decided to move in with him. *So much in love you thought it might kill you?*

No, her sister replied. *I don't see the point.*

How can you say that? It's the whole *point. Of everything.*

Everything? Jacqueline frowned. *Seems like there should be more to it than that, Ant.*

Now, sitting amid the indifferent rush of traffic, Antoinette wipes her face on the sleeve of her shirt and sighs.

Seems like there should be a lot more.

2

Antoinette's about to slide the key into the lock when the front door swings suddenly inwards, and she bites her lip, spine straightening in reflex, only to find not Paul standing there, but Greta. Tall and curveless in clinging black lace, her glossy midnight bob even more severe than usual, one arm swaying in a studied gesture of listless welcome.

'Ant, I'm *aghast*.' Her lazy German accent thickens with emotion. 'Not you and Paul, of *all* people?'

'You've gotten the gory details, then,' Antoinette mutters as she walks into the flat. There's not much room in the entrance hall, not with all the books piled precariously high against one wall, so Greta steps backwards to let her pass, wobbling a little on her platform heels.

'I have heard Paul's *interpretation* of events.'

'Is he here?'

Greta blinks. 'Paul feels it might be *wise* if the two of you did not *see* each other so soon. Wounds still *wet*, ja? He wondered if

I would not *mind* being here for you instead.'

'What, did he think I would trash the place? Steal his precious vinyl collection?'

'Scheisse! Don't crucify the *messenger*, Ant.'

She's right, none of this is Greta's fault. But Antoinette can't help it; everything about the woman seems to grate. It always has, right from that very first night at Abyss with Paul so eager-pleased to introduce them and Greta smiling lean and cool, extending a black-nailed hand to clasp her own. *Enraptured to finally meet you, Ant.* Those grey eyes dark with shadow and fierce as kitten teeth. *Utterly enraptured.*

Antoinette tried to like the woman, if only for Paul's sake, but it was hard. Greta was hard. There was a veneer, impenetrable as one-way glass and twice as intimidating, which Antoinette never seemed to get beyond. And, of course, there was the Thing. The Greta-and-Paul Thing. Ancient history, each of them swore any time Antoinette brought it up, so she never found out what had really gone on between them, how serious it might have been, or exactly why it ended.

Greta and me work best as friends, Ant, that's all there is to it.

Paul belongs to you now, ja? So why all this stirring about at the past, like a child with a stick in a mud puddle? Why does it matter so dreadfully much?

Because of the glances swapped over drinks, the enigmatic smiles and private in-jokes. Paul and Greta. Greta and Paul. With Antoinette scraping handholds in the slim space between. She could never talk about it with Paul, and she sure as hell doesn't have to explain anything to Greta.

'I just need to grab some stuff, then I'm leaving,' she says, but Greta has her by the elbow and is moving with surprising swiftness into the kitchen where a bottle of Bacardi waits beside two half-filled glasses. She pulls out a chair.

'Here, sit down. Tell me all.'

'Greta, I really don't want—'

'But you *must*.' Her kohl-rimmed eyes are vulture-keen. 'You cannot keep this inside of you. It is *toxic*, it will *fester*. You need to *expel* it.'

'I already have. Jacqueline and me, we sat up for most of last night—'

'Mein Gott!' Greta laughs around the curve of her glass, leaving a red smear of lipstick like a fresh-made wound. 'That frigid little nun? What would *Jacqueline* know about love, what would *Jacqueline* know about heartbreak?'

Shut up, Antoinette wants to say, *don't talk about my sister like that*. But guilt pinches her tongue—hasn't she thought just the same thing herself, too many times to count? What *would* Jacqueline know?

'Please, Ant.' Greta takes her hand, traces a nail along the lines of her palm. 'We are friends, ja?'

Friends? Antoinette stares. Since when does Greta care if they are friends?

'Come. Tell me what has happened.'

KIRSTYN McDERMOTT

There's something different about the woman sitting across from her, an openness to that narrow, artfully made-up face that Antoinette hasn't seen before. And maybe it's because of this, and maybe it's because she really does want a chance to tell her side of the story, to balance out whatever poison Paul has been spilling in Greta's ear, that Antoinette sits back in her chair and takes a large gulp of rum.

'It wasn't planned,' she says. 'Remember a few months ago, that time I was really sick? I had to miss Jai's spoken word thing.'

Greta smirked. 'I thought that was simply a cover story.'

No, Antoinette tells her, she wishes. More like a chronic dose of stomach flu, stuck home for a week within stumbling distance of the bathroom and stir crazy after the third day. Paul deserting the flat each morning with his MacBook—*love you, Ant, but I can't work with you filling my space like this*—leaving her in the hands of boredom and bedbound curiosity. Easy enough to find the flashdrive where his backups were kept; even easier to sneak a copy onto her laptop.

'Such a *betrayal*.' Greta shakes her head.

'I just wanted to read the bloody thing,' Antoinette says. 'After all these years, I hadn't seen even a single sentence.'

'Because he did not want *anyone* to see this book until it was finished. Not you, not even me.'

Not even me. Antoinette lets that go, swallows another mouthful of rum instead. 'I know. But I just wanted to see.'

Greta leans forward. 'Tell me, is it very good, his book? What is it about?'

'It's about…' Antoinette shrugs. 'It's kind of an autobiography, I think. Names are changed, sometimes, but you can tell who he's writing about. Him and me—and you, Greta. Everyone we know is in that book, one way or another. It's not very flattering, and it's also … it's not very good.'

'So this is why? Because it doesn't *flatter* you?'

'No!' Antoinette fumbles for the right words. 'It's not what it's about, it's the way it's written. The writing itself is just … it's not good.'

'Who are you to decide this?'

'The one paying the bills while he sits on his butt and churns out that crap!'

'Ant!'

'I mean it, Greta, it's rubbish. No one who doesn't already know him would have a clue what he's on about, and even then it's just petty and pretentious and boring. No wonder he didn't want me to see it.'

'But he is not finished, it is not fair to judge him now.'

No, and that's what Antoinette told herself as she scrolled through the disjointed and rambling mess, the confusion of in-jokes and circular references: *it isn't finished, it isn't done.* And maybe it was because he was too closed in, too closed off, to see the truth of it. Maybe outside feedback was just what he needed. A fresh pair of eyes, a sympathetic edit even. And so.

'And so?' Greta echoes.

'I started to fiddle.'

Just small things, she hastens to explain. At least in the beginning. Rearranging sentences and resolving ambiguities, adding shades of clarity and trimming back where the writing seemed too overdone, too heavy-handed—and she always intended to tell him. Always. Even as the changes became more and more significant, even as characters were radically modified or replaced entirely, as superfluous scenes or chapters were deleted whole and absolute, she meant to tell him.

'It was just a matter of finding the right moment,' she says. 'I thought maybe we would sit down one day and go through it together.'

Greta raises a thinly plucked brow. 'Did you *really* think this would happen? That Paul would *thank* you for this *fiddling* of yours?'

Probably not, she admits, and maybe that's why it went so far. Sneaking sessions on her laptop whenever Paul was out of the flat, begging off nights out clubbing with friends on pretext of exhaustion, snatching all the time she could to type and type and type until ... until. It wasn't Paul's novel she was working on anymore; it was hers. A completely different beast to the one he'd originally conceived, different and—though she felt guilty even to think it—far better.

'Better?' Greta snorts. 'You told him this?'

'I didn't tell him anything,' Antoinette says. 'He didn't give me a chance.'

You thieving little bitch.

His lips twisting around the words as she came into the kitchen last night after work. Her laptop open on the table in front of him with what could only be one file splashed across its screen. *Paul*, his name barely out of her mouth before she saw what he was shifting from hand to clenching hand. One of the bookends Antoinette bought him last Christmas, a heavy slab of black marble with more sharp edges than not, and his face was so cold, so dark with menace, that she backed instinctively away as he raised his fist.

Paul. Wait, I—

Antoinette shrieked as he brought the thing down with a crash onto her laptop. Again and again and again, until the machine was nothing more than a dead, shattered screen amid a wreckage of cracked plastic and broken circuitry. And her novel dead along with it—she'd printed no hard copies, made no backups, because either of these would have made what she was doing too *real*. Which Paul must have guessed, to judge by the sneer on his face.

Was that important to you, Ant? As important as me?

Oh, so sick to her stomach then, and even now in the retelling.

'He didn't have to destroy it, Greta. It's not like I was going to try and publish it or anything, and he still has his version. This was just for me, you know, a private thing?' She sniffs, wipes her nose on her sleeve. 'It was the first time I've ever tried to write something like that. It was fun, more than fun, it was … something that was *mine*. Something that came from *me*. I felt like I was a kid again, making up stories and people and … I can't really explain it, how I felt, how good it made me feel. And now it's gone.'

'Ja, it was cruel, what he did.' Greta frowns, her chin dipping in a sharp little nod. 'But perhaps this can be *reconciled* as a sacrifice?'

'A sacrifice? Greta, what—'

'Ja, ja, a *sacrifice*.' She lifts her hand in a plea for patience. 'You did not mean the *plagiarism*, you did not intend to *publish* behind Paul's back.'

'It wasn't plagiarism, it was—'

'So what does it *matter* if the rotten thing no longer exists? Tell me, what has been lost, truly? *You* did an unforgiveable thing, *Paul* did an unforgiveable thing, and these two things, they cancel each other out. You sacrifice this writing of yours, and your love, the love between you and Paul, that can be saved. It is a *good* thing.'

'Greta, no. You don't understand.'

'I am too blunt, ja? Always I am blunt. But this is too *important*, what you and Paul have is too *important* for prancing around in circles like the Russian bear.'

'No,' Antoinette says. 'We don't have anything. He's been seeing someone else for the past couple of months, he told me last night.'

'Ah.' The other woman shakes her head. 'Silly boy, to confess such a thing.' But her face holds no surprise, not the slimmest hint of shock.

'You knew? Greta, you *knew*?'

'Of course I knew, I am his friend.'

'I thought *we* were supposed to be friends, too.'

'No, you are not to do this!' Greta near bounces to her feet and begins to pace about the kitchen, her arms waving in the air. 'I *am* your friend, Ant, but I am *his* friend also, and I *detest* being stuck in the middle of the two of you, I *detest* it! But what am I to do? He *confides* in me, he *begs* me not to tell you, and so I do not tell. But I do *try* to help, I do *try* to make him see what he is doing, the *stupidity* of it, to make him *end* it. I do *that* for you.'

Antoinette braces herself, needing to ask the one question Paul has so far refused to answer—*who is she? who is this other girl?*—and Greta is so worked up the suspicion moves swift and clear to the front of her mind. 'It's not you, is it Greta? Please, tell me it's not you.'

'Scheisse!' Of course it isn't her, the woman snaps; why must Antoinette keep harping on that? Not Greta, not for a long time, just some pretty little morsel he picked up at Abyss—or was it Heresies?—no matter, because it is over with, *finished*, Paul is sincere about that. It only happened because he thought Ant was drifting away, never coming out to clubs anymore, always finding reasons to stay at home, to avoid his company—but that was all because of the book, wasn't it? Her book, *his* book, and how can Ant blame him for being so upset, thrown over for a pile of words?

'That's a good enough excuse, is it?' Antoinette retorts. 'He gets to go out and fuck some suicide girl every time he feels insecure?'

Greta throws up her hands. 'Did I *say* it was a good excuse? It is a *reason*, that is all, an *explanation* for what he did, not an *absolution*. Oh Ant, this is all such a mess, such a tangle and you must help to fix it, because you are a part of it.'

'I don't want to fix it.'

'But you love him.'

'I don't care if I love him! I don't want to love him!'

Even cushioned with anger it hurts to say the words, to hear them, and Antoinette knows with gut-sinking certainty that if Paul was standing here before her, if he had the balls to stay and plead his own case instead of sending Greta as proxy, then she would have little hope of resistance. Poised on the edge of her life here, Paul and their flat and the history that seeps from every wall, every photograph stuck careless to the fridge, every half-burned candle and guilty wine stain on the carpet, how easy it would be to close her eyes and jump, to allow herself the exhilaration of free-fall.

Easy, sure. Until the ground came up to meet her.

'I'm sorry, Greta,' Antoinette says. 'I have to get going, I'm working later.'

She heads down to the bedroom, eyes blurry with nascent tears. Her hip catches on the little hall cupboard like it has a hundred times before and she swears, rubbing at the familiar bloom of pain.

Greta is close behind. 'Please, Ant, don't be childish. He loves you, you *know* that he loves you.'

'Yeah? Why isn't he here, then?'

'He is a boy, he is too proud.'

Antoinette wrestles her largest suitcase out from under the bed, wipes off the worst of the dust, and surveys the room. So much stuff, too much even for this monstrous piece of luggage to swallow, so it'll be just another exercise in snatch-and-grab.

Not even thinking about what she's taking, what she's leaving behind, just filling the case with whatever comes to hand—this and this and this. How in hell has she acquired so much crap in the first place?

'Listen to me.' Greta pushes in front of her, hands firm on bony hips. 'You must let him have his pride.'

A candid happy-snap is wedged into the dresser mirror. Taken just a few months ago at Abyss: Antoinette grinning drunk and red-eyed from the flash, her right hand a frozen, unfocused blur of pale skin as she reaches for Paul's face. Paul, whose gaze is turned not to her, not to the camera, but to something across the room.

To someone.

'He can keep his pride, Greta.' She tears the photograph in half and half again, watches the pieces flutter lifeless to the floor. 'Just make sure he knows, he won't be getting any more of mine.'

Jacqueline checks the motel room lock for the third time that evening then calls home on her iPhone. There are four rings before the machine answers and her own clipped voice echoes in her ear.

This is Jacqueline Paige. Please leave your name, number and a short message, and your call will be returned as soon as possible.

Carefully, she recites the message she's prepared for Ant. Each word chosen to show that she cares, but stripped of any intimation that Jacqueline might be checking up on her. Checking up is what their mother would do. No, Jacqueline simply wants to make sure that Ant is all right. Wants her to know that Jacqueline is here if she needs to talk. Not that she expects Ant to call back tonight. It's after six and if her sister isn't answering then she must have already left for work. This is a good thing. Perhaps she won't spend the next week sulking about Jacqueline's flat with her hair unwashed and her fingernails gnawed to the quick, mooning over her moronic boyfriend.

Her moronic *ex*-boyfriend. Jacqueline hopes it stays that way.

Of course, for all she knows, they might have patched things up already. Paul would only need to come crawling over with an apology and a bunch of day-old flowers for Ant to fall sobbing into his arms. Her sister is so emotional. So impulsive. Moving in with a man she's barely known for five minutes. Paying the bills while he sits on his backside and potters away at his precious book. Ant waited tables for almost two years after high school, living at home and saving up to backpack around the world. She kept journals of all the places she wanted to visit, all the things she longed to see. Before Paul, it was all she talked about. Jacqueline never understood how her sister could give up her dream like that.

Once Paul's novel is published, we'll travel the world together.

Their mother was simply livid: Ant was a foolish, lovesick child, Paul a useless, exploitative deadbeat; Jacqueline should talk to Ant, should make her see reason. The phone calls were relentless and seething, but Jacqueline's support for her younger sister never wavered. She couldn't *allow* it to waver. No matter that she found herself in silent agreement with their mother half the time—they were *sisters*, a united front their sole defence against such maternal onslaughts. If they let slip even once, the breach would lie between them for good.

A frightening thought; Sally Paige is all too adept at handling a wedge.

Jacqueline stretches both arms to the ceiling, trying to work some of the tension out of her neck. She isn't looking forward to tomorrow. The phone at Ryan Jellicoe's place went unanswered all afternoon and, predictably, none of her calls to his mobile were returned. Her final message was simple: she's here in Brisbane and will be coming to see him in the morning. To see the paintings. To see if there is anything he needs, anything at all. Because she's here to help.

'You didn't have to warn him,' Dante says when she reports in. 'He'll probably piss right off now.'

'It will be worse to show up unannounced,' she argues. 'He'll just slam the door in my face—if he even bothers to answer.'

'I don't care if you have to get a battering ram. Get in there and see what he's up to. I want photos of the work and I want—'

'You sent me up here to do a job, Dante. Please, let me do it.'

'Don't make me wish I'd gone myself, Jacks.'

She can picture him pacing the floor, teeth grinding mercilessly in time with his steps. One furious hand skimming back and forth over his platinum crew cut. Jacqueline takes a breath. 'I'll call tomorrow and let you know what happens.'

'And remind him about the fucking contracts, yeah?'

'I will. I'll remind him.'

'Should have made him sign them in blood.'

The phone clicks in her ear. Jacqueline switches it off. Places it on the bedside table. She's had enough contact with the outside world, at least for tonight. She can sympathise with Ryan Jellicoe and his avoidance strategies.

At least the motel is bearable, her room small but clean. The shower leaves something to be desired in terms of water pressure, but it does run hot for the entire fifteen minutes she stands beneath it. Things could be worse, considering how strained Seventh Circle's budget is these days. At least Dante is covering costs up front. Her own credit cards are close to maxing out and she doesn't get paid until next week. Even then, most of it will go on bills.

Jacqueline turns off the water. Steps out of the shower. She dries herself with a towel that has seen softer days. Rubs at the line of muscle still stretched taut across her shoulders. She needs the promotion Dante has been hinting at. She needs the extra money that will come with it. If she can fix the Ryan Jellicoe situation, extract this particular thorn from Dante's side, then the Gallery Manager job must be as good as hers. The only other option is Becca, who is surely no option at all. Fine Arts degree or not, the girl has worked at Seventh Circle for less than a year. What would she know about management?

Yet Jacqueline sees the way she fawns over Dante. The way that round, sunflower face turns to follow his every move. And how he all but glows beneath its gaze. No, smoothing things over with Ryan Jellicoe is vital. There won't be enough blame in the world if she fails.

Jacqueline sighs, massaging the bony place where her skull meets her spine. Her head has felt strange ever since the plane. Ever since the *episode*. Foggy and full, packed with cotton wool and thumbtacks. She grabs her toiletries case, then kills the harsh en suite light and retreats to the room. Her newly-washed hair lies heavy and damp against the bare skin of her back, the ends brushing almost to her waist as she arranges herself cross-legged in the centre of the bed. The weight comforts her. It feels like armour.

She closes her eyes. Takes a deep breath. Holds it.

Imagines herself floating above the mattress. Rising weightless as helium. Her body sitting awkward and empty below. Its sharp, angular bones. Its pasty, fishbelly skin. The sags and creases and stubborn pinch of flab no amount of sit-ups can shift. Three years shy of thirty and her flesh is already giving in.

She exhales. Takes another breath. Looks closer.

Studies each curve and hollow, catalogues each fissure and epidermal flaw. Closer and closer until her body begins to lose cohesion, becomes nothing more than a discordant collection of lines and shapes. Pieces of a puzzle not hers to solve. Disassociation, disconnection, divorce.

There. Now.

Jacqueline opens her eyes.

The toiletries case is right by her ankle. With careful fingers, she slides the razor blade from its wrapping. The metal is thin and double-edged. It warms beneath her touch. Half a sigh drifts from her lips. Her inner thighs are pale and smooth, cross-hatched by fine lines even whiter than the skin they have scarred. The freshest, still blushing pink near the edges, are on her right leg; Jacqueline lowers the blade to her left.

Draws it slowly across. Once, twice, and once again.

Tonight, three will be enough.

She watches the slow bead of blood. Concentrates herself around the burn in her thighs. Feels herself drifting away from herself. She needs this. Needs to dismantle the artifice, however briefly. To cut through the costumes and taxing displays of survival. So pure, this release bestowed by the blade. By the delicate taste of blood on her fingers. Pure and secret and hers alone to savour. No one to see, no one to know.

No one to judge.

She knows what people think of her. Those fleeting lovers and infrequent friends. Even Ant must think it at times. The words hover behind their eyes: *snow queen, ice princess*. But snow melts, ice cracks. Far safer to be rock. Granite or black-mirrored obsidian. Impregnable and solid, slow to erode.

Jacqueline, the stone maiden, etching away at herself.

3

In the kitchen, the message light on the answering machine is flashing red and Antoinette pauses for a second, heart beating hard, before she presses the button. But it's only Jacqueline, her tone cheerful and light, passing on the name of the motel and her room number just in case, and asking if it wouldn't be too much trouble for Ant to finish off the double-chocolate ice cream in the freezer. Jacqueline feels bad about leaving it on its own; she wouldn't want it to feel abandoned.

Antoinette smiles despite herself. Did she really expect the message to be from Paul? Worse, did she *want* it to be?

'No,' she mumbles. 'Only a little.'

It's past two in the morning, but sleep will be a while coming yet. Her mind is too wired, her thoughts strung-out and tumbling strong; never mind the exhaustion that seeps through her bones, or the bright caustic ache in her feet. Antoinette grabs a glass from the sink and stalks into the living room, pulls open the door of the drinks cabinet. It's well-stocked—it's always well-stocked, even though she hardly ever sees her sister drink anything from it—and the bottle of Smirnoff is almost full.

The vodka burns down her throat and she's tempted to cut the next shot with ice, but no. Because fire is what she needs right now. Fire, to cleanse her mind and scorch away all the moon-eyed, idiotic musings that have sauntered through her brain all night. With no less than three orders misheard and a bottle of wine smashed on its way from the bar, she was nearly in tears when Michelle finally hooked her arm. *You see to that tame lot in the corner*, the older waitress instructed, *I'll handle your pricks at Table 9.* But Antoinette's focus was shot, her concentration wavering in less time than it took to navigate from one side of Simpatico to the other and, at the end of the night, Michelle was waiting by the back door. *I'm taking your shift tomorrow night*, waving a hand as Antoinette started to protest. *Get yourself together, girl. You're back on Monday and don't think Ronan won't sack you on the spot if this shit happens again.*

Antoinette grimaces, splashing more vodka into her glass, over her hand, as she slumps onto the couch. Tomorrow, she'll get herself together. Tomorrow and tomorrow and tomorrow. She picks up the remote and turns on the television, flicks through sport replays and music videos, late night movies and infomercials, before sending the screen back to black. The flat is quiet and empty. Antoinette shivers; she hasn't felt this lonely in a long, long time and she wonders what Paul is doing right now. Out clubbing maybe, writhing about with some perky-cute gothling beneath the flash and stutter of strobes, or maybe back at home already. Maybe sleeping, maybe alone. Maybe neither.

Antoinette bites her lip. She is *not* going to start crying again.

Standing up instead, too fast, swaying across the room on less-than-steady feet to slide open the glass balcony door. Colder than she expected, close to freezing or so it feels in her thin polyester blouse; she won't be staying out here for long. But the view of the bay is so beautiful, even at night. The reflection of lights on water, the moon a scarce shave off full—does Jacqueline know how lucky she is? Antoinette could never afford the rent on a place like this, not on waitress wages. Not even now, without Paul to support.

'I don't want to be a waitress.'

The wind lifts her words away and she rubs her arms, feeling the shiver of gooseflesh on her skin. All those tiny bumps, like a story written in braille if only she knew how to read it. If only she knew how to *write* it.

You're not a writer, Ant. You're nothing but a common thief.

Antoinette sips her drink, remembering the glow of triumph on Paul's face as he stood over her shattered laptop. He was right about one thing, him and Greta both: the novel was never hers. Stillborn from the moment she touched it, a cobbled-together freakshow hybrid which could never have lived to draw breath. But so what? It didn't mean that she couldn't *be* a writer, that she couldn't create something new, something original.

Something that would be *hers*.

She used to make up stuff all the time when she was a kid.

Whimsical flights of fancy peopled with talking animals and strange, imaginary creatures, stories told simply to entertain herself—and Jacqueline too, her older sister sitting cross-legged at her side, chin cupped in hands: *And then what? And then what happened?* Finer details elude her now, yet she can almost feel the warm, delicious sensation that would unfurl within her tummy as the words tumbled from her mouth, as her tongue strove to keep up with the images flicking through her mind.

A sensation she felt once more—or very nearly, perhaps the barest shadow, the barest shimmer of it—when she began to tinker with Paul's novel. When she began to make it her own.

Swallowing the last of her drink, Antoinette stumbles back through the balcony door and closes it behind her. The night air has chilled the room, so she makes her way down the hall, fingers sliding along the wall for balance, down to the tiny study with its fold-up futon that takes up almost every square inch of floorspace when it's not being a sofa. Right now her suitcase is spilling its guts all over the mattress, and she sorts through the pitch-dark tangle of velvet and lace, the handful of CDs and all the junk swept from the top of the dresser back home—*home! ha!*—finds something woolly with sleeves and pulls it on.

Briefly, she considers booting up Jacqueline's computer, but squeezing herself behind the desk with the futon still unfolded seems an unlikely possibility, and she can't face cleaning away all her stuff right now. There's an expensive-looking fountain pen in the desk drawer, though, along with a small stack of notebooks—all brand new, in various sizes and colours; her sister obviously has stationery issues—and Antoinette chooses one with a stiff lilac cover. Mostly because its spine is a spiral, fat and powder blue, which makes a satisfying sound when she runs her fingernail along it. Which she does, all the way back to the living room.

But the first page of the notebook proves too great a challenge. Blank and fresh and daunting, daring her to make a mark, to make it count. Antoinette doodles flowers along the edges instead, five-petalled daisies and fat black roses, their thorny stems twisting upon themselves, dripping leaves like tears. She writes her name in the centre of them, wobbly calligraphic swirls and a heart to dot the *i*. Writes *PAUL* underneath, then shakes her head, sharp, and turns the letters to solid inky blocks: four little tombstones, all in a row. She turns to a new page and waits, waits, waits.

For the words that will not come.

You're not a writer, Ant.

'Shut up,' she mutters.

The bottle of Smirnoff is still right there on the coffee table, the wisdom of another drink debatable, but what the hell, one in all in. No idea where she left her glass, though, and sculling from the bottle seems a level lower than she feels like stooping to even now, so Antoinette pushes herself up from the couch, wanders unsteadily into the kitchen for a fresh one. She grabs a bottle of orange juice while she's there—continuing with straight shots is beyond her endurance—along with the tub of ice cream, and is reaching into the cutlery drawer for a spoon when the new glass slips from her overburdened grasp, falls and shatters all over the tiled floor.

'Shit!' Antoinette freezes, excruciatingly aware of her bare and vulnerable feet. She dumps the juice and ice cream onto the bench, well away from the edge because all she needs is for them to topple as well, then lowers herself to a crouch. The glass seems to have broken into manageable enough pieces, large and easy to spot. She gathers them together, shuffling inch by careful inch across the floor, head tilting to catch them all in the reflection of the overhead light.

Well, almost all.

It's the blood she notices first, the sneaky red snail-smear trailing behind her. No pain at all until she sits down and turns over her foot, until she actually sees the wound sliced through the pad of her heel, white-edged and deep, the offending shard still lodged within. Antoinette grasps the tip and pulls, hissing through gritted teeth as the splinter slides loose, because *now* it hurts, the pain so fine and diamond-bright, and the resulting crimson flow brings a surge of bile to her throat; her head feels too light, too heavy, all at the same time.

Ohhhhhh.

Oh no, you are not going to pass out, you silly cow.

She forces herself to her feet, to one foot at least, and hobbles to the bathroom for gauze and antiseptic wash. Because better safe than sorrier-than-thou, as Paul would say—a fresh threat of tears served along with that thought—and Antoinette perches on the side of the bathtub, wraps the gauze around her injured heel. There's a stab of pain as she stands, slightly woozy and putting too much weight on her bad foot, and for a moment she can almost see him in front of her, can almost feel his hands on her waist, holding her together.

Ant, baby, you're my favourite kind of disaster area.

'Paul,' she whispers. 'Paul, it hurts.'

Shhh, baby, I know. How about I kiss it better?

And *this* is what she wants to write about, this is the story she wants to tell. How it was when they first met, how it might have been, how it *should* have been. This is what she wants to pin down with words, what she wants to preserve.

Back on the couch, foot propped up by a cushion, Antoinette flips to a new page in the notebook. *Paul*, she writes again. Frowns and crosses it out. Turns the page. She closes her eyes, conjures an image behind their lids: a boy with ivory skin and irises of pale, arctic blue; a boy whose hands are always gentle, and whose wild, blue-black hair isn't poured from a bottle every six-to-eight weeks. So clear now, she can picture him in the room with her, leaning with one hip against the wall, leather pants slung low, the crooked flash of a smile. So clear, she can almost smell the salt on his skin.

Paul, yet not Paul.

Paul as he might have been once, right at the beginning of things, or maybe only ever how she wished him to be. Paul, with all the rough edges shaved away, all the sniping and petty selfishness that set in over the past few months—the past few *years*, if she's honest with herself; a trait there from the start if only recently aimed in her direction. Paul, without the petulant attitude and apparent inability to comprehend any point of view aside from his own.

A delicious fantasy, if one too fragile to exist beyond the pages on which she now begins to write. Paul-not-Paul: a boy who loves her, absolutely and forever; a boy who could never so much as dream of betrayal, who would sooner carve out his own heart than inflict the slightest wound on hers.

Everything she desires, everything she needs; nothing she does not.

Her hand moves fast, the ink smearing in places as she rushes to capture all that she holds in her head, and Antoinette wonders how much of it will even be intelligible later. She feels odd, like something more potent than vodka lurks in her veins. The words flow through her like smoke. But it's not enough to merely describe him, this strange and beautiful boy. She weaves him a story as well, a past cut from old cloth with every stain and painful rip excised or hidden, tucked sly behind fresh and clever seams.

Paul made perfect—*this* is what she needs right now. Because if it's impossible to stop loving him, to simply turn her emotions off at the switch, then maybe a sneaky bit of re-wiring will work just as well. The object of her love no longer a flesh-and-flawed boy but instead a most perfect version of him. A creature against which the real Paul will stand little chance, even if he gets down on his knees and begs her to come back.

He cheated on you, Ant. Jacqueline, last night, a frown shadowing her usually calm features. *How can you ever trust him again?*

No, she can't trust him, but neither can she trust herself. Because if he knocked on the door right now, greeted her with outstretched arms and that slow, easy grin—Antoinette shakes her head.

Deep inside, pressure builds.

She keeps writing, ignoring the sparks of pain in her hand, the winch-tight ache across her shoulders from sitting curled over for so long. Knowing that most of it has to be rubbish, the words no better than ashes and dust, because nothing that comes this easily can possibly be any good—*can it? can it?*—but writing anyway, compelled to get everything out and onto the page.

The pressure expands within her, fills every space, pushes at her skin. It feels like dread and delirium and desire, and yet like none of these things, like no thing she has ever felt before—or nearly so: a subtle taste of the familiar lingers at the margins, coupled now with the iron-sharp flavour of threat. She is saturated, swollen, ready to split apart, to fly apart until—*oh!*—this last fleeting sensation rushes through her, quick and sudden as thought: *it is done.*

Antoinette straightens, lays down her pen. Her right hand is a cramped, arthritic claw, the hand of a crone; her fingers all but scream as she flexes them. How long has she been writing? Long enough to have filled near half the notebook with her messy scrawl, long enough for the night to have slipped away, for the thin grey light of just-before-dawn to inch its way around the sides of the blinds. Long enough to write herself halfway to sober as well, her head swollen and heavy on her shoulders, her mouth parched. The heel of her injured foot throbs, the bandage is dark and damp to the touch, and there's a bloody stain on the cushion beneath it. Clotted red soaked into fine cream jacquard; Jacqueline is going to kill her.

Cushion tucked under her arm, Antoinette limps back to the bathroom. She tries to rinse the blood out of the fabric, scrubbing at it with her short-bitten nails, but only succeeds in spreading the stain around. She swears, tosses the cushion into the shower for a later attempt. Is it salt that's good for bloodstains, or baking soda? Whatever, she'll google it tomorrow—today—whenever. Her foot is easier to clean, the wound not as bad as she remembers, not anywhere near as bad as it feels to walk on. It only bleeds a little after the dried and scabby crust is washed away, and this time she pads it with cotton wool before wrapping a fresh length of gauze all the way up to her ankle.

Good enough. She splashes her face with cold water. Glares at herself in the mirror. Enough, full-stop. Enough drinking and weeping and wallowing about in her own misery. Paul isn't worth it. Time to snap out of it, girlie-girl. Time to get a life.

But first, she needs some sleep.

Her clothes and other assorted chattels are still staging their hostile takeover of the futon, and Antoinette is too exhausted to even contemplate its liberation. Across the hall, the door to her sister's room is neatly closed. Behind it, there's a queen-sized bed with a comfy mattress and fat, Euro-style pillows—a far more tempting crash zone than the small, cramped study—and Antoinette doesn't have to think twice. The smooth metal handle zaps her fingers with static and she hisses, shaking off the charge as the door swings open to reveal a figure, solid and backlit through the half-drawn curtains, sitting hunched on the end of the bed.

Antoinette freezes. The nape of her neck prickles with sudden sweat.

He lifts his head, turns part-way towards her. Shadows move across his bare skin, and within the depths of those too-pale eyes.

'P-Paul?' Her voice squeaks. She clears her throat. 'How did you…'

Faltering, realising her mistake even as the words die on her lips. Not Paul. Not *her* Paul. Or maybe now more hers than ever.

Then she's running. No thought beyond getting herself to the front door, *through* the front door and out into the thin dawn light, the close confines of the flat too easy to be trapped within. But the security chain is still drawn, her fingers clumsy in their panic, and by the time she has it free his arms are around her waist, dragging her away. She fights back, or tries to, fingernails and elbows and knees the sharpest weapons at her disposal, and *stop it*, he says, and *please*. He pulls her down to the floor, both of them falling in a barely controlled collapse, his weight knocking all the breath from her body. She could laugh, she really could, to think that she's always considered herself more than capable in the self-defence department, one tough cookie if it ever came to the crunch—because how bloody helpless does she feel now?

'Don't hurt me,' she whispers. 'Please don't hurt me.'

'Shhh.' He takes her face in his hands, hands fine-boned but stronger than the world, and tilts her gaze to meet his own. Even in her terror, Antoinette marvels at those eyes, those black-rimmed irises of cool and pale blue. Arctic eyes, husky eyes, brilliant with unspilled tears. 'Please,' he echoes. 'I'm scared too.'

Maybe it's something in his voice, harmless and uncomprehending as a kicked puppy, or the gentle-firm way he's holding her, pinning her moveless to the carpet the way you might keep a panic-struck bird from breaking a wing. Something in his voice, his touch, that makes her stop and look at him, really *look* at him, at that face which is so familiar, yet wholly new. The differences are subtle but definite: his features more finely wrought, their symmetry close to perfect; his skin beyond pale, almost inhumanly white, and flawless but for an inch-long scratch below his right eye, still beading crimson along its edge.

Antoinette swallows, the stale aftertaste of fear lying flat on her tongue.

'Are you hurt?' he asks, relaxing his hold when she shakes her head. A heartbeat later and he's on his feet, his movements too quick, too fluid to follow. He reaches out an arm and she takes it, feels his hand close around her wrist as he helps her stand.

Her sore foot protests sharply and she half-shifts, half-stumbles against him. 'You *are* hurt.' He points to the bandage which is bloody again and starting to unravel.

'No,' she says. 'I mean, that's not from just now.'

'Come on, I'll clean it for you.' His arm slips around her waist, and she actually takes two dazed and limping steps at his side before asking him to stop, to please just *stop* and *wait* a second.

'Is it bad?' he asks. 'I can carry you.'

'No, it's not that. I just need … please, just stop. Stop everything.' She pushes him back, a gentle shove to arm's length so she can see him more clearly, the whole of him. 'My god.' Not exactly the same, but close enough, more than close enough: they could be brothers, the two of them; stand them side by side and that's what anyone would think, couldn't help but think. One of them taller, cast from finer clay maybe, but undoubtedly brothers, brothers if not twins.

Paul and Not Paul.

'What are you?' A thought not intended for words but finding them anyway, just as her hands find the bare, milk-smooth skin of his shoulders, his chest, his hips. The flesh is solid and warm, and feels as real as her own. Only dimly does she register the fact that he's naked, the observation devoid of promise or threat. What does matter are the marks which redden his skin: scratches that match the one beneath his eye, an angry carpet burn on his knee. Perfect, he was *perfect* until she went and injured him, *marred* him, idiot girl that she is. 'I'm sorry,' she says, knowing it's not enough but repeating it anyway as his eyes gloss over and he dips his head, blue-black hair falling like bowerbird feathers into his face.

'I don't know,' he whispers. 'I don't know what I am.'

Antoinette wraps her arms around him and squeezes tight, a desperate-fierce hug to make it all go away. Because she doesn't know what he is either, and for that she's sorry as well. 'It's cold,' she says at last. 'Aren't you cold?'

'No, are you?'

He steps from her grasp and she almost falls, her vision darkening around the edges as the walls start to sway inwards and the floor tilts beneath her feet. Her hands shake and she pushes her knees together to stop them from buckling, bites her tongue in an effort to hold onto consciousness. 'Little help?' she murmurs, but he's already there, one arm firm on her waist as he steers her back down to the hall to Jacqueline's room. The bed has never seemed bigger and Antoinette curls up right in the middle, hands tucked close to her chin. He draws the curtains and pulls the doona over her. 'Sleep now,' he says, his lips brushing warm and dry across her cheek. Down near her feet, the mattress sinks beneath his weight.

Sleep, yes. She hasn't felt so utterly wasted for ages, or maybe never; not even the nights spent clubbing till dawn—not even those nights when she managed to score a dex or two—ever strung her this far out. But how *can* she sleep, right now, with her own breathing, blood-bearing miracle perched at the end of the bed like something out of a trashy teen vampire flick? How can she...

'Hey, Antoinette?'

She starts, the path to dreamland not so elusive after all.

'What's *my* name?' he asks, as if the thought has only just now occurred to him. But the question feels too big, too complicated; nothing her poor, fried brain wants to ponder right this second, so she throws him an old scrap of a syllable instead, the first and last thing that comes to mind—*Paul*—and buries her face into the pillow.

Paul, he might have echoed as she drifted away. And then, *no*, he might have whispered, scornful and proud. *No, I don't think so.*

4

acqueline wonders if she should have had the taxi wait. The address matches the details in her diary, but the place isn't what she expected. More bungalow than house, its wooden boards are the pink of early dawn. The lawn is neatly mown. Flanked on three sides by colourful gardens. Small concrete statues, some partially painted, congregate in groups. Others peer out from beneath plants. Fairies and frogs. Mermaids draped dry over rocks. A baby dragon still emerging from its shell, a flower clutched between its paws.

An enormous loquat tree looms beside the front gate, its branches low and heavy with fruit. Jacqueline ducks beneath it. Follows the narrow path that takes her straight to the front porch. Plastic frangipanis are threaded unevenly through the patchy screen door. She steels herself. Resists the temptation to retrieve her diary and confirm yet again that she's at the right house. Beneath her finger, the doorbell chimes the hallelujah chorus.

She chooses to read that as irony.

To read it *all* as irony, as one huge postmodern practical joke, because what other explanation can there be?

Then inner door swings open and a short, plump woman peers up at Jacqueline through the flymesh and flowers. 'Yes, what?' Behind fuchsia-framed glasses the size of beer coasters, her eyes have the suspicious squint of a sun-snared owl.

Jacqueline clears her throat. 'Does Ryan Jellicoe live here?'

'No, he doesn't. Who are you?'

'I'm sorry, I must have been given the wrong address.' She reaches into her bag for her phone. To find out how on earth Dante managed to send her to Sunny Kitsch Central. Damn it, why hadn't she asked the taxi to wait?

The woman opens the screen door a few inches. 'I'm Ryan's sister. He gives out my address a fair bit.' She sniffs. 'Like when he doesn't want people to know how to find him.'

'Oh.' Jacqueline decides to let the last remark run free. Instead, she offers her name and where she's from. Holds out a hand which is stared at but not shaken. Allows it to drop back to her side. 'I must have copied the wrong details from our files. Ryan would definitely want Seventh Circle to know where to find him. We're putting on his show next month and there's still a lot to organise before—'

'Yes, I know all about your little *show*.' The woman smiles in a way Jacqueline finds impossible to read.

'But Ryan knows I'm here to see him. I called last night.'

'Talk to you, did he?'

'I left a message. I'm sure he's very busy.'

'He's always *very* busy.'

There's a mocking twist in her tone that sets Jacqueline's teeth on edge. 'How about I just call Ryan,' she says, brandishing her phone at the woman. 'I'm sure we can clear this up here and now.'

Seconds roll slow and sullen between them. Jacqueline holds her ground. Finally the woman concedes that a phone call might be in order, but that she'll be the one to make it. Ryan's *her* brother; it's *her* he'll want to speak to.

'Fine,' Jacqueline says. 'Thank you.'

The woman vanishes into the depths of the house, letting the screen door bang behind her. A few moments later, her voice drifts back out to the porch. There are no words Jacqueline can pick clear of the one-sided conversation but the tone is enough. Sharp, strident. Absolutely not happy. Jacqueline sighs. Pats at her forehead with the back of her hand. It's not yet ten o'clock and already the temperature must be nearing thirty degrees. The air is thick and humid, iron lung oppressive. How people can live up here is beyond her. How they can even *think* in this heat, let alone get up every day and face the world—

Footsteps sound from within the house. The screen door swings open.

'He'll have you over.' Ryan Jellicoe's sister steps outside, keys jangling loose in one hand. 'But don't expect to be seeing any of his pictures.'

ॐ

Ten minutes cramped in the passenger seat of the woman's pokey red hatchback is enough to make Jacqueline queasy, even with the windows at half-mast. The heat, the confinement, the sweaty clutch of her blouse against her skin—all of it is too much. She presses a surreptitious palm to her thigh. To the cuts beneath her skirt. The pain is dull but immediate. A comfort, a focus. Jacqueline closes her eyes and nips at the soft, inner flesh of her bottom lip. Imagines the pain as a living creature—an octopus perhaps, or giant squid—some strong, sinuous beast with salted water in its heart. She can almost feel its enormous limbs unfurling themselves across her lap, curling about her shoulders.

Keeping her safe. Keeping her whole.

'Here we are then.'

They've stopped moving. Jacqueline opens her eyes. For one absurd moment, as Ryan Jellicoe's sister climbs out of the car and marches around to the passenger side, it seems as though the woman is actually intending to open Jacqueline's door for her. But no, of course not. 'You coming or what?' she simply barks, waiting with hands on hips for Jacqueline to join her.

They're parked outside an old Queenslander, the rickety wooden box perched high on stilts like an overly ambitious cubby house. Jacqueline follows the woman up the stairs to the huge, enclosed verandah that appears to encircle the entire house. The front door is really just a screen, dilapidated grey mesh framed by cracked and peeling woodwork.

'Ryan?' His sister rattles the door in its frame. It doesn't open.

There are flecks of peeled paint on Jacqueline's hand from where she held onto the stair railing. She brushes her palms together. Watches white scraps fall like dandruff to the floorboards.

'Ryan!' the woman shouts again. 'Ryan, love, it's me.'

'Out here.' The voice is close, coming from where the verandah turns to run along the far side of the house. Ryan Jellicoe's sister glares at Jacqueline then leads the way, sandals slapping the soles of her feet with a damp, fleshy sound that's almost obscene.

Her brother is slouched in a rattan chair. Three glasses of what looks to be iced water sit on the table in front of him. He has something small and round and green in his hands—a ball perhaps, or perhaps not. The way he's playing with it, turning it over and over and over, Jacqueline can't really tell. His fingers are long and tanned. They move with a juggler's grace.

'I'm Ryan,' he says.

'Good to meet you at last,' she replies. 'Jacqueline Paige. I've left some messages on your voicemail.'

'Sure you have.' He smiles, crows feet crinkling at the corners of his eyes. He looks older than she expected. Somewhere in his late thirties, wiry and well-worn, though some of that might only be the effect of the sun. His skin holds a tan that belongs on someone who works outdoors for a living. Blond dreadlocks hang down past his shoulders, swaying as he leans forward. 'Lime?'

'Pardon me?'

Ryan waves the green sphere. 'For your G and T.' He produces a folding knife from his pocket and flips it open. Cuts the fruit into thick wedges.

'Thanks, but no,' Jacqueline says. 'Not in this heat.'

'Best weather for drinking, you ask me.' He winks, slow and lazy, then crushes a chunk of lime into each of the three glasses.

'I'll have hers, love.' Ryan Jellicoe's sister pushes past. Slumps into one of the empty chairs. A land-bound seal would possess more grace.

A scowl shadows Ryan's face. 'You've met Alice, then.' He picks up one of the drinks and holds it out to Jacqueline. 'C'mon, it's not getting any cooler round here.' The glass is sweating nearly as much as she is and almost slips from her grasp as she raises it to her mouth. The taste is too bitter, even with the lime. More gin than tonic and Jacqueline is used to neither. She grimaces. Returns the drink to the table.

'Your knees broke or what?' He nods at the third, still empty chair.

Jacqueline sits down and crosses her legs. Watches him watch her cross them. Straightens her back. 'Ryan, there are some things we need to discuss.' She smiles. 'There's not a lot of time left before your show and I have to tell you, Dante is worried. He's concerned that—'

'He's *concerned* he'll lose his dosh,' Alice chimes in.

Jacqueline nods curtly at the woman. 'The money is a factor, granted. Seventh Circle is a business after all, not a charitable foundation, and Dante has already invested a sizeable amount to see this show go ahead. I do think the finances are secondary, though; right now, he's more concerned about Ryan's reputation.'

'*Ryan's* reputation, yeah right.' Alice stabs a pudgy finger onto the tabletop. 'Listen to me, missy: we know how much his paintings are worth, as opposed to what Dante's gonna give him. Your boss needs to be asking a lot more, or taking a smaller cut, one or the other.'

Jacqueline turns back to Ryan. 'If you want to discuss pricing, I'm sure that will be fine. You need to understand, though, that the market is rather tight at the moment. Dante is trying to position your work—'

'That's not what we've been told,' Alice says. 'There's a place right here in Brisbane would kill to have Ryan's stuff on their walls. *And* they'll represent him properly, the way he deserves.'

Jacqueline turns to the woman. 'That might be problematic, Alice. We have … well, there are contracts in place.'

'Contracts, yeah right. Our *lawyer* might have something to say about those *contracts*. I'm sure he can find us a loophole or two.'

'You may be right,' Jacqueline says. 'But really, do you want to go down that road? Legal fees and courtrooms, dragging it out for possibly years. Dante won't take that lying down, you know. He has lawyers of his own.' Ryan is staring out over the road, his drink more than half gone. Jacqueline wonders when he stopped paying attention. 'You don't want to go through all that, do you? Ryan?'

His gaze snaps back to her, slips down over her breasts, her legs, then back up to her face. He grins and his teeth are straight and white like an American movie star. For a moment he looks all of seventeen years old. 'Are you doing anything tonight?'

'Ryan, be serious,' Alice says.

Jacqueline resists an urge to throttle the woman. To throw her bodily down the stairs and watch her flail and sear on the concrete driveway below. With sister dearest out of the way, Jacqueline has few qualms about her ability to handle Ryan Jellicoe, thank you kindly. Casually, she reaches down to wipe a line of sweat from the back of her crossed leg. Her skirt hitches a little higher up her thigh as she straightens. She neglects to smooth it down again.

'There's this club in the valley,' Ryan says. 'Couple of mates doing a gig there tonight, thought you might want to come along. They're good.'

'I don't know.' Jacqueline curves her lips into a regretful smile. 'I need to report back to Dante this afternoon. If there isn't good news, he'll most likely want me straight back on a plane to Melbourne.'

'Good news, eh?' Ryan scratches his chin. 'And what do you reckon your boss's idea of good news is, then?'

'A reassurance that things are still on track. If I could tell him that I've seen your painting, the one that's to be the focus of the show?'

'It's not ready to be seen.'

The man's jaw tightens and Jacqueline calmly backtracks. Assures him that she understands, absolutely she understands. Perhaps some of the other paintings then, just the ones he's happy for her to view? Anything at all, as long as she has something to tell Dante. Surely, he can meet her halfway?

Alice bangs her empty glass down on the table. 'You won't see squat till certain contracts get changed—take that back to Dante and see how he likes it.' All the muscles in her face conspire to a self-satisfied sneer. 'Time to go, my brother has work to be getting on with. You've wasted enough of his day.'

But it's Ryan who gets to his feet. 'Alice, zip your fucking lip.' He holds out his right hand to Jacqueline. She takes it. Allows him to pull her up and out of her chair in a single, fluid motion. Sweat shifts between their palms and for the first time she notices the tattoo on the inside of his wrist, an elongated blue sun that ripples above the flex of his tendons. Finally, belatedly, he releases his grip. 'C'mon then, girl, let's you and me go take a gander at some etchings.'

His studio occupies the entire rear of the house, an area which must have originally been three separate rooms. Patches of raw, exposed wood remain where dividing walls once stood. At the far end, angled towards one of several curtainless windows, twin easels support what can only be the painting she's been sent to reconnoitre. Wider than the spread of her arms and almost as tall, the canvas is shrouded in a grey, paint-spattered sheet. Pointedly, Jacqueline averts her gaze. Allows it to drift instead over the smaller canvases that lie stacked against the outer walls, their faces turned uniformly away. The jars of brushes and half-curled tubes of paint cluttering the corners and windowsills. The single mattress with its colourfully stained and crumpled sheet.

'Sometimes I crash in here,' Ryan says. 'Easier'n cleaning myself up for bed.'

Jacqueline smiles. 'I can imagine.'

'Ryan?' Alice pokes her head around the door. 'Ryan, I got things of my own to do today. You gonna be long with her?'

Jacqueline opens her mouth to tell the woman not to wait on her account, that she's quite capable of calling a taxi, but she doesn't get the chance.

Ryan whips around, his face dark with fury. 'Get the fuck out of here, Alice!'

'I only—'

'Piss *off*!' Right in her face, so close that Jacqueline sees spittle arc through the air and land on Alice's cheek. Her heart beats faster. Her breath sticks in her throat. The woman backs quickly out of sight and Ryan slams the door. Hard enough to make all the windows rattle in their frames.

'Sorry,' he mutters. 'She knows I don't want her in here, I don't *ever* want her in here.' He turns to face her, hands spreading in a gesture she takes for contrition. 'She doesn't understand art, never has. Doesn't get the process, you know?'

Jacqueline nods. 'Sure.'

'Only reason she's interested now is there's money involved.'

'I imagine that interests a lot of people. More so than art, that is.'

Ryan grins. 'Someone in mind?'

Jacqueline takes a couple of steps towards the nearest stack of canvases. The topmost bears a word scrawled in red across its back: *median* or perhaps *meridian*. 'Dante does care more about the money, your sister was right about that. Art is his business, and a status symbol. To be honest, I doubt he'd spot the difference between a genuine Jackson Pollock and a mass-produced Chinese knock-off. If he could sell them for the same price, he'd quite likely argue there was no real difference at all.' She points a toe at the canvas in front of her. 'Could I…?'

Ryan moves to her side. 'Yeah, I got that about Dante. A real bottom-line guy.'

He bends and flips the painting around to face them. A sunset, all bloody reds and rich, bruised purples, casts its dying light over a city which has long since ceased to breathe. Skyscrapers loom, their glassless windows gaping black as missing teeth, above a river the colour of raw sewage. A post-urban wasteland, concrete and iron decaying to rubble and rust—and amid it all, faces peering out. Or what might be faces; what might be nothing more than wishful thinking. What might be nothing ever again.

'It's Brisbane,' Ryan says. 'One day.'

Jacqueline nods. 'What you have to understand about Dante, though, is that he's good at his business. *Very* good. You need him, Ryan, you really do.'

He shrugs, noncommittal, then turns over another canvas. And another. He leads her around the room, becoming more animated as each new painting, each vision of his tragic, post-apocalyptic city, is revealed. They're good, better than good. They're grand and

KIRSTYN McDERMOTT

dismal and undeniably beautiful, although Jacqueline can't but help feel that something is missing. A unity, a narrative. Perhaps when they're hung. Perhaps when the centrepiece is there to tie them all together. *If* the centrepiece ties them together. Jacqueline glances at the shrouded bulk straddling the two easels. Her fingers ache to lift a corner of the sheet.

'You coming out tonight, then?' Ryan asks.

'I might.'

'Better than hanging around some roach motel, yeah?'

'It would be that.' The heat in the studio is intense. Sweat beads on her face faster than she can pat it dry, and the skin on her back, her chest, feels clammy and close. Jacqueline wonders how the man can stand to work in here. She tilts her chin towards the concealed canvas. 'Just a peek, Ryan? For me, not Dante. I promise I won't say a word to him about it.' Smiling, she draws a lazy cross over her left breast.

Ryan watches her finger complete its path before lifting his eyes to hers. 'Sorry, but it's not done yet and I don't show anything that isn't done. Not to anyone, yeah?'

'We open in less than eight weeks, Ryan, and we need to allow time for everything to be crated and shipped...'

'Hey now, don't get yourself in a knot. It'll be done.' He reaches up with both hands to scratch at his scalp. Nervous serpents, his dreads twitch with each movement. 'Less than a week, maybe, I get my blood up. You can see it then if you're hanging around that long. You gonna be hanging around that long?'

Jacqueline tries not to think of the heat and the humidity. How, after a week of it, she might be little more than a puddle on the motel's cheap polyester carpet. Instead, she nods. 'I'll be here, at your disposal. Anything you need.' The grin that splits his face is wolfish. A startling flash of tooth and fire that sparks something equally unexpected deep in her loins. Uncertain, Jacqueline laughs. 'Well, *nearly* anything you need.'

'What do I need, what do I need?' Ryan stalks across the room. Squeezes both her hands in his. 'I need you to come out with me tonight, girl. I need inspiration, I need to dance. C'mon, you can be my muse, my Calliope.' He's laughing now as well—Ryan Jellicoe, Court Jester—but still his hands swallow hers.

'All right.' She pulls free, grinning despite herself. 'Tell me where the club is.'

'That's my girl!' Ryan retrieves a small scrap of canvas from the mess that litters the floor. Using a stub of charcoal wetted against his tongue, he sketches a series of intersecting lines. Streets, Jacqueline realises as he starts to label them. One near the middle he marks with a big fat asterisk and a scribbled name. 'Here you go.'

The tips of her fingers blacken as she turns the map around. '*Merde*? That's really the name of the place?'

'Hey, you're in Brisbane now; no one knows *shit* up here.' Ryan snorts at his own joke, then snatches the canvas back. Still grinning, he signs his name in the bottom right corner. 'There, you see, that'll be a worth a mint one day. Isn't that right, *Alice*?'

The last word is shouted over her shoulder, and Jacqueline turns in time to catch a glimpse of a shadow beneath the studio door before it slips away. Sister dearest, indeed. How long had the woman been standing there, ear pressed to the dry and splintery wood? Jacqueline suppresses a shudder. Her skin crawls.

There is always a game; there is always an audience.

Her own private mantra, for as long as she can remember. It wouldn't do for her to forget it, not now. Jacqueline tucks the map into her bag. Feels her composure return. Ryan Jellicoe may have slipped briefly beneath her skin for a few scattered, heat-swollen moments, but what of it? She is beginning to sense the rules now, the conditions and boundaries. Gentle flirtation and the padding of egos.

It's a game she knows she can play. It's a game she knows she can win.

5

Waking to darkness and disorientation, Antoinette spends a few seconds fumbling for a reading light that isn't there, before remembering and rolling across to the other side of the bed. Jacqueline's side, the side with the art nouveau lamp Antoinette bought as a housewarming present, its green-glass shade casting a faintly olivine glow once her fingers find the switch.

The room is as empty as the rest of the bed.

And, just for a second, Antoinette doubts. Allows herself to think that maybe, just maybe, it was all a dream, some crazy-eyed fantasy spun from alcohol and grief and the kind of imagination that's better left to bounce against padded walls.

But only for a second.

Because she *knows*, because she *feels*. It's real. *He* is real. He must be.

Antoinette gets out of bed, wincing as her injured foot hits the floor. Still in her work clothes, she feels stale and constricted, her white blouse now crumpled, smelling of old sweat, and she reaches up beneath it, rubs at the spots where her bra has dug into sleep-soft flesh. A shower is what she needs, coconut bodywash and water so hot it all but blisters skin; a shower, and a clock—because she has no idea what time it is, what *day* even—but there's one thing she needs even more.

The hall is dark except for a slim line of light shining beneath the closed study door. Without allowing herself time for second thoughts, Antoinette limps across and turns the handle, belatedly rapping her knuckles on the door as she pushes it open. 'Hello? You in here?'

He turns to face her, swivelling in his chair with an easy, open grin. 'Lo! Sleeping beauty awakens!'

He's tidied the room, returned the futon to its sofa state and piled her stuff neatly on top of it. Behind him, Jacqueline's computer hums, what looks like a page from Wikipedia open on the screen, but that isn't what grabs Antoinette's attention, what makes her burst into laughter.

'I'm sorry,' she says, covering her mouth with her hands. 'Is that my dressing gown?'

'I was cold.' He pulls the faded pink terrycloth tighter across his chest. 'It's all I could find that would fit. Sort of.'

Antoinette tries to stop smirking. The robe is absurd, purple appliqué ponies cavorting across a background the colour of fairy floss, and she would have sent it off to Vinnies years ago except that it was a thirteenth birthday present from her grandmother—her mother's mother, who died soon afterwards. At least two sizes too big back then, it fits her comfortably now, and despite the numerous coffee stains and the rip on one sleeve—inexpertly repaired but holding—she can't bear to let it go.

On him, it looks at once ludicrous and strangely endearing.

'We'll have to get you some clothes,' Antoinette says.

His grin returns, wider than ever, as he rises from the chair. 'If you say so.' It only takes him a couple of steps to reach her, and Antoinette puts out her hand when he gets near, flattens a palm against his chest. Still warm, still solid.

'Can I just…' She leans forward and presses her ear over the place where his heart should be, her breath held tight in her lungs. Listening, listening, and when she hears it, the faint but steady rhythm, it sounds like magic. *Feels* like magic, the shiver that spreads across her skin, that thrums through her bones. Because can there be any other word for it? One day he wasn't here—wasn't *anywhere*—and now he's standing before her, hand cradling her head as this unseen muscle beats and beats and beats, the fact of him so real, so *big*, it leaves no space for questioning.

'Incredible,' Antoinette whispers.

He takes her chin in his hand, tilts her gaze to meet his own. 'Yours,' he says, and lowers his head towards hers.

Jacqueline inches away from the boy newly slumped on the couch at her side. His sweaty arm rubs against hers and she wrinkles her nose at the odour that wafts from his body. He grins at her, head bobbing in time with the music. At least in Merde's upstairs lounge the sound of the band is somewhat muted, their drums and synths blending to a harmless, syncopated beat. The vocal drone is just another instrument. Woodwind perhaps, or pipe organ.

'You want a drink?' the boy yells in her ear.

'No thanks.' Jacqueline smiles, carefully bland. She looks towards the staircase where Ryan disappeared too long ago. The band that's playing isn't the one his friends are in. He's gone to find out when they'll be on.

'You look thirsty,' the boy yells at her again. 'Thirsty and hot.'

'I'm not drinking tonight,' she says. Not tonight, not ever if she can avoid it. She hates the way alcohol makes her feel. Light-headed and loose. Disconnected from everything, including herself. 'Thanks anyway.'

But he's already on his feet. 'S'kay, I'll get you a Coke then.'

Jacqueline starts to protest, but he's already making his way towards the bar. Long and lanky, his limbs move as though they're attached to strings. The girl on the adjacent couch begins to laugh, a harsh and barking sound. 'Don't sweat it; Scott totally crushes on newbs.' She's lying on her back, legs hooked over the arm of the couch and swinging gently. Her skirt puddles in her lap. Her calves are smooth and well-defined, criss-crossed by the strappy Egyptian-style sandals she's wearing.

Jacqueline leans closer. 'Jane, isn't it?'

The girl shakes her head. She wears dreadlocks, like Ryan, only hers are shorter and multicoloured. '*Zane*. With a Z.'

'Sorry,' Jacqueline says. 'I must have misheard.'

The girl shrugs, as though it doesn't really matter, but there's a keen, catlike gleam in her eyes. 'So you're this big shot gallery chick, right?'

'My boss is the big shot. I just do his dirty work.'

'You reckon he might be interested in someone other'n Ryan?'

'I don't know, I can't really speak for—'

'Hang on, look.' Zane swings her legs around and sits up. She undoes the drawstring on the patchwork pouch she wears slung across her chest and pulls out a handful of photographs. Passes them to Jacqueline. Her fingernails are short and grimy. Her cuticles are ragged. 'My website's on the back, yeah?'

The light's dim up here and tinted scarlet, making it hard for Jacqueline to discern much detail from prints which appear second-rate to begin with. Shots of boxes, and open suitcases, filled with a variety of different objects. Dolls, or parts of dolls, and scissors clutter one of them. Another seems filled with brightly coloured shapes and shiny pieces of metal. 'You're a photographer?'

Zane shakes her head. 'No, see, I make what's *in* the photos. But you really need to look at them for real, you know? You need to be in the same space. I thought maybe while you were up here, you might like to check them out.'

Jacqueline shuffles through the photos, flips one of them over. The website address appears to have been stamped on by hand, letter by individual letter. 'I can certainly pass these on to my boss. He's always looking for new work.'

'Look, I know the photos are crap. But if you just came by...'

'I'm not sure I'll have time. I'm just here for Ryan.'

'What if I bring a couple of them to you?' Zane leans forward. Hunger pinches her face. 'Where you staying?'

Jacqueline tries not to recoil. 'Ah, I'm not sure that—'

'Give it up, Zaney.' The boy, Scott, sidles between them with drinks in hand. 'No one cares about your stupid puzzle boxes.' He places one of the glasses on the table in front of Jacqueline. 'One Coke for the lady, straight up.'

'They're *not* puzzle boxes!' Scowling, the girl aims a kick at him. Misses and hits the table instead. The glass wobbles and Jacqueline reaches to steady it, the photographs dropping to the floor as she does.

'Scott, you dick,' Zane snaps. She crouches beside Jacqueline's legs to pick up the scattered prints. 'They're not puzzle boxes,' she says again. 'They're more like dioramas, but complicated, you know. Layered. You should see them.' She offers the photos to Jacqueline, thrusts them towards her.

'Zane, put those away.' The voice is sudden and commanding, and Jacqueline turns to see Ryan standing with arms crossed beside the couch. 'No one's doing business here tonight.'

'I was only showing her.' The girl pouts, then actually flutters her eyelashes at him. 'Hey, Ryan, you think I could, like, bring a couple cases round to your place? *Creeping Beauty*, maybe, or *Malice in Wonderland*, that be okay? So she can get to see them while she's here?'

Ryan grins. 'A time to every purpose, little thing.' He bends and kisses the top of her head, right where her dreads morph from pink to peacock blue, rendered purplish in this light. The expression on his face is amused, indulgent. An expression Jacqueline imagines a father might reserve for his favourite child. Except there's nothing *daughterly* about the way Zane looks at him. Watching them, Jacqueline wonders about conduits, and whether it would prove help or hindrance to get the girl onside.

Ryan straightens. 'Come on,' he says to Jacqueline. 'My mates'll be on soon. Let's head down, grab us a good possie, eh?'

Downstairs is the last place she wants to be. Amid the heat and the noise and the crush of the clammy, pulsating bodies that throng before the stage. But Jacqueline smiles and gets to her feet. Tonight, her primary concern is to keep Ryan happy. As she sidles her way out of the circle of couches, Jacqueline catches Zane's eye. The girl's mouth is now a hard, thin line, and her gaze has daggers in it.

Antoinette steps from the shower and grabs one of the ivory-coloured towels from its rail. She still feels bad about ducking away from him like that, slipping mercurial through his arms just as his lips were so obviously about to touch hers, but it was too sudden, and too strange. Kissing him would have been a kind of weirdness she doesn't want to consider just now.

Her heel looks much better at least, now that she's cleaned away the dried and crusted blood. It still hurts to put weight on, but the pain is old, dullish, the edges of the wound crinkled white from the shower. There are butterfly stitches in the medicine cabinet and Antoinette uses three of them, smears on some Savlon and wraps a fresh length of gauze around her foot, hoping the cut won't open up again. Doctors and stitches and shots, oh my! Antoinette shudders.

She rubs at her hair, squeezing as much water from it as she can. It's too long, the curls too thick, and will take ages to dry, but she's forgotten her anti-frizz stuff back at home—back at *Paul's*—and blow-drying would be a disaster without it. Antoinette swipes a hand across the mirror, cuts a swathe through the steam. Maybe she should hack it all away, short as she can stand it. She bundles her hair together, piles it up on top of her head: Raggedy Ann gone gothic, sure, but certainly easier to care for, easier to dye as well. Already time for a touch up, she notes, a fresh coat of black to conceal the creep of mousy brown.

Antoinette laughs. All that's happened in the past couple of days, and she's worried about the colour of her hair? She pokes out her tongue at her reflection, then wraps herself in the towel and opens the bathroom door.

There's music coming from the living room. The new Emilie Autumn album which she bought only a week ago and has barely found time to play, all violins and high-strung harpsichord, higher-strung vocals soaring over the top. Antoinette closes her eyes, opens her senses. She can feel him somehow, can almost visualise him standing by the glass balcony doors, looking out into the night, a glass of red wine in his hand. Like there's a thread joining the two of them, some unseen umbilicus anchoring him to her. It's an odd feeling, and not an entirely comfortable one.

Antoinette slips into the study and quickly dresses—her favourite black jeans and an old Cure shirt she bought on eBay, a black sweater she's had so long it's almost grey—then notices that the computer is still humming, its monitor in sleep mode. Curious, she taps at the space bar and a website flashes onto the screen. Paul's blog, the latest entry dated Saturday—yesterday? Yes, the clock confirms, today is still Sunday, at least for another sixteen minutes.

angry, sad and bitter about the waste of too much time, i sit here and stare at the screen in the hope it will give me the answers i need or, failing that, solace. nothing can ever be the same. nothing should ever be the same. sharklike, i swim forward, always forward. otherwise, i remind myself, i will drown.

Quasi-cryptic, lower-case melodrama, typical Paul, and Antoinette stops reading after the first paragraph. Closes the browser and flicks the monitor off at the switch, mildly surprised at the hurt she doesn't feel. *Sharkboy*. She snorts.

In the living room, she finds him waiting on the couch, still wrapped in her pink dressing gown. Antoinette smiles. 'Hey.'

'Hey yourself,' he says. There are two wine glasses on the coffee table, one of them empty, along with an open bottle of red. 'Want some?'

'Okay.' She sits beside him with her legs crossed beneath her, watching the tendons shift in his hands as he pours the wine and passes over the glass. Their fingers brush as she takes it from him and she's amazed all over again by how undeniably *real* he is. 'Why were you looking at Paul's blog?'

He raises an eyebrow. '*Paul's* blog?'

'Well.' Antoinette sips her wine. 'You know.'

'It was trippy,' he says. 'I remember what's in it, but I don't remember writing it—or *living* it, not for real. Everything felt sort of second-hand, third-hand even. Like someone telling me about what someone else has done, except that someone is also me. Does that make sense?'

'Not really,' she says. 'Sorry.'

'It's okay, I can't explain it properly anyway.' He stares into his wine, black hair falling over his face like a curtain, the cast of his mouth so despondent, she wants to reach out and hug him. She shifts her position, and his head snaps up again, blue eyes sharp as splinters. 'What am I, Antoinette? *Who* am I?'

She shakes her head, apologising yet again as she thinks back to the night before, all that manic scribbling, the pressure building in her skull, her chest, her gut, as she wrote, filling page after frantic page, the sensation nothing she can put into words for him now. It feels too intimate, too distant, all at the same time. 'I never gave you a name,' she says. 'I just ... you were just ... you just *were*.'

He tilts his head, a half-smile quirking his mouth. 'I still am.'

⌀

A runnel of sweat slides down Jacqueline's spine. Her hair hangs wet and limp, sticking to her face and the nape of her neck. Ryan is pressed close against her back, his body moving in time with the music. His fist punches the air with every drum beat. There are people in front of her. Behind her. Pushing and pulsing. She feels small and swallowed whole. The water someone pressed into her hand earlier is long gone. She clutches the empty bottle as though it's a talisman.

She tries to match herself to the rhythm. Tries to move the way the crowd is moving. Loose and fluid. But her foot is trapped beneath someone else's and she stumbles. Almost falls. Ryan catches her, his hands strong around her arms.

'You okay, girl?' he yells into her ear.

She nods, far from okay. 'I might take a break.'

He grins and tosses his head, unhearing.

Around her, the crowd continues to pulse and sway. There are no gaps to weave herself between. No avenues of escape that won't involve shoving and squeezing and the sharpness of elbows. On stage, the singer leans into his microphone, his vocals distorted to an electronic screech. Ryan's hands slide down her arms, coming to rest on her hips. Jacqueline closes her eyes. Tries not to notice the way her head seems to float away from her body.

Loose and fluid. She licks the sweat from her lips. Fluid and loose.

∂

'Loki?' Antoinette echoes. 'That's really what you want to call yourself?'

'I like it,' he says. 'It's mythic, and strong.'

'I already know two guys who go by the name of Loki.'

'Now you know three.'

Antoinette is doubtful. 'It's a bit … pretentious, maybe?'

'I like it,' he says again. She opens her mouth, wanting to say something about the types of boys who dub themselves *Loki* or *Thorne* or *Vlad*—pick a cliché, any cliché, paint it black and watch it insist it isn't a *goth*—but he reaches out and touches a finger to her lips. 'You had the chance to name me. Now it's my turn.' His finger slides across her cheekbone, dips down to run along her jaw. 'I choose Loki.' Smiling, he cups her chin with his hand, moves a little closer. Beneath them, the couch shifts and creaks.

'All right,' Antoinette says, *all right*, as she pulls away from him, wedging herself into the corner with her knees pulled up between them. 'Whatever, look, just stop doing that, okay? Give me some space.'

He leans back. 'I don't understand.'

'Neither do I.' She pulls a cushion onto her lap, hugs it close. 'Why am I here? Why did you *bring* me here?'

Antoinette looks away, unable to meet his eyes for the confusion that shines there, teary bright and oh so wounded, so she takes his hand instead. Traces the grooves on his palm, the sweeping curve of his lifeline, bifurcated near the base just like Paul's was—just like Paul's *is*, she reminds herself with no small amount of wonder, the seep of past tense startling and unexpected.

'Antoinette?' he asks, *Loki* asks. 'Talk to me.'

She squeezes his hand, their fingers interlacing. His skin is so pale compared to her own, so utterly unblemished—*a stone-smooth pallor which sunlight cannot penetrate*, she recalls writing, though the specifics of much else now elude her. The harder she tries to remember, the quicker the phrases seem to twist away, slippery as shoals of fish, and Antoinette gives up, frustrated and fearful.

'Have you seen my notebook?' she asks, scanning the room, trying to think where she might have left it. Because knowing exactly what she wrote, being able to see the precise words that conjured him, this creature who now sits beside her—*her* creature, her *Loki*—suddenly seems of vital importance.

Jacqueline fades in and out. The lights, the music, the texture of the patchy velour couch beneath her cheek, all pull at her from different directions. The girl with hair like shivery, coloured serpents crouches down in front of her, mouth moving—*how you going down there?*—and Jacqueline smiles at her. 'Ryan?'

The girl shakes her head. Snakes whip about her face. *He's gone to find you some water. You don't look so good.*

Jacqueline keeps smiling. 'I'm fine.'

Yeah, right. The girl presses a cold hand to Jacqueline's face, a hand that feels like glass. *And I'm the Virgin Mary.*

She might be, the way the lights shine around her head. A crimson halo, a corona made from dust and darkspun dreams. Zaney, she remembers, the girl is called Zaney. And something else. 'You make puzzle boxes,' Jacqueline says.

The girl rolls her eyes but it doesn't matter because now Jacqueline can see Ryan Jellicoe over on the other side of the room. He's holding some boy by the shirt with one hand, pushing him hard up against the wall. His mouth moves and he's pointing, pointing towards Jacqueline, and the boy is shaking his head, his mouth moving as well. Then Ryan Jellicoe does something, something with his shoulder and his knee, too fast for her to catch and then the boy is on the floor, and now Ryan Jellicoe is stalking in her direction with a face full of thunder and demons.

And. Jacqueline. Fades.

Antoinette flips through the notebook again, cover to lilac cover. It's definitely the same one she was using last night, inky flowers filling the first page, along with her own name and the lopsided heart and the four little blocks that no longer spell P-A-U-L, but the rest of the pages are blank. Not *new*, though, not *pristine*. Rumpled and worn, like they've been written on, then thoroughly, impossibly, erased, and if she tilts the book to the light *just so*, Antoinette can even make out the imprint of curves and strokes, faded little ghosts of words that *must* once have been.

'It was already like this?' she asks. 'You're sure?'

'I guess,' he says. 'I found it under the table while I was cleaning up but I didn't even open it. Just put it in here with the rest of your things.'

Antoinette throws him a glance. 'I still can't believe you cleaned up. Without the threat of corporal punishment even.'

He blinks. 'I'm not *him*, you know.'

'I know. Sorry, it's just…'

'I'll *never* be him.'

Antoinette sighs. 'I don't want you to be him, believe me. That's the very last thing I want.' She closes the notebook, tosses it onto the desk. 'Bloody useless.'

'It's all disappeared, everything you wrote?'

'Every last word.'

'How? Where did they go?'

'I don't know, Loki! Where did they come from in the first place? Where did *you* come from? You need to stop looking at me like I should have all the answers, because I don't even know where to start.'

Except he's not looking at her like that, not anymore. The grin that brightens his face is so broad and wild and infectious, so full of delight, that she can't help smiling in return. 'What?' she asks. 'What did I say?'

'You called me Loki,' he says. 'That's the first time you've used my name.'

6

acqueline stares at the mug of green tea Ryan has set in front of her. She isn't sure she wants to drink it. She isn't sure she wants to drink anything that she hasn't prepared for herself ever again. Ryan sits down opposite with a plate of toast. Reaches across the scarred wooden table top for her hand.

She snatches it away. 'Don't. Please.'

He sighs. 'Drink your tea, you'll feel better.'

Jacqueline crosses her arms. Her blue silk cocktail frock was overdressed for the valley at night; in Ryan's kitchen, with the midday sun blazing through the windows, she feels like a Christmas decoration left up past Easter. She wants to go back to the motel. She wants to take a shower.

'Really,' she says. 'I'll just call a taxi.'

Ryan shakes his head. 'Least I can do is give you a lift. Just let me finish my toast.' He picks up a piece, thickly slathered with peanut butter. Waves it at her. 'Sure you don't want some?'

Jacqueline looks away. The sight of the food is nauseating; the sound of Ryan's chewing makes her stomach roll. There's not much of last night that she can remember with any clarity. The light and the heat. The press of bodies. Little else. She can't even picture the boy who gave her the bottle of water that turned out to be spiked. Something low grade, Ryan assured her this morning, relatively harmless. Just some stupid prank gone wrong. Nothing happened, he promised, nothing at all.

We just came back here and talked till you passed out.

What did we talk about? What did I say?

The usual stuff and nonsense. Girl, you were pretty out of it.

Steam curls from her mug, the smell of tea grassy and sharp. Jacqueline takes a tentative sip. 'Ryan?'

'Yeah?'

'You said it was a prank. What did you mean?'

He takes another bite of his toast, chewing slowly while he studies her face. Swallows, then wipes his mouth with the back of his hand. 'What you need to get about me is, most days, I'm an arsehole.'

Jacqueline frowns. 'Pardon?'

The drink-spiking, he explains, case in point. He doesn't like being watched, doesn't like being *handled* and, yeah, maybe he is starting to have second thoughts about schlepping his paintings halfway across the country for a bunch of Melbourne hipsters to gawk over. And when, after all the sniping emails and passive aggressive phone messages, she rocked up to *his* home town, then yeah, maybe he thinks it's time to take her down a peg or two. Nothing too freaky; he only wanted to embarrass her.

'*You* drugged me?' Jacqueline doesn't want to believe it.

'No, I called it off. Thought I did, anyways.'

Because once she came to his house and they got to talking, he changed his mind about her pretty quick smart. Only someone didn't get the message, or someone thought they'd have some fun with the Melbourne girl anyway; whatever, *someone* has been dealt with. So, yeah, he's sorry about the whole mess, the way it panned out.

'But, hey,' he says. 'Points for honesty?'

Jacqueline squares her jaw. She wants to leave immediately. No, not quite immediately. First, she wants to stand up, reach across the table and slap him. Watch her handprint bloom across his cheek. Tell him where he can stick his damn paintings. But she can't afford to burn any bridges here; Dante would never forgive her. *Lighten the hell up, Jacks*, she can hear him saying. *This prima donna shit is part of your job, so just swallow it and deal.*

She takes a deep breath. 'You're right, Ryan. You are an arsehole.'

He smiles. 'I am.'

Her chair scrapes on the linoleum as she pushes it back from the table. She stands up, arms folded across her chest. 'I need to go. Now.'

Ryan chews his toast, slowly, his gaze not wavering from her own. 'How's about my painting then?'

KIRSTYN McDERMOTT

'What painting?'

'The one you came all this way to spy on. Could show it to you now, if you like.'

'I thought it wasn't finished.'

'It isn't.' He brushes the crumbs from his hands with three quick slaps. 'You could see it anyway.'

Jacqueline regards him evenly. There's an upper hand in the balance here, and she senses the scales tipping in her favour. 'Later,' she tells him, then stalks barefoot into the living room where she left her shoes and bag.

She's buckling the strap on the second sandal, hoping the four-inch stilettos won't prove too much for her compromised equilibrium, when she hears Ryan push his own chair back from the table. Jacqueline retrieves her phone from her bag. Holds it up to him as he walks into the room. 'Do I need to call a taxi?'

He pauses, then shakes his head. 'Give me a sec to find my keys.'

It's a fifteen-minute drive to the motel in Ascot and Jacqueline spends most of it with her head turned towards the window, watching suburbs melt past in the sun. Brisbane in February. If she never comes here again in her life, she will die happy. At least Ryan's car has air conditioning, which he obligingly turns up to maximum. 'Not much for the heat, are you, girl?'

'Not much.'

She parries further attempts at conversation with equally terse responses, and he soon stops trying. Switches the radio on instead. Turns the volume up loud, filling the car with the kind of abrasive, masculine rock that scrapes on Jacqueline like asphalt over skin. Strident guitars and sandpaper vocals. Flame trees and weary drivers.

Jacqueline sighs. Lifts a hand to shield her eyes from the glare.

'Number eleven,' she says—almost shouts—when they reach the motel.

Ryan pulls up in the parking space outside her room and kills the engine. 'Look,' he says. 'I'm sorry, okay? It was a shitty thing to do to someone.'

'Yes,' she replies. 'It was.'

The car grows warm in the silence. Jacqueline reaches for the door handle, pulls it towards her just as Ryan grabs her other arm.

'Look,' he says again. 'This hasn't mucked everything up, has it?'

'Meaning what?'

He rubs at his chin. 'You gonna tell Dante to cancel my show?'

Jacqueline curbs a smile. If only she wielded that sort of influence. 'Isn't that what you want?' she asks. 'This whole song and dance number you've been running for the past few months. You've been practically daring us to rip up your contract.'

'Yeah.' Ryan slumps in his seat. 'Yeah, I guess.'

'Do you want to tell me what's going on?'

He shrugs. 'I dunno. These past couple of months, nothing seems to be coming out right. Like it's just cut me off, you know?'

'Cut you off?'

'The painting. It doesn't wanna play anymore. Or I've lost sight of what I was doing in the first place, maybe, or I never knew.'

Jacqueline shifts to face him. Her hem rides up on her thighs and she pulls it back down. It doesn't pull far. 'If you want some feedback, I'd be more than happy to—'

'Feedback.' Ryan grimaces. 'What I want is an exit strategy.'

'You don't mean that,' Jacqueline says. 'I've seen your work and it's good, it really is. How about I come by tomorrow morning? You can show me the painting then, and we can talk things over. Perhaps the show doesn't even need it. There are already enough canvases in your studio to fill Seventh Circle twice over.'

'It needs it,' he says. 'You know it needs it. No centrepiece, no show. Right?'

Jacqueline bites her lip. 'Let's talk about it tomorrow.'

'Tomorrow. Yeah, sure.'

He looks deflated, *defeated*. She touches his knee, lightly. Right where a stripe of sunlight falls across his skin, setting the hairs aglow. His skin is warm. His muscles twitch.

'I'm exhausted, Ryan. My eyes hurt. I need to sleep.'

He looks down at her hand. 'Yeah, I reckon you do at that.' He traces a finger over her skin, describing extended figure eights between her knuckles. 'Smooth,' he says. 'Soft.'

Jacqueline pulls away. Opens the door and pushes herself from the car with less grace than she'd like. Leans back in to retrieve her bag from the footwell. 'I'll see you tomorrow morning, then?'

'Want me to come pick you up?'

'All right,' she says. 'Around nine?'

He laughs. 'Christ, up with the birds, eh? How about ten?'

'All right,' she says again. 'See you then.'

Antoinette sits outside in the car for several minutes, watching the darkened flat that used to be her home. Paul will be out at his Monday night critiquing-slash-drinking session with his writer buddies, she knows that, but still she waits, watching for the sudden switch of a light, the movement of a silhouette beyond the glass. She yawns, tired despite having slept most of yet another day away. Tired down to her bones, her body clock all screwed up, and it will take some time to set it right.

At least she doesn't have to work tonight, though the favours she owes Michelle are multiplying like amoeba. *You need to let him go*, was the lecture when Antoinette called that afternoon, *you don't heal a broken heart by picking at the wound*. And *I know*, Antoinette told her, and *it isn't that, honest*. Explaining about her foot, about how she really should let it rest just one more night, and promising to make it up to Michelle any way she liked—which means she now has to pull a double-shift on Wednesday, but she'll hobble across that bridge when she gets to it.

'Come on, girlie-girl,' she tells herself. 'Get this over with.'

She wrestles the two suitcases from the back seat. They're both large—Jacqueline took the smallest with her to Brisbane—and Antoinette dreads the weight of them once full, but the fewer trips she makes back here the better. Without bothering to knock, she unlocks the front door and pushes inside.

The flat is dark and empty and feels like … nothing.

Surprised, Antoinette flicks on the hall light. Just a couple of days ago, the place was full of jagged edges and pointed corners, heavy with grief and the salt-sharp taste of regret. There are still memories aplenty—the empty peg on the wall where she used to hang her coat; the geisha-girl painting they bought at a garage sale for five dollars, haggled down from ten; the deadly, hip-bruising cupboard—but now they seem like *old* memories, smooth and threadbare and worn, leached of any emotion stronger than a vague nostalgia.

Antoinette supposes she should feel grateful—and mostly she is—but there's a small part of her that also feels robbed, like something precious has been lost, or stolen, or was maybe never there in the first place.

In the bedroom, she throws the suitcases onto the unmade bed, side by side with bellies eager for filling. This, too, is easier than she thought it would be: all her clothes pulled from the wardrobe, from the chest of drawers that she scavenged out of hard rubbish but which Paul could keep, from underneath the bed itself. Neatly folding everything into the first suitcase, deciding to leave the coat hangers with their awkward elbows behind, impressed with how much the thing can swallow.

When it comes to Paul's clothes, she chooses carefully.

A black woollen jumper she bought him a couple of years ago, an old pair of jeans he hasn't worn for ages, a couple of T-shirts from the bottom drawer. A handful of socks and jocks that won't be missed, and a pair of black Converse sneakers that have been living under the bed for so long she has to blow an entire tribe of dust bunnies from their laces before stuffing them down the side of the suitcase. A few more odds and sods, nothing he wears very often, nothing he should miss. Her hand pauses over the leather jacket hanging on the back of the door, but only for a moment.

That really would feel like stealing.

Antoinette sits on the end of the bed, head in her hands, thinking of what else she needs to take with her. There's too much to consider: personal things like books and DVDs and CDs and all the little knick-knacks and bits of junk she's carried along throughout her life; and then the household stuff, not so much the furniture which was mostly here when she moved in, but all the mundane minutiae, cups and saucepans and towels and blankets and crappy paintings of Japanese girls in cheap wooden frames.

She'd like to abandon it all. Just take what she's already packed and leave the rest for Paul to do with what he will. A clean break, a fresh start, the notion exquisite but impossible; she won't be able to afford to replace everything she'll need in whatever place she eventually finds for herself—and for *Loki*, she supposes with a jolt. She has no idea what to do about *Loki*, her new and needy shadow with his strong, blue-veined hands and eyes that trace her every step.

Never mind the *way* he looks at her, eyes fox-sharp and fox-hungry, the colour of winter skies and low horizons, holding her gaze throughout the night as questions spilled relentless from his mouth. *How did you* and *why did you* and *what am I*, and even though most of her answers were merely variations on the theme of *I don't know*, still he kept on asking.

Tell me more. Tell me everything. Tell me again.

And so she did. Curled on the couch until the thin light of dawn broke over the bay: her life, her memories, all the messy, painful stuff with Paul, hashed through again for him or, rather, *with* him. For as she spoke he would nod and sigh, and *I remember*, he would say, pressing her hand to his cheek. *Or I know. I remember knowing.* His skin so warm beneath her fingers, vellum-soft, as he asked her again to tell him of his creation, her eager young Sunday schooler begging for serpents and fruit.

Tell me more. Tell me everything.

Enough. Antoinette gets up, tosses the two lacquered jewellery boxes from the top of the dresser into a suitcase, not caring how they rattle, nothing in them more valuable than amethyst and sterling silver anyway. There's an old Poppy Z Brite paperback on her bedside table, a novel she's read almost to death, its broken spine so creased the title is all but rubbed away. *Lost Souls*, comfort reading for the shy and cynical, and surely there's a couple more rounds left in it, so she throws the book into the case as well, then tugs the zipper closed.

And that's the bedroom done at least.

Dispirited, she shuffles into the kitchen and checks there's enough milk in the fridge before switching on the kettle. She should take the toaster with her—Jacqueline gave them that—and there are her favourite mugs as well, not to forget the three googly-eyed bat magnets she found at a two-dollar shop, or the Halloween-themed potholders with their black cats and pumpkins. So much stuff. She's going to need more than a couple of suitcases to remove herself completely from this place; she's going to need boxes and bubblewrap and possibly someone with a station wagon.

And she's going to need to sit down with Paul and talk.

It makes her tired just to think about it. It makes her feel old.

Antoinette stirs three heaped sugars into her coffee. Ever-expanding hips be damned, tonight she needs it sweet. There's a picture frame lying face-down on the kitchen table. Bright red with bleeding black hearts she painted on using nail-polish their first Valentine's together, it used to hang in the living room near the stereo. She picks it up and turns it over, wanting to see again the photo of the two of them Paul took at arm's length the time they drove down to Phillip Island to see the fairy penguins, their hearts as big and open and clear as the blue summer sky spread above them.

Except the photo isn't in the frame.

There's only a piece of plain white paper pressed behind the glass. Antoinette frowns and unclips the backplate. Not *plain* paper after all, not with the faint grey Kodak logo stamped all over the underside, but the kind she used to print the photo onto in the first place, and that's just too weird. Taking the frame down, she can understand. Removing the photo, even putting another snapshot in its place, fine. But replacing it with nothing, just a blank white space? That she cannot begin to fathom.

'None of your business,' she tells herself. 'Not anymore.'

It seems odd, not the words themselves, but the absence of an echoing pang. Only three days since Paul kicked her out, only three days since it felt like the tears would never stop, like the ragged hole behind her ribs would never heal, and surely it can't be this easy? This odd oasis of calm in which she finds herself can only be a temporary reprieve, some species of shock limping in a little late for the bell, or maybe just a reaction to the much, *much* stranger things that have come to come pass since Friday night. In a world where fantasy turns flesh-and-blood, after all, who's to say what is and isn't normal?

Antoinette shakes her head. She needs to get moving, needs to get these clothes back to him—back to *Loki*—so he can get out of her dressing gown once and for all. He was still wearing it when she dragged herself out of bed late that afternoon, still or *again*, because his hair was wet and smelling of shampoo, dripping down his narrow back when she poked her head through the study door to see if he wanted coffee. His smile less effusive than the day before, cast fresh with caution, with uncertainty, and it pained her to see that, to know she was the cause.

I don't drink coffee, Antoinette. I decided I didn't like it.

So she made him hot chocolate instead—which he did like, very much—and though she was curious about her things still piled untouched on the futon, she didn't ask where he slept, or even if.

Antoinette puts the picture frame back together, white paper and all, folding the metal clips down with a careful thumbnail before returning it to the table. She tips the rest of her coffee into the sink and is rinsing out the mug when she hears a key turn in the front door lock, followed by the familiar creak of hinges and the stamping of boots on the doormat.

'Greta?' Paul calls, slamming the door shut. 'Greta, that you?'

Antoinette squares her shoulders, remembering again the face he wore last time she saw him, blunt with anger and contempt, and she turns, steeling herself for the reprise, as he walks through the doorway and stops short, his mouth falling open in a round, startled *oh*.

7

ecovering, Paul throws her a scowl. 'You might have called first.' He's carrying a plastic bag of what smells like Indian takeaway, one of the containers leaking orange.

'I didn't think you'd be here. Isn't Monday your—'

'I didn't feel like it.'

'Oh.' She can't help but compare the two of them in her mind, Paul and Loki, Loki and Paul; would like to stand them side by side, face to face, measure one against the other and see what has been changed, what has been kept.

'Greta's coming over,' Paul says. 'She's downloaded the latest *True Blood*.'

'I was about to go anyway.'

He puts the bag of Indian on the table. 'Leave your keys, okay?'

'What? Why?'

'I don't want you sneaking in here all the time, messing around.'

'I wasn't *sneaking*, Paul. I just needed some more of my stuff, and I thought it would be easier if I came by when you were out, that's all.'

'Sure, you did.'

'I was going to write you a note, let you know I'd been by.'

'Like you did yesterday, you mean? I must have missed that.'

'I wasn't here yesterday.'

'When did you swap this over, then?' Paul snatches the picture frame from the table and thrusts it towards her, its empty face a blank and glassy accusation. 'And all that shit you left in the bathroom, ash or whatever it was? If you think playing voodoo is gonna get us back together, Ant, you're more fucked up than I thought.'

She pushes the frame away. 'I haven't the foggiest what you're on about.'

'Those bloody rose petals. What did you do, burn them? Mix them with ink or something? It took me all day to clean that shit up.'

Rose petals. Bathroom. The dozen long-stemmed blooms he gave her on the first anniversary of their moving in together, the ones she so carefully plucked once they started to curl, drying enough to fill a tall glass vase which she kept on the windowsill, their fading scent bolstered by a few drops of essential oil every other week. And now they're gone, burnt to ash, is that what he's saying?

'It wasn't me,' she tells him. 'I wasn't here yesterday, I told you.'

'Then who? Fucking Cinderella?'

Antoinette glares at him. 'Greta has a key.'

'Greta?' Paul snorts. 'Oh sure, that makes a whole lot of sense. Christ, Ant, do you think I'm a moron?'

And no, it doesn't make any sense, but yes, she's starting to think maybe he *is* a moron—or at least he's been acting like one—and she tells him this, tells him to stop acting like a *baby*, and then they're fighting again, snapping at each other like maltreated hounds. The same old litany of complaints and resentments, the *you nevers* and the *I should haves*, voices pitching higher and louder with each fresh-aired grievance, until suddenly the picture frame is hurled across the room, slamming into the pantry door with a shriek of broken glass, and Antoinette jumps, a startled cry of her own caught in her throat.

'Well,' she says after a beat. 'That was grown-up.'

Paul sticks out his hand. 'Give me the keys.'

'No.' Anger simmers beneath her skin, a not entirely unpleasant sensation. 'I've still got stuff here. You'll get the keys once I'm done.'

His jaw clenches, eyes narrowed to hateful shards. The last time he looked at her like that, hovering over the innards of her shattered laptop, there was fear at the back of her throat, fear and dread and the incipient scratch of tears. Now there's only the slow, clean burn of anger and, after a breath or two, not even that, just a hollow throb deep in the very centre of her. She stares at him, at the red flush of his cheeks, the pulse of a single vein at his temple. Was it only Saturday she spent so many wretched hours sobbing over this man, over the mess she made of their life together? It seems an age ago now. It seems almost … inconsequential.

'I'm sorry,' Antoinette says, and she means it, though exactly what she's sorry for, she can't quite define.

'Get out,' Paul growls. 'You can come back for the rest of your gear later.'

'Fine. I'll just grab what I've already packed.'

He follows her into the bedroom, suspicious old fishwife watching her every step and struggle as she lugs the suitcases one at a time down the hall, not once offering to help, but also not demanding to inspect their contents, and for that she's thankful—explaining why she has some of his clothes in her cases is not a conversation she feels up to dodging right now. Gritting her teeth, she heaves them in silence down the front stairs and into her faithful old Laser—one in the boot, one across the back seat—thinking how at least she'll have Loki to lend a hand at the other end.

Paul remains at the front door, arms folded. The porchlight stains his skin jaundice, throws sharp and ugly shadows across his face. She doesn't wonder what she ever saw in him—she *knows* what she saw in him—she just wonders where it went, and how.

'We have to talk properly at some stage.' Antoinette walks back up the front path, keeping her voice low. 'Work out what to do with some of the shared stuff, take my name off the bills. That sort of thing.'

He shrugs, the barest hitch of his shoulders. 'Whatever.'

'So, I'll call you? Next time I need to come over?'

'Make it snappy, yeah? I don't want your shit gathering dust here for the next twelve months while you mope around at your sister's.'

'Actually, I already have a place.' An impulsive lie, unthinking, unplanned, but more than enough to wipe that condescending smirk from his face, and so she runs with it. 'A friend of Jacqueline's is backpacking through Europe for a while and they're letting me take over their lease. It's a great little flat in St Kilda. Dirt cheap rent, just around the corner from the Esplanade. I move in next week, so...'

'Wow,' Paul says, deadpan. 'Jacqueline has friends?'

Antoinette sighs. 'Look, can we just be civil about all this? I'll get my stuff out of here as soon as I can and then we can both go on with our lives.'

'Got yourself one of those as well, did you? A life?'

He's such a fucking baby. How she managed to put up with all this for so long is beyond her comprehension right now, but she bites her tongue. Antoinette wouldn't put it past him to simply toss what's left of her stuff out on the street for the urban scavengers to pick through. Toss it out or else build himself a merry little bonfire in the back courtyard, invite Greta and Jai and the rest of their snarky, black-taloned clique around to toast marshmallows and burn white sage and generally cleanse the place of all things Evil Ex-Girlfriend.

'Paul,' she says. 'Listen, I think we—'

But he's already retreating into the flat, top lip curling into a sneer, and when he slams the door in her face, Antoinette doesn't think she's ever heard anything sound so final.

✄

Zane stomps up the front stairs to Ryan's place, her rainbow-laced sneakers slapping hard against the bare wood. Jacqueline follows at a slower pace, a dozen careful steps behind. She feels tired, in a used up sort of way. A lingering effect of the drink-spiking, perhaps, or merely due to what little sleep she managed to scrape together from broken and dream-worried scraps.

It was the girl who picked her up that morning. Thumping on the motel door at quarter to ten and flicking a salute when Jacqueline finally opened it. *Your chariot awaits, m'lady.* A chariot littered with empty cans of Coke Zero and crumpled chocolate wrappers. Three small suitcases lay flat along its back seat. They reminded Jacqueline of old-fashioned school ports, or the sample bags of a sales rep down on her luck.

Zane carries them with her now. One in each hand, the third tucked beneath her left arm. The screen door is ajar and the girl snags the corner with her foot. Pulls it open enough to wedge a hip inside. 'Ryan? You here?' A male voice answers from within the house, words Jacqueline doesn't catch, but Zane grins and bumps the door wide. Bustles herself and her cases over the threshold. Glances back with an impatient jerk of her chin. 'You expecting a personal invitation?'

Ryan is in his studio.

The smell of oil paint hangs fresh in the air and the large canvas still sits on its easels. Still faces the mid-morning sun that streams through the windows on the far side of the room. It's naked now, the cloth that once shrouded it crumpled in the corner. Jacqueline can feel her skin begin to itch. She wants to see that painting. She needs to see it.

'Hey,' Ryan says. He's wiping a brush on a soft piece of rag. Green paint stains his fingers. 'How you feeling?'

Jacqueline ignores the question. 'You've been working.'

'He's always working,' the girl says. 'Even when he's not. Can't turn it off, can you, Ryan?' She taps the side of her head. 'Man's a machine, for reals. Runs on pure imagination.'

Ryan snorts. 'That's enough out of you, little thing.' He regards Jacqueline with red-rimmed eyes. There's more paint on his chin. On his forehead. 'Been up all night, trying to sort it. Too wired to sleep, too buzzed.'

'A machine.' Zane grins. 'Like I said.'

Ignoring her, Ryan steps closer to Jacqueline. He reaches out, his hand almost on her arm before he seems to think better of it. Changes the gesture to a wave, motions for her to follow. 'Look,' he says, walking over to the huge canvas. 'Just look and tell me what you reckon.'

The painting is another cityscape, another of Ryan's ruined Brisbanes. The angle feels familiar, a tourist shot for a place no sane person would want to visit, with the river curving through the foreground, its bridges near to crumbling, and above it all the loom of long-vacant buildings. Except here there are signs of life, slight but certain. Green foliage spills from the balconies of abandoned apartments. Creeps like ivy over vertical concrete walls. Lush and vibrant, glossed with the gold of a rising sun. A reclamation at once relentless and, possibly, redemptive.

'It's only a start,' Ryan tells her. 'I've been messing with the light. Trying to get the balance right before I expand on it.'

'More plants?'

'Birds too, maybe some critters even, if it won't look too naff.' Absently, he shoves a hand into his dreads and shakes them. ''Cause this is what it'd be like, yeah? Take us out of the picture and everything doesn't just stop. My perspective was wrong—no, not *wrong*, just not *complete*, if you get me. It was, I dunno—'

'Arrogant,' Jacqueline offers.

Ryan lifts an eyebrow, then nods. 'Yeah, okay. Arrogant.'

She smiles, just a little. 'This is really excellent work. Complex, considered. Dante will love it; he'll call it transcendent.'

'That'll help me sleep at night.'

'Ryan—'

'I know, I know.' He holds up his hands. 'You need to ignore half what comes out of my mouth, most days. You really do.'

'Because you're an arsehole.'

Those straight, white teeth of his flash. 'Because I'm an arsehole.'

'Right.' Jacqueline steps closer to the painting. Steps further away from the man who created it. There's a scent about him, sharp and teasing and naggingly familiar. Something like eucalyptus but not quite. It makes her uncomfortable. Not the scent so much, but the way it snags at her. She wants to bury her face in his dreads and breathe deep. She wants to shove him from the verandah and hear him scream.

Her phone rings, muffled yet insistent, from within the side pocket of her bag.

Jacqueline fishes it free: *Antoinette calling*. She loosens a tight-held breath. Dante has rung three times since the weekend. Left at least a dozen text messages. She's yet to reply to any of them. Later, she tells herself, when she has something to report.

'You need to get that?' Ryan nods at the phone in her hand.

Jacqueline shakes her head. Diverts her sister to voicemail with the flick of a thumb. Slips the phone back into her bag. Later, later. 'How long do you need to finish the painting?'

'A week or so. But I want to go back to some of the others as well.'

'Do you think that's necessary?'

'Nothing heavy-handed. A bit of foreshadowing, a few hints to what's coming.'

'There's not a lot of time, Ryan. There's still the transportation—'

'Yeah, I get it. I need to work fast. I can do that.'

'The paint needs to dry fast, too.'

'It'll be dry. Not cured, not sealable, but dry enough to cart across country, you get people who know what they're doing.'

'It's not as though we hire Mini Movers for these jobs, Ryan.'

He rubs at his chin, his eyes fixed on the canvas before them. His jaw clenches, loosens and clenches again. A vein pulses at his temple. Jacqueline takes a step towards him. Places her hand on his shoulder. The light cotton weave of his T-shirt is warm and damp beneath her skin.

'It's really good.' She squeezes, feels his bones shift. 'I mean it.'

Ryan covers her hand with his own, then lifts it, presses her fingers against his stubble-rough cheek. 'Thanks.'

Behind them, Zane coughs. Scuffs her sneaker along the floorboards until Ryan turns to face her, Jacqueline's hand still clutched within his own. 'Zaney wants to know if you'd like to take a gander at her cases while you're here. Only she's too shy to ask for herself.'

'That's me,' the girl retorts. 'Shrinking fucking violet.'

Jacqueline considers the three suitcases stacked against the wall. One of them is the bright candy pink of Barbie doll boxes, the other two a more sombre charcoal. Vaguely, she recalls the photographs thrust into her hands at Merde. Those, along with the voracious expression the girl wore that night. The same one that's tightening her face now. 'I've already told you I'm not a commissioning agent for Seventh Circle,' she says. 'Dante's the one you need to talk to.'

'But you can take a look, right?' Zane isn't actually begging, but her tone is probably as close to it as she gets. 'Come on, you gotta be curious.'

Jacqueline really isn't. After three years of working with Dante, she knows there's little chance he'll give a damn about whatever it is the girl has tucked away inside those cases. Her boss prefers his art adversarial, his gestures grand and overly dramatic and—for preference—flavoured with a not insubstantial dose of testosterone. But she wonders again about the relationship between

Zane and Ryan. About whether snubbing the girl would be likely to get the artist offside as well.

'All right,' she says. 'But no promises.'

Wordless, Zane marches over to her suitcases and lines them up side by side on the floor. Snaps them open and lifts their lids before stepping back, hands on hips. 'They're sort of a sequence, these three. You need to start from the left and work your way over. Or you don't *need* to, but it's better if you—'

'Stop now.' Ryan places a hand on the back of Zane's neck. Squeezes, gentle as a mother cat. 'How's about getting us something to drink, eh? Let Jacqueline take her own time with these.'

Zane grins at him. Turns to Jacqueline with barely the scrap of a smile left over. 'You want Coke? Or juice, I think there's some left in the fridge.'

'Juice will be good. Thanks.'

'Put something extra in mine, little thing.'

Jacqueline waits until she can no longer hear the smack of sneaker on wood before approaching the cases. Hot pink flanked by grey. A wound within necrotic flesh. She crouches before the first one.

Inside, a female figure crouches as well, face tilted upwards. Made from some kind of flesh-coloured compound that looks soft and malleable. Able to be hurt. Silver fish-hooks sink into the figure, golden chains pull in opposite directions. Flesh stretches, skin draws taut. Breast. Hip. Throat. An elbow tugged akimbo.

One hook remains unseen, swallowed between the figure's thighs. The chains seem to float in space, not quite reaching walls which are painted a dark and clotted red. Jacqueline squints. Sees the fishing line deftly strung from the end of each chain to its ultimate anchor point. The entire inner lid of the case is a sheet of mirrored glass. When it's closed, the figure inside will be forced to stare at herself.

'She's young,' Ryan says. 'Over-estimates the value of shock.'

The interior of the second case, the pink case, is covered with photos torn from magazines. A roughly equal mixture of pornography and high fashion, Jacqueline guesses. A collage of women, or at least their composite parts. Open mouths modelling lipstick or offering blowjobs. Hard to tell which. The case is filled with doll parts. Barbie dolls, baby dolls, Bratz dolls—all naked, all torn to pieces. Legs, torsos, arms, heads with flat, unblinking eyes but hair still long and glossy and smooth.

'Too obvious,' Jacqueline murmurs. 'She's trying too hard.'

'Yeah,' Ryan says. 'I know.'

The third case is painted a dull matte black, inside and out. Dozens of small keys, the kind to fit luggage locks, hang from the lid. More fishing line. Little red beads, suspended like drops of blood. And on the floor, another mirror. Round. Its gilded frame is fancy but old, the gold flaking to base metal. Tilted slightly to reflect the face of the viewer, although Jacqueline isn't at the right angle.

She sighs. Rubs her forehead, already beading with sweat.

'Here.' Ryan reaches out a hand.

Jacqueline takes it, allows him to pull her to her feet.

'She's young,' he says again. 'She'll get there, she wants it bad enough.'

'Not with Dante. This isn't the kind of thing that grabs him.'

'Doubt there's anyone it would grab too hard right now.' He bends down and runs a finger through the dangling keys. They jingle like coins in a pocket. Like thin brass chimes in a breeze. 'It's not there, it's not nearly there.'

'So why let her bring these over? Why raise her hopes for nothing?'

'Not for nothing.' He frowns. 'Be honest with her, yeah? Don't hold back. She's straight out of high school, some white-bread art program that didn't teach her squat 'cept how to be teacher's pet monster. Girl needs a reality check. She needs to hit the ground for once.'

'That's cruel.'

'No, it's not,' he says. 'Zane has something, when she's not trying so bloody hard, when she just lets it ride her instead of trying to force everything into these clever little schoolgirl shapes. If I didn't believe that, I wouldn't give a rat's arse what she did with herself. So you tell her, yeah? Tell her exactly what you think about these stupid doll coffins.'

'Why don't *you* tell her?'

'That's not my role. I'm here to pick up the pieces and make sure she doesn't give up the first time she gets bit.'

'Leaving me to wear the black hat.'

'Why not?' He smiles, brushes her cheek with the back of his hand. 'You'll be the one riding off into the sunset at the end of it.'

Jacqueline steps from his reach. She feels queasy all of a sudden, stomach rebellious, skin flushed. Pressure builds at her temples. Her ears are filled with a low background hum. She shakes her head. 'What other *roles* are you playing with that girl, Ryan?'

'That any kind of concern of yours?'

'Anything that might distract you is a concern of mine.'

His smile twists sideways but as he opens his mouth to answer, the sound of footsteps filters down the hall. 'Not my type of distraction,' he whispers, then winks and turns towards the door as Zane comes shuffling slowly through, three near-to-brimming glasses in her skinny hands. Ryan takes one and the girl offers a second to Jacqueline, her eyes bright with anticipation.

'So?' she asks. 'What did you think?'

Jacqueline accepts the glass. Her hand shakes and juice spills over onto her fingers, sticky and cold. Ice clanks against the sides. The humming in her head is louder now. White noise like the crash of waves on rocks. 'I, ah...' She coughs, sips at her drink. Some kind of tropical mix, sweet with pineapple where she expected the tart snap of orange. Her mouth is still dry. 'They're not the right kind of work for Seventh Circle.'

Zane falters, but only for a moment. 'Why not?'

'They've yet to mature. The pieces certainly have potential, but they're not ... you're not ... I mean...' Jacqueline blinks and colours bloom behind her lids. Mute firecracker flashes that linger even after she opens her eyes again. Her vision distorts. Wavers, flickers. The walls twist and warp, shifting in and out of focus.

She holds her breath. Presses the glass against her forehead.

'Are you okay?'

Ryan looms in front of her, so suddenly that she stumbles backwards. A wave of disorientation crashes over her, through her, and now it's not the walls that are slipping, but Jacqueline herself. *No*, she says, tries to say, tries to force the word through the closed, dry flesh of her throat. *No*, as she falls, as the glass falls, as juice splashes wet and cold onto her legs. *No*, arms outstretched, lurid pink case, doll parts jutting hard and plastic into her palms, scattering beneath her clumsy weight.

From somewhere too distant to matter, Ryan is calling her name.

But Jacqueline is fixated on her hands. The translucent shiver of skin and flesh, the X-ray delicacy of bone, holding them up to the light that surrounds her now like a caul. Hard, white light she has never known before and would give almost anything to never know again. *No*, she says. *Stop*, and, *please*, as she squeezes her eyes shut. It makes no difference. The light follows, searing, scraping at her flesh. Filling her head with the incoherent hiss of a thousand dying stars.

hold on hold on hold on

Stern and familiar, the voice winds around her, through her, within her.

hold on hold on hold on

And Jacqueline wants to listen, wants desperately to obey those words and cling tight to consciousness, to her own fading, falling self. But the light is so hard and so bright and so cold.

And it wants her more.

8

Antoinette delivers a second round of cappuccinos to the couple at Table 3, then hurries back to the counter to plate the slice of flourless orange that will go with the latte Jackson is making for the woman at Table 5.

'That it for coffees?' he asks, steaming the milk.

'That's it.'

'Traffic kinda slow today, huh?'

Antoinette sprinkles icing sugar over the cake and spoons a dollop of fresh cream onto the side. 'It's Tuesday, and the weather doesn't exactly help.' A fat summer rain that's been falling since she woke up this morning, the splatter of water against window the only sound in a flat that was still empty when she left for work. If it wasn't for the feeling inside her belly, the solid, shifting weight she's come to think of as the Loki-stone, she could almost imagine that he never—

Jackson nudged her elbow. 'You hear me?'

'Sorry, what?'

'Take a break, I can hold the fort.'

'You sure?' There should be three of them front of house this shift, but Steff called in sick at the last moment and Antoinette's reluctant to leave Jackson out here on his own, no matter how sluggish the punters.

'Fifteen minutes,' he says. 'You look like you need it.'

Which is surely a roundabout way of saying she looks like hell, no matter how sweet the smile he flashes as he slides the plate smoothly from her grasp, and fifteen minutes won't even begin to make amends on that score. She wipes her hands on her apron and pours herself a glass of water. Normally she'd venture out back to the beer garden, but the rain will sound like marbles on the laserlite roofing, so instead she retrieves her bag from the staff pigeonholes and tucks herself into the desperate little table for one-and-a-half that lurks by the kitchen door.

Three missed calls on her mobile: two from numbers she doesn't recognise and the third from her mother, the latter followed up by a text demanding that Antoinette call back as soon as possible. *Important!* Everything is always *important* with her mother, though Antoinette wonders if this latest urgency means she has called the flat—called *Paul's* flat—and been caught up on the not-so-breaking news. If she isn't planning a celebration dinner right this moment. Antoinette shakes her head. Time enough to deal with her mother later, much later if she can manage it. Certainly after she's had a chance to talk to Jacqueline, to tell her...

What exactly?

Hey, sis, guess what I made in school today?

Whatever, she'll think of something. Right now she just needs to hear her sister's voice, calm and cool and definitely-can-do.

Antoinette flips her mobile shut and dumps it onto the tabletop, turns it slowly around and around, an electronic death-watch beetle spinning helpless on its back. Briefly, she considers trying Jacqueline again, but the three texts she's sent since this morning will be irritation enough and she knows that her sister will call as soon as she gets a free minute. If she gets a free minute. If Mr BrisVegas doesn't need his hand held and his ego stroked every tick of the damn clock.

If. If. If. Way too many of those in her life right now.

'Here you go.' Jackson, sneaking sly beneath her notice, placing a mug of coffee in front of her. 'Flat white with two, right?'

Antoinette smiles. 'Thanks.'

'Hey, you want to do something later on, grab a drink maybe?' Fiddling with the wide silver ring that he wears on his thumb, twisting it around and around and around, fast enough to leave a groove, and the hope on his face so clear and sweet she feels like a dick for having to crush it.

'Sorry, Jackson. I can't.' She rips open the sugar sachets and stirs them into her coffee. 'Things with me are a bit, um, complicated right now.'

'Yeah, I know. Michelle filled me in.'

But of course she did. 'You don't know the half of it. Hell, *I* don't even know the half of it.'

Jackson nods sagely. 'Getting dumped sucks every kind of arse; been there, done that, got the scars to show for it.' He slaps a flattened palm to his chest. 'But you should give yourself a night off from the heavy stuff, you know, get some distance? No pressure, no strings, just a couple of mates out having a drink.'

Which is a nice enough save, and so she lets him have it, never mind what other designs he may have had. 'I'm okay,' she says. 'Really.'

''Course you are, but the offer stands anyway.' He grins, bumps her on the shoulder with a loose-curled fist. 'You know where to find me.'

She starts to thank him, and maybe to say something else besides, something to put him more firmly off her scent because a new entanglement—even one with *no pressure, no strings*, if ever such beast can be said to exist—is the very last thing she needs right now. But before she can find the words, her Nokia starts to buzz, starts to skitter across the table like it's making a run for it, and she scoops it into her hands. Frowning at the number on the screen—yet another mystery caller—she flips the phone open and lifts it to her ear.

'Antoinette? It's me.'

Only a beat to recognise him above the background hum which sounds like the rush of traffic, or maybe the shunt and shudder of train wheels; only a beat to realise that too-familiar voice does not belong to Paul.

'Loki? Where are you?' She mouths an apology to Jackson,

makes her *I have to take this call* face, and he smiles and hooks his thumb over his shoulder—*I need to get back to work anyway*—then saunters off to the front of the restaurant.

'I had some stuff to do,' Loki is saying. 'Didn't want to wake you.'

'I thought you were…' *Gone*, the word on the tip of her tongue but that's not right, not *gone*. Not with the Loki-stone anchored inside her, its subtle tug and pull a constant reminder of his presence, of his *absence*.

'What time will you be home tonight?' Loki asks.

'Um, seven-thirty, eight o'clock, depending on the trams.'

'Cool, I'll take care of dinner.'

'You will?' Too late to keep the surprise from her voice, and Loki's sigh sounds like static in her ear.

'I'm not *him*, Antoinette. You need to remember that.'

'I do,' she says. 'I mean, I know. I'm sorry.'

'Look, I gotta go. I'm using some guy's phone here.'

'Where *are* you?' she asks again, but he's already hung up. No point calling him back, what with the borrowed mobile probably returned to its owner by now and Loki loping off on whatever errands he's managed to amass for himself in the whole three days of his existence. Instead, she sends another quick text to Jacqueline—*not working tnite, pls call, need to talk*—then leans back against the wall and closes her eyes.

Three days.

Astonishing, how soon the magical becomes mundane.

❧

It takes Jacqueline a few moments to recognise the woman leaning over her. Ryan Jellicoe's sister—what was her name? Alice? yes, Alice—stooping to press the back of one hand to Jacqueline's cheek.

'How you feeling?' the woman asks.

'I…' Jacqueline coughs, her throat too dry for words. She's lying on her back in a strange bed, in a strange room. A sheet is pulled up to her waist. The ceiling is made from wide wooden boards painted the colour of old milk. A fan spins lazily in its centre, stirring the soupy air above her. There's a window opposite, its Holland blind drawn all the way down. She has no idea where she is.

'Here, have some of this.' Alice is holding a glass of orange liquid. She slips a hand beneath Jacqueline's head and gently lifts. Presses the glass to her lips. 'Careful, not too much.'

The juice is cold and sweet. It almost hurts to swallow. 'What happened?' she whispers. 'I don't … I remember falling.'

'What about before that? You remember what you were doing? Anything weird, funny sounds or smells even?'

Light, she remembers that, and colours. There was something terrible about the light. Something horrible and frightening that she really doesn't want to consider right now. Or ever. 'I was looking at the painting,' she tells Alice. 'No, I was looking at the suitcases. I remember feeling hot, and then dizzy.' *And lost.* She shakes her head. 'Sorry, it's all a bit fuzzy.'

Alice puts the glass down on the beside table. Ice clanks against the sides. 'My brother says you fainted. You ever have anything like this happen before?'

Jacqueline swallows hard. 'No.'

'How about your family, any history of seizures? Epilepsy, anything like that?'

'No, nothing. Why are you—'

'Hey there.' Ryan appears in the doorway, silhouetted against the light from the hall outside. 'Thought I heard voices.' He crosses the room and sits himself on the end of the bed. The oily scent of turpentine slicks the air.

Jacqueline pushes herself up on her elbows. 'Can someone please tell me what's going on?'

'You passed out,' Ryan says. 'Might've been the heat, I dunno. One minute you were fine and then you started acting kinda woozy, and—bam—you're down. I tried to stop you, catch you, whatever, but it was all too quick.' His gaze drops to his hands. 'Sorry if you've got some bumps and bruises; my reactions aren't so hot these days.'

'Bruises might be the least of it.' Alice grasps Jacqueline by the chin and stares into her eyes. 'How's your sight? Any blurriness or double-vision? You have a headache? Feel like you're gonna be sick?'

Concussion, Jacqueline realises. The woman is worried she has concussion. 'Did I hit my head?'

'No,' Ryan says. He glares at his sister. 'I already told you, she fell on her arms, kinda onto her chest, into a pile of plastic dolls. Her head didn't hit anything hard. I was there, I saw it. She's fine, she just fainted.'

'People don't take four hours to come out of a *faint*,' Alice says.

'Wait.' Jacqueline is sure she couldn't have heard correctly. She glances at her wrist, at the bare spot where her watch would be sitting if she hadn't left it back at the motel when Zane rushed her out of the door that morning. 'Four hours?'

'Give or take,' Alice says. 'You sure you don't have a headache?'

'No.' It's not really a lie. The woolly sensation isn't something she would define as an *ache* precisely. It feels more like she's floating. Not free, but tethered to the earth by the most tenuous of lines.

Alice frowns. 'I still say she should see a doctor.'

'No!' Her voice is too loud, tinged with alarm.

Ryan gives his sister a told-you-so look. 'It's okay. No doctors, no hospitals. Don't worry, I keep my promises.'

'Promises?' Jacqueline shakes her head. 'I don't understand.'

'You've been drifting in and out,' Ryan says. 'Mostly out. I was talking to Zane about driving you to hospital, maybe even calling the ambos, and then you kinda freaked out. Grabbed my arm, wouldn't calm down till I promised not to take you anywhere.' He rubs his wrist and grins. 'You've got some grip on you, girl. I might be the one ending up with bruises.'

Jacqueline tries to return his smile but it feels wrong on her mouth.

'Zane helped me bring you in here. Thought you'd be more comfortable in a bed than out there on the floor at any rate.'

'Is she still here? Zane?' Jacqueline looks over his shoulder towards the door, half expecting the girl to pop into sight at the sound of her name. Possibly still brandishing a suitcase or two.

'Nah, she, um, she had to leave. Busy little thing, you know.' Ryan's eyes flicker away for a second she wonders what it is he's keeping to himself. 'Anyways, I called Alice. She's got her first aid certificate.'

His sister nods. 'Did a refresher just last month.'

'Well, ah, thanks for taking care of me.' Jacqueline tries to sit up, wondering what time it is exactly. Where her shoes are. Her bag. But Alice's hands are on her shoulders before she's even halfway to vertical, pushing her back down into the pillow. The expression on the woman's face is even more forceful.

'You're not going nowhere.'

'But I—'

'Might still be concussed. Someone needs to keep an eye on you for the next few hours, make sure you don't have an ... *embolism* or something.' She pauses, head tilted to the side. 'You're not taking medication, are you? Stuff that might have side effects? Dizzy spells, fainting and whatnot?'

Behind his sister's back, Ryan is slowly shaking his head. A subtle movement, close to pleading. She thinks about the drug that was slipped into her drink at Merde. About possible lingering side effects. Wonders if Ryan is thinking about it too and whether this is another reason he was reluctant to take her to hospital. Could he be that self-centred?

Yes, of course he could. And so can she.

'Look,' she says to Alice. 'I think I may have just fainted. I've been working too hard lately and Ryan's probably right about the heat. I don't function very well in this sort of climate, I'm afraid.'

The woman purses her lips. 'I'm going to get my thermometer. Make sure you don't have a fever.'

'Put the kettle on while you're at it?' Ryan's voice pitches up just enough at the end to blur the line between command and request. 'We could all do with a cuppa, I reckon.'

Alice snorts. 'I could do with a lot more than that.'

Ryan waits for his sister to leave the room. When he finally speaks, his voice is soft and subdued. 'Thanks,' he says. 'If Alice knew I had anything to do with drugs … she had a fella OD on her a while back. Pretty serious, they were; cut her up real bad to lose him like that.'

'I'm sorry.' It's all she can think to say.

'Yeah.' He scratches his chin. 'She'd never have another thing to do with me, she found that out.'

'I didn't think…' Jacqueline moves onto her side. It feels a less vulnerable position. 'You didn't seem very fond of your sister the other day.'

'It's complicated between me and her.' His smile this time is grim. 'But we're family and I don't want to let her down—she's had more'n enough people in her life do that already.' He squeezes her hand. His nails are grimy with paint, his fingers a patchwork of hues. 'I appreciate you not saying anything.'

There's a shiftiness in the way he looks at her. A cast to his face that might be guilt or might equally be guile; Jacqueline doesn't know him well enough to judge. She decides to ask point blank.

'Did I really make you promise not to take me to hospital?'

'Yeah, why?'

'So what happened the other night hasn't anything to do with it?'

Ryan shakes his head. 'It's not that. I mean, what you were given, it was an upper. Some mild hallucinogenic effects maybe, lots of happy-happy—nothing lasting, I give you my word.' He's twisting a dreadlock around his first two fingers, pulling it tighter with each word.

'But?' she prods.

'Okay, sure, it crossed my mind that if a hospital ran any sort of test, there might still be traces of it in your system.' He shrugs. 'Kind of awkward to explain, don't you reckon?'

'For one of us, sure.'

'Yeah,' Ryan says. 'Look, I owe you. Big time.'

Jacqueline holds his gaze for few unblinking seconds. 'Agreed.'

'What?'

'Agreed,' she repeats. 'You owe me. You owe me a painting—an entire show, actually—and you owe me the complete absence of any further … bullshit.'

He laughs. 'A woman after my own heart.'

'It's not your *heart* I'm after, Ryan.'

'It'll be done,' he says. 'I'm working my arse off out there and it feels *good*, you know? For the first time in weeks, it *feels* like I'm working. I tell you, it's gonna be bloody magnificent.'

'I'm glad to hear it,' Jacqueline says. 'I'll be gladder still to see it.'

'You will, don't worry. You're no small part of this now, girl.'

'Someone had to come up here and kick you into gear.'

'It's not just that.' A feverish new light glitters in his eyes. 'I called you a muse the day we met, remember? I was only mucking about, but—'

Footsteps sound in the hall outside. Alice walks slowly into the room, carrying a digital thermometer in one hand and a bright yellow mug in the other. 'I put a fair bit of sugar in this,' she tells Jacqueline. 'It'll do you good. Boost your glucose levels.'

'Think you might be getting your concussion mixed up with your diabetes there, Alice,' Ryan says.

The woman glares at her brother, then thrusts the thermometer towards Jacqueline. 'Under your tongue.'

It would seem fruitless to argue, so Jacqueline accepts the instrument. Sticks it obediently into her mouth. The plastic is smooth and doesn't chink against her teeth like she remembers glass thermometers doing when she was young. *Don't bite down*, her mother's voice nevertheless chides from the back of her mind, *the mercury will poison you*. Although Jacqueline herself was seldom sick, Ant managed to drag home every stray virus and bug that crossed her path and the merest hint of an overly flushed cheek would send their mother running for the thermometer. Jacqueline's temperature never once rose above thirty-seven.

It doesn't now. Alice looks supremely disappointed.

'You should stay for a bit anyway,' Ryan says. 'Get some proper rest.'

'I can't, I should call Dante and—'

'You need supervision,' Alice interrupts. 'Just to be safe.'

'I feel fine.' This time Jacqueline really is lying. Exhaustion has crept up on her yet again. Her limbs feel leaden. The close, building heat in the bedroom doesn't help and she reaches for the glass of juice. Takes a sip. The ice has melted away to almost nothing.

'You don't look so great,' Ryan says. 'Why not sleep off the rest of the day? I'm gonna be out in my studio working, so it's no skin off my nose. I'll wake you later and you can talk to Dante. What's a few more hours gonna hurt?'

Jacqueline swallows another mouthful of juice. Returns the glass to the bedside table. She feels drained all of a sudden. No, not all of a sudden—she's been battling this for weeks. Constant exhaustion. Frayed nerves. Pressure, building deep within her. She thinks of the razor blades back at the motel. Pictures them waiting calm and precise within their white plastic case. Longs for them.

The need frightens her. It's only been three days.

'A couple of hours then,' she tells Ryan. 'Promise you'll wake me?'

He crosses a finger over his heart. 'Get some sleep, girl.'

Jacqueline nods. Closes her eyes and concentrates on the soft *shick-shick-shick* of the ceiling fan as it wafts air over her face, cooling the sweat along her hairline. She is only vaguely aware of Ryan and Alice leaving the room, of the door clicking shut behind them, as the tethering line within her slips loose.

And she begins to drift.

Impossible. Antoinette checks again, sorting through the rest of her keys as if the one to her sister's front door might have miraculously managed to swap positions and hide itself among them. The fuzzy purple bat which hangs off her keyring regards her with a puzzled, possibly mocking expression.

'You can shut up,' she tells it, digging through her backpack in case the key fell off somehow and is rattling around in the bottom with the rest of her crap. An unlikely story, sure, but so is the fact that the bloody thing is missing in the first place. Behind her, footsteps sound on the stairs and she turns, wondering if Jacqueline left a spare key with one of her neighbours.

'Hey,' Loki says. 'You're early.' He takes the steps two at a time, his long legs making easy work of the remaining flight. A plastic bag thumps against his thigh and the spicy aroma of Indian fills the alcove. 'I was going to have this all dished up and ready for you.'

Antoinette frowns, pieces clicking into place. 'You took my key.'

'Sorry,' Loki says. 'I didn't think you'd get back here before me.' He digs into the pocket of his jeans, retrieves a bright green key and sidles past her to stick it into the lock. Antoinette starts to tell him to wait, that's wrong, Jacqueline's key is nothing like that, but the latch is already turning, the door swinging open and Loki stepping backwards into a bow with arm still outstretched.

After you, madame.

In the kitchen he plucks the original key from his pocket and places it on the bench in front of her. 'I got another one cut,' he explains, spreading out the take away containers and popping their lids. He offers her a small paper bag, brown and spotted with grease. 'Pappadum?'

Shaking her head, Antoinette picks up the familiar silver key and slides it back onto her ring. 'When did you take it?'

'This morning. You were still asleep and I didn't want to wake you.' He opens the cutlery drawer, then pauses. 'Wait. You're mad at me?'

'Yes, I'm mad at you. You can't just rifle through my stuff without asking, Loki.'

'I didn't rifle through anything. Your keys were on the coffee table.'

'Fine, but how was I to know you'd taken it? What if I'd gone out for milk or something before work and couldn't get back in the flat?'

'I left a note.'

'What? Where?'

Pointing, one long skinny finger directing her gaze to the fridge, to a page of pale blue paper that he's probably torn from one of the blank notebooks in the study, now pinned in place by a couple of art magnets Antoinette gave her sister when Jacqueline scored the gallery job. Munch's screaming, colour-smeared face at the top, Van Gogh's golden sunflower down below, and between them a wavering, childish scrawl like nothing she would have expected to come from Loki's hand.

A— Stuff to do. Borrowed your key. Be back before you get home tonight. L xx

Antoinette sighs. 'I never saw that.'

'It's okay,' Loki says. 'I should have mentioned it again when I rang.'

'It's a good idea, you having your own key. I should have thought of it.'

'You've got a lot on your mind.' Loki takes a step closer. 'You don't need to worry about me as well.'

'Right,' she says, swivelling to grab some plates from the cupboard. 'How about this dinner, then?'

There's way too much for the two of them—chicken korma, beef vindaloo, lamb madras, her favourite eggplant and tomato curry, plus a wealth of saffron rice and three types of naan bread—but Loki offers only a fleeting smile when she jokes about having more than enough provisions to survive the inevitable zombie apocalypse. He spoons small portions onto his plate and eats with the care and deliberation of a restaurant critic, discarding some dishes after only one bite, taking second and third helpings of others.

'I like this.' He waves a piece of garlic naan at her and uses it to mop up a thick puddle of korma sauce from his plate, then points at the container of vindaloo with his other hand. 'Not so much that.'

'It's never been one of my favourites, either,' she tells him.

He swallows, wipes his mouth with a paper towel. 'Paul liked it.'

'Paul did.'

'But I don't.' His pale blue eyes focus on hers, unblinking, unwavering. 'I honestly don't like it, Antoinette. I'm not just saying that to be, I don't know, *contrary* or whatever.'

'All right,' she says. 'I believe you.'

If cats could grin, she suspects they would look just like Loki does now, lips curled in a satisfied, semi-private smirk. He forks another piece of chicken from its container and chews slowly.

'Hang on.' Antoinette waves her hand over the food. 'Where did you get the money for all this, anyway?'

'I borrowed it from your purse this morning.'

'You *borrowed* it?'

'Yes, borrowed.' Loki hitches a shoulder. 'I'll pay you back.'

'How will you ... never mind, just ask me next time.' She gets up from the stool and carries her plate over to the sink, scrapes at the remaining sauce-soaked rice. The money isn't the point, she wants to tell him—even though it is, to a degree; the cost of tonight's banquet likely more than she would spend in a week of home-cooked pasta and stir-fries—it's the *presumption* of it.

The fact that he didn't even think it important enough to rate a mention on his lousy note.

Loki grabs her wrist, his fingers gentle but firm. 'Let me wash up.'

'It's fine.'

'Antoinette, please.'

'All right, whatever.' She turns and begins to put the lids back on the takeaway containers. At least there'll be leftovers for tomorrow, and Jacqueline's bound to have some rice in the cupboard they can boil up to go with. Tomorrow, shit—she'll be working Michelle's payback dinner shift along with her own daytime roster. It wipes her out just thinking about it.

'Can I borrow your car?' Loki asks, his voice raised over the rush of tap water.

'My *car*?'

'Yeah, you don't need it, do you? You catch the tram to work.'

Antoinette stares at him. 'Do you even know how to drive?'

'Of course.' He grins. 'I'm a great driver.'

'No,' she says. 'I mean, you might be, but you don't have a licence.' Or a birth certificate or a tax file number or any other piece of evidence to prove he even *exists*, because of course he shouldn't, he bloody well *can't* exist in the world as she knew it just a sly handful of days ago, and what the hell are they going to do about that? These days, no one can so much as hire a DVD without needing a personal paper trail.

'I'll be careful,' Loki is saying.

'It's too risky. Why do you want the car?'

'Just some stuff I need to do.'

'Stuff. Like the stuff you had to do today?'

'Yeah. Like that.'

'Bloody hell, Loki, you've only been breathing for three bloody days. What sort of *stuff* can you possibly have to do?'

His eyes narrow. 'You don't have to yell.'

'I wasn't yelling, I...' Except she is, her voice pitched close to *screeching*, as Paul used to call it, that horrible harridan word never failing to stop her in her tracks, push her brusquely on to the back foot, no matter how justified her anger. Antoinette gnaws on her bottom lip. 'I'm sorry, I didn't mean to yell at you. I'm just worried.'

'I told you, there's no need to worry about me.'

'But I do, Loki. What if someone sees you? Someone who knows me, who knows Paul?' She frowns. 'You probably shouldn't be going outside at all.'

'What am I, some kind of pet you need to keep locked up in case the landlord finds out?'

'That's not what I meant.'

'Do I get my own litter box at least?'

'Loki, stop it.'

'What does it matter if anyone sees me? They'll think I'm Paul, or someone who looks like him. So what?'

'It's not that simple, what if—'

From its perch on the wall, the kitchen phone starts to ring—*Jacqueline, finally*—and Antoinette reaches for the handset.

Loki scowls. 'They can leave a message, you know.'

'It's probably my sister. I've been calling her all day.'

He turns his back and sweeps the dishes into the sink, muttering words she can't quite catch over the clatter of cutlery.

Antoinette sighs and presses the call button. 'Hello?'

'Antoinette? What are you doing there?' A woman's voice, its syllables sharp and clipped and grating as always. Antoinette's stomach clenches. Not Jacqueline, no, and how she wishes she'd listened to Loki now. She closes her eyes and forces a smile to her mouth, hoping it will colour her tone with audible cheer.

'Hi Mum,' she says. 'How are you?'

9

'Where's your sister?' Sally Paige demands. 'I've been leaving messages for you both all over the place.'

'Sorry,' Antoinette says. 'I was going to call you back after I ate.'

'And Jacqueline? I suppose she's avoiding me, too?'

'No one's avoiding you, Mum. Jacqueline's in Brisbane for a few days; I'm house sitting for her.'

'Brisbane? What's she doing up there?'

'It's a work thing. I'm sure she meant to tell you.'

Her mother makes a sound somewhere between a snort and a sigh. 'Yes, I'm sure she did.'

'It was all pretty rushed. She'll probably give you a call later on tonight, maybe tomorrow. She's got her hands full up there, from what I gather.'

'When does she get back?'

'I don't think she knows. Whenever the job is done, I guess.' She mouths an apology to Loki, up to his elbows in suds with a scowl still darkening his features, then carries the handset into the living room.

'I wanted you both to come over for dinner,' her mother is saying. 'But if she's away … can you come tomorrow? I'll make a roast.'

'I'm working tomorrow night, Mum. How about we wait until Jacqueline's back? You don't need to cook; the two of us can take you out somewhere nice. Somewhere in the city maybe?'

Because the last thing she feels like doing is trekking all the way out to the Dandenongs. More than an hour each way even using EastLink—*if* the traffic is good, which it almost certainly won't be on the drive down—plus the ill-lit winding road up the mountain to her mother's place, the draughty old house where she and Jacqueline grew up, the house neither of them could wait to leave.

'That won't do,' her mother insists. 'There are matters of some importance that I need to discuss with you—with the both of you in fact, but I can't wait for your sister to decide to grace us with her presence.'

'She can't help being sent on a business trip, Mum.'

'How about you? Are you free on Thursday, or even Friday? You can't possibly be working all the time.'

Antoinette relents. Sally Paige with a bee in her bonnet isn't a force to be easily dissuaded. 'I could maybe do Friday. But I don't finish until seven, so it'll be fairly late by the time I get up there.'

'That will be perfect. I find myself eating later these days, anyway.'

'Don't go to any trouble, Mum. If it's only the two of us, I could just pick up a pizza on the way over. That place in Monbulk is still open, isn't it?'

'I don't eat *cheese*.' Her mother sounds appalled, as if Antoinette has suggested bringing along a kitten on a spit. 'I haven't eaten cheese for over a year. It's a nightmare for your digestive system. No, I'll make a roast, and pancakes for breakfast. With that maple syrup you like.'

Antoinette stifles a groan. 'Mum, I don't think I'll be able to stay over. I'm working both nights this weekend and there's things I need to do here on Saturday.'

'What things? You're house sitting; it's like being on holidays.'

'Mum—'

'And I don't like the idea of you driving home so late. Not all alone.'

'All right, we'll see how it goes.'

'I'll make up your bed.'

Antoinette clenches her teeth. Better to save the argument for Friday, when she might just be able to grab her keys and slip out the door before her mother manages to turn on the guilt full force. *Matters of some importance.* Sounds suspiciously like another of what passes for a Sally Paige heart-to-heart. A stellar evening of *why haven't you?* and *why don't you?* and *what are you planning to do with your life, really?*

'Look, Mum, I have to go. My, ah, my dinner's getting cold.'

'But I'll see you on Friday? You promise?'

Those last words spoken in such an odd, near plaintive tone, a tone so unlike her mother, so *unsuited* to her, that Antoinette pauses, ears pricked to the hiss of dead air over the line like it might hold a subtext.

'Antoinette? Did you hear me?'

'Yes,' she says. 'I promise.'

The storm must have woken her, Jacqueline realises as a flash of lightning illuminates the room. It's followed almost immediately by a deafening crack and rumble that sounds as though it's directly above the house. Rain drums almost as loudly onto the roof. Spatters against the window in thick, angry drops. Without the lightning, the room is dark. Night time dark.

'Damn it, Ryan,' Jacqueline mutters. She throws off the sheet and slips from the bed. Tucks in her blouse and straightens her skirt. Her throat feels raw, her mouth mossy with sleep. She locates the glass of juice on the bedside table and drinks what remains in two greedy swallows. The liquid is almost warm. Pulp sticks to her teeth. She grimaces, running her tongue around her gums as she shuffles cautiously across to the bedroom door. Once in the hall, Jacqueline can see artificial light shining from the back of the house. Ryan's studio. Smoothing her hair as best she can with only her fingers, she walks towards it.

The large canvas is still uncovered. Unattended as well, its creator sprawled belly-down and shirtless on the mattress at the far end of the studio. His eyes are closed. His back rises and falls so gently it takes her a moment or two to catch its movement. She's amazed that anyone can sleep through a tropical storm like the one currently raging beyond the house's flimsy walls. Another clap of thunder splits open the sky. Ryan doesn't so much as flinch.

There's no clock in the studio but outside the sky is black, the world illuminated only by the rain-hazed glow of streetlights. It feels very late. She should call a taxi. Get herself back to the motel and wash away the day's grime and confusion beneath a hot shower. Tomorrow—she can't think about tomorrow just yet. She spots her bag over against the wall, near the doorway where Zane's suitcases had been. Beside it are Jacqueline's shoes, arranged neatly side by side with her phone perched across their toes. Ryan must have done that, or Zane, after Jacqueline fainted. Maybe even Alice, tidying up while waiting for her patient to awaken.

No, not Alice, because Ryan doesn't let her inside his studio. Unlike Zane, unlike Jacqueline, unlike however many others to whom he happily swings wide the door. How that must make his sister burn—which is perhaps all the motivation Ryan needs. Jacqueline shakes her head. With a mother like her own, familial power plays are a game she understands only too well.

And she has no intention of joining anyone else's team.

She picks up her phone and slips into her shoes. Slings her bag over her shoulder. Her phone screen is blank and she wonders if the charge has run out. She switches it on, pleased to see the battery icon displaying half its life. Not so pleased to find that it's almost one o'clock. As the device searches for a signal, Jacqueline considers the back of Ryan's painting.

I'm working my arse off out there.

She activates the camera. Dante will need to be shown something.

Taking care not to tread on the myriad tubes of paint that litter the floor, Jacqueline makes her way around to the front of the canvas. Ryan really has been busy. The city is no longer simply abandoned. It's flooded. The Brisbane River now swollen and stretched, swallowing the foundations of the metropolis it once wound through. The water itself is calm. Settled and still. As though it has always been this way. As though it always will be this way. A tangle of greenery bursts from a glassless window. Vines fall towards the water below, tendrils reaching for its surface.

It's not finished, but she can see how it will be.

Jacqueline steps back a couple of paces. Raises her phone and tries to frame as much of the painting as she can within the small camera window. Then almost drops it as the device start to shrill, vibrating unexpectedly in her hands. Text messages, several of them, tumbling in on top of each other now a signal has been found. Antoinette, her mother, Dante—of course, *Dante*—and even a couple of voicemail alerts advising, no doubt, of messages left by the same.

She groans. Tomorrow looms too close for any sort of comfort.

'What do you reckon, then?'

Jacqueline peers around the side of the canvas. Ryan's eyes

are open and serious. Yawning, he pushes himself up from the mattress.

'I didn't mean to wake you,' she tells him. 'I was just calling a taxi.'

'In this weather? An ark might be better.'

There's a tattoo on the left side of his chest. A tree, stylised and vaguely Celtic. Black ink fading to blue beneath the skin. She watches its movement over his muscles as he crosses the room to join her.

'There's still a lot to do,' he says.

She nods. 'The river is a dramatic change.'

'Yeah, but it feels right. The city was too passive before, you know?'

'Passive?'

'I'd left the possibility of choice, that we left because we wanted to, not because we had to. Not because we were pushed.'

'Repelled.'

'*Ex*pelled.' He frowns. 'Expulsion, maybe that should be the title.'

'Of the painting?'

'Of the show.'

Jacqueline hesitates. 'Ryan ... the show's already being promoted. *Null and Void*. You can't change the name at this stage.' She braces herself for resistance, for further argument, but Ryan only smiles.

'Okay,' he says.

'Okay?'

'What's a bloody name matter, anyway?' He nudges her arm with his elbow. 'Besides, I owe you, girl. You did this, you opened this for me.'

'I don't understand.'

'The stuff you were saying before, when you were still kinda out of it. Delirious, Alice said, but what would she know about it?'

Her stomach clenches. 'What … stuff?'

'Don't worry, nothing incriminating. A lot of talk about floating, about drowning. And not being able to find your way back.'

'My way back? To where?'

Ryan shrugs. 'You weren't making too much sense. But it set me thinking, about the floods we had up here, and some dots got themselves joined. I was never gonna do anything with the floods—it felt too cynical, too exploitative—but the reference is powerful here, don't you reckon? It's an anchor. It makes this possibility real, more real than a Brisbane left to rot for unimagined reasons.'

'It is powerful,' Jacqueline agrees. Privately, she wonders if *unimagined* reasons would be even more so. 'But it's late and I really need to go, Ryan. We can talk more about this tomorrow.'

'Mmm.' His face seems distant as he studies the painting. Tanned fingers scratch at his stomach. Circle his navel and pluck at the hair that grows in a scraggily line below it. A thoughtless gesture. And far too intimate.

Jacqueline clears her throat. 'Would you mind if I took a couple of photos before I go? To send to Dante in the morning.'

'What?' He turns away from the painting. Glares at the device in her hand as though she is offering him something poisonous. 'No, no way. This isn't something you can capture with a bloody phone.'

'Ryan, this is important. I need to show him *something*.'

He sighs. Rattles his dreads with his hand. 'Yeah, look, I got this mate, pretty handy with a camera. I'll give him a bell tomorrow and get him over here, get him to take some shots with his proper kit. Good ones, high res. That be okay?'

'And you'll email them to Dante?'

'Sure.' He crosses a hand over his chest. Over the tree. 'Promise.'

Which is probably not worth much, but she's too tired to argue any longer. She flicks through her contacts. Retrieves the number of the taxi company.

'You're not really going?' Ryan asks.

'It's late.'

'So, stay the rest of the night.'

Jacqueline looks up at him. Considers the sly quirk of his mouth. His bare, lean-muscled torso. His skin the colour of perfectly toasted bread. She could stay. Split herself beneath him, fall back and allow her flesh to lead the way. Not the sort of release her razors could deliver, but still.

But still. Ryan seems the type to confuse sex too easily with significance. With the sort of power she's not about to relinquish. Not when she can feel the balance of the game shifting. Control returning to her hands. Tomorrow, she'll ring Dante, make her apologies, give him the good news. Ring Ant as well and perhaps even their mother, find out what the state of emergency is back home.

Tomorrow, she can fix everything. But not if she stays. Not if she slips any further. Jacqueline shakes her head. 'I have to go.'

She taps the call icon, holds her phone to her ear. Outside, there's a bright flash of lightning followed a few seconds later by the rumble of thunder. Slightly muted now, as the storm moves across Brisbane, washing the city clean.

Her phone rings just as Jacqueline is cutting into her poached eggs. The yolks flow thick and yellow, dripping onto the toast beneath.

Dante calling.

Damn. She was planning to ring him after breakfast. He never turns up at Seventh Circle much before ten anyway, and her appetite upon waking was unusually sharp. Ravenous, even. Perhaps not surprising, considering how little—and how badly—she's been eating up here. Jacqueline puts down her cutlery. Takes a small mouthful of water, then picks up the phone. She's not entirely prepared for this conversation but if she lets the call go through to voicemail yet again, the next communiqué from her boss might well be a termination notice.

'Dante, how—'

'Well, look who managed to answer her phone for once.'

'I'm sorry about that.'

'You get my messages yesterday? My texts?'

'Yes.' His messages. Light on detail, heavy on anger. All variations on the theme of *call me right the fuck now*. 'But not until late. Things have been … complicated. With Ryan, I mean, and the painting. I was going to ring—'

'Save it, Jacks. Crazy suitcase girl already filled me in on your *complications*.'

'Zane?' Her face flushes, her skin feels damp and prickly. She's thankful that the café has air conditioning. 'Zane talked to you? How?'

'That's what I'd like to know,' he snaps. 'Called my private number, from *your* phone, Jacks. Trying to tell me how *brilliant* her work is, and how you've *personally recommended* I take a look at it.'

'That's not true, I never said—'

'Had to listen to the whole spiel to get any decent intel on was happening up there, considering I've heard squat from you, and it turns out *that's* because you're sleeping off some kind of drug-fucked hangover in Jellicoe's bed. I sent you up there to sort this shit out once and for all, and you bloody well go native.'

Jacqueline closes her eyes. 'That's not what happened.'

'Whatever. Fact is, you're no longer reliable.'

'Ryan's close to finished his painting. The painting.'

There's a pause. When Dante speaks again his voice seems a little calmer. Or perhaps that's only wishful thinking. 'How close?'

'A week, Ryan says.' Although that was before he painted the flood. Before he allowed the river to swallow the city up to its knees. She didn't ask how much greenery he still intended to add. *Birds too, maybe some critters even.*

'A week?' Dante echoes. 'That's definite?'

'Give or take a couple of days. He wants to do some more work on a few of the smaller pieces as well.'

'What? We've got six weeks till doors open on this thing. Shit, not even six.'

'He knows that.' Jacqueline tries to sound assured. Assuring. 'It's only some minor tweaks, to improve cohesion. It'll be fine, I promise.'

'Your promises aren't worth much right now, darling. I want photos, I want to see what's going on with this.'

'Ryan said he would email you something today.'

Dante snorts. 'What *he* says is worth even less. Get over there and take some shots, text them to me. Within the hour, Jacks, I mean it.'

'I'm not sure Ryan will agree to that. He has concerns about image quality.'

More silence, stretching across the seconds.

'You're done,' Dante says at last. His voice is flat as iron. Colder, harder. 'I want you back here. Now.'

Jacqueline's mouth is dry. She takes another sip of water and swallows, tries to find words to salvage the situation. 'I thought the idea was for me to keep an eye on Ryan until he finishes.'

'The *idea* was for you to remind the lazy rat-bastard that he has a contract to honour, a contract I will waste no second thoughts on suing his arse over.'

'I don't think the contract was ever really the issue. He was just stalled on the painting. Creatively, I mean.'

'Well, you seem to have *un*stalled him, darling. That's wonderful, that's fine and fucking dandy; have a gold star. But that doesn't mean you get yourself a sweet little Contiki tour at my expense.'

'No, it's not—'

'Listen to me carefully,' Dante says, his voice somewhere between a whisper and a snarl. 'I cannot trust you. And if I cannot trust you, you are absolutely no use to me up there. Bec will book your flight. This conversation is over.'

Jacqueline opens her mouth to ask him to wait, to let her explain, but it's too late. She can already hear the phone changing hands. Can hear Dante's muffled instructions for Becca—*get her on a plane, pronto*—and then the girl is on the line.

'Give me two secs, will you Jacqueline? I'm checking flights for you now.'

'How … how bad is it?'

'Mmm, yes.' Becca pauses, then lowers her voice. 'Pretty bad. He's seriously pissed—you really should have called before now.'

'I'm sorry if he took it out on you.'

'Me?' She sounds amused. 'He's been like a kitten to *me*. I think he's saving the weapons of mass destruction for when you get back.'

Jacqueline sighs. 'That's something to look forward to.'

'Um, I can't get you on a flight today, not for what Dante's authorised me to spend. How does tomorrow morning at 9.15 sound?'

As though she has any choice in the matter. 'It's fine.'

'Cool. I'll book it now and text you the details.'

'I'll see you tomorrow, then.'

'You're going to come in to the gallery?'

'The sooner the better, don't you think?'

'Listen,' Becca says. 'You really need to get some photos for Dante. Right now, he doesn't think you've done anything to fix up the Jellicoe mess; he thinks you've made it worse.'

'Ryan is going to email him photos this afternoon,' Jacqueline tells her. The words sound doubtful even to her ears. But she still has time. One last day, one last night to rescue what she can before tucking her tail between her legs and slinking dutifully back home. As much as she hates Brisbane, that's not how she wants to leave the place. Not defeated. Not shamed.

'Good,' Becca is saying. 'That's good. Because from how Dante's been carrying on, I'm not sure you'll even have a job if he doesn't.'

'Thanks for the advice. I'll keep it in mind.'

'I'm only trying to help.'

'Yes. I'm quite sure you are.'

Stupid, she admonishes herself even as she cuts off the call. Becca was hardly making a threat of her own. At most she was relaying something she's heard Dante say. Yet Jacqueline couldn't help but detect a certain glee in the girl's tone. An edge to her words that sounded suspiciously like schadenfreude. After all, if Jacqueline loses her job, it's Becca who'll most likely reap the benefits.

'No,' Jacqueline whispers. 'It's not over yet.'

The cuts on her thigh are almost fully healed and barely itch as she scratches at them through her skirt. She forces herself to stop. To place both hands on the table and think. She will call Ryan. Explain the situation. Make sure he keeps his promise about the photos. He owes her one, she will remind him. By the time she gets back to Melbourne, Dante will have seen them. Will have seen that the central painting is near completion. And, hopefully, that it was worth the wait.

Good. A plan. A good plan. She can fix this.

Smooth everything over, yes.

Jacqueline stares at her plate. The eggs have cooled, their yolks congealed. Beside the toast, fried spinach wilts in a pool of grease, topped with half a tomato. She picks up her cutlery again. Hunger may be a distant concern, but her body needs food regardless. Sustenance. Energy. Strength. Yes, to all the above.

Still, the eggs sit thick and tasteless in her mouth. Closing her eyes, Jacqueline forces herself to swallow.

10

Antoinette is still rubbing dry her hair when her mobile starts to chime. Wrapping the towel around herself, she hurries from the bathroom, swearing as she jags her arm on the door handle, hard to enough to hurt, hard enough to likely leave a bruise—*honestly, could she be any clumsier?*—and into the bedroom where her mobile sits buzzing on the nightstand. The chiming is almost through its final cycle as she grabs the Nokia and flips it open, lifting it to her ear in one quick motion, no time to even check the caller. 'Hello?'

'Ant? It's me.'

'Jacqueline? Hey, how are you?' Only slightly disappointed and only then because she was hoping it might be Loki, some stranger's mobile fresh in hand and a mouth full of reasons as to why she woke up to an empty apartment yet again. Not even a note this time, the magnets securing nothing but flat, white space.

'I'm good,' her sister says. 'Sorry I didn't call back yesterday.'

'That's okay. Problem child giving you grief?'

A pause. 'Something like that. Is anything wrong?'

'No, not really. Just...'

And now it's Antoinette's turn to pause, to stall with her tongue pressed tight against the back of her teeth, because all of a sudden she hasn't the faintest idea what to say. Everything she planned to tell her sister yesterday—about Loki and all the rest of it, about the strange and scary and utterly *magical* thing her life has become—all those careful words she rehearsed over and over in the fraught and sleepless dark, all of it's gone now, evaporated like morning mist.

'I miss you,' she says. 'That's all.'

Jacqueline laughs, a sound oddly flat and mirthless. 'I've been away less than a week.'

'I know, I just ... I needed to talk and you weren't here.'

'It must be hard. This business with Paul.'

'Yeah,' she says, caught off guard. 'I guess.' Because it should be hard. Hard and painful and bitter as wormwood in absinthe, and yet ... and yet. She wonders what's wrong with her, that she has so easily pushed it all aside, a broken heart and the tattered ruins of her life, that she can no longer bring herself to care.

Less than a week—she's mourned dead goldfish longer than that.

'Did our mother ring you as well?' Jacqueline is asking.

'Yeah, she wants me to come over for dinner on Friday.'

'Really? Just you?'

'Well, the both of us, but since you're away … hey, how come you never told her you were off to Brissie?'

'I meant to. Or I didn't mean *not* to. You know how she is.'

'Yeah,' Antoinette says. Air travel has always been a source of anxiety and distrust for Sally Paige, along with doctors, internet banking, and people who own large dogs, to name but a few. 'Do you know when you'll be coming home?'

'I—I'm not sure yet. Soon, perhaps.'

'So things are going well?'

'Well enough.'

Right then Antoinette decides it'll be better to wait until Jacqueline gets back before she says anything about … anything. Face to face with Loki, with the living, breathing *fact* of him, there'll be less she will have to explain, less convincing she'll need to do because, after all, there will be *Loki*. And maybe it's because of this decision, because of the secret she now tucks away inside herself—not the only secret she's ever kept from her older sister, but definitely the biggest—that a vague remoteness seems to insinuate itself between them.

They chat some more, swap banalities about the weather and work and the weird dislocation of being away from home, while Antoinette finds a clean blouse—her last; she really should've put on a washload last night—and returns to the bathroom to scrub a stain from the hem of her most comfortable skirt. Mobile switched to loudspeaker, she pulls her hair into a ponytail, capturing escapee curls with bobby pins while they're still damp enough to manage.

'What are you doing?' Jacqueline asks.

'Um, my hair. Why?'

'You sound so far away.'

'I've got you on hands-free. In the bathroom.' Antoinette picks up her mobile again, switches off the speaker. 'Better?'

'I should go,' Jacqueline says. 'I don't want to make you late for work.'

'It's okay, I've got ages yet.'

'Oh.'

Silence, or nearly so. Just the sound of something which might be bad reception or might be a person breathing too heavily, too harshly, holding back sobs maybe, and Antoinette's about to ask if everything is really okay up in Brisbane when her sister speaks again, her voice strong and clear and certain.

'Well, it's good you're all right. Honestly, Ant, I'm sorry I didn't have a chance to ring before now. I feel terrible about that.'

'You really don't need to check up on me, you know.'

'I know. But I like to. That's what big sisters are for.'

Antoinette smiles. 'And you wonder why I've missed you.'

After they exchange goodbyes, she makes herself a coffee before sitting down at Jacqueline's computer. There actually is time to kill before she needs to catch a tram, time enough to browse a few real estate sites and see what local rents are looking like—because, really, once her sister gets back, this apartment will start to feel very crowded, very soon. But every click of the mouse twists her stomach into tighter and tighter knots. Anything with even a glimmer of promise is priced way beyond what she can afford on her own, and the few places within her budget seem cramped and depressing, shoebox meets studio, and she wonders how the hell Jacqueline manages to live so close to the city.

'I need a better job,' Antoinette mutters.

She'll have to expand her search, look further out, further even than she was living with Paul maybe, but she's had enough for now. Instead she checks her email, deleting spam and the random newsletters she only occasionally reads, as well as a whole bunch of posts from mailing lists she can't be bothered catching up on, finding nothing left of interest besides her shift schedule for next week and a reminder to make an appointment for her annual dental check-up.

With a sigh, she logs onto Facebook.

Is it possible for the blisters on my blisters to have blisters?

Her status update from early last week, home after a late night out wearing a new pair of too-cheap shoes for the first and last time. Her fingers hover over the keyboard for a few seconds, then slide away. She can think of nothing to replace it with right now, nothing she cares to share with—

Antoinette frowns. Her number of friends has more than halved. She opens the list and scans the names that are left. Paul and everyone who knows him, it seems, have defriended themselves sometime in the past week. No word of explanation, no parting message. Just gone. With the somewhat mystifying exception of Greta, who remains like the sole witness to another life, a pouting and black-lipped anachronism among old school acquaintances, work buddies, and the occasional random stranger.

'Well, fuck you too,' she says to them, the missing and the mute. 'Passive aggressive bunch of wankers.'

Because it doesn't matter, and whatever Paul told them matters even less; if they can cut her loose like that, without even feeling the need to hear her side of the story, then really: fuck them all. Swallowing back a lump that definitely, absolutely bloody well is *not* the beginning of tears, she opens Greta's page, starts to write a message on her wall—*So why are YOU still here?*—then deletes it.

Enough, girlie-girl; they're not worth it. They never were.

Antoinette shuts down the computer, glances at her watch and swears again. The internet has sucked away every spare minute she had and then some, her chances of catching the earlier tram now close to zero, but still she races through the apartment, shoving on shoes, stuffing pantyhose into her bag for the dinner shift and grabbing her keys from the kitchen bench. Keys which feel slightly wrong in her hand, less weighty, less bulky, her fist enclosing them too completely and she opens her fingers again, frowning at the jagged metal shapes that cross her palm. The bulbous, black head of her car key is a noticeable absentee.

Loki.

Her teeth are clenched so hard they hurt, and she closes her eyes, forces herself to take long, slow breaths. Inside her skull, his name ricochets like something sharp, like something keen-edged and cornered and utterly beyond control.

Loki Loki Loki

Finally. Jacqueline checks her watch and stands up. Shades her eyes from the afternoon sun as Ryan's car pulls into the driveway. She's spent almost two hours waiting on his verandah, shifting position to follow the shade as it moved around the house, for what little that was worth. She frees her skirt from the damp skin of her thighs. Wipes the sheen from her cheeks.

'Hey,' Ryan calls up to her. 'This is a surprise.'

Another man gets out of the passenger side. Shorter than Ryan, but with the same lean, muscular build, his bare arms bright with tattoos from shoulder to wrist. He opens the rear door and pulls out a bulky canvas bag.

'I've been trying to reach you all day,' Jacqueline says as the two of them climb the stairs towards her. 'You ever answer your phone?'

'Didn't have it with me,' Ryan says. 'You been here long?'

'No. Not long.'

'This is my mate, Tim. Gonna take those photos you wanted.'

'You're Jackie,' Tim says. 'Been hearing a lot about you.'

'*Jacqueline.*' She shakes the hand he offers. Holds her smile even as the sweat slides between their palms. 'Thanks for taking care of the photos. I appreciate it.'

'No worries. Jells and me go way back.'

She steps back to allow them to move past her onto the landing. Ryan sorts through his keys and unlocks the front door. The air inside the house is stale and still, no cooler than being outside, and Jacqueline feels foolish for having expected even a minor respite from the heat.

'Ryan,' she says. 'Can I talk to you for a second?'

'What's up?'

'It's, ah, confidential.' She glances at Tim. 'I'm sorry.'

The man grins and holds up two hands. 'Secret artist business, I get it. You want me to go set up, Jells?'

Ryan nods. 'Yeah, cool. I'll bring you a cold one, yeah?'

'Wouldn't say no.' Tim hefts his bag onto his shoulder. 'Nice to meet you, Jackie.' He taps two fingers against his brow in a quick salute before disappearing into the back of house.

Jacqueline turns to Ryan. 'You told him my name was Jackie?'

'He remembers what he remembers.'

'And how about your memory? Anything you've forgotten to mention?'

'Like what?'

'Did Zane use my phone yesterday? To ring Dante perhaps?'

Ryan sucks air through his teeth. 'I was kinda hoping nothing'd come of that.'

'Well, something has,' Jacqueline says. 'What exactly did she tell him?'

He shrugs, confessing that he didn't hear much, that he only walked in right at the end while Zane was trying to convince

Dante to look at her stuff. An afterthought, apparently; the girl just called Dante to see if he might know why Jacqueline passed out. In case she had a condition they should know about, epilepsy or diabetes or what have you. In case there was something they should do to make sure she wasn't about to up and die on them.

'And you believed her?'

'Yeah, right.' Ryan laughs. 'Took the phone off her is what I did, kicked her pushy arse out the door. She's gonna go far, that girl, but she needs to smarten the hell up. There'll be a few words to that effect, next time I run into her.'

'Don't bother,' Jacqueline tells him. 'It hardly matters now.'

'Why's that?'

'I'm flying back to Melbourne in the morning.'

'Since when? Thought you were meant to be lighting a fire under my arse or whatever.'

'Dante thinks I've done enough. He wants me home.'

'Yeah?' Ryan tilts his head. Rubs a paint-smeared thumb over his lower lip. 'What if I tell him I want you to stay?'

'Why would you do that?'

'Because it's true.'

Jacqueline stares at him, attempting to gauge these bolder rules. 'I don't think that would help at all,' she says. 'But if he gets those photos this afternoon, then I might still have a decent chance of keeping my job.'

'See, now I feel like a right shit.'

'Is that a step up or a step down from being an arsehole?'

He smiles. 'Touché.'

'Just make sure those photos are good ones, all right? Dante needs to be reassured that there's still a viable show here.'

'Why don't you stick around? Pick the shots you want to send to him, and later we'll go out and have a drink. Tim knows this bar, says they got a tree growing right in the middle of the place. For real.'

'I don't think that's a good idea.'

'Nah, it goes up through the roof. There's a skylight or something.'

'I mean, I don't think it's a good idea to have a drink with you.'

'I knew what you meant.' He steps closer, places a hand on her shoulder. 'Just … this is gonna sound like a line, but I really don't want you to go.'

'Ryan, I—'

He kisses her. She could have dodged. Could, with some grace even, have slipped sideways, moved beyond his reach. Instead, she allows his mouth to find hers. Notes the firm, insistent press of his lips, the scrape of his stubble against her chin. His dreads fall gently against her face, their now familiar scent clear and sharp. Not eucalyptus, she realises at last, but ti-tree oil. A short-lived cure *de jour* from her childhood, their mother dabbing it on scratches and scrapes and mosquito bites for one whole summer before moving on to some other miraculous all-natural alternative.

Ryan slides his hands to her hips, tries to pull her body closer, but Jacqueline steps away. From him, and from the nascent warmth between her thighs. The time for playing that particular game is over; too many complications sit between them now, and she has too little interest in disentanglement.

'Enough,' she says, crossing her arms.

'Really?' Ryan asks. His eyes gleam. 'I got the feeling there was maybe a little something going on here.' He flicks his index finger back and forth between the two of them. 'Did I get that wrong?'

Jacqueline considers the possible scenarios. The possible outcomes. Leverage. Complications. Consequences. Narrows down the response most likely to flatter and please. Most likely to keep him onside. 'Perhaps not entirely *wrong*,' she says. 'But I still have to leave tomorrow, and you're still a client. I don't see too many ways for this not to end in a mess.'

Ryan grins. 'I like mess.'

'You like distraction. Procrastination as well, it seems.'

'No, I like *you*.' He taps his forehead. 'I like how you make me think.'

'Now *that* sounds like a line.'

'Maybe. Don't mean it isn't true.' His smile softens. 'Come on, girl, you can't say you don't feel something happening here.'

Jacqueline isn't sure how to respond, so elects to say nothing. Simply stands with lips pressed close together, arms still crossed over her chest. Holding his gaze, unblinking, as the seconds swell long and slow between them.

'Okay,' Ryan says at last. 'But how about this: after the show, when the monkeys have danced and the organ grinders have counted their pennies and packed up their music boxes, how about you let me take you out to dinner?'

'I don't—'

'No expectations, and no more of this *client* bullshit getting in the way. A clean slate, yeah? A do-over, you and me.'

'Fine,' Jacqueline tells him, *if that's what it takes, then fine.* Because she's exhausted. Because her bones feel like undercooked spaghetti, spongy and brittle all at the same time, and it's easier to simply agree, then worry about wriggling out of it later. Right now, all she wants to do is wind up this disaster of a trip and crawl back to Melbourne. Face up to whatever fire and brimstone Dante has brewing for her, and hope she can finagle her way back into his good graces.

'You promise?' Ryan is asking. His right hand carves the air between them and she pauses only briefly before meeting it with her own. He squeezes her fingers. Circles his thumb slowly over the back of her hand.

'I promise,' she lies.

A flash of headlights as she leaves Simpatico, accompanied by the triple staccato beep of a car horn, and Antoinette shades her eyes with one hand, squints at the red hatchback parked in the loading zone. 'Ant,' Greta calls, waving a lace-gloved hand from the driver's side window, 'Come, please. We need to talk.' Black-lipped smile, black-bobbed hair flawless as usual, glinting dark beneath the streetlights, and Antoinette sighs, rubs her bare arms as she crosses the street.

'It's late, Greta. I'm on my way home.'

'Ja, ja, but please come in the car. I shall take you.'

The way Greta drives, zipping at speed around corners, running lights even as the amber flashes to scarlet, Antoinette is glad of the late hour, of the traffic moving sparse along the roads. Pausing only to heed the flat, robotic instructions of the GPS unit, Greta rattles on about Paul, Paul, Paul: how *angry* he still is about all of it—*livid, Ant, positively fuming*—how hurt as well, wounded beyond measure, but how she thought he was beginning to calm down until this last thing, this thing with the coat.

'I cannot understand.' Shadowed gaze flicking towards the rear-view mirror, small hands wrenching the steering wheel around another bend. 'I cannot *understand* why you would *do* such a thing.'

'Wait. What are you talking about?'

'His coat, his lovely *leather* coat. Left in so many *shreds*, like some *creature* clawed it to bits and pieces.'

Antoinette frowns. 'It wasn't me.'

'But who else would have a *reason*?'

'Paul's not the nicest guy, you know. Maybe he pissed someone off.'

'But things of *yours* were missing. Who else would *take* them?'

'Oh, for godsake! Paul was *there* the other night when I came and picked up my stuff. Is he still trying to say I broke in and trashed the place?'

Greta throws her a glance, eyebrows drawn crypto-quizzical. 'The other *night*? No, no, Ant—I am talking about what happened *today*.'

'Today? I've been at work all day.'

'Really?' Doubtful now, aggression veering towards uncertainty. 'But, *all day*? When you have only now just finished?'

'That's right,' Antoinette says. '*All day*.' Echoing the other woman's emphasis, lunch *and* dinner, thanks very much for asking, a bloody neverending nightmare of a double shift that Greta is more than welcome to verify with the restaurant tomorrow if she cares to—if Antoinette's word isn't enough, and there's no reason to think that it will be, not so long as Paul has a tongue to counter it.

'That is not fair, Ant. I am your friend as well—'

'Yeah right. You'd *live* inside his arse if you could.' Turning to stare out of the window, prickly silence broken only by toneless machine directions and the overly dramatic sighs of Greta as she speeds them through the streets. Why the woman even bothered to come is beyond Antoinette. Greta should be glad of the split, delighted to have Paul all to herself once again. And maybe she was, maybe all this shit was down to her after all: Greta with her spare key and the pocket knife she carries to cut the tips off her thin black cigars, the knife or maybe just a pair of kitchen scissors clutched in a black-taloned hand, silver blades slicing through leather and blame laid where it could never be forgiven.

Greta, sowing salt on fields already razed. Just to be sure.

But then, why is she here?

Question is, girlie-girl, why do you care?

She doesn't. Whatever happened at Paul's place, whoever tore up his precious jacket, it has absolutely *nothing* to do with her. Managing to hold onto this conviction right up until they pull over outside the apartment block, most of the windows dark at this time of night, but the ones to her sister's living room still bright-lit and only partially curtained, the glass door open and there on the balcony, a tall and slim-shouldered silhouette, standing motionless in the still air.

Why do you want the car?

Just some stuff I need to do.

She opens the car door, the interior light flickering yellow and wan, and above her the balcony figure raises a hand, waves it, quick side-to-side gesture like a metronome, like Paul—

'Ant, *truly*, I am sorry.' Greta, reaching to grasp Antoinette by the arm, lace-cold fingers squeezing tight. 'Paul thought—and I … well. It is a *puzzle* then, a little mystery for us, ja?'

Antoinette pulls away, muttering her thanks as she exits the car—for the lift, for the apology even, because the woman does look contrite, *truly*, gnawing waxy black from her bottom lip to reveal the pink glistening beneath, wet and oddly vulnerable—and by the time she looks up again, the balcony is empty, the door closed and curtained against the night.

'I shall talk to Paul,' Greta insists. 'I can do that, at the least.'

'Just leave it. Seriously, we're over. We're *done*.'

At that Greta narrows her eyes, narrows her mouth to a thin line, turning frontwards with both hands clamped to the steering wheel, and Antoinette sighs—*why are you here, Greta? what could you possibly want?*—the car door heavy in her exhausted fingers, slipping as she moves to close it and slamming hard. In darkness and silence, the sound echoes, sharp and clear as a slap across the face.

Loki, a glass of red wine in each hand, smiling wide as she stalks into the kitchen and slings her bag onto the bench. 'Hey—'

'Give me back my car key,' she says, holding out a flattened palm.

He puts one of the glasses down onto the bench, takes a slow and deliberate sip from the other before digging into the pocket of his jeans. 'I needed it.' He drops the key into her hand. 'I told you.'

'And I told you it was way too risky.'

'Nothing happened, everything's fine.'

'Oh yeah, everything's just peachy.'

'What do you—'

'I know you went to the flat today. What the hell were you thinking?'

'I was *thinking* you might like the rest of your things.'

'God, Loki, I could have gotten them anytime. What if Paul had been there, what if he'd seen you?'

'I'm not stupid.' Wounded, his glare, but sharp-edged all the same. Relating how he watched, waited for Paul to leave the flat, library-bound no doubt with laptop bag slung over his shoulder and a scowl on his face. Waiting out a further ten minutes, just to be certain, before letting himself in with the key Antoinette buried in the garden all those years ago.

'Wait,' she says, startled. 'How did you know about that?' The *spare* spare key—*For Emergency Use Only*—tucked safe inside an empty mustard jar and dug into the ground beneath the geranium that grew rampant and pink beside their front gate. Her mother's trick, interring keys; safer than tucking them beneath doormats or windowsills or potted plants, though Antoinette had all but forgotten about the one she'd buried, had never even told Paul for fear he would think it childish.

Loki taps his forehead. 'What you know, I know.'

'Really?' News to her, and troubling. 'I didn't realise it worked like that.'

'It's not like I can read your mind or anything.'

'But you know … what, exactly?'

He shrugs. 'If it's about Paul, about you and Paul, then it's in my head. Only … it feels vague somehow, like it's not really mine to have.'

'I don't understand.'

'And you think I do?' he says. 'I have all these memories, all this stuff that I know—or *think* that I know—only none of it's for real. I haven't done any of it myself, haven't learned anything directly. It's all just … here.'

Free hand holding his head now, fingers caged around his temple, flexing slightly as he tries to explain how it feels: not *wrong* exactly, but off kilter, out of sync with whatever slim sense of self he's managed to so far patch together. Too many recollections, flattened like photographs, like leaves pressed dry between pages in his mind, and Loki impelled to revisit—no, to *visit*, for the *first* time—as much as he can, to overlay abstraction with solid experience and, finally, make his mind his own.

'Mine,' he repeats. 'Not *his*, not anymore.'

'I'm sorry,' Antoinette says. 'I didn't know.' She retrieves the second glass of wine, takes a large and decidedly uncivilised gulp. Most of her anger dissipated now, cooled by the lines that crease his brow and drag at the corners of his mouth, by her frank inability to imagine what it's actually like, being him, that bright new skull crammed with pre-owned memories and hand-me-down thoughts. But still: 'Please don't go back there, Loki. It's too risky.'

'I've no reason to go back.' He taps at his forehead again, quick staccato pecks so hard they're audible. 'There's nothing else I need from that place, nothing else I want.'

'Good.' More wine, a smaller sip this time while she ponders, debates whether or not to bring it up, but what the hell. Pennies and pounds. 'Why did you shred his jacket?'

Another shrug, his gaze sliding from hers. 'Why not?'

'Loki...'

'I don't know.'

Black hair falling in shards across his face, like bars, like splinters, and now it seems too important a point to set quietly aside. Antoinette pushes, prods, trying to tease an explanation from him until finally—

'It's not like I planned it,' he snaps. Insisting there was no plan, no intentions of any kind until he spied the thing slung across the back of the couch, felt the tug of black leather, worn and warm, at his core. The jacket one of his most beloved possessions—one of *Paul's* most beloved possessions—and yet he recoiled from the touch of it, from the tentative brush of finger over hide. He didn't want it anymore, this second skin, this second-*hand* skin, but equally he did not want Paul to have it. And so: the saw-toothed kitchen knife cutting through leather like flesh, catching on the lining, but cutting all the same, and it felt good, cathartic.

'I felt free of it,' he finishes. 'Free of *him*.'

Antoinette refills his glass, tops up her own. 'I made a right royal mess of things, didn't I?'

'Of what?'

'Of you.' The wine is sour on her tongue. 'Whatever it was, however I managed to do it, seems I've fucked it all up.' Her nose tingles, her eyes sting, but damn her to hell before she starts to cry. She just wants her sister to be here, longs to be able to dump the whole mess in Jacqueline's lap—*look, here, sorry*—and let those elegant, careful fingers pick through the tangles and snarls.

'Hey,' Loki says, and, 'No,' and then his mouth is pressed to hers, one hand gently cupping her chin as his hair falls forward, curtaining their faces, and *why not*, she thinks. This is why she made him, isn't it? Her Paul-not-Paul, her beautiful doppelganger with his tongue that tastes of wine and spices warmed sharp in the sun, his silk-smooth cheeks and his hands that now move over her body, that now slide down her back, curving around her hips to pull her close. Half-moan, half-growl, the mewl of her name in his throat, and really: why the hell not?

So she returns his kisses, not precisely eager but willing enough, right arm twisting awkward to return her glass to the bench against which she now finds herself pinned, the weight of him urgent and close, and she opens her mouth to him, moves her tongue in a way she can only hope doesn't seem half as mechanical as it feels, slips wine-splashed fingers under his shirt to trace the vertebrae that bump beneath his feverish, fish-pale skin.

'Come on,' he whispers. A thumb hooked into the waistband of her skirt, pulling her towards the hall, towards the bedroom, and she follows, matching him kiss for fervent kiss because why not, because even if this is not entirely what she wants then it's certainly just what he needs.

And maybe it's what she needs as well.

Except.

Except, except, *oh*, it's all too much: his lips sliding along the hollows of her throat, sexy and lush and tickling precisely the way she likes it—the way she *should* like it—his fingers unbuttoning her blouse, thumbs circling persuasive over her nipples, hard little nubs pushing keen through the fabric of her bra, and she presses her body against him, runs her hands through his hair as she whispers his name—

Loki Loki Loki

—spurs to her own unbloodied side because she *wants* to want this, she does.

She really does.

Mouth finding hers, he lowers her to the bed, a motion so smooth, so graceful, it feels ludicrous. It feels wrong, she feels wrong, miscast in some fantasy of her own foolish devising, with poor Loki following a script she can read two heartbeats in advance, and 'I'm sorry,' she gasps, laughter bursting rough and wild from deep within her belly, unbidden, uncontrolled, and far too violent to tamp back down in any kind of a hurry.

'What?' Loki draws back, arousal mixing with confusion in his face. 'Did I do something wrong?'

Which only makes it worse.

'I'm sorry,' she repeats, finally, hand pressed to her aching diaphragm. 'It's not you—' Biting off the words, *it's me*, because she can feel them about to set her off all over again, and trying instead to explain the strange and inescapable sense that it was all staged, each movement of their bodies prearranged, each whisper and sigh placed *just so*, because surely … surely he must have felt it too?

'No.' Loki shakes his head. 'I don't know what you mean.'

Taking his hand, because she can't make it any clearer; there simply aren't the words. 'It's probably just me,' she says. 'I'm over-tired, not thinking straight.' A small lie, she hopes, to ward off the hurt. A small lie, because she fears the larger truth behind it.

Loki squeezes her fingers. 'You don't love me.'

'Of course I do.' And she does, a fierce and protective love, the force of which surprises even her.

'But it's not the same, is it?'

'The same as what?'

'The same as how I love you.'

'Oh, Loki.' Her voice is thin, exasperated, and she feels him recoil beside her, his hand slip from hers. 'I do love you, I do, it's just—'

'You don't want me. Not like this.'

Antoinette starts to tell him, *no, that's not true, maybe I just need more time to get used to things, to get used to you*, but his face is an open wound and she can't bring herself to salt it any longer. False hope, false promises; Loki doesn't deserve any of it. 'No,' she says. 'Not like that.'

'And that isn't going to change.'

Words like stones in her mouth, cold and heavy and easier to swallow than spit out, but spit them out she does. 'Probably not. I don't—no, it won't.'

Loki sighs. 'You made me to love you. I can't *not* love you.'

No accusation in his voice, merely a dull finality that's somehow even worse, and Antoinette fights the urge to hug him, to wrap her arms around his shoulders and hold him close, because right now he needs that like a hole in his head. Apologising instead, *sorry* and *sorry* and *sorry*, that pathetic dead-mouse word all she can find to offer him, until he shakes his head and crosses a finger over her lips.

'Stop,' he says. 'You didn't mean to do it.'

'No, but—'

Stop, again, pale blue eyes now damp and glimmering, and so she does.

eventh Circle is all but empty when Jacqueline walks through its doors. No clients, no tyre-kickers, just Becca sitting at the little desk at the back of the gallery, tapping away on her iPad. She looks up at the sound of suitcase wheels rumbling over the entrance tiles and her eyes widen. 'Jacqueline,' she whispers, glancing at the floating staircase that leads up to Dante's office. She drops the iPad. Scuttles around the desk with her hands held out in front of her. A gesture not so much of welcome, but of warding. 'What on earth's been going on?'

Jacqueline pauses. 'Didn't the photos come through?'

'Oh, they came *through*.' Becca flicks her hair, a habit that never fails to irritate. The girl wears her hair long, with a heavy fringe that falls over half her face, and bleached within an inch of its life. Her lips are bright red. Glossy as patent leather. 'I haven't seen them myself, but—'

'The prodigal daughter returns!'

Dante stands at the top of the stairs, one hand on hip. There's nothing good about the expression that tightens his face. Jacqueline waves, a pathetic waggle of fingers that she immediately regrets.

'Up here,' her boss snaps. 'Pronto.'

He disappears into his office and Jacqueline takes a deep breath. 'Time to face the music, then.'

Becca squeezes her shoulder. 'He's been like that all morning.'

Jacqueline forces herself to remain still beneath the girl's touch. To smile and nod as though everything is fine. Nothing more than she expected. Nothing she can't handle. She nudges her suitcase with her foot. 'I'll leave this down here.'

'No probs.' Becca smiles. Her fingernails are painted a dark, bluish purple. Jacqueline watches them curl around the handle of the case. Watches the girl drag it away behind her desk. 'Good luck,' Becca mouths.

Jacqueline straightens her back. Beneath her heels, the stairs sound hollow and insubstantial. She tightens her grip on the handrail as she climbs. Dante is at his desk, hunched over his laptop. His finger hooks the air between them, draws her closer.

'You wanna tell me what this is all about?'

Photos of Ryan Jellicoe's painting splash across the screen. A distance shot of the entire canvas, plus several close-ups that Dante now cycles through.

'It's almost finished,' Jacqueline says. 'He wanted to add some more detail to the foliage, I believe. But it's just about done.'

'He's changing the rest as well?'

'Not all of them. Half a dozen, perhaps. He wants to tease out the narrative, unify the show along those same lines.'

Dante rakes a hand over his crew cut. 'This is completely fucked, Jacks.'

'I don't think it will take that long to—'

'It's got nothing to do with time.'

'I don't understand.'

'It's this fucking *response to tragedy* bullshit.' His fingers bob air quotes, savage stabbing gestures that match his tone. 'This isn't the show I commissioned. I want the dead city, the dystopia. I want the bloody *grunt*, not this bleeding-heart, back-to-nature crap.'

'That's not what he's trying to say—'

'I don't want to hear it. I sent you up there to hustle his arse, *not* to give him editorial notes and *not* to change the whole damn show.'

'I didn't—'

'*Jacqueline was the best.*' Dante reads off the screen. '*Please thank her for me. I wouldn't have come up with it if she wasn't here.*'

Jacqueline winces. 'Ryan said that?'

'Ryan said that.'

'I don't know why he would, honestly. I didn't tell him to change anything; he came up with it all on his own.'

'Whatever, Jacks.' Dante flaps a dismissive hand.

'I'm serious. He wouldn't even let me see the canvas until—'

'Leave it. Just come up with a fix.'

'A fix?'

'We have to spin this to the punters somehow.' He looks through the images again. His nose wrinkles with disdain. 'I mean, look at this shit. Is that a fucking *parrot* sitting on that lamp post?'

Jacqueline leans closer. Squints at the red and green splodge of paint Dante is pointing at. 'I think you're worrying about nothing. These photos don't really capture the work. Once you see it in person…'

He straightens, suddenly. 'Don't tell me what I will and won't see. I've been doing this a long time, babe, and I *know* from photos. Point blank, this is *not* the show I thought I was getting. This is the very *opposite* of the show I thought I was getting, and there's squat I can do about it now.'

His teeth grind together. The muscles on each side of his jaw twitch. Jacqueline says nothing. There are no words she can offer which won't be mangled and spurned and thrown right back at her feet. She wishes she could see the entire email Ryan sent. Wishes she knew precisely what it was he said about her.

Dante rubs a hand over his scalp again. 'Look, you might as well go home.'

'Sorry?'

'Becca's got a handle on things. You weren't meant to be here today anyhow.'

'I thought I could catch up on the accounts. Now that I *am* here, it seems silly to just—'

'I think Becca got those done yesterday.'

'Oh.' Becca. *Becca* did the accounts. 'I wasn't aware she knew how.'

'It's not rocket science, babe.' Her boss sits down at his desk and starts tapping away at the keyboard. 'Didn't know how long you'd be flitting about up there, did we? Bills gotta be paid, yeah?'

'Perhaps I should go over everything,' she offers. 'Just to make sure she—'

'Jesus!' His head snaps up. 'Territorial much? Becca did the accounts and I checked them; it's not the end of the goddamn world. Go home and get some sleep. Looks like you could use it.'

Jacqueline straightens. 'All right, then. An afternoon off would be good, actually. It's been a long week.'

'Take tomorrow as well, yeah?' Dante turns back to his screen. 'Becca's on for a full day; no need for you to come in as well.'

'Really? Don't you think—'

His iPhone rings, the klaxon call of an old rotary-dial phone. Her boss plucks the thing from his pocket and swears. Taps the screen and holds it to his ear. 'Susie-Q, I was just thinking about you.'

Susan Keyes, the money behind Seventh Circle. Behind Segue, the sister gallery Dante is angling to open by the end of the year, as well. He catches Jacqueline's eye. Jerks his head towards the open office door. *Monday*, he mouths, before turning his shoulder against her. 'No, my lovely, it's all in hand. I'm literally looking at the proofs as we speak.'

Jacqueline backs out of the office. Closes the door behind her and walks down the stairs to where Becca waits with eyes wide and inquisitive.

'How'd it go?'

'Are you working this weekend?' Jacqueline asks.

'Only Saturday,' the girl says brightly. 'Dante's going to man the ship himself on Sunday. It's nice of him to give you a few days off after your trip—sounds like it was all pretty arduous.'

Jacqueline can't tell whether or not she's being sarcastic. She opens her bag and retrieves her collection of CabCharge receipts, neatly held together with a paperclip. 'I didn't get a chance to give these to Dante.'

'I'll make sure he gets them.' Becca takes the receipts from her. Flicks them between her fingers. 'So, you have any plans?'

'Plans?'

'For your time off?'

Jacqueline shakes her head. All she wants to do is go home and stand beneath a scalding-hot shower for several million hours. Sleep in her own bed for a few million more. Recover herself from the mess and sweat-slicked confusion that was Brisbane. That was Ryan Jellicoe. Recover and regroup. A few solitary days on her own, without the need to even speak to anyone, not even—

Ant. She'd almost forgotten about her sister in the spare room.

'Jacks? Are you okay?'

Becca is reaching for her again. Dark nails inch close to her wrist.

'Don't call me that,' Jacqueline snaps.

The girl snatches back her hand. Her red mouth rounds to a near perfect circle.

Jacqueline swallows. 'Sorry.'

'I was only trying to be friendly.' Her tone is far from it now.

'I know. I'm tired and ... I'm sorry, honestly.'

The girl nods and walks back to her desk. Tosses the CabCharge receipts on top. 'So, we'll see you next week, then.' She brings Jacqueline's suitcase around, taking small, delicate steps in her spiked heels. 'Don't forget this.'

'Thanks.' Jacqueline grips the handle tightly. 'Tell Dante not to worry about the Ryan Jellicoe show. Whatever he needs fixed, I'll handle it.'

'I'm sure you will,' Becca says.

Jacqueline wheels her case through the gallery doors. Pauses to wave a polite goodbye. The girl returns a thin smile, the press of her lips as cold and hard as the glass that slides shut in front of Jacqueline's face.

Her apartment is a mess. Boxes stacked in the corners of the living room. Clothes draped like discarded skins over furniture. Dirty dishes, most of them glasses, crowd the sink and kitchen bench, which makes Jacqueline wonder at the vast depths her sister's sorrow needs for drowning. To be fair, she can't wholly blame Ant for the state of the place. If her sister knew Jacqueline was coming home early, then she would have tidied. Would have insisted on picking Jacqueline up at the airport. Would, no doubt, have wanted to talk the entire drive home—the kind of rambling, broken-hearted babble Jacqueline was not yet prepared to face.

A messy apartment is a small price to pay for solitude.

For a few precious hours in which to gather herself before becoming—again, always, still—Big Sister.

She tugs her suitcase towards the bedroom, planning to unpack before tackling the kitchen. Only in the hall does she register the muted spatter of water coming from the bathroom. Jacqueline's stomach sinks. Ant is supposed to be working day shifts all this week and yet here she is, treating herself to a mid-afternoon shower. Goodness knows what time she managed to drag herself out of bed. A wisp of steam curls beneath the door.

'Fine,' Jacqueline mutters. 'That's just fine.'

Her bedroom appears to have been recently occupied by an invading army. The bed is unmade, the doona sloughed halfway off the mattress. A near-empty wine glass perches close to the edge of the side table. In front of the wardrobe, a suitcase gapes like some huge, stomach-slit beast, spilling a tangle of clothes and boots over the floor. It looks like her sister's room always did when they both lived with their mother.

Except this is *not* her sister's room.

Jacqueline feels intensely, absurdly violated. She leaves her own small case outside in the hall and returns to the kitchen. Fills the kettle and opens the fridge to check for milk. The smell of stale curry is sickening. Wrinkling her nose, she extracts the half-dozen or so takeaway containers that have been crammed onto the shelves. One of the lids must be loose as too late she notices the thin trail of yellow sauce following her to the rubbish bin.

'Damn it, Ant!' Her eyes prickle. She bites the inside of her cheek, hard. Draws herself along the pain as though it is a lifeline.

Down the other end of the apartment, the bathroom door opens.

Jacqueline braces herself. Forces fresh air into her lungs. 'It's only me,' she calls. Her voice is strong and calm. 'Everything wrapped up earlier than expected.'

No answer beyond the heavy fall of footsteps and the closing of a second door. The door to the *spare* room, where her sister should have been staying all along. Should she have made that clear? Should she have needed to? Jacqueline runs water from the kitchen tap. Waits for it to heat and then foams the dishcloth with detergent. The spilled curry turns the cloth a bright yellow. Not the sort of stain that will rinse out and so, once the floor is clean, she throws it into the bin with the containers. Locates the plug beneath an unrinsed cereal bowl. Starts to fill the sink with suds and steam.

Behind her, a throat is cleared.

'I thought you were working today,' she says, turning to face—not her sister but *Paul*. Standing beside the kitchen bench in his customary black T-shirt and jeans, hair loose and still dripping from the shower. That same smug grin on his face that she's always detested.

'Oh,' she says. 'You two are back together?'

'It's not what you think.'

'Is she here?'

'At the restaurant. She'll be home for dinner.'

'Home?' She raises an eyebrow. 'Here, you mean? Is there something wrong with your place?'

He shakes his head. 'I need to explain.'

'Never mind.' She doesn't want to hear his excuses. His flimsy justifications for behaving the way he did. Artistic temperament? Wounded pride? Fear of abandonment? Bad enough her sister obviously deemed such offerings worthy of forgiveness. Bad enough she will have to listen to Ant rationalise it all herself anyway. Validation for the lovelorn. For the terminally lost.

Jacqueline turns back to the sink. Flicks off the tap and begins to pile dishes into the near-scalding water. She's furious. At Paul. At her sister. At Dante and Ryan Jellicoe and sweet little Becca in whose mouth butter wouldn't so much as soften. But mostly at herself, for allowing everything to spin so completely out of control. Beneath the suds, her hands tremble. She considers the razor blades hidden in her toiletries bag.

She needs time. She needs to be alone.

'Here,' Paul says, close by her side. 'Let me.'

Jacqueline swivels on her heel. Looks up into a face that looms higher than she remembers. That seems somehow different. Finer-boned or whiter-skinned, with eyes pale as polar ice. Were they always like that? She would have sworn his eyes were brown.

Brown or hazel. Some dull, muddy colour. A vague recollection of a Halloween party skitters across her mind. Ant with her face and forearms powdered and irises tinted a disconcerting shade of red.

'Are you wearing contacts?' she asks him.

This smile is nothing she has seen before. Cautiously open and more genuine than she would have thought Paul capable of being. He takes her hands from the sink. Dries their reddened skin on his shirt.

'I need to explain,' he says again. 'Please.'

Jacqueline stares at him. Takes in his inexplicable height, his strangely altered features. The way his fingers close around hers in a manner that asks permission even as the liberty is taken. And there's something else. An air about him, or perhaps *the* air about him. Crisp and sharp and *new*. She has no words to describe it. Knows only that the man standing in front of her is not Paul. Was never *Paul*.

'Who are you?' Her voice is barely a whisper.

'Come with me,' he says.

Jacqueline allows him to lead her away from the sink, out of the kitchen. She isn't afraid—she can never *be* afraid—not of him. She has no idea where such conviction comes from, only that it fits within her as close and faultless as truth.

Antoinette pours herself more wine, reaches across her sister's coffee table to top up Loki as well. Jacqueline covers her glass with a flattened palm even though it's still full, barely a mouthful missing and not worth the addition of anything more. Her sister's usual trick, the sly and careful nursing of one solitary drink all through the meal, or night out, or whatever the occasion happens to be, and even then it'll be rare to see the glass emptied. Antoinette doesn't know why she bothers.

'I can't believe you're so cool with all this,' she says.

Jacqueline shrugs. 'He's here, isn't he? Hard to refute that.' She sits with the purple notebook open in her lap, flips each page and runs her fingertips over the lines which themselves hold nothing but those shallow grooves and indentations, braille in reverse, and Antoinette wishes she would leave the bloody thing alone for five minutes.

'There's nothing, not a single word left.'

'Yes.' Jacqueline says. 'But I wonder…'

'I didn't really think you'd believe me.' Antoinette glances at Loki. 'Believe us, I mean. Thought I'd have to, you know, prove it somehow, get the two of them together or something, side by side.'

'But you said he shouldn't see me,' Loki says.

'He *shouldn't*,' Antoinette tells him. 'I just meant, I didn't think she would be so easy to convince.'

'Loki explained it all,' Jacqueline says, dismissive. 'I wish we could still see what you wrote. You can't remember any of it?'

'Not really. Not the details.'

This is freaking her out all over again. Arriving home from work to find not just Loki but her *sister*, the two of them sitting side by side on the couch like old friends, like co-conspirators, the murmur of their voices trailing off as she came into the living room. And Jacqueline laughing, rising gracefully to pull her into a hug, words warm as breath in her ear. *Close your mouth, Ant, something will fall in.* She should be glad, relieved that Loki has already done most of the heavy lifting, because she sure as hell hasn't been able to think of the right way to explain things. Still, it seems too easy, her sister's calm acceptance of the situation, of *Loki*—as if he's no more than a stray dog dragged home from the pound.

'I've got an idea.' Jacqueline sets her glass down on the coffee table, tucks the notebook beneath her arm as she rises. 'Back in a minute.'

Antoinette waits until her sister has left the room before turning to Loki, turning *on* Loki. 'What did you tell her? I mean, what did you *say*, exactly?'

'The truth.'

'And she believed you, just like that?'

Loki sips at his wine. 'She's very perceptive.'

'But it's insane. If she came up to me out of the blue and said, hey look, here's this guy I somehow *made*, somehow magicked into existence or whatever, I mean … it's *insane*. I don't get how she can just *believe* it.'

'Hard to argue with what's right in front of your face.' He pats his chest, his hand falling over the heart that beats unquestionably beneath that black cotton shirt, beneath skin and muscle and ribcage, and Antoinette finds herself marvelling afresh at the miracle sitting on the couch opposite her. Loki smiles. 'See?'

She shakes her head. 'It's not like you have my name stamped on your arse. *Trademark Antoinette Paige*, or some shit. You could be just a person for all anyone could really tell.'

'You don't think I'm a *person*?'

It's a gift, this ability she has of finding precisely the wrong words to say at any given moment. Words that wound with such blind precision, she might have spent months honing their edge.

'I'm sorry,' she tells him. 'That came out wrong.'

'You sure it didn't come out exactly right?'

'Loki, you know I wouldn't…'

His gaze shifts past her, scowl softening to a smile as Jacqueline walks back into the room. Shaking her head, she settles down beside him again with one leg crossed over the other, one stock-inged foot rocking gently in his direction.

'It didn't work.' She opens the notebook to a once-white page, holds up the pencil she must have used to colour it a uniform, shimmery grey. 'I saw it in a film once. I thought we might be able to show up the indentations from the pen, even if the ink itself has … evaporated? But no luck.'

Antoinette leans close, squinting as she tries to make out words or letters or anything approaching some kind of sense from the textured stripes of lead. There are markings, sure; swirls and scratches and dots that tantalise and tease, but nothing legible. Nothing to illuminate the shape of her thoughts that night, if thoughts are what they could be called, those vodka-fuelled fantasies from which she had so unwittingly spun the creature—the *person*—now calling himself Loki.

'Useless.' She slumps back in her chair.

'But worth a try,' Loki says, touching her sister's wrist.

'I don't think it really matters.' Jacqueline frowns. 'What I mean is, the words themselves may not be very important. I know you both think it was a … spell? Or some such? But—'

Antoinette snorts. 'A spell?'

'That was me,' Loki says. 'That was my word.'

'I didn't cast a *spell*, Loki. You think I'm what, some kind of witch?'

'That's not what I said. You were the one talking about magic.'

'For want of a better word, god! I didn't mean that I literally—'

'Enough,' Jacqueline says. 'Both of you, stop it.' She closes the notebook, slides it across the coffee table. 'It would be *nice* to know what Ant wrote—nice for Loki to see the words that shaped him, so to speak—but it doesn't matter. It wouldn't explain *how* he was made, or what happens to him now.'

'You weren't even here,' Antoinette protests. 'How can you know anything?'

Jacqueline sighs and leans back against the couch. Fine lines crease her forehead, pull the corners of her mouth into a taut and thoughtful expression that Antoinette knows only too well. Her sister, contemplating what needs to be said, each potential word and phrase weighed and measured according to some precise internal scale of her own, and it drives Antoinette mad sometimes, this over-thinking of anything even vaguely important, when she should just bloody well come out and—

'Tell us,' Loki says, his voice soft, smooth and firm as a hand gloved in leather, and Jacqueline turns to look at him, her eyes snapping back into focus.

'Yes,' she says and then, to Antoinette: 'Remember when we were little, really little? Remember the fendlies?'

Antoinette starts to shake her head, starts to say that she doesn't have the foggiest what her sister is on about, and yet that word—*fendlies*—feels strange and familiar both at once, its flint-sharp edge striking a place laid so deep in her memory it defies articulation. Throws off merely a spark, vivid and certain but too brief to catch hold, too painful to fan and, *no*, she warns herself. *Not that, not there.*

You don't want to see that.

'You must remember something,' Jacqueline says.

'No.' Antoinette swallows the last of her wine in two large gulps and deposits the empty glass on the floor. 'I don't remember anything.' Not sunlight flickering through trees or the shriek of girlish laughter, not the glimmer of glass-bright eyes or the silken warmth of fur against her cheek.

'What are the fendlies?' Loki asks.

'We were only children,' Jacqueline tells him. 'I wasn't even in school yet, so four years old perhaps? Which would have made you about two, Ant?'

Antoinette crosses her arms. 'How can you expect me to remember if I was only two?'

Her sister ignores her. 'There weren't any other children around where we lived and our mother didn't believe in playgroups or kindergarten, or perhaps she couldn't afford to send us, so we only had each other. The fendlies were … well, Ant was only little. She couldn't say *friends* properly, or *friendly*. So, friendly ones became *fendly* ones. *Fendlies*, you see?'

Loki nods, glances at Antoinette. 'None of this rings a bell?'

She shakes her head. A dull, throbbing pain has set up camp behind her eyes and she just wants them to shut up, her sister and Loki both, to shut up and go away and leave her alone.

'They weren't real,' Jacqueline continues. 'She made them up. They weren't human, either, most of them. More along the lines of animals, or … other things. Like the puppets from *Sesame Street*.'

'So?' Antoinette snaps. 'Lots of kids have imaginary friends.'

Her sister stares at her. 'But, Ant, I could see them as well.'

'You could *see* them?' Loki echoes.

'I used to think I imagined it all,' Jacqueline says. 'We were both so little and it's not as though I can remember all that clearly anymore either. I told myself that I must have simply been pretending along with Ant, convincing myself that the fendlies were really there—you know, the way children do with monsters under the bed, or Santa Claus—because anything else was impossible, wasn't it?' She reaches out and touches his face, trails the tips of her fingers along his jawline. 'Until now. Until you.'

He smiles, captures her hand with his own and squeezes. 'I'm not impossible?'

'Perhaps, but you're most definitely here.'

Antoinette wonders at the effect Loki is having on her sister. She has never seen Jacqueline so at ease with someone who is, after all, a near perfect stranger. Her relaxed posture, the way she allows her hand to sit so still within his, the curious, almost coy tilt of her head when she speaks to him—all of it so utterly unlike the sister-shaped space that Antoinette keeps in her heart.

'What happened to them?' Loki asks her. 'The fendlies, where are they now?'

'I told you, I don't remember.' Antoinette's headache intensifies and there's a taste like sour milk in the back of her mouth.

'They disappeared,' Jacqueline says. 'They weren't like you, they didn't stay with us. Once we finished playing, they ... they just went away.'

'Is that what will happen to me, Antoinette?' The fear in his voice wounds her to the quick. 'Am I going to just disappear?'

You don't want to see that.

'I don't know!' She lurches to her feet, struggling against the nausea that locks around her throat as she tries to tell them again that she doesn't remember anything, doesn't *know* anything, not about the fendlies or Loki or the barbed, blackened place in her mind whose perimeter hurts too much to even tiptoe around, let alone get close enough to—

Then she's running. Down the hall with one hand clamped

over her mouth, smashing her hip on the bathroom vanity as she makes for the toilet in the corner and half-kneels, half-falls onto the tiles before it. Not much in her belly past the tuna salad she had for lunch, but still she retches until her muscles ache and her throat is raw with bile, until Jacqueline is there with a glass of water and a cool, damp cloth to wipe her face.

'It's all right,' her sister tells her. 'Everything will be all right.'

Antoinette spits into the bowl. 'I don't want to talk about this anymore.'

'You're okay, though? Antoinette?' Loki is standing in the doorway, the expression on his face every bit as scared and confused as she feels, every bit as lost, and she gets to her feet, wills her knees not to buckle as she shuffles over to him. In her arms, he feels solid and warm and fixed. He feels *real* in a way that she knows—that she forces herself to *remember*, skimming as close to the blackness as she dares—the fendlies never were.

'You're not going to disappear,' she whispers, hugging him even tighter. 'You're staying right here with us, I promise.'

As exhausted as she is, Jacqueline cannot sleep. Not with Ant in the bed beside her. Sighing, shuffling, stretching her legs every five minutes. After meeting Loki, Jacqueline assumed he was the reason behind the annexation of her room—a queen bed providing greater comfort for an eager new couple than the futon—but apparently, perplexingly, not.

You sure you don't mind? Ant asked as they brushed their teeth. *I can sleep on the couch if you want the bed to yourself.*

Of course I don't mind. You're my sister.

It's just, with me and Loki … it's a bit awkward, you know.

But Jacqueline didn't know. Still doesn't know. She rolls over towards her sister. The room is dark, but she can make out enough detail to see that Ant is lying on her back. Most likely staring sleepless at the ceiling. 'You made him for yourself, right?' Jacqueline asks. 'To replace Paul?'

'Something like that,' Ant replies. 'I told you, I was pretty wasted. It's not like I had an actual plan or anything.'

'Yet here he is. And Paul is out of the picture?'

'Definitely.'

'You're sure about that?'

'What are you saying?'

'Only that you seem to have gotten over him very quickly. Perhaps there's still a torch burning there, perhaps that's why you won't let yourself have Loki.'

'It's not that.' Her sister sighs. 'I don't love Paul, but I don't hate him either. When I think about him, about us, I don't feel anything except tired. It's different with Loki. I do love him, just not … you know.'

'Not the way he loves you.'

'Don't think for a second I feel good about that.'

'Why not make him happy, then?'

'What, just lead him on? Brilliant idea, Jacqueline.'

'Oh, for crying out loud, it's just *sex*—and I'm sure you've equipped the man with superlative skills in that department.'

Silence. Served with bristles and spikes.

Jacqueline wishes she could take back her words. 'That was harsh, I'm sorry. But I don't understand, Ant, I honestly don't. He's beautiful and sexy, and he knows how you feel about him—or, rather, how you don't feel—and he *still* wants you. You *made* him to want you. What's the harm in having a bit of fun, the both of you?'

'You're right, you don't understand.' Her sister's voice is thin and drawn, as though it might snap if rubbed in the wrong spot. 'I'm not like you, Jacqueline. If I'm in love with someone, then sex is more than just *a bit of fun*. It actually means something. I'm pretty sure Loki would feel the same.'

'So if he *didn't* love you, then…'

'God, why don't *you* fuck him, you're so bloody keen!' The mattress creaks as her sister rolls heavily onto her side. Turns her back and curls herself foetal beneath the covers. 'I need to get some sleep.'

Jacqueline hesitates, balancing words on her tongue. 'That's not what I meant,' she whispers at last. Reaches out her hand in the darkness and rests it on her sister's shoulder. 'I'm sorry, honestly.'

Ant shrugs but doesn't pull away. 'If you ever let yourself fall in love, even for a day, then maybe you'd understand.'

'Maybe.' The word barely audible. She squeezes Ant's shoulder then tucks both hands beneath her own chin, pressing tight enough to feel the pulse of blood in her throat. Lies there motionless, thinking of Loki. That sharp, pale face. Those ice-cut eyes and lips lush as slivers of fruit. The odd twist of longing that drew her to him earlier that afternoon, that somehow draws her still.

Maybe. The syllables echo. Swell with possibilities unbidden, unwanted. Yet she cannot bring herself to shut them out.

Maybe.

12

Jacqueline takes off her sandals. Digs her feet into the warm, dry sand and smiles. Loki nudges her with his elbow. 'Glad I dragged you down here?'

'I am,' she says. If he hadn't coaxed her out of the door and onto a tram, she would likely still be hip-deep in the chaos of her apartment. Growing ever more frustrated in her attempts to restore order. The place simply isn't big enough for the three of them—and even if she could conjure up the space to stow each box and suitcase neatly away, she knows Ant will simply haul it all back out again whenever she wants to find something.

It's impossible. She needs to talk to her sister. Set some boundaries.

'Hey,' Loki says. 'You feel like an ice cream?'

He's gone before she can answer. Loping up the boardwalk towards the Mr Whippy van parked by the pier. Jacqueline turns back to the beach, shielding her eyes from the sun. It's not as crowded as she expected St Kilda to be on such a glorious summer day, and she has to remind herself that it's only Friday afternoon. Most people will still be at work.

Speaking of which.

Jacqueline retrieves her phone from her bag. No messages. No missed calls. She hesitates, then redials the last number on her call list. It goes straight to voicemail, to the terse recorded greeting that she knows too well, and she hangs up before the beep. He must be working. Sweltering in his studio with only the smell of paint for company and no patience for distraction. Which, she tells herself, is a good thing. He'll call when he finally takes a break. When he switches on his phone and hears the message she left this morning. He'll call, or he won't. In any case, her days of playing phone tag with Ryan Jellicoe are over.

Instead, she flicks through her contacts to Seventh Circle. Becca answers on the third ring, her voice losing its polished tone when Jacqueline announces herself. 'Dante is in a meeting,' the girl informs her. 'For the rest of the day.'

'That's all right, I was hoping to talk to you.'

'Me?'

'I wanted to apologise for being so snippy yesterday. I really appreciate you keeping on top of things while I've been away. I know it can't have been easy, putting in all those extra hours.'

'Oh.' Becca pauses, long enough to melt the frost from her tongue. 'Thanks, Jacqueline, that's really nice of you to say. But it's been fantastic, getting to see how everything happens behind the scenes. Dante's been unbelievably supportive too. There's this certificate? Business administration, something like that? Anyway, he thinks maybe I can do that through the gallery as a trainee.'

'A trainee?'

'That way the government pays for part of it, or something.'

Jacqueline bristles. Dante has never once offered *her* any sort of training or qualifications upgrade, but less than a week alone with Sunflower Girl and he's tossing business certificates around like confetti. 'Listen, Becca?' She keeps her tone light. 'Has Ryan Jellicoe been in touch by any chance?'

'I don't think so. Why?'

'He said he might give me a status update before the weekend, that's all. I thought he might have called the gallery instead of my phone.'

'Okay, well if he … sorry, Jacqueline, there's a client just walked in.'

'I'll let you go. But if you do hear from Ryan—'

'I'll be sure to have him call you.' The girl has already switched to the cool, rounded vowels of *how may I assist you*, and a moment later Jacqueline finds herself wishing goodbye to an empty line.

'Nice speaking to you as well,' she mutters.

'I thought you were supposed to be on holiday?'

Jacqueline starts, almost dropping her phone in the sand. 'Don't do that!' she snaps as Loki steps out from behind her. In each hand he holds a large soft-serve cone, one of them coated with chocolate, the other chopped nuts.

'Don't bring you ice cream?'

'Don't sneak up on me.'

'Sorry.' He grins. 'Chocolate or nuts? I forgot to ask.'

She doesn't feel like either, but chooses the cone with the chocolate because it doesn't appear to be melting quite as fast. 'I'm not on holiday,' she says. 'I'm on leave. Forced leave.'

'That's not what you told Antoinette this morning.'

'She has enough on her plate without worrying about me.'

Loki bites the top from his ice cream. Makes a face as though he's been tricked into swallowing a mouthful of soap. 'What the hell do they call this?'

Jacqueline points to the side of the van. 'Ninety-five percent fat free?'

'*Taste free* would be more accurate. You gonna eat yours?'

'After such a glowing endorsement?'

Grimacing with disgust, Loki collects her untouched cone and promptly dumps it onto the sand along with his own. 'Seagulls can have them, they get desperate enough.' He wipes his hands on his shirt, picks up her sandals. 'Come on, let's take a stroll.'

Jacqueline returns her phone to her bag. 'Where?'

'Wherever we end up.' He smiles, a bright flash of teeth she can't help but return. His fingers find hers. Pull her into motion. 'You know, I don't have much on *my* plate right now.'

'Mmm.' Sand shifts beneath her shoeless feet. Her toes curl with each step. Two young girls play in the shallows, squealing as each incoming wave foams and splashes against their legs. Their mother stands watch nearby, her face concealed by a floppy-brimmed hat.

Jacqueline looks away.

'So you could talk to me,' Loki prods. 'No worries at all.'

'Talk to you? I barely know you.'

He squeezes her hand. 'That should make it easier.'

Remarkably, it does. They walk almost the entire length of the beach, stopping just shy of the marina where sand gives way to scrub and stone, and the words fall from Jacqueline's mouth as effortless as breath. Loki remains silent. Allows her simply to speak. No interruptions, no commentary beyond the occasional murmur of acknowledgement or request for clarification, and perhaps because of this she finds herself telling him everything. Ryan Jellicoe, the surreal nightmare that was Brisbane, the fear that her job might be secured by only the slimmest of threads.

Even, with only a minor hesitation, her concerns about her health. The sudden, inexplicable headaches and dizzy spells. The blackouts.

'Scary,' Loki says.

'Yes.' Jacqueline pauses. 'You're not going to insist I see a doctor?'

'Is that what you want me to say?'

'No,' she admits. 'Anyway, I'm sure it's only due to stress. I'll manage.'

'Maybe you should talk to Antoinette.'

'But *I'm* the older sister.' She steps onto the footpath that runs parallel to the beach. Braces herself on his shoulder and dusts the sand from her feet. Slips back into her sandals. 'I'm the one who solves the problems. I'm the one who fixes things. Ant needs me to be strong, and I need to be there for her. The other way around, we don't make any sense to each other. Trust me.'

Loki stares at her, bemused.

'Stop it,' she tells him. 'I'm not a science experiment.'

'Come on.' He grabs her hand again. 'There's a café up on Acland Street, makes awesome cakes. Pretty good coffee, too.' They follow the foreshore a while, doubling back towards Luna Park. Faint screams from the rollercoaster reach over the growl of passing traffic. 'You know,' Loki says. 'You really need to stop calling her *Ant*. She hates it.'

'She does?' Jacqueline is genuinely surprised. Ant has been Ant for as long as she can remember. 'She told you that?'

He shrugs. 'It's just something I *know*. She thinks it's an ugly nickname; too short, too blunt. It makes her feel … insignificant? Close to insignificant. Overlooked maybe, taken for granted? It's hard to express. I don't think she's expressed it herself, not even to herself.'

'Well, I … what should I call her?'

'Antoinette?'

'That's a lot of syllables.'

'About as many as *Jac-que-line*.'

'Sure. But consider the alternatives. My boss calls me *Jacks*.' She grimaces. 'Jackie is just as bad—which is how they tried to shorten it in high school. Sounds like, I don't know, someone who isn't *me*.'

'I think you both have beautiful names.'

'Of course you do,' she laughs. 'Honestly, our mother is so damn pretentious. Antoinette, Jacqueline, Charles. She's never even been to France and yet it's her favourite place in the whole world.'

'Charles?'

Jacqueline raises an eyebrow. 'You don't know about Charles?'

'Should I?'

'He was our brother; my *twin* brother. I thought this might have been something you already...'

Loki taps two fingers against his temple. 'It's not Wikipedia in here. Mostly, I know stuff about me and Antoinette.' His tone grows bitter. Thin as the edge of a blade. 'About Antoinette and *him*, anyway. I'm trying to separate all that from me—from who I am—but it's hard.'

'Because you have his memories?'

'No. Because I don't have any of my own.'

Uncomfortable, she fixes her gaze on the path ahead. The shopping strip is busier, the perennial café crowd filling alfresco tables with chatter and cigarettes. Too many people, too much noise. Jacqueline feels hemmed in, unsure of herself. Unsure of her next step.

'Sorry,' Loki says. 'You said Charles *was* your brother?'

'I don't remember him very well. We weren't even four when he died.'

'Was he sick?'

'He drowned.' Jacqueline dodges a large pram parked right in the middle of the sidewalk. A woman bends over it, fussing with the child inside. 'In the bath, just another of those awful domestic accidents, you know? I don't think our mother's ever gotten over it. Perhaps, if our father hadn't left her so soon afterwards...'

'You ever see him?'

Jacqueline snorts. 'Not so much as a phone call. We expect he's still alive, only because we assume we would have heard from someone if he wasn't. It's not as though our mother would be hard to find.'

Loki squeezes her hand. 'I'm sorry about your brother.'

'Thanks, but honestly, it happened such a long time ago. I rarely think about him these days, although...' She searches for the right words. For *any* words to fit the queer tugging sensation that she sometimes feels. A nameless, formless dragging down, as though there's a tiny black hole planted deep in the centre of her. As though Charles took something of hers with him when he died. She asked Ant about it once but her sister only shook her head.

I really don't remember him, Jacqueline.

But you adored him. Of the two of us, I think he was your favourite.

I'm sorry, I must have been too young.

'It doesn't matter,' she tells Loki. 'It's ancient history.'

'Hey,' he says, stopping in front of a clothes shop. Music pumps into the street through the open door. He points to a male mannequin in the window. 'What do you think of that jacket?'

'It's very nice,' Jacqueline responds. Thigh-length black leather. A flash of burgundy on the lining. 'Also, very expensive, I'm sure.' Inside her bag, her phone bleats the arrival of a text. Ryan, hopefully.

'I'm trying it on,' Loki says. He drops her hand. Disappears inside the shop.

Jacqueline takes out her phone. The message is from Ant, short and not so sweet: *Mum called. Knows you're home. Have to come tonight.* Dinner with their mother is not high on her list of sure-fire tips to avoid stress. Simply thinking about the emotional thrust and parry likely to be involved makes the muscles running down the back of her neck tighten. Her fingers hover over the screen. She could refuse. Could say that she has other plans. Could...

Fine, she types. *See you after work. Will polish the armour.* Sends it.

In the shop window, a slender blonde girl with lips the colour of strawberry bubblegum is removing the leather jacket from the mannequin. Jacqueline watches as she turns back to the floor, back to Loki. As she grins and holds the jacket up for him to slide into. Her pink mouth moves. She runs her hands over his shoulders and straightens the lapels. Points to a mirror hanging framed on the wall. Loki laughs and shakes his head. Jacqueline wishes she could hear the words that pass between them, but she prefers to stay out on the street. If she isn't in the shop, Loki can't ask her to pay for the jacket. If she isn't in the shop, she won't have to tell him *no*.

She doubts very much if her sister has let him borrow a credit card.

But he doesn't so much as glance in Jacqueline's direction. Simply removes the jacket and returns it to the blonde who folds it across her arm and sashays over to the counter. Loki follows. Says something that makes the girl laugh and smooth her hair. Loki laughs as well. With expert fingers, she removes the swing-tags and the security clip, then pulls a bag from beneath the counter. Folds the jacket, slides it inside. Passes the bag to Loki, whose smile is bright enough by now to power a small city. He reaches out, touches the girl's face. Brushes the backs of his fingers against her cheek. Takes the bag with him as he leaves. Outside, he squints and turns away from the sun.

Jacqueline stares. 'Did you pay for that? I didn't see you pay for that.'

'It was a gift.'

'A gift? Do you know her?'

Loki shrugs. 'She said I had amazing eyes.'

Inside the shop, the girl is holding the security clip in front of her face. She looks confused, distracted. Her gaze shifts to the window, to the jacketless mannequin and beyond, to where Loki and Jacqueline stand on the sidewalk. Loki grins and lifts his hand, waves back through the glass. The girl blinks. Her own smile falters and her forehead creases.

'Come on.' Loki slips his elbow through Jacqueline's and begins to walk. 'You want to grab that coffee?'

'Did you just *steal* a leather jacket?' she asks.

'I told you, it was a gift.'

'But it must be worth, what? Seven, eight hundred dollars? You can't just walk into a shop and have a perfect stranger decide to *give* you an eight-hundred-dollar jacket simply because she likes your eyes.'

'You were there. What did you see happen?'

'I saw...' Jacqueline shakes her head. 'I saw her give you the jacket.'

'Right then.'

'But I—'

He stops. Places a finger against her mouth. 'She said I looked good in the jacket. I told her I didn't have any money. She said I could have it anyway—that I *should* have it anyway. People are allowed to be nice sometimes, you know.'

Jacqueline says nothing. If Loki is lying then so are her own eyes. 'I'm tired,' she says. 'Let's go home.'

'Okay.' As they walk, he catches her hand in his. 'Was that your artist dude before?'

'Hmm?'

'You were looking at your phone.'

'Oh, no, that was Ant. Our mother wants us over for dinner tonight.'

'Can I come?'

Jacqueline laughs. 'You're *volunteering* for An Evening with Sally Paige? But she hates you.'

'She's never met me.' His voice flattens, and cools. 'She's only met *him*.'

Jacqueline winces. 'I'm sorry, Loki.' She needs to do better than that. Needs to remember how he feels about Paul. About not being Paul. 'You realise that we can't explain you to our mother, though? If you do come, you'll have to pretend to be him. Let her think you are him. It might be easier for you to stay home.'

'I don't mind,' Loki says. '*She* doesn't matter, what *she thinks* doesn't matter. Only, I have some memories—of her, of her house—and I need to make them real. I need to make them mine. Understand?'

'Not entirely,' Jacqueline admits. 'But it's important to you, I understand that.'

'You'll tell Antoinette? I don't think she'll be too happy about it.'

'She'll be fine. You can run interference for us.'

'I'm serious.' He stops walking, turns to look at her.

And perhaps she can see how someone might be moved to hand over an expensive leather jacket. For those eyes, for those long, black lashes. Those lips, soft and certain to yield if pressed against her own.

You fuck him, you're so bloody keen.

She moves closer. The air around them stills. 'Ant might have made you, Loki, but that doesn't mean she owns you.'

'I never said she did. I just…' He turns his head away. 'I can't hurt her. Not ever.'

'No,' Jacqueline tells him. 'Neither can I.'

ℒ

Antoinette spots an opening and abruptly changes lanes, resists the urge to raise a middle finger to the jerk in the car behind her who thinks that leaning on his horn will solve anyone's problems. There was no danger of a collision, not in this peak hour crawl-along, and she still has to get across at least one more lane in the next few kilometres before her exit.

Beside her, Jacqueline sucks air through clenched teeth. 'Careful.'

'Anytime you want to learn to drive will be fine by me,' Antoinette says. Still pissed her sister didn't take her side in the argument with Loki, those precious fifteen minutes wasted on debating whether or not he should accompany them to dinner with their mother, fifteen minutes that might have seen them get ahead of the worst of the traffic.

Loki leans forward from the back seat. 'You don't drive?'

'It makes me anxious,' Jacqueline tells him.

Antoinette catches his eye in the rear-view mirror. 'You didn't know that?' He shakes his head, sits back and returns his attention to the passing scenery, what little there is of it out here on the freeway. She still hasn't gotten a handle on the vagaries of what Loki does and doesn't already know, the extent of his data cache, so to speak, his pre-loaded software—not that she'll ever admit to thinking in such terms.

You don't think I'm a person?

She's hurt him way too much already.

She glances at Jacqueline, sitting with hands calmly clasped in her lap, face turned to the passenger side window. Her sister is wearing the dress their mother gave her last Christmas, coffee and cream roses on a bright orange background, an ugly combination not helped by pale yellow lace that trims the bodice and runs in triplicate around the hem. For Antoinette, it was a bottle of red wine and—*because you don't seem too fussy about your figure these days*—a box of Belgian seashell chocolates.

'You know you only encourage her,' Antoinette says.

Jacqueline looks around. 'Hmm?'

'The dress. You keep wearing those hideous things, she'll just keep buying them for you. It's a vicious circle.'

'No skin off my nose.'

'Listen, I'm sorry about before.'

'I'm not the one you should apologise to.'

Antoinette grimaces. Tonight will be bad enough without having Jacqueline offside. Her sister, who knows better than anyone how to handle their mother, how to deflect the worst of her barbs and defuse all the dire and well-hidden explosives that Antoinette would otherwise blithely stomp right over, who somehow manages to keep the peace and her temper both.

'Loki?' Antoinette checks the mirror. 'I'm sorry, okay? It's just weird, having you meet my mum. Like it wasn't bad enough the first time.'

Loki grimaces. 'The first time?'

'You know what I mean,' Antoinette says. 'With Paul, the first time she met Paul.' Rushing on even as he opens his mouth, even as his eyes flash with wounded, wrathful pride. 'And, yes, I know you're not *him*, Loki. Believe me, I know that. But tonight, you're going to be, right? You have to *be Paul* because I don't know how else I'm supposed to explain to her that … what? What the hell am I supposed to say? *Hi Mum, meet my imaginary friend?*'

'I'm not imaginary,' Loki mutters.

'Calm down,' Jacqueline says. 'It'll be fine.'

'But what if she sees him and knows? What if she can tell?'

'She won't.'

'You did. You knew straight off, you said.'

'I saw a lot more of that imbecile than she ever did. Besides, Loki wasn't trying to convince me he was anyone other than himself.'

'Neither of you have to worry,' Loki interrupts. 'I know how to be Paul. I know how to be Paul better than I know anything else.'

'Okay, but—*shit*.' Snug in its nest in the centre console, her mobile starts to chirp and she reaches for it, fingers scrabbling as she tries to keep focus on the exit lane opening up to her left.

'Give it to me.' Jacqueline grabs the Nokia from her hand. 'It's Greta, should I answer?'

'God no, just let it ring.'

Greta, again. Add this to the two missed calls earlier today, plus the half dozen or so increasingly urgent texts that followed. Greta, wanting to talk, wanting to meet for purposes unspecified, some mysterious agenda of her own, or maybe in cahoots with

Paul on matters more nefarious, and when is she going to get the message that Antoinette is just not interested? If Paul does need to talk with her, he can bloody well get in touch himself, and if not, if it is just Greta with some fresh-killed scheme to get them back together, then she can take a flying—

'Greta?' Loki leans forward again. 'What does she want?'

'Who knows?' Antoinette mutters.

Jacqueline returns the mobile to the console. 'She's that weird German girl, right? The one who sniffs around Paul like she's his personal guard dog?'

'She's not *that* weird,' Antoinette says.

'Remember Paul's birthday last year? She was wearing that little stuffed bat around as a brooch. A *real* bat, Ant, a real *dead* bat.'

'So?' Hackles raised now, automatically defensive. Most of the time, her sister is cool about the whole goth thing, but still there's the occasional eyebrow lifted over a choice of corset or platform boot, the subtle makeup tips that always favour toning it down somehow, the suggestion from time to time that she consider running a colour other than black through her hair—*you never know, Ant, it might suit you*—and it grates, as much as she laughs it off, it does grate. 'What's the difference between a stuffed bat and that jacket Loki has on? It's all dead animal.'

Jacqueline nods like she's never before considered this point, and maybe she hasn't. 'I suppose that's one way to look at it.'

Antoinette glances at Loki in the mirror. He catches her eye and grins. 'Better than wearing a *live* bat as a brooch,' he says.

'Hell no, that'd be awesome. You could have it wear a little silver collar and leash, let it fly around and everything. And, hey, it's way cooler than skulking about with an overgrown mouse on your shoulder.'

'Oh yeah.' Loki rolls his eyes dramatically. 'Rats are so twentieth century.'

'I've changed my mind,' Jacqueline says. 'You're *all* weird.'

And if this is a truce, Antoinette will take it. She doesn't know exactly what Jacqueline and Loki got up to today, but the new and tender bond between them is only too obvious. Curious looks and cautious smiles, the two of them circling each other like the courtship of strange, uncertain creatures, and part of her is amused by the dance, part of her disconcerted by the flicker of yearning in her sister's face whenever Loki grins. Yearning enough to cover the cost of the leather that hugs his shoulders like it was made to measure—because no way did some St Kilda salesgirl just hand it over on a wink and a promise, even though Antoinette can't for the life of her understand why her sister would lie about such a thing.

Unless she fears Antoinette would be jealous.

Which she isn't, not even remotely. Not of Loki or Jacqueline or whatever might have seeded itself in the soil of their trepidatious hearts, not of *that* at all. But still it sits, raw and chafing behind her ribs, that same familiar anxiety. Paul and Greta; Jacqueline and Loki—and Antoinette shunted straight to a place soundless and cold, the realm of the third wheel.

Stupid. Stupid and insecure. What does she think this is, high school all over again?

Grimly, Antoinette steers the car along the winding mountain road, only half listening as her sister recounts tales of their mother driving like a demon back in the day, rounding blind corners like she owned the road and riding the horn as hard as the accelerator. 'This, from a woman afraid to set foot in an airport,' Jacqueline says with a shudder. 'I used to let Ant have the front seat. Couldn't bear to see what we might be about to slam into.'

The last of the twilight is fading from the sky by the time they arrive. Antoinette pulls into the car port beside her mother's old green Commodore and switches off the ignition. 'Last words, anyone?'

'Very funny,' Jacqueline says, unbuckling her seat belt.

Gravel crunches beneath their shoes as they walk up to the front door. Loki grabs Antoinette's hand. 'Paul Morgenstern, at your service.'

She smiles. 'Thanks, Loki. Really, I mean it.'

Jacqueline steps forward, small fist raised, but before she has a chance to place knuckle to wood, the door swings open, spilling a wan yellow light onto the porch.

'You're late,' says the woman standing in the entrance way. The emaciated, spindle-shanked woman whose creased and hollowed face, whose grey and short-cropped hair, bears such meagre resemblance to the mother Antoinette knows, that she finds herself rendered mute, stunned into gaping silence.

'Close your mouth, dear,' Sally Paige says. 'Something will fall in.'

13

'I expected you an hour ago,' their mother says, clasping first Antoinette and then Jacqueline in her awkward, stiff-armed embrace. For Loki, for *Paul*, there's merely a glare and the curtest of nods. 'This long in the oven, my lamb will be all dried out.'

Far from it; the roast is pink-centred and pretty much perfect, but their mother still eats very little of the thin sliver she carves for herself. Merely sits at the table with shoulders slightly hunched, cutting the meat into smaller and smaller squares and pushing them around on her plate until they're barely distinguishable from the mash of potato and carrot and thick, brown gravy. She murmurs a begrudging acknowledgement when Loki compliments her cooking, points her fork at the serving platter and instructs him to help himself when he asks for seconds.

Antoinette doesn't like the way her mother keeps looking at him. Covert, suspicious glances, as if there's something about him that bothers her, something she can't quite put her finger on, but give her a minute…

Jacqueline nudges her beneath the table, a light tap of shoe against shin. 'Don't you think so, Ant?'

'I'm sorry?'

'Our mother's new haircut. I was saying how much it suits her.'

'Oh. Oh, yeah, definitely.'

Antoinette forces a smile, studies again the short curls-slash-cowlicks that adorn their mother's skull. So different from the frizzy, flyaway locks which were a Sally Paige trademark going on just about forever, prematurely grey and falling near to her waist, steel-wool medusa spirals she refused to colour even though they made her look twice her age in a *good* light. Shorn away now, hacked away—Antoinette would lay even money that her mother's own hands did the deed—leaving this abrupt new style which makes her look so much worse. Thinner and older and alarmingly less substantial without her wild, windblown mane.

But it's not just the new haircut, emphasising as it does those eyes sunk deep in shadows, those cheekbones knifing through wrinkle-sagged skin, and Antoinette makes a surreptitious count on her fingers. Christmas, the last time they were up here on the mountain—sitting around this table with homemade fruitcake and egg custard thick enough to stand a spoon in—which means not quite two months. Scant time, it seems, for age to steal in and so ruthlessly stamp its mark.

'It's easier,' their mother says, raking bony fingers across her scalp. 'Too many mornings spent battling the knots and snarls, you get sick of it. I don't do more than shower and run a comb through these days.' Wrists balanced on the edge of table, she offers a cool, deadpan stare to both her daughters. 'Of course, I *have* worn it like this since the new year.'

'We'd come up here more often if we could,' Jacqueline says.

Antoinette swallows a mouthful of orange juice, wishing she had thought to bring a bottle of wine. Or vodka. 'Yeah, we've both been slammed with work.'

'Is this a *new* job, Antoinette?' her mother asks.

'No, still the same place. Simpatico.'

'Oh.' The waning smile, the lowered gaze; Sally Paige does crestfallen particularly well. 'I thought … I mean, I'm sure Jacqueline is very busy jet-setting about the place with *her* career, but I didn't think waitressing was that demanding an occupation.'

'I've been pulling a lot of extra shifts lately,' Antoinette lies. 'Trying to put some money aside, you know?'

'It must be a strain, with the two of you to support.'

'Oh, Mum, can we please not—'

'Didn't you tell her?' Loki interrupts, turning his thousand-watt grin towards the woman now scowling at him from the head of the table. 'I have a job too, Mrs Paige. So it's all cool. We're not exactly rolling in moolah, but—'

'Really?' Sally Paige raises an eyebrow. 'What about your book?'

'All done,' Loki says. 'Sitting with my agent as we speak.'

'I see. And now you have a job as well.'

'Yep. Nothing flash, just writing copy for an environmental agency. Ground level stuff, but room to move up if I play my cards right.' His smile doesn't waver, not for a second. 'I know you've been worried about me and Antoinette, Mrs Paige—and I don't blame you being a bit dirty on the guy who stole away your youngest daughter—but it's all good. I swear.'

Antoinette struggles to keep a straight face. He has Paul down pat and pitch perfect, each idiosyncratic nuance and subtle rhythm of speech, even the way he sits, that same stoop-shouldered slouch that always made her want to rope her ex to a cross-post—*straighten up, scarecrow boy*—his whole performance so uncanny, it gives her chills.

'Well, isn't that lovely,' her mother says. 'Antoinette, you should take some time off, now that Paul's working. Come up here and have a holiday with me.'

'Mum, I told you, I'm—we're—trying to save some money.'

'You have the rest of your life to do that. Why don't you—'

'Mother,' Jacqueline breaks in, her foot making a gentle but pointed return to Antoinette's leg. 'Ant didn't want to say anything in case it falls through, but she's going to apply for university next semester.'

Their mother sits back in her chair. 'University?'

'Um, yeah.' Antoinette scrambles for an answer. 'That's why I'm saving all I can now, because I'll probably have to stop working if I get in. Stop, or else cut my hours right down. You know, so my studies won't suffer.'

'I see,' their mother says. 'What course are you going to do?'

'Psychology.'

'Psychology?'

'Yeah, if I get accepted.' Antoinette hasn't a clue where *that* came from, and even Jacqueline looks mildly surprised. *Psychology* simply the first idea to strap on its skates and glide across her otherwise barren mind, but at least it puts on a good show. Impressive enough to placate Sally Paige while still managing to sound feasible; a course she might actually be able to get into—and complete—a course with a career waiting at the end. Tick, tick, tick.

'You want to be a psychologist?'

'Maybe. There, um, there are lots of options, really.'

Her mother contemplates this for a moment before conceding a slight and careworn smile. 'That's good, dear. I'm glad to see you finally putting some thought into the future. It'll happen without you, otherwise, and before you know it…'

Abruptly, she clears her throat, then lays her cutlery across her plate and pushes it aside, holds a crumpled napkin to her mouth like she might be about to bring up what meagre amount of food she actually put into her stomach.

'Mum?' Antoinette reaches for her mother's free hand, stricken and trembling on the tablecloth, but physical affection has never been a strong suit in their family and she pauses, never really sure when—if ever—her touch might be welcome. And in that moment of hesitation, Jacqueline is up and by their mother's side with a glass of juice, pulp sloshing thick and orange up the sides, and Loki too has scraped back his chair—'Mrs Paige? Can

I get you some water maybe?'—but Sally Paige just coughs and waves them both away.

'I'll live,' she croaks. 'I'll live for now.' Turning to Loki with eyes reddened and watery, but still sharp, scrutinising his face as she wipes at the corners of her mouth with the napkin, dab dab dab, before scrunching it into her fist. Antoinette feels her own stomach churn. *She can see. She knows.*

'Paul,' her mother says. 'I need to talk to my girls for a bit. Alone.'

Loki looks to Antoinette, his face an open question.

'Mum, he's part of the family. Whatever it is—'

'No,' her mother says. 'He is *not* part of the family, he's … I'm sorry, Paul, I don't like to be rude but it *was* meant to be just the three of us tonight.'

Antoinette starts to protest, but Loki holds up his hand, cuts her off with a brittle shake of his head. 'No worries, Mrs Paige.' His smile is stiff, marched all the way past polite and back to barely civil. 'How about I clean up? Let you all get on with talking about whatever it is you need to talk about.'

He picks up the congealing remains of the roast and carries them from the room.

'Way to make him feel welcome, Mum.' Antoinette gets to her feet and begins stacking their plates. 'As per usual.'

Her mother coughs again. 'I didn't ask for you to bring him.'

'He's my *boyfriend*.' A dissonant, discordant word because this is *Loki* now, Loki and not Paul, but the track is too familiar, its grooves worn too deep to skip at speed. 'What part of that is so hard for you to understand?'

'The part where you let him walk all over you.'

'I don't—'

'Ant,' Jacqueline says. 'Why don't you go and make us some tea? We'll be in the living room.' *Take a few minutes*, her unspoken subtext. *Take a few minutes and calm yourself down.*

Antoinette grabs an armful of dishes and storms into the kitchen where Loki already has the kettle on, cups and spoons lined up and waiting. He's even found her mother's tea tray, the one with the border of yellow roses. 'I'm sorry,' she tells him. 'She was truly awful.'

He shrugs. 'She's been worse.'

The water boils and Antoinette takes her time making the tea, showing Loki where the dishwashing liquid lives and what Tupperware to use for leftovers, until he takes her by the shoulders and plants an unexpected kiss on her forehead. 'Get back out there, you.'

She hugs him. A fierce, impulsive embrace that she wants never to break, never or at least not until she feels something more for this inexplicable creature beyond the effortless affection she could almost class as maternal. Because he deserves more, this kind and gentle boy who loves her and has never hurt her, who *could never* hurt her, because he is *not Paul*.

But there's nothing, just a cauterised line of scar tissue in the hollow where her heart used to beat. 'I'm sorry,' she says again, stepping away.

Loki turns to the sink, turns his back, turns the taps on full.

Antoinette picks up the tray and carries it through to the living room where her sister and her mother wait in opposing chairs, their faces blank and smooth as queens on a chessboard. 'Here we are now,' she quips, distributing the cups and settling herself on the middle cushion of the sofa. 'Entertain us.'

Jacqueline looks puzzled, and Antoinette isn't surprised the reference is beyond her; it's hard to imagine a person less interested in music, more oblivious to pop culture of all kinds, than her sister. But the expression on their mother's face stops her smile in its tracks. Eyes dull, lips drawn tight and bloodless, Sally Paige is a woman resigned. She places her tea on the little round table beside her chair, then considers each of her daughters in turn.

'I have cancer,' she tells them. 'It's terminal.'

Cancer. Jacqueline holds the word inside her head. Turns it over. Examines its hard, impenetrable surface. It is a stone, that word. Hard and cold. A heaviness in her skull. It sits there, beyond denial, despite her sister's best efforts to the contrary.

Yes, their mother is certain. No, there is nothing to be done; the thing has worked its way too far into her body. Into her organs. Into her glands. Into every cell it has convinced to turn traitor. No, chemo is out of the question. Surgery, too. It is too aggressive, has been caught too late. It's all over bar the shouting. Bar what comes next. What comes last.

'There is *nothing* to be done,' she repeats as Ant opens her mouth with yet another protest, another *but*, another *what if*, another *have you tried*. Their mother knew something was wrong before Christmas. Well before, she insists. Knew also that it was too late even then. 'You live in a body as long as me, you can feel when the warranty's about to run out.'

'You're not even sixty,' Ant says. She wipes at her eyes. Smears a thin streak of black liner across her cheek.

Their mother sighs. 'Feels I've lived a lot longer than that, believe you me.'

'What do you need us to do?' Jacqueline asks.

'Don't you start. How many times do I have to say it?'

'I'm talking about palliative care. Have you organised anything?'

'I have Dr Chiang for that side of things. He's prescribing me drugs for the pain, says he can give me something stronger when it's needed. You remember Dr Chiang?'

Jacqueline remembers him. A nice man, a good doctor. She remembers his kind, soft-lined face. His hands which were always warm, always gentle. His sad, sympathetic smile as he talked her through the results. So many tests, so many procedures. All of them leading down a singular dead-end path. *I'm sorry, Miss Paige, but it's extremely unlikely you will ever be able to have children*. She remembers, too, the lecture from her mother as they drove home. Her admonition that Jacqueline not consider her circumstance to be a Get Out of Jail Free card. That there are worse things to be caught from sex than pregnancy. That—when the time comes, of course—she should be careful nevertheless. Protect herself. Always protect herself.

What would her mother think now, if she knew of all the times her eldest daughter had ignored that advice? Those hurried, hopeful encounters in her teens. The desperate calculation of her early twenties. Until she could no longer convince herself that Dr Chiang may have been wrong. Until, finally, she forced herself to give it up. To pack it away. The desire, the longing, the *need* which she felt for near her entire life. Curled within her heart. Within her broken, bloodless womb. Only rarely, now, does she hear them. The ghosts of those children she can never conceive.

Jacqueline clears her throat. Pushes such thoughts aside. 'Have you thought about where to go?' she asks her mother.

'I have everything right here, I don't need to go anywhere.'

'Mum,' Ant's voice is wavering. 'You can't just … you need people to take care of you. People whose job that is, you know?'

'What, you think I want to die in some hospital? In one of those horrible homes, stinking of disinfectant and stale piss?' Their mother snorts. 'I think not, missy. I intend to die right here, right in my own bed.'

'All right,' Jacqueline assures her. 'No one is saying—'

'You can't make me go to one of those places. Neither of you can make me. I still have all my faculties; you don't have the right to shuffle me off to some *nursing* home just because it's more convenient. It's my right to refuse whatever care I please.' Her mother coughs, loud and phlegm-filled, then sits back in her chair. Crosses her arms over her chest. 'It's my *legal* right, I checked with my solicitor.'

Ant looks as though someone has slapped her. Pale, eyes wide and brimming with tears. Jacqueline moves to sit beside her. Takes her sister's hand. 'We're not saying that.'

Their mother glares at them. Her lower lip quivers.

'What we're saying…' Jacqueline pauses. 'What we're saying is that you do need to think about it. That *we all* need to think about it. If you want to stay here, that's fine and we're not going to make you leave—'

'Damn right, you're not.'

'—but you *are* going to need help. Professional help. This is going to get worse, a lot worse. You have to know that.'

'Jacqueline…' her sister says. 'I don't think…'

'You have to know it as well, Ant.'

In the silence that follows, their mother coughs again. Grimaces and clutches her side. 'I'm tired,' she tells them. 'I need to sleep.'

Jacqueline rises from the couch. Steps swiftly across the room to offer an arm to her mother. The older woman's fingers seem little more than skin and bones as she digs in. Hauls herself to her feet. 'I've made up your beds,' she says. Nods towards the kitchen. 'Don't know where *he's* expecting to lay himself down.'

'Loki can have my room,' Ant says. 'I'll share with Jacqueline.'

'*Loki?*' That keen, bright stare is vintage Sally Paige.

'It's a nickname.' Jacqueline rolls her eyes. 'Don't even ask.'

Ant swallows, hard. 'Yeah, you don't want to know.'

Their mother laughs. It's not a happy sound. 'You'll both be here in the morning, then? Not planning to sneak off early on me?'

'Mum!' Ant sounds hurt.

'Of course not,' Jacqueline says. 'We'll be here for breakfast.'

'Good, because I'm making pancakes. I bought maple syrup. The real stuff, not that maple-*flavoured* rubbish.'

'Mum, you're sick,' Ant says. 'Really, you don't have to get up and make us breakfast when you're sick.'

Again, that laugh. Brittle as burnt sugar. 'I'm not *sick*, dear. What I have, it isn't anything you recover from.' Their mother reaches out a skeletal hand. Touches her youngest daughter on the cheek. 'I'm going to *die*, Antoinette; I'm going to die *soon*. Don't kid yourself into thinking anything else.'

Finally, Ant stops sobbing. Jacqueline smooths her sister's curls away from her flush-damp face. Shifts herself away from the sag in the centre of the mattress. The old single bed really is too small for the both of them.

Ant sniffs. Rubs at her eyes. 'The worst thing is that I don't even know how I really feel. I mean, that's not the *worst* worst thing, obviously, but I just ... it's like there's this voice in my head saying, *your mother is dying, you should be feeling awful*—and I *do* feel awful, but I don't know if I feel awful *because* of Mum, or because I'm not feeling awful *enough* about Mum.'

Jacqueline smiles. 'You think too much about these things.'

'It's not funny.'

'I'm not laughing at you, honestly.'

'I don't understand why she didn't see anyone sooner. All this time, she said she knew something was wrong. Why didn't she just see someone?'

'You know how she is about hospitals. I think Dr Chiang's the only doctor she's ever remotely trusted. Even then, she had to be at death's door to call him.' Jacqueline bites her lip. 'Sorry. Poor choice of words.'

Ant wipes at her eyes. 'What are we going to do?'

'It depends on what she wants,' Jacqueline says. 'We can't force her to do anything against her will.'

'But she can't just stay up here on her own. God, that's bloody medieval.'

'We can make some calls on Monday. I'm sure there are services that provide palliative care at home. Perhaps a live-in nurse, if she'll agree to that.'

'Sounds expensive. I don't … I mean, do you have any money, Jacqueline? Mum can't have much put aside, not with just the bit of bookkeeping she's been doing. How do we pay for something like that?'

Jacqueline shakes her head. 'We'll find a way. There's this house for a start.'

'She'll never sell it. You heard her, she wants to die here.'

'Perhaps we can convince her to take out a mortgage against it.' She rubs her temples. 'Look, Ant, I don't have the answers right now. But there will *be* some, I promise. Tomorrow, when we get back, we'll go online. See what options are out there for people in our mother's ... situation.'

'Okay.' Her sister frowns. 'This is why she wanted me to come and stay with her, wasn't it? Remember, over dinner?'

'Possibly. Yes, I would say so.' There's a weird, nameless tightness in her chest. Not jealousy. Not even its weaker sister, envy. But certainly a distant cousin. 'You notice that she didn't ask me.'

'Oh, Jacqueline, it's because of your job. She knows it's hard for you to get time off from the gallery, whereas I'm *only a waitress*.' Ant grimaces. 'Why on earth did you tell her I was applying for uni?'

'I thought she would ease up on you for a while.'

'And when the truth came out?'

'Well.' Jacqueline presses her lips together. 'That's not something you'll have to worry about anymore.'

'That's awful!' Her sister looks stunned. Genuinely shocked.

'That's honest,' she tells her. 'Besides, it doesn't have to be a lie. You're bright, Ant, and you did fine in school. There's no reason why you couldn't apply to do, what was it again? Psychology?'

'And what about Loki? How am I supposed to study full-time *and* earn enough to take care of the both of us? It's not like he can actually go out and get a job. He doesn't have a shred of paper to prove he even *exists*.'

Jacqueline recalls the blonde girl from the clothing shop. Her fervent smile as she helped Loki into what would soon become his leather jacket. 'I don't think you need to worry about Loki. I suspect he's more than capable of taking care of himself.'

'What's that supposed to mean?'

'I know you think it, Ant, but I didn't buy him that new jacket. Honestly.'

'Where did he get the money then?'

'He didn't.'

'Are you saying he *stole* it?'

'No, he . . .' There aren't any words for how the salesgirl looked as she handed Loki the bag. Eagerness comes close, gratitude even closer. But neither feel right. 'It's almost as though he ... *charmed* her, the girl in the shop. I know it doesn't make sense, but it seems as though she wanted him to have the jacket. As though she was glad to give it to him. Needed for him to have it, almost.' Jacqeuline shrugs. None of those words are right either. 'Sorry, I'm not explaining it very well.'

'So, what, he just asked for the thing and she gave it to him?'

'I think so. I didn't hear what was said, but that's what it looked like.'

'He can *do* that?' Ant's voice has dropped to a whisper. 'He can just ask for things and people give them to him?'

'Don't look at me,' Jacqueline says. 'You're the one who made him.'

'You say that like I knew what I was doing.' Ant sighs. A forlorn, drawn-out breath that hurts to hear. 'I never know what the hell I'm doing these days. I'm just so bloody tired all the time, I don't even have the energy to *think*. It feels like I've been living on autopilot, you know, just going through the motions and waiting for … god, I don't even know what it is I'm supposed to be waiting for.' Tears well fresh in her eyes. 'And now there's Loki, and this … *thing* with Mum, and it's all such a huge mess, I don't know what to do with any of it.'

'It's all right.' Jacqueline holds her sister's hands between her own. 'We'll figure everything out, I promise. We—' On the bedside table, her phone chimes to life. Automatically, she reaches across and scoops it up. *Ryan Jellicoe calling*. 'Sorry, Ant, I really need to answer this.' Her sister rolls her eyes. Jacqueline pushes herself up from the bed. Mouths another apology as she taps the screen. Heads towards the bedroom door and the lightless hall beyond.

'Ryan? Thanks for calling me back.' She closes the door behind her.

'Jacqueline, girl, I've missed you.'

'Always the charmer,' she says, and grimaces. That last word makes her think of Loki. It tastes foreign in her mouth. The door to Ant's old bedroom is shut, the gap beneath it dark.

'Always,' Ryan echoes. She can picture the grin on his face too well.

'I wanted to thank you for sending those photos through to Dante.'

'Yeah, he left me a message. Gotta say, your boss doesn't sound like the happiest little Vegemite right about now.'

Jacqueline wanders back down the hall to the main part of the house. Everything is quiet and still. She has forgotten what it's like up here on the mountain after dark. No sound of passing traffic. No ambient noise beyond the occasional shriek of a nightbird or the scrabble of possum claws on the roof. 'Dante is never happy,' she tells Ryan. 'But the photos help. He's reassured that there'll be a show at least.'

'Even if he doesn't much care for what he's gonna be sticking on his walls.'

She takes a breath. 'He said that?'

'Didn't have to. Could hear it in his voice.' Ryan chuckles. 'Tosser, going on about *new directions* and *re-visioning* and god knows what else. Bloody message went on for about five minutes. Already told him I was only gonna be talking to you from now on.'

'When did you—'

'In the email, when I sent the shots. Except I used his lingo, yeah? *I prefer to liaise solely with Jacqueline from this point.* So it's sorted, right? Bastard can't sack you if the talent insists on keeping you around. I can do prima donna with the best of them, girl, don't you worry about that.'

Jacqueline swallows a groan. 'Ryan, I really wish you hadn't. I appreciate the vote of confidence but that's not how it works.'

'Hey, c'mon, lighten up. You should see what I've been doing up here the last couple of days. That big canvas is almost done, I reckon.'

'That's great.' She forces herself to smile. Hopes he can hear it in her voice. 'That's really good to hear. But honestly, I think…'

There's a dull thumping noise in the background, followed by muffled shouts. Muffled laughter.

'Hey, you there?' Ryan asks. 'Look, I got some people rocking up here, we're heading into the Valley.'

'Sounds like fun,' she tells him. 'But tomorrow, can you do something for me?'

'Ask and you shall receive.'

'Call Dante. Tell him you're looking forward to the show. And that you're happy to work with *anyone* from Seventh Circle.'

'I'm not crawling on my knees to that prick.'

'He's not a prick. He's funding your damn show and you're acting like some spoiled five-year-old who's been told he can't have ice cream for dinner.'

Silence, pierced only by a faint shriek of laughter that sounds suspiciously like Zane. Jacqueline cringes. How quickly the girl has managed to make amends. Then Ryan's familiar chuckle fills the line. Fills her head. 'You're good for my ego,' he says. 'Good for kicking it up the arse as needs be.'

'Ryan—'

'No, look, I'm not gonna call him. But if he rings again, I'll answer.'

'Don't mention me. Honestly, it won't help anyone.'

'Sure, whatever you say. But our deal stands, yeah?'

'Our deal?'

'Dinner, just you and me. After all this shit has blown over.' That chuckle again, throaty and rough with self-confidence. 'No ice cream till I've eaten all my vegies, that's a promise, girl.'

Her smile this time is genuine. 'I'll hold you to that.'

More muffled shouts. Another shriek. And Ryan, his voice low and apologetic, threading like silk through her ear. 'Gotta go, the natives are restless. But we'll talk soon, yeah?' He ends the call without waiting for goodbyes.

Jacqueline switches off the phone and heads to the kitchen for a glass of water. She should get one for Ant as well. Perhaps make them both a mug of warm milk. Stir in some honey and cinnamon—her sister would like that. But as her fingers search for the lightswitch, a large shadow moves across the kitchen window. Moves towards her, silent and swift, and a startled cry lodges in her throat.

'Shhh,' Loki whispers. His eyes glimmer in the darkness, cold as distant stars.

14

'm sorry I scared you,' Loki says again. He's still staring out of the kitchen window, fixated on the backyard and the looming bushland that surrounds the house. Jacqueline stirs the milk on the stove. With the pantry bereft of cinnamon, she's had to use nutmeg with extra honey instead. Three mugs wait on the counter top.

'We should go for a walk,' Loki says.

'Why on earth would we do that?'

'To see what's out there.'

'This place backs right onto National Park land. There's nothing out there but trees.' Her mother has let the yard go in recent years. Small shrubs and saplings now invade well within the perimeter. The grass is overgrown, clumped and heavy with seed. Jacqueline shivers. 'Snakes and spiders are about all you're likely to run into.'

'Where does the parkland begin?' Loki asks.

'Quite a way back. This house is built on a fairly large lot.'

'It must have been fantastic when you were kids.'

'What do you mean?'

'All that bush to muck about in. Like having your own private kingdom up here on the mountain.'

'Not really,' Sweet-scented steam begins to rise from the saucepan and Jacqueline turns down the heat. 'It wasn't ... we didn't play out there very often. Our mother used to worry about us getting lost or hurt or...' A flash of memory. Shadows and sunlight. Her sister's tearful face. She pushes it aside. 'We didn't much like it out there anyway. I think Ant was afraid.'

Loki turns around, visibly curious. 'Afraid? Of what?'

'Who knows? We were only little girls.' She rolls her eyes. 'Little girls with a chronically paranoid mother.'

'It can't be easy for you, finding out about her health like this.'

'It's especially bad for Ant. She's always been closer to our mother than me, always ... well, she's the youngest after all. Isn't that the natural way of things? The youngest is always the favourite?'

'I wouldn't know.' Loki stares at her. An odd, oblique cast to his face.

Jacqueline meets his gaze. 'What does it feel like?'

'What does *what* feel like?'

'Being ... what you are.'

He folds his arms over his chest. Leans back against the sink. 'Disconnected,' he replies at last. 'I feel like I'm floating on top of things, like I could slip off the edge at any second. Take the wrong step, *be* the wrong step. I'm not really part of this world, I know that. I feel it. There's this … pressure? I don't know, something like pressure, around me all the time.'

Jacqueline swallows. His words scrape along bone. 'You have to be careful,' she says. 'You have to think about everything you do, everything you say, in case it might be wrong. In case it won't fit.'

'In case *I* won't fit. And I need to fit. I need to know that…'

'That you belong,' she finishes. 'That you are accepted.'

'Accept*able*.' Loki tilts his head to the side. Regards her with new and narrowed eyes. 'This world, being part of this world? It's like I've been given an instruction manual, written in Chinese, translated into French. With all the diagrams printed backwards. I can *see* how I'm supposed to act, the person I'm *meant* to be, but…' He spreads his hands before him, palms out. A helpless gesture. Lost and flailing.

Too easily, Jacqueline finds the words to throw to him. 'But you have no idea if you're doing it right. If there will ever come a time when you won't have to wonder if you're doing it right.'

He stares at her for several heartbeats. Then nods, a gesture closer to acknowledgement than affirmation. 'How long has it been?'

On the stove, the milk boils over with a hiss. Jacqueline swears and lifts the saucepan from the element. Turns off the heat. Loki is at her side almost immediately, a damp cloth in hand as he wipes at the spillage, catches the drips from the bottom of the pan. The smell of scorched milk stains the air.

'When did she make you?' he asks.

'She didn't,' Jacqueline says brusquely. Because, really, what was she thinking? No sense in such ridiculous suspicions. Merely paranoia, which she now pushes aside.

'But you just said—'

'Just because I can understand how you feel, doesn't mean I'm *like* you.'

'Doesn't it?'

'I'm her sister, Loki. Her *older* sister.'

She moves across to the waiting mugs and begins to pour. The milk-skin sloughs off into the last. Sits wrinkled and yellowed on the surface. She pinches it between finger and thumb, intending to drop it back into the saucepan, but Loki grabs her wrist. Lowers his mouth and sucks the milk from her fingers. His tongue is warm, almost rough. Cat tongue, cat eyes, holding her gaze with his own as he licks his lips.

'I'm older than her as well,' he says. 'Objectively speaking.'

'Stop it.' She pulls away. Dumps the saucepan into the sink and fills it with water. 'It's impossible.'

'*Impossible* seems to be in flux these days.'

Her hands are trembling as she turns off the tap, dries them with one of her mother's jumble sale tea towels. The green crocheted edge is fraying at one corner. She picks at a loose thread. Watches it unravel. 'I'm her sister, Loki. I have a whole lifetime of memories of being her sister.'

'Yeah.' His smile is bitter. Cold. 'You don't need to tell me about memories.'

'Stop it,' she says again. Her voice is barely a whisper now and it's not just her stomach that seems hollow. Her entire body feels scraped out. She is a shell, a girl-shaped husk. Perhaps she always has been.

'I'm sorry,' Loki says. 'This wasn't the best time to—'

'You're wrong.' Jacqueline straightens her shoulders. 'I'm not like you, I'm not some cheap, pirated copy Ant conjured up to make her feel better. I'm real. I've always been real.'

His jaw clenches and he turns back to the window. Back to the night beyond. She takes a mug in each hand, leaves the third behind for him to do with what he chooses. She's already in the hall when Loki calls her name. 'We don't belong in this world,' he says. 'Tell me I'm wrong about that.'

Jacqueline says nothing. Endeavours to *think* nothing as she makes her way carefully back through the house to her old room. The light is still on but Ant has fallen asleep. Curled on her side with fists tucked up beneath her chin. Jacqueline places one of the mugs on the small student desk at which she had spent so many long, arduous hours. First high school, then university. Countless projects and essays, not to mention revision for exams. Those memories are real. They are hers. Hers *alone*. She takes a sip of warm milk and wrinkles her nose, regretting the nutmeg. Two more mouthfuls before her mug joins its mate on the desktop, and she switches off the bedroom light.

Ant grumbles but doesn't wake as Jacqueline wedges herself between her sister and the wall. Pulls the doona over them both and presses her face to the warm, solid curve of her sister's back. Pushes away thoughts of Loki and his ridiculous ideas. If she was home, if she was alone, she could banish it all. Two, three strokes of a blade would be enough to release her.

If she was home. If she was alone.

Jacqueline closes her eyes. Concentrates instead on keeping still. On matching the slow, comforting rhythms of her sister's breath.

'I love you,' she whispers. The truth of that is a comfort as well.

Antoinette follows Loki and her sister up the stairs to Jacqueline's apartment, balancing the foil-wrapped plate of pancakes on one hand as she reaches into her pocket for her mobile with the other. A text from Greta, the first for the day; she doesn't even bother to open it, makes a mental note to figure out how to block the girl's number. As if there isn't enough for her to worry about now. The look on her mother's face as they left the house still burns cold in her memory, that hard veneer of abandonment, like she expected never to see them again, like that's all she has ever expected. The way she thrust the plate into Antoinette's hands, warm and weighty with leftover pancakes, the bottle of maple syrup close behind.

Waste not, want not. I didn't make them to be thrown away.

Sally Paige, up with the birds as usual, up before either of her daughters managed to drag themselves, stiff-limbed and poorly slept, into the kitchen to find her stirring an industrial-sized bowl of batter beside a warming frypan. Way too much for any of them to finish, even with Loki showing up to shovel half a dozen syrup-soaked slabs into his belly. The breakfast table a tense and lockjawed arena, with Jacqueline and Loki swapping the occasional frostbitten glare—how Antoinette longs for a moment alone with her sister to get the story behind *that* development—and Sally Paige hunkered taciturn over her plate, cutting her single, unladen pancake into bite-sized shapes which would, like her dinner the night before, remain largely uneaten.

Not that Antoinette had much of an appetite herself. Not with her mother sitting right there, skin-and-bone shadow of the woman Antoinette knew, the morning light scalpel sharp and granting no favours to sunken eyes and hollow, wrinkle-hung cheeks. But still as stubborn as she is sick, quick to scuttle any suggestion that there might be possible avenues of treatment yet to be explored.

It's my time, Antoinette. You need to accept that.

Her face set against further argument as, beneath the table, Jacqueline kicked Antoinette's shin. *Leave it*, both clear command and silent appeal, *please leave it for now*, and so Antoinette did.

But she can't just accept it—they need to do *something*. Maybe hunt down Dr Chiang and give him a call, find out all the gory details their mother insists on keeping from them: how bad the situation is, exactly; what options there might be for them to consider—because there *have* to be options. This is the twenty-first century, for godsake, there has to be something modern medicine can offer Sally Paige beyond packing her off to die like some gangrenous, gut-shot beast. Maybe—

Up ahead, Jacqueline cries out. A soft, breathless *oh*, half-moan, half-sigh, and Antoinette looks up in time to see her sister falling, face-down, that too-slight body folding like a puppet whose strings have been abruptly severed.

Antoinette runs. Pancakes and mobile clattering to the ground as she reaches out her arms, too late, way too late, but it doesn't matter—Loki is already there, lithe catlike crouch as he spins on his heels to catch Jacqueline one heart-stopping moment before her head hits the edge of a step.

'What happened?' Antoinette scoots down beside her sister as Loki turns her over, cradles her limp body into his lap. Jacqueline's eyes are closed, her lips quiver soundlessly. 'Did she trip?'

Loki shakes his head. 'She just fell.'

'What do you mean? How did she fall?' Antoinette can hear the pitch of her own voice ascending, an unbearable waspy-whiny buzz, and she forces herself to breathe. 'Loki, what happened?'

He doesn't answer, just slides his arms beneath her sister's body and lifts, rising to his feet in one graceful motion as if she is something empty and weightless, a Jacqueline doll made of plastic and air. 'Get the door,' he says.

Rummaging in her bag for the keys, Antoinette stumbles up the remaining steps to the apartment. She swings the door open then moves aside to let Loki through, wincing at the mess left in his wake—scattered pancakes and shards of broken plate, her Nokia in pieces down on the landing—before following him inside to the living room. Gently, he lays Jacqueline down onto the couch and brushes the tangle of hair away from her face, folds those small, white hands carefully over her belly.

Jacqueline moans, a slurred mouthful of speech that Antoinette isn't able to decipher beyond one word which might have been *blind*, or might have been *blood*, or might have been nothing meaningful at all.

'What happened?' Antoinette asks again. 'Is she hurt?'

'She'll be okay, she'll come out of it soon.'

Loki pats Jacqueline on the cheek, leans forward and whispers her name, whispers it again and again as if the third time really might be the charm, but she doesn't respond, doesn't open her eyes, doesn't move at all. Just lies there on the couch, a strange and waxen sister-shape silent now but for the shallow rasp of her breath. Antoinette's stomach sinks. 'This isn't right. I'm calling an ambulance.'

'Wait.' Loki springs to his feet, snatches her arm before she even has a chance to take more than two steps. 'It's okay, she's going to be okay. I promise.'

'You can't know that, Loki. You can't know...'

But he does, or at least he knows something. His gaze shifts between Jacqueline and herself, guarded yet torn, and she can almost see the gears grinding inside his skull as he weighs allegiances, attempts to level whatever complicated scale he's constructed to keep everything balanced within his head.

'Loki?' Antoinette grabs his chin, turns his face directly to hers. 'This isn't about choosing a side. We're sisters; stuff like this has no sides.'

'She didn't want you to know.'

The ground tilts beneath her feet. 'That doesn't matter. Whatever it is, Loki, you need to tell me.' Her voice wobbles and she clears her throat, imagines herself not Antoinette but *Sally* Paige, iron-willed with tongue to match. 'You need to tell me *right now*.'

When her sister finally wakes up, Antoinette almost bursts into tears. The thin coil of dread that has cinched itself tighter and tighter around her heart loosens, dissolves to relief, as Jacqueline opens her eyes and blinks, glazed and unfocused, at the room about her. 'Ant?' she whispers. 'Did I … how did we…?'

'You fell on the stairs.' Antoinette squeezes her sister's shoulder. 'Why didn't you tell me, you idiot?'

'Tell you what?'

'That you've been having seizures.'

'Don't be silly.' Jacqueline winces as she pushes herself upright. 'I must have fainted, that's all. I didn't eat very much at breakfast and—'

'You can stop there,' Antoinette tells her. 'Loki's already filled me in.'

'Oh.' Jacqueline tugs at her skirt, straightens the hem along the line of her knees. 'I asked him not to do that. I wanted to tell you myself.'

'When? This has been going on for a month or more, he says.'

'Not constantly. The last week has been the worst by far, and I did mean to tell you as soon as I got back from Brisbane, but then Loki was here and...' Her sister pauses, a frown pinching at her features. 'In any case, now you know.'

'And you're going to see a doctor, right? First thing Monday, you're going to make an appointment—'

'I have to go back to work on Monday.'

'So call in sick, for godsake. This is serious, Jacqueline, you can't just brush it off like nothing's wrong. You would have hit your head on a bloody concrete step today if Loki hadn't caught you. You could be in hospital right now with concussion or a skull fracture or ... or worse.' Tears burn angry tracks down her cheeks and she wipes them away with the back of her hand. 'You and Mum. You're both as bad as each other with this shit.'

'We're not your responsibility,' Jacqueline says quietly.

'Responsibility?' Laughter builds in her chest, bubbles into her throat and she lets it loose; it's either that or choke on it. 'You think this is about me feeling responsible? Nothing at all to do with the fact that you're my *sister*? That maybe, just maybe, I love you and don't want to see you *fucking die*?'

'Ant, please. You need to calm down.'

'You need to see a doctor.'

'Can we talk about this later?' Jacqueline stands up, wobbling like some Friday night margarita maiden, downing a drink for every spike-heeled inch stacked beneath her feet. 'I have a headache coming on.'

Antoinette blocks her sister's path. 'When later?'

'When I *feel* like it.'

Words spat with more venom than Antoinette has ever heard from Jacqueline before and in her eyes a flash of anger mixed with something near to loathing—but just a flash, she tells herself, come and gone so quick she can't be sure she saw it right, can't be sure she saw it at all—because now there's only Jacqueline, that serene and depthless gaze as familiar to Antoinette as her own reflection … and yet. There's an edge, new and startling like a hairline crack in polished glass, visible at just the right angle, in just the right light, but now, forever, impossible to overlook.

'Ant,' Jacqueline says. 'When you made him, was it…'

The front door opens and closes, footsteps pad down the hall and Jacqueline shakes her head, raises a finger briefly to her lips as Loki strolls into the living room. 'Thought I heard voices,' he says. 'You're awake.'

'I'm awake,' Jacqueline agrees.

In one hand, he carries a dustpan and the plastic shopping bag he's filled with ruined pancake and rattling ceramic shards; in the other, what used to be Antoinette's mobile, the flip-top now irrevocably severed from the keypad. Loki offers the pieces to her on a flattened palm, swings his head from side to side in slow and rueful parody of regret.

'I'm sorry,' he says, deadpan. 'I don't think it can be saved.'

15

Jacqueline minimises her browser as Loki taps on the study door. Opens it without giving her a chance to answer. 'You want anything? Tea? Wine?'

'No.' She nods at the glass of water by her wrist. 'I'm fine.'

He doesn't move. 'What are you doing in here?'

'Researching palliative care.' A lie, but one of omission. She did begin by looking into home nursing services. Hospices as well, because despite what their mother has said, there might come a time for that and there's no harm in having the information at hand. None of them deem it useful to show costs on their website, of course; she will have to call them on Monday to make such tawdry enquiries. She wonders if she can apply for another credit card.

Loki is still leaning into the room. 'How are you feeling?'

'A little better. Tired, but my headache is mostly gone.'

'You want to do something later? Go out and catch a movie?'

'I don't feel that much better.'

'I could run down the street and rent something.'

She shakes her head. 'I'm going to have an early night, try to catch up on some sleep.'

'Okay,' he says. 'Maybe I'll just watch some TV, then.'

Jacqueline swivels in her chair. 'I don't need a babysitter, Loki. If you want to go out and do something, then go. You have my blessing.'

He hesitates. 'Antoinette wanted me to keep an eye on you.'

Ah, yes. Those anxious, sidelong glances as her sister readied herself for work that evening. The whispered exchange of words with Loki at the front door just before she left. A goodbye smile stretched thin enough to snap.

'Ant doesn't need to worry about me,' she tells him. 'Neither do you.'

He stares at her with those opaque, impenetrable eyes. Jacqueline turns back to the computer. After a moment he leaves the room, the door latching softly behind him. She pulls up the browser again. Thinks for a moment, then types a new string of words into Google. Clicks through a handful of links, all of which prove as useless and irrelevant as her previous searches. Whatever kind of creature Loki might be, the internet knows nothing of him. Or else she simply doesn't know where—know *how*—to look.

Either way, she is wasting her time.

Frustrated, Jacqueline holds up her left hand and studies again the thin, jagged scar that runs across the pad of her thumb. Faded after all this time but still visible at the right angle. Still clearly there. A fall from a bicycle. A broken bottle in long grass. Mercurochrome and butterfly stitches beneath a gauntlet of white gauze. Fourteen years old, that scar. Evidence of a memory which *must* be real—her sister doesn't possess such attention for detail.

Of course, the scar remains a part of *her*. It offers no external, conclusive proof of anything. She wishes she hadn't thrown away the diary kept for those three months at the beginning of high school. A dull record certainly, little more than an itemised account of time passed, but a record nonetheless. Better than the drawer full of pretty, unfilled notebooks she has collected since. Each one bought in the hope it would inspire. Would unlock the creative, whimsical side of herself which so many frustrated art teachers assured her must exist.

Let yourself wander. Draw the first thing that comes to mind; write the first words that pop into your brain.

But her thoughts would remain staunchly unliberated, as blank and empty as the page in front of her.

Jacqueline's hand trembles. She rounds it into a fist. Enough.

Antoinette is just about to tell the smarmy hipster dickhead in the checked fedora *exactly* what he can do with his prawn and coriander risotto when Michelle nudges her aside with a subtle hip-bump and scoops the dish off the table. 'I'm very sorry for the inconvenience, sir,' she says, turning on her best silver service smile. 'Chef can whip you up another with vegetable stock right away.'

Antoinette's already back in the kitchen, waiting on the mains for her moon-eyed couple at Table 7, by the time Michelle catches her up. 'What the hell is wrong with you tonight?'

'Bloody liar never said a word about chicken stock till he tasted it.'

'Since when does that matter?'

'If he changed his mind, he should have just said so instead of trying to make out like he only ordered it because I told him it was made with veggie stock. As if he can even tell—'

'Some vegetarians can taste—'

'Vegetarian? Yeah, right. Last time I checked, *prawns* weren't growing in the fucking dirt.'

'Hey,' Michelle says. 'Don't take your crap out on me.'

Antoinette presses her lips together, draws a deep breath through her nose and holds it for a couple of seconds. 'I'm sorry,' she says at last. 'I just ... you wouldn't believe the week I've had.'

'Honey, you *have* to let him go. He's not worth your sanity.'

It takes her a moment to realise that Michelle is talking about Paul, not Loki—though the shoe would seem to fit either troublesome foot right now—and Antoinette shakes her head, bites down on the words lining up eagerly at the tip of her tongue. How simple it would be to play the cancer card, the *mother*-with-cancer card at that, a sympathy pass almost too perfect to shuffle back into the deck. But spouting advice to the lovelorn is one thing; dealing with illness and death is something else and, for all the months they've waited tables together, she isn't sure Michelle is that kind of a friend.

'It's not Paul,' she tells her. 'Of all the stuff I've been dumped with lately, Paul's the very least of it. Believe me.'

'Well, if you ever need to talk…' The smile on Michelle's face is fleeting, coloured more by obligation than any deep-welled concern, and Antoinette knows she's made the right decision.

'Thanks,' she says. 'But I'll muddle through.'

The service bell chimes and Michelle collects the dishes that slide across the line counter. 'I don't doubt it, honey.'

At least that makes one of us. Dredging up her own version of the silver service smile—dented and tarnished, but the best she's going to manage tonight—Antoinette grabs her Table 7 mains and follows Michelle back out to front of house. Behind the bar, Jackson catches her eye, brows drawn in silent question as he loads a tray with wine glasses. She shakes her head slightly—*nothing to see here*—then concentrates on making it through the rest of her shift.

Hair dripping cold down her spine, Jacqueline opens the bathroom door and calls Loki's name. No answer. Calls louder, with the same result. Satisfied that he is still out doing whatever it is that Loki does, she unwinds her towel and returns it to the rail. Flicks off the harsh fluorescent light but leaves the exhaust fan running to dispel the steam, then walks naked through the unlit apartment to her bedroom.

This is the first time she's been here by herself since returning from Brisbane. The space around her feels swollen with silence. With solitude.

She switches on the beside lamp. The green glow from its shade is a familiar reassurance. All of her sister's things have been hidden away, if only temporarily. Stuffed into the wardrobe, shoved beneath the bed. The floor is empty and clean, the bed made. A keen new blade waits on the pillow. Unwrapped, fresh from its little plastic case.

Jacqueline sits, crossing her legs beneath her. Smooths the doona where it has rumpled. Holding the razor between thumb and forefinger, she closes her eyes. Breathes. Loosens her thoughts.

And, at long last, allows herself to slide.

Antoinette swears beneath her breath as she pushes through Simpatico's rear door, wiping at the tears that edge, angry-hot, from the corners of her eyes. Fuck Ronan and his official warnings. Almost two years she's worked at this place, two years of putting up with shit from prissy clientele and even prissier chefs, of rushing in to cover emergency holes in staff schedules because someone has woken up with a hangover or needs to stay home with a sick brat. Heaven forbid she be allowed to stumble through a couple of bad nights without Ronan feeling it his sacred managerial duty to keep her back for a private reading of the riot act.

'Ream you a new one, did he?' a voice asks close beside her.

Antoinette jumps, swears again, as Jackson steps out of the shadows beside the bins. Cigarette smoke—not entirely tobacco; she can smell that much—drifts with him, curls from his mouth as he apologises, says he didn't mean to scare her.

'Just be glad I didn't have my pepper spray handy.'

'Pepper spray?' Jackson carefully extinguishes the glowing end of his cigarette against the side of one of the bins before tucking the butt into his sleeve. 'Had you pegged as being more a switchblade kind of girl. Either that or a katana.' He mimes a couple of samurai sword passes. Badly.

Antoinette laughs. 'You should be so lucky.'

'A guy can hope,' he says, grinning. 'You doing anything right now?'

'Other than going home to crash for about a bazillion years?'

'Some of the others went down the road for a drink. Thought I'd hang back, see if you wanted to come with.'

Now it's her turn to apologise. Sorry, really, and thanks for the offer but being around a whole bunch of shiny happy people right now? Probably not such a great idea, she tells him, heading towards her tram stop on the off chance she hasn't missed the last service and won't have to flag down a taxi. Jackson keeps pace, keeps smiling, and 'What about just one person?' he asks, holding up an index finger even as she turns with *no* already shaping her lips, *no* and *sorry*, but 'Come on,' he says. 'Just me, just one drink. You look like you're sorely in need.'

And there's more than a thimbleful of truth in that.

'Okay,' Antoinette reaches out to tap the end of his finger with her own. 'Just one drink.'

Jacqueline wraps her arms around her knees. Pulls herself into a tight and trembling ball. Her flesh is stubborn. Solid. It contains her. Constrains her. Refuses even the most transitory of escapes. This has never happened before. Not since that first time, age fifteen with a paring knife snuck from the kitchen. Moonlight through curtains and breath sucked hard through teeth as her virgin thigh split beneath the blade. As blood-drops bloomed like berries, smeared warm beneath her fingers.

As she discovered there were more ways than one for a woman to bleed.

But now, tonight, too many cuts. Seven, perhaps eight, and none of them with more to offer beyond a simple flash of pain. No transcendence, no ecstatic emergence from the shells in which she has cocooned herself. The cascading matryoshka sequence of Jacqueline, Jacqueline, Jacqueline, all those artfully constructed personas that stifle and strangle. Squeeze her into close, constricting forms until she cannot even breathe without second-guessing whether or not she is doing it right.

Tonight, each fresh cut proved merely an anchor line. Dragging her further and further down. Holding her there in the blue and the brine and the cold.

She gets up from the bed. Her thighs burn. Blood spots the doona cover and she frowns, lays a tissue over the mark. She can see to that later. In the living room, she takes the bottle of vodka from the drinks cabinet. Unscrews the lid and sniffs. The alcohol claws at her nostrils. Claws more going down her throat. Jacqueline coughs, unable to fathom why her sister likes this stuff so much. Smirnoff, black label, the only bottle she has ever had to replace. The others—Tanqueray and Bacardi, Glen Fiddich and Baileys, the Midori with which Dante presented her last Christmas—all remain at their carefully balanced levels. Enough splashed down the sink for the sake of seeming regularly sampled at least.

Jacqueline seldom touches alcohol. A mouthful of wine when it's pressed upon her, not much more than that. The vodka sloshes in her stomach like molten fire. Warm tendrils thread through her veins. She has cared for a thoroughly drunken sister on enough occasions to know bodily surrender when she sees it. Perhaps tonight she can lose herself in the bottle, if not the blade.

She crosses the room to the balcony doors. Presses her torso against the glass. Her skin prickles. Outside, below and beyond, the bay spreads to the horizon. A runnel of blood slides down her thigh, tickles the back of her knee. Too deep, that final slice. Too desperate.

Jacqueline raises the bottle to her lips and swallows a second mouthful.

Then a third.

Last call, and Antoinette rolls her eyes as Jackson places yet another glass of the paint stripper that passes for house red on the table in front of her. 'What happened to one drink?' Thick-tongued and muzzy-minded, she speaks slowly, trying to keep her words this side of a slur. Judging by the smirk on Jackson's face, she hasn't come close to succeeding.

'Fuck one drink,' he shouts over the clamour of the pub. 'One drink is for pussies.'

Antoinette laughs, downs half her wine in a couple of gulps so fast the stuff barely skims her tastebuds. They've done very little but talk meaningless shit for the past hour or two and god how she's missed this, the effortless ebb and flow of ephemeral banter. No weighty pauses for thought, no grave descents into the oh-so-serious, no need for eggshell diplomacy. Just the simple freedom to leave her brain in neutral, to abandon conversational threads in favour of irrelevant segues, to snicker at Jackson's filthy jokes and crack worse ones of her own.

Right now, she feels more like herself than she has for months.

Perversely, the thought makes her sad.

Which might be why, when Jackson nods at her empty glass and suggests they could very well kick on back at his place, she grins and sways to her feet, half-stumbling around the leg of her barstool.

'Whoa, careful there.' He grabs her elbow, steadying her with a hand so flushed she can feel the heat of it through her blouse. Antoinette sways towards him, smiles as he shifts his grip, slides his arm through hers in a slow and purposeful motion that leaves no doubt as to whether or not the brush of finger against breast might have been accidental. 'Come, fair princess. Your pumpkin awaits.'

'You okay to drive?'

'Abso-ma-lutely,' he says, baring straight white teeth as he ushers her through the dregs of the two o'clock swill, and she's pretty sure he's lying, pretty sure she doesn't really care. So obvious now that Jackson is in fact a wolf. Muzzle-deep in the endgame, sleek nice-boy pelt shed in favour of claw and slavering fang, but that's okay, that's just peaches and cream as far as she's concerned. Because waiting back home are Loki and Jacqueline, prickle-backed twins emanating their own peculiar versions of the silent treatment while the apartment walls pull in around them, closer than shrink-wrap, with Antoinette squeezed breathless in between.

Right now, the forest is more welcoming than the path.

Jacqueline is cold. She knows she should go inside. Should put something on before she catches her death. But the balcony is quiet. The bottle of vodka significantly diminished. She doesn't even know if she can stand up without her head falling from her shoulders. She runs a finger over her bottom teeth. Feels their hard, sharp edges. Bites down. The pain is a distant thing. Fragile. Futile.

Everything is futile.

Behind her, the living room is splashed with light. She turns in her chair. Careful, slow. The ground seems a long way down.

'Jacqueline?' Loki stands in the middle of the room. He is holding something long and red. It falls from his hands like the bloody, shorn scalp of a girl entowered. 'Are you all right?'

Jacqueline laughs. Tells him that she's fine. Or thinks she tells him. Her tongue is dead weight. She braces herself on the arms of the chair. It wobbles as she tries to push herself to her feet. Or she wobbles. Hard to tell. Either way, she ends up back on her backside, laughing. *Sorry*, she thinks she says to Loki. *I appear to be indisposed.*

'Stay there,' he says.

He drapes the red thing over the couch and leaves. Jacqueline looks out at the bay. A breeze has picked up, chill and needling. She really should go inside. In a minute, in a minute. She closes her eyes.

'Here. Jacqueline, try to stand up.'

Loki has brought her kimono with him. He helps her to her feet. Helps her slip her arms through the sleeves. The pale cream silk is almost as cold as the breeze. She shivers. Leans against him as he shuffles them both through the balcony door and into the living room. The red thing is a dress, she sees. The satin shiny as varnished nails. Black sequins glitter at the bodice. *Pretty.* She reaches out a hand but they've already left it behind. The hall is dark. A surge of nausea grips her and she falters. Sags in Loki's arms. *Wait.* One hand over her mouth. *I feel…*

'Hold on,' he says, picking her up. Not a good idea. The burn of vomit already in her mouth by the time they reach the bathroom. On her knees, crouched over the toilet. Water—and worse—spattering back onto her face as she heaves. Her stomach spasms, violently, again and again. There is nothing left of her inside. She rolls away, head still spinning. The tiles are icy against her bare legs.

'Here.' Loki holds a glass of water to her lips. 'Rinse your mouth.'

'Have you checked for fillings?' she asks weakly.

He smiles. Makes her take the water. Waits for her to spit before he flushes the toilet and helps her to her feet. Waits, too, while she brushes her teeth and splashes her face clean. She keeps her eyes averted from the mirror. The fluorescent lights are too bright. Too clinical.

In the bedroom, the lamp is still dimmed to a dusky green glow. Jacqueline allows Loki to lead her over to the bed and sit her down. But she refuses to let go of him and so he sits beside her. Leans across, places the water on the bedside table. She didn't realise he'd brought it with him.

'You should sleep,' he says. 'You'll feel better once you've slept.'

'Liar.' Jacqueline rests her head on his shoulder. Men are so *hard*. Muscle stretched solid over bone. She places a hand on his thigh and squeezes. He tenses beneath her touch. His flesh is warm. Immutable. She stares at him with eyes that refuse to focus. His smooth white skin, the dark fall of his hair. If she had a type, Loki would not be it. But, oh, the smell of him.

'Jacqueline,' he says. 'You should lie down.'

Smiling, she takes hold of his shoulder. Swings herself into his lap. Not so much graceful as gravity assisted. Loki grasps her waist—it's either that or let her tumble to floor. Jacqueline laughs, wriggles in close. He's hard *everywhere*. She kisses him, her tongue sliding between his lips, tasting him. The kimono slides from her shoulders and she takes his hands, guides them up to her breasts. Circles her groin against his. Loki moans, a torn and broken sound trapped deep in his throat.

Then he pushes her away.

'I'm sorry,' he whispers. Picks her up, lifts her right off his lap and places her gently onto the bed as though she is made of nothing but air. 'This can't be.' He tucks her hair behind her ears, rearranges her kimono over her chest.

Jacqueline slaps his hands away. 'I'm not a doll.'

'I'm sorry,' he says again. His eyes are wet. 'I can't hurt her.'

'Hurt who?'

He stares at her. A gaze filled with longing, with desire beaten down and muzzled. She reaches for his face and he flinches. 'Don't,' he whispers. 'Please, she…' His arms are wrapped around his stomach. His fingernails dig into his ribs as though he's the one being hurt, or should be.

Realisation creeps in. 'You mean Ant, don't you?'

Loki nods. He doesn't meet her eye.

'But she doesn't…' Jacqueline chews on her lip. Tries to think of the least horrible words for what she needs to say. It would help if her mind would keep still. If it didn't insist on wandering off under its own drunken steam. 'My sister doesn't feel that way about you, Loki. She loves you, I'm sure, but it's not … it's not *that* kind of love.'

'You think I don't know that?'

'But then why…' She reaches out again. More cautious this time, her hand coming to rest on his shoulder. A fresh spark of heat quickens within her. 'I honestly don't think she would mind.'

'I belong to her,' he says. 'This would be a betrayal.'

'Even if she doesn't want you?'

'Even then.'

Jacqueline snorts. 'Martyrdom doesn't suit you, Loki.'

He lifts his head. Glares at her with eyes that bite colder than hoarfrost. 'You say that like it's something I've chosen.' She doesn't understand. Not until he sighs and shifts around to face her, takes both her hands in his and kisses her fingers with a gentleness she finds unnerving. 'I *can't* hurt her like that, Jacqueline. It's not a matter of choice, or doing the right thing. It's more like, I don't know…'

'A compulsion?' she offers.

'Close. There's resistance. It feels … unpleasant.'

'So it hurts? You hurt my sister, and you feel pain. Is that how it works?'

Loki grimaces. 'Pain is too simple. It feels like I'm about to be torn apart, pulled to pieces. Like there's this line and I can come right up to it, put my toes right on the edge but if I was to take one step more, even the smallest nudge forward, then...' He shudders. The dread in is his voice is unmistakeable. 'I don't ever want to know what's on the other side of that line.'

Jacqueline feels sick again. She closes her eyes. Swallows the bile that rises in her throat. She remembers the hard, white light that threatened to claim her in Brisbane, the promise of annihilation at its core. 'I'm sorry,' she says. The words are inadequate. Worn out. Still, she says them.

He squeezes her hands one last time then lets them drop. 'You really should try to get some sleep.'

She lies down, rolls onto her side. Catches Loki frowning at her exposed thigh. At the cuts and the dried blood. She waits for him to comment, but he says nothing. Simply stands and draws the doona up to her waist, then switches off the bedside lamp. Darkness, it appears, is not her friend. A wave of vertigo washes over her; her stomach cramps.

'Loki?'

'Still here.'

'Can you stay with me?'

'Antoinette isn't home yet. I should wait up.'

'Just until I fall asleep? Please?'

She feels the mattress sink beneath his weight. Shuffles over to give him room. He is a barricade, solid and warm. She curls herself against his back, presses her cheek to the ridge of his spine. 'You really think I'm like you?' she whispers. 'You really think Ant made me?'

'What do you think?' he asks. 'What do you feel?'

Jacqueline swallows. Dizziness is giving way to a headache, a dull pulse of pain taking roost behind her right eye. She buries her face into Loki's back, inhaling the strange, not-quite-sweet scent of him. She thinks about lights and lines, passing through and crossing over. About Loki, about the connection that sparks between them, brighter than desire. Simpler as well.

It's impossible.

Impossible seems to be in flux these days.

'I'm scared,' she says. 'I'm scared of what comes next.'

16

I diot, Antoinette tells herself as she sneaks into the apartment. It's not like her mother will be waiting in the kitchen with arms crossed or that Jacqueline gives a damn in whose bed she decided to spend the night. Nevertheless, there's an element of relief in finding the place silent and empty, the door to her sister's room still closed. She puts on the kettle and searches the cupboards for camomile tea, thinking she might flake out on the couch for a while, try to catch up on some of the sleep she didn't get staring at the ceiling of Jackson's bedroom for half the night. Antoinette still isn't sure what happened with that.

The sex wasn't awful, exactly, just *weird*. Mechanical and disconnected, at least from where she was lying. Jackson more than enthusiastic, his mouth wet and eager, his hands skilfully persistent, and it wasn't like she didn't *want* to, not like the thought hadn't slunk across her mind once or twice before last night—those full lips and honey-smooth skin, those eyes stolen straight from a Manga comic—but all the same it felt … not wrong, not bad, just *weird*.

You okay? You want to stop?

Jackson uncertain, anxious even, as he picked up on her vibe, maybe wondering just how wasted she actually was, running desperate calculations of responsibility and regret, and so she kissed him, moaned and arched her back and pulled him deeper into her, wanting him to finish and be done before she lost control of herself.

Before she started to laugh.

Afterwards, he kissed her neck, one finger circling her nipple until she told him that it tickled.

You sure you're okay? You were pretty quiet.

I'm fine.

Short, clipped words too much like her mother would have spoken them, too much like Jacqueline even, and she forced a smile, told him that really, it was good, it was fun. Stopped herself just short of *we should do this again sometime*, giggles catching like burrs in her throat, as he stroked her hair like it was the mane of some horse he'd just dismounted—*good girl, have a sugar cube*—before he kissed her on the forehead and got up to take a piss.

She should have gotten up herself. Dressed and called a taxi, written the night off as a Bad Idea. No, not bad, that was hardly fair; just weird. But so much easier to stay where she was, to keep that smile on her face as Jackson padded in and slipped beneath the blankets. Her wolf now fat-bellied and fed, shrunk down and squeezed back into his boy-skin. And so she stayed, and must have dozed off at some point because one minute the room was dark and the next the sun was streaming through the gap in the curtains, and as she swung her legs out of the bed, Jackson mumbled something in his sleep and she stopped and stared at him, ran her eyes over the muscled curves of his shoulder, remembered the rhythms of him moving inside her.

And felt nothing. Nothing at all.

Antoinette carries her tea into the living room. There's a dress draped over the couch, slinky red satin with corset-style ties at the back and a sequined pattern of black roses swirling over the bodice. Gorgeous, but too small for her to even consider trying on. More Jacqueline's size but like nothing she could ever imagine her sister wearing. Too revealing, too sexy, the colour far too bold. At the Halloween party she and Paul threw a couple of years ago, her sister turned up as Jackie Kennedy, elegant pink two-piece perfect down to the final stitch and button, pill-box hat slanted just-so, and a look of priceless horror on her face when Antoinette suggested they finish her off with a spatter of fake blood.

It's Halloween, Jacqueline!

It's replica Chanel, Ant. Do you know how much this is worth?

She hangs the red dress over one of the chairs then settles down on the couch with her tea. Her eyelids scrape like sandpaper, her limbs feel leaden. Out in the hall, the door to her sister's bedroom opens, but it's Loki who walks into the living room, face creased with sleep and hair dishevelled.

'Hey,' she says.

KIRSTYN McDERMOTT

'Hey.' He shuffles over to the couch, sits down beside her. 'Where've you been? I was worried about you.'

'Some of us went out for drinks after work.' She hesitates, unsure of the boundaries between them. The tension in her belly, the perpetual weight of the Loki-stone that most of the time she's able to ignore, shifts and eases. This close to him, the tug of it is stronger but, paradoxically, less insistent. 'Sorry, I should have called or something, but I lost track of time…'

'You crashed on someone's sofa?'

'Something like that.'

Loki lays himself down, rests his head in her lap. 'You don't need to lie to me, Antoinette. I'll understand if you were with someone.'

'Sorry.' She combs his ink-black locks with her fingers, untangles the snarls gathered near the nape of his neck. 'It wasn't anything. I had too much to drink.'

'You don't have to explain either.'

Apologising once again, she separates his hair into strands, begins to weave them into loose plaits. 'Hey, did I hear you coming out of my sister's room just now?'

'It's not like that.' His tone slightly defensive but tinged with a genuine and unexpected tenderness. 'She was feeling pretty rotten last night. I don't think that much vodka agrees with her.'

'Jacqueline got drunk?' Antoinette's never seen her sister wasted before, never even known her to be on the wrong side of tipsy. 'Was that a good idea? I mean, so soon after her … her seizure?'

'She doesn't think it was a seizure.' A curtness to his voice, a tone that—with Paul—always signalled the need for time out, for a change of subject at least, and Antoinette decides to take the hint. For all of Loki's hard-fought points of difference, some things have stayed very much the same.

'What's with the dress?' She nods at the chair opposite.

'I saw it in a shop window, thought it might cheer her up. It'll look great on her, don't you reckon?'

'Um, yeah, but it's not really her style. I'm not sure she—'

'Maybe you don't know your sister as well as you think.'

'What's that supposed to mean?'

'She's more than you imagine her to be, that's all. More than she imagines herself to be as well, which is the real shame of it.'

Antoinette stares at the dress she still cannot picture her sister wearing. All that glossy red satin, the sequins and ties, the bodice that would surely plunge too deeply for Jacqueline to dare. 'Hang on.' She frowns. '*When* did you get the dress?'

'Last night. Jumped a tram out to Fitzroy. There's this bar, they serve absinthe from a fountain right in front of—'

'Jacqueline went too?'

'Nah, just me. I think she wanted to be alone.'

'Alone with a bottle of vodka. For godsake, Loki, you promised me you'd keep an eye on her. You *promised*.'

'She didn't need keeping an eye on.' He sits up, too sudden, and Antoinette winces as the plait she's working on catches and pulls, leaves a couple of loose strands wound round her fingers.

Loki scowls and rubs at his scalp. 'Nothing happened, Antoinette. So, she got a little wasted, so what? She's not a kid.'

'But she never gets drunk. This isn't like her, she isn't—'

'Isn't what? The sister you want her to be?'

'What are you talking about?'

'Antoinette.'

'No, really, what the hell has this got to do with—'

'Antoinette,' he repeats, louder, eyebrows lifting as he nods over her shoulder and she turns in her seat, follows his gaze across the room to where Jacqueline now stands in the doorway. Though *stands* too upright a word for the way her sister slouches against the jamb, one hand all but digging into the wooden frame, the other cinching her pink kimono tight like it might be stolen from her at any moment, like they might be the ones to steal it.

'Don't stop on my account,' she says, regarding them with eyes bloodshot and sunken. 'While you're at it, perhaps you should both decide what I'm allowed to have for breakfast.'

Not that Jacqueline wants breakfast. The thought of eating any kind of food is enough to make her stomach recoil. Her head pounds. A blunt, unmitigated throbbing worse than any of her recent migraines. She almost regrets leaving her bed. Wishes she'd simply rolled over after Loki's getting up woke her. Buried herself in pillows and blankets until the world returned to normal.

'You look awful,' Ant says. She's already up and crossing the room. Loki as well. Guilt flickers in their eyes.

'I'll live,' Jacqueline tells her. 'What was it you two were discussing? Something about me needing a chaperone?'

'Only last night,' her sister says. 'I was worried about you after your—' She glances at Loki. 'After you collapsed, or fainted, or whatever it was. I didn't think you should be alone, you know, in case…'

'In case?'

'If it happened again. If no one was around to help you.'

'And would it? Happen again?'

'How am I supposed to know? You're the one who's been keeping it all state-secret for god knows how long.'

Jacqueline glares at her sister. '*You* don't get to lecture *me* about secrets.'

'Sorry, what? I tell you *everything*. There's not a single thing—'

'You never told me about Loki.'

'You weren't *here*. It was kind of hard to explain over the phone.'

'You didn't even try.'

Loki steps forward. 'Please.' Steps between them, his expression anxious. Almost childlike. He takes Jacqueline by the hand. Rubs his fingers over her knuckles the way he rubbed the bones of her neck during the night when she woke to nausea and dread. 'You need to tell her,' he says.

'Tell me what?' her sister demands. 'What *else* is there?'

'As though you don't already know.'

'Lina.' He called her that as she heaved over the toilet for the second time, his hand moving in circles over her back. *Lina, my Lina, Lina Lina Lina*. She's still unsure about it. The sound is beautiful, the cadence subtle. Light. It feels like another woman's name. A woman she could never be. 'Lina,' he says again. 'Tell her.'

'What is it?' Ant asks. 'What's wrong?' Her voice shakes. With anger, yes, and hurt. But also confusion, a very real and fearful bewilderment.

Jacqueline pauses, uncertain. Loki squeezes her hand. *Trust me.* And she does. Trusts him, trusts the connection that draws them together. The connection she can no longer dismiss as ordinary desire or lust. Moreover, she trusts what she feels within herself. And what she doesn't.

'Am I...' She pauses, her tongue dry and stilted. 'Am I like him? Did you make me like you made him?'

For a moment, Ant still looks confused. Then her face clears. 'Did I *make* you? You can't seriously think that.'

Jacqueline squares her jaw. Waits for an answer.

'It doesn't make any sense,' her sister says. 'You're older than me.'

'Loki's *older* than you. So to speak.'

'He's been here all of five minutes. You've been here my whole life, Jacqueline. Bloody hell, this is absurd.'

'I only have your word for that.'

'What? No, we grew up together, we went to the same schools. There's not a single month of my life we haven't seen each other, talked to each other at least. Come on, all those years? When was I supposed to have—'

'Loki remembers things. Things he wasn't here to remember.'

'That's not the same! Loki, tell her how crazy this is.'

He shakes his head. His gaze darts between the two of them. Uneasy, torn.

'Don't force him to choose sides,' Jacqueline says. 'It's not fair.'

'Sides? There aren't any sides to this; there's just what's real and what's batshit fucking insane.'

'What about the fendlies?' Loki asks softly.

Ant stares at him. 'What?'

'The fendlies,' he repeats. 'You don't remember making *them*.'

'That's different. That's…' Ant squeezes her eyes shut for a couple of seconds. 'I kind of remember, just not … it's not very clear.'

'Maybe you don't remember making Jacqueline, either.'

'No!' She shakes her head, vehement. 'She's my sister, she's *always* been my sister. Jacqueline, you have a *birth certificate*, for godsake.'

Jacqueline glares at her. 'Because those can never be faked.'

'And baby photos, photos of you and Mum and Dad from before I was even born. Remember those tiny plaster casts Mum made of your hands and feet? Stuff like that can be faked too, I suppose?'

'I don't…' Her stomach rolls. Pain forms a vice around her temples. She tries once again to recall something she has kept from her childhood. A memento, a favourite toy or book. Some useless, forgotten bauble. 'I don't have anything from that long ago,' she says at last. 'I remember things, yes, but perhaps that's all it is. A collection of unlived memories.'

Ant snorts. 'You don't have anything, because you constantly throw stuff out, you always have. *I'm too old for this now*; *this isn't who I am anymore*; et-bloody-cetera. You don't even keep birthday cards.'

'You don't understand how it feels,' Jacqueline whispers. Because there are no words to explain it. Only the gaps between the words, beyond articulation. Those formless, indifferent spaces where, until Loki, she has always dwelt alone.

'We're not saying you did it deliberately,' he tells her sister.

'I didn't do it at all!'

'I don't feel real.' Her own voice fights her now. Loki frowns. He hates that word, she knows that, but it's all she has. 'I've never felt real.'

Ant isn't listening. Instead she's talking about their mother. Who would need to be in on the whole thing, right? Lying to them and everyone she knew for however many years Jacqueline decides it has been, pretending she has two troublesome daughters instead of just one, forging paperwork and god knows what else. Does that sound remotely like the Sally Paige they know and love?

'Maybe,' Loki says. 'If she did it for you. If you were so lonely, if you wanted a sister so badly that you went and made one, then maybe she did it for you.'

Ant looks as though she could rip his throat out. 'You're not helping,' she says through gritted teeth. Then she turns to Jacqueline. 'What about Charlie? Am I supposed to have made our brother as well?'

'I don't...' Deep inside, that familiar, twin-shaped pang.

'Because Charlie isn't just a memory, Jacqueline. He lived, and he died—for real. His grave's down in Springvale, you know that.' Her sister points towards the front door. 'Should we go and visit, take some flowers? Will that be proof enough for you?'

Jacqueline presses fingers to her temples. 'You could have made him ... the both of us at the same time...' She feels like vomiting again. Loki touches her shoulder. She shrugs him off.

'Well, why isn't he here?' Ant is asking. 'If I made him, why isn't he here with us right now? Why would I just let him—'

'I don't know!' Her voice pitches so high it cracks. 'What happened to the fendlies when you got bored of playing with them, or when you just wandered off, forgot they were even there?'

Her sister looks stricken.

'Is that what happened to Charles?' Jacqueline wipes at her eyes, surprised to find them wet. 'Is that what's happening to me? Now that you have Loki, perhaps you don't need a sister anymore. Is that it?'

'Lina,' Loki warns, but she's finished. She's done. Each terror and nightmare-fed doubt sliced open. Pegged out for inspection. But still the tears won't stop. She dries her face with a kimono sleeve. Breathes.

'I think…' She can't even look at her sister. It's easier to turn away. To walk away, to force one foot in front of the other until she reaches the kitchen. Open the cupboard. Find a glass. Fill it from the tap. Drink. Drink some more. Behind her, feet stomp down the hall, keys jangle in someone's hand. Jacqueline stays by the sink and closes her eyes.

'Fuck this,' Ant mutters.

'Where are you going?' Loki asks.

'To get some bloody proof, if that's what she needs.'

'Wait, let me…'

The front door slams shut. Jacqueline can hear the faint echoes of their footsteps going down the stairs. She finishes the water. Tucks her hair behind her ears. Then she bends neatly over the sink and allows her rebellious stomach to do its worst.

When her third series of knocks goes unanswered, Antoinette sorts through her keys for familiar, tarnished brass—the oldest one on her ring, the key she's had since she was twelve years old and could be trusted not to lose it—and lets herself into her mother's house. 'Mum? You home?'

No answer, even though the Commodore is in the driveway. She checks the kitchen window, in case her mother has got it into her head to do some gardening out back, to weed the dande-lions or prune the oleander shrubs that grow half wild along the perimeter. But no, the yard is empty and overgrown, littered with mutant, misshapen lemons from the tree by the porch—and it's these that really get to her. Normally the fruit would be collected long before it fell, squeezed into juice or boiled for chutney, or simply left in a bowl handy for cooking, and it hurts to see so much of it left to just rot in the grass. Hurts to know how ill her mother must be to let them lie.

Antoinette taps on the bedroom door, waits a beat before opening it. 'It's only me,' she calls softly, but the room is empty, the bed made. There's a small army of pill bottles lined up on the side table, most of them the shop-bought vitamins her mother has been swallowing her entire life, although there are a couple with more ominous labels. Prescription labels, plain and white with black type far too small to read from this distance, but she isn't about to take another step unbidden and instead retreats, closing the door behind her.

Sally Paige's bedroom has always been sacrosanct.

Back in the kitchen, she puts the kettle on. The only coffee in the house is instant and most likely stale, the half-empty jar kept solely for the benefit of guests, but it'll still deliver a much-needed dose of caffeine. The house is so quiet. So still. Her mother must be visiting a neighbour, Mrs Jeminson from down the road maybe, if they're still on speaking terms after the incident with, what was it, geranium cuttings? Antoinette has lost track of how many people have made it onto the Sally Paige blacklist, let alone for what obscure slights and misdemeanours.

The coffee is vile, bitter stuff. She stirs in extra sugar and tops up the milk, then takes it with her into the living room. The mahogany cabinet in the corner is where her mother stows Family Business, its two bottom drawers filled with photographs and greeting cards, old letters and other various keepsakes. It's the photographs she's after. Those of Jacqueline and Charlie as babies, as toddlers, taken before she was born or not long after, some concrete evidence to wave in her sister's face—*look, you were here first*—to make her see the ludicrous depths of her paranoia.

To make Loki see it as well.

How can she even think it, she yelled at him as he followed her down to the car. *And you, encouraging her like that.*

Why won't you admit the possibility that we're right?

Because you're not. Stabbing two fingers into his chest, right into the middle of his sternum. *I would feel her, the same as I feel you.*

After all this time? Maybe you're just used to her.

Antoinette chewed on her anger all the way to the Dandenongs, seething and singing along with early Nine Inch Nails jacked up as loud as she could stand it. Anger as black and bitter as her mother's coffee, but better that than face up to the hurt that lurked beneath it, the raw bloom of betrayal.

But now, as she pulls a thick, mustard-coloured album from the drawer and begins to turn its pages, the anger dissolves and drips away. Past the photographs of her parents looking far too young to be believed, past the candid wedding day shots where her mother's smile shone wider and happier than it possibly ever has since, she comes at last to the baby snaps. Not all that many—Sally Paige now uncomfortable around cameras, it seems—but enough.

Here, the sequence she remembers. Half a dozen shots of the twins in a bubble bath, their mother crouching beside the tub with her belly still clearly full of Antoinette, a taut, unwilling grimace on her face as her husband presumably exhorts her to *say cheese*. Jacqueline and Charlie themselves all grins and giggles and shiny pink baby skin, Charlie brandishing a handful of bubbles in one photo, dumping them on his sister's head in the next, while Jacqueline stares at the camera with huge, astonished eyes. *J & C–15 months*, penned in careful Sally Paige script.

Antoinette closes the album and gulps down a mouthful of coffee. Wills her hands to stop shaking. She doesn't like thinking about Charlie. Dreads the greasy, suffocating darkness that slides over her whenever she does, the anxious clawing at her guts and the voice in her head that's more vibration than speech.

runstopbadrunstopbad

It's why she always rolls her eyes whenever Jai or any of his death fetish circle-jerkers start up their necrophilic spiels: death as friend, mother, lover; death as guardian or guide; death come with gentle arms to kiss your brow and usher you into the sweet unknown. Rolls her eyes or just walks away, depending on what mood she's in, because fuck that Sandman shit; death is not your valentine.

runstopbadrunstopbad

Death is what comes for your four-year-old brother in the bath and holds his face under the water until his tiny lungs fill and choke and burst.

runstopbadrunstopbad

The back door slams.

Antoinette jumps, coffee splashing from her mug. 'Mum?' She rubs the spill into the carpet with her foot. 'Is that you?'

No answer, still, but she follows the sound of running water and finds her mother standing at the kitchen sink, lathering her hands with eucalyptus-scented soap. She tilts her head a little as Antoinette comes into the room but doesn't look around. 'I didn't expect another visit so soon.'

'Where were you? I couldn't find you.'

'Out back.' Her mother has blue socks on her feet. She must have taken off her shoes before coming into the house. Not something she usually does, not unless the shoes are particularly filthy.

'How far out back?'

'I went for a walk in the bush.' Her mother rinses her hands, turns and grabs a tea towel from the dish rack to dry them. 'It relaxes me.'

Antoinette hates the reserve. The shadows that move between the trees, the constant rustle and crack of the underbrush, the chance of being bitten or stung by some small, unseen and possibly deadly creature—it's incomprehensible how anyone could find strolling through such an environment *relaxing*.

'I'm feeling fine, by the way,' her mother says.

'Sorry, I just … that's good, that's really good.' Although *fine* is far from how she looks. Thin and hollow-eyed, her once-tanned skin fading to grey, Sally Paige is a woman being worn away from the inside out.

'Your sister with you?' her mother asks.

'Uh, no, she had some things to catch up on. For work.'

'On a Sunday?'

'Yeah, tell me about it. Her boss is an arsehole.'

Her mother nods at the photo album tucked beneath Antoinette's arm. 'What are you doing with that old thing?'

'Can I borrow it? I … um … I want to show Loki some of the photos from when we were kids. Thought he'd get a kick out of them.'

'Loki. That's Paul's new nickname?'

Antoinette winces. 'Yeah, a bit silly, I know.'

Her mother stares at her, doubtful. 'Here,' she says at last. 'Give me that rubbish.' Antoinette shifts the album beneath her arm, but it's the coffee mug her mother wants. She plucks it from her hand like it might be diseased, takes one small and suspicious sniff before tossing the contents down the drain and setting it aside. 'I'll make us some proper tea,' she says, filling the kettle. 'Then we can talk.'

'I can't stay very long.' Not with Jacqueline most likely climbing the walls back home, paranoia goading her to ever greater heights.

'You can stay as long as we need.'

'No, Mum, really I—'

'Stop it!' Sally Paige now at full steam and close to boiling, stabbing the air with a forefinger so thin it might be nothing but wrinkles and knobbly bone. 'Do you think I'm such a moron, I can't see what's sitting at my own dinner table?'

Antoinette is stunned. 'I don't...'

'Stupid, thoughtless fool of a girl. I know exactly what you've done. I know exactly where that *boy* of yours came from.'

17

Her mother starts to cough, a brutal hacking and hitching of shoulders, shaking her head as Antoinette takes a step forward. 'I'll be all right,' she insists, slapping at her chest. But the coughing has deflated her, diminished her; she sags panting against the kitchen counter like a runner at the end of her race. Beside her, the kettle shrieks and steams. 'When?' she asks. 'When did you perfect him?'

Antoinette frowns. '*Perfect?*'

'Create him, bring him into being, however you want to say it.' Her mother dismisses the words with a wave of her hand. 'When did you do it? How long has he been in the world?'

'I didn't—'

'Enough.' She grabs Antoinette's chin, fixes her with a merciless Sally Paige stare. 'Don't try to tell me that he's Paul, or Paul's long lost brother, or even some tall-dark-and-handsome who just so happens to bear a striking resemblance. I'm your mother, Antoinette, and *I know*. Now, stop playing games and tell me the truth.'

And so she does. Her confession albeit stilted, nudged through every pause and reluctant hesitation by a dogged Sally Paige who appears to have already guessed the broader strokes anyway. Paul dumping her. Antoinette devastated and alone. Loki spun from grief and disillusioned desire. That only a week has passed comes as a surprise, and even Antoinette needs to count back on her fingers. Really, only one week? There are raised eyebrows over the notebook as well, and the vanished words. *Clever*, her mother acknowledges. *Clever to do it like that.*

'I didn't mean to do it,' Antoinette says. 'I didn't even know it was something I could do.'

'No, you never *mean* to do it. That's your problem.'

'What are you talking about?'

Her mother just stares for a moment, the expression on her face at once thoughtful and strange. Like she's scared, or sad, or both. 'Do you remember, when you were a child? Those things…'

'The fendlies? Not really, no. Little bits and pieces if I think about it hard enough. Jacqueline remembers more than I do.'

'Your sister remembers the fendlies?'

'Not well. Until Loki, she figured she imagined them.'

Her mother nods. 'But now she knows the truth. Because of him.'

'She, ah…' Antoinette is unsure how much she can reveal before landing herself on the wrong side of the Sisters Against Sally Paige alliance. But so many chips on the table already, her bank running close to dry, and besides—the realisation tinged by no small amount of wonder—her mother might actually be able to help for once. 'That's why I need the photos, to show Jacqueline. She thinks, um, she thinks that I somehow made her as well.'

'Ridiculous,' her mother says. 'She's older than you by almost two years.'

'She reckons I made her with a head full of fake memories. I thought if I showed her the photos, you know, physical evidence that she *was* alive before I was born…'

'Good idea, you do that.'

'Maybe you could come with me? Since you know about it all anyway? If the two of us sit down and talk to her, make her see how impossible…'

Her mother is already shaking her head. 'I can't. I'm sorry.'

'I know you hate going into the city, but Mum, this is important. Jacqueline's seriously freaking out about this. She's afraid she's not even real.'

'Convince her she's wrong.'

'I've tried, she won't listen to me. If you could just—'

'No, it won't work.'

'She's your daughter, she needs you. Why won't you even try?'

'Because she'll know I'm lying.' Her mother rubs at her forehead in the same distracted manner that Jacqueline does, those hard sandpaper strokes Antoinette catches herself making when she's stressed or frustrated or just too tired to think. Her stomach dips; she feels the urge to hang onto something solid.

'Lying about what?' she whispers.

Her mother coughs again, thumps herself once on the chest. 'Jacqueline isn't *your* perfection, Antoinette. *You* didn't make her. That, I managed all on my own, her and Charlie both.'

Loki was right. The grease has helped. Jacqueline still feels quite seedy but at least her stomach has decided to tackle the bacon and eggs and hashbrowns rather than reject them. She puts her sunglasses back on as they leave the café. It's too bright outside. The sky too blue.

Jacqueline takes Loki's hand as they walk. 'Thank you.'

'For what?'

'Throwing me in the shower. Forcing me out here.'

'I wasn't going to let you hole up in that apartment all day.'

She squeezes his fingers. 'I feel odd.'

'It's called a hangover.'

'No,' she says. 'Not that. More than that. What was that word you used? Flux, yes. That's how I feel.'

'You feel like you're in flux?'

'Like I *am* flux.' She sighs. 'I don't know who I'm supposed to be.'

'Why do you have to be anyone? Why can't you just be you?'

Jacqueline stops. Drags on Loki's arm so that he has to stop as well. It's a clear, sunny morning and Port Melbourne is packed. Brunchers and joggers. Couples pushing oversized prams or dangling toddlers from their wrists. So many people, so many lives. How do *they* know who they are? How do they not spend every moment wondering how they should act or speak or carry themselves? How they should dress or style their hair? How they should *breathe*?

Loki pulls her from the path of two girls giggling over a phone. One of them knocks Jacqueline's elbow. Keeps walking. Keeps giggling. Jacqueline wants to grab her oblivious blonde head and smash it into the footpath.

'What is it?' Loki asks. 'What's wrong?'

Jacqueline blinks at him. Adrenaline seeps from her system as the urge to violence flickers. Fades. She has no idea where it came from. Loki brushes her cheek with the backs of his fingers.

'You're crying.' He shows her his hand, damp with tears.

Jacqueline blinks again. 'I never cry,' she tells him.

Perfections. Sally Paige's name for them, and her mother's, and her grandmother's—but not her *great*-grandmother's apparently, because sometimes it skips a generation; skips it or finds a heart stubborn enough, stony enough to offer resistance—a lineage of women passing along this gift, this *curse* as Sally Paige sees it, spitting the word from her mouth like something rancid and foul. Never the men of the family, never their dull and mundane sons—those lines stop dead; cauterisation by Y chromosome—and so it's been whittled down over the centuries, cornered and corralled into the blood of fewer and fewer daughters.

The ability to take what should only be imagined and *perfect* it, to craft dreams and desires into flesh and bone, into life and breath. To force a small chink in the world and fill it with what doesn't belong.

'Grandma could do this as well?' Antoinette struggles to hold it all in her mind. The knowledge is big enough to swallow her without even chewing. 'Who else?'

Her mother sips at her tea. There's no one she knows, not in this country anyway. There's a woman over in America—Georgia or Louisiana, she can't remember—the descendant of some great-great-aunt or other, and a handful back in Europe as well. No names, no more details than that, so Antoinette might as well close her mouth and forget the questions.

'But—'

'No. This is nearly at an end with us, and good riddance to it. You ever get pregnant, my girl, you best take one of those tests they have now, tells you the sex before it's more than a tadpole wriggling inside you. If it's a boy, you have my blessing. Otherwise, you make the right decision. Do what you need to.'

Antoinette stares into her empty tea cup, at the few leaves that sit limp and wet on the bottom. She doesn't want to consider the decision Sally Paige might have made with such a test at her disposal.

'You think I'm an evil old woman.'

'I ... I don't know what to think.'

'Your new boy. Loki. What did you give for him, you figured that out yet?'

'What do you mean, *give for him?*'

'That's how it works, even if we try to convince ourselves otherwise.'

It's the difference between a perfection and a whimsy, she explains. Those *fendlies* Antoinette used to make, they were whimsies—thoughtless, tattery scraps of imagination that little girls fashion as playthings, barely aware of what they're doing. It's often the first sign a child carries the curse. Of course, grown women have been known to make their own whimsies to play with, albeit of a less *innocent* nature.

And here Sally Paige offers a sneer, thin and fleeting; Antoinette can't tell whether her mother is revolted or amused.

A girl makes a whimsy, she continues, it doesn't take much from her. A bit of energy maybe, for the fancier ones. A bit of breath, like she's been walking up hill for too long. Then a few minutes or hours later, maybe even as much as a day if her concentration holds that long, they just disappear. Those ones, the whimsies, they're not alive. They're no more real than what a child might construct with Lego blocks. Strange and colourful creations to be briefly fussed over, then pulled apart and thrown back into the mix.

But a perfection is different. Permanent, fixed, part of the world.

A woman doesn't get to make something like that for free.

'So,' her mother says. 'Why *exactly* did you create Loki?'

Antoinette shifts in her seat. 'I told you, I was drunk. I don't really remember much of the specifics and all my notes—'

'Stop making excuses. You know why you did it.'

Shaking her head, because she doesn't want to talk about it, not with Sally Paige of all people; cold, pragmatic Sally Paige who wouldn't have the first clue what it was like to fall in love. Except … she remembers the wedding photos, and the young woman in the white flouncy dress with a smile so radiant and broad, her face must have ached for days afterwards. That young woman, now this old woman who winces whenever she sits down, or stands up, who hides behind a battered, hand-me-down, Sally Paige face. Antoinette doesn't know *this* woman at all.

And maybe that makes the difference.

'I made Loki because I loved Paul.' Antoinette pauses, searching for the right words, because the right words seem so very important to find. 'I loved him so much, more than, well, everything. I wanted to keep loving him, only I wanted him to be, I don't know, better? Someone who would love me as much as I loved him, who wouldn't ever cheat on me. Wouldn't hurt me or take me for granted.' She laughs bitterly. 'You know, the standard *Cosmo* bullshit.'

Her mother laughs as well. It's not a pretty sound. 'What about now? Do you still love him?'

'Paul? Or Loki?'

'Either. Both.'

'No,' Antoinette sighs. 'With Paul, there's absolutely nothing left. When I think about him, I can remember what it felt like, what *I* felt like, but now it's all gone. And Loki's a disaster. He loves me, I mean, *he loves me*, god, so much. And I look at him and I *want* to love him like that, I really do, but…' Her nose itches with the threat of tears, and she pushes the heels of her hands into her eye sockets, presses and presses until light flares behind her lids. It doesn't help. 'I've tried, believe me, but it's not there. I don't love him. I don't think I ever can.'

'Stop snivelling,' her mother says. 'Love is what you wanted, my girl, and love is what you gave.'

The wooden floor echoes beneath each tap of her shoe. Jacqueline likes the sound. Likes that she makes it. There aren't as many people inside the Ian Potter Centre as she feared from the high-density crowd outside in Fed Square. Without some blockbuster exhibition as drawcard, a gallery of Australian art obviously cannot compete with alfresco dining or fire-eating, unicycled street buskers.

'I like it here,' Loki says. 'There's nothing I remember.'

Jacqueline smiles.

Take me someplace that makes you happy, he told her. This was the first spot that popped into her head. She wonders why she doesn't come here more often.

Loki catches her hand. 'Art's not just a job for you, is it?'

'No,' she replies. 'When I'm in a place like this, or even working at Seventh Circle, I feel connected. Involved. I understand this world. I feel part of it.'

'But you're not an artist yourself? You don't paint, or draw, or sculpt. You don't even own a camera.' He gestures to the walls.

To the series of oblique, unframed prints that wind around them. *Found images* the artist calls them. Unfocused, hipshot compositions too clever to be entirely accidental. 'You could take photographs like this, Lina. Hell, anyone could.'

Jacqueline pokes him in the ribs. 'Shows how much you know about art.'

He grins. 'Enlighten me.'

'Execution is only half the story,' she says. 'It *tells* the story. But if you don't *have* a story inside to tell . . .' She shrugs. The photo in front of them might be a mermaid's tail, flash-blurred beneath sun-sparkled water. 'I can handle a brush very well, actually. Give me a painting and I'll make a copy so fine you'll be hard pressed to spot the original. *You* will, that is; I couldn't fool an expert. But give me a blank canvas, and I have nothing to say.'

'Frustrating much?'

'Not really,' Jacqueline tells him. 'Keeping still, keeping quiet, listening, watching; there's something to be said for all of that. I like seeing how other people imagine the world. How they make the world.'

Loki is silent as they move through the galleries. He gives the exhibits only a cursory glance. Mostly, he frowns at his shoes.

'Are you bored?' she asks after a while. 'We can leave if you like.'

'I don't want to leave.' He stops. 'Show me your favourite piece.'

'In this room?'

'In the whole gallery. You know, burning building, can only save one thing, blah blah blah. And I don't want to see the most important thing, or the most valuable thing—I want to see the thing *you* love most.'

Jacqueline doesn't need to think about it. 'Follow me,' she says.

To Antoinette, it reads like a bad joke. To get the thing you want, you forfeit whatever it is that made you want it in the first place? Not quite so simple, according to her mother, but near enough to smell the cigar smoke. There *are* a few clever, careful women who navigate the process with skill, shoring up what they can, salvaging what remains; or at least rumours of clever, careful women. Sally Paige has never heard a single name herself, only whispers about a sister of an aunt of a cousin who once ... but it hardly matters. Rumour is poisonous enough.

Rumour and hope and the stubborn, stupid hearts of girls barely grown.

'But why?' Antoinette can't fathom it. The rank unfairness of it. 'Why do it if you know it won't work out? If *I* had known, if *you* had taught me about this instead of leaving me to scrabble in the dark, I never would have—'

'Don't go blaming me. We all think we'll be the one. You would have too.'

That one clever, careful woman whose love is so strong, desire so bold, whose need is a blistering, unquenchable force that will be ripped from her hands only when they are bloodless and cold. The woman who'll not only end up with the whole damn cake in her lap, but a silver fork with which to shovel it into her mouth.

'It's the lie we want to believe,' her mother says. 'Love will conquer all.'

Antoinette feels numb. She presses a hand to her chest, wanting nothing more than to rip through her own skin, to rend flesh and crack rib until her fist closes at last around the Loki-stone and crushes it, tears it in pieces from her body.

'It wouldn't do any good.' Sally Paige playing mirrors, spindle-fingers curled loose between her breasts. 'This isn't Kmart, dear, you can't bring him back for a refund. What's paid stays paid.'

'Do you...' Antoinette wets her lips. 'Can you feel her? Jacqueline?'

Her mother nods. 'Every single day.'

'I don't understand. Why make a baby—two babies—like that?'

Because Sally Paige longed desperately for motherhood. Because after almost eight years of marriage and just about every humiliating test and procedure the medical profession could dig up to throw at her, it seemed the only conceivable option. Because when a husband begins to regard his wife like he might a defective washing machine, when she finds his gaze trailing after young lasses with babe-swollen bellies ... well, it doesn't take a genius to calculate the end result of that equation.

Besides, she *knew* it would work. Sally Paige would be that clever, careful woman that others would come to whisper about.

A mother's love couldn't be bartered, of that she was certain. It was something innate, a property entwined so irrevocably around the core of her being that having it torn loose was unimaginable.

Impossible, she told herself. *Promised* herself.

Such pretty, sweet-tasting lies.

'All that love,' she says. 'All that longing. It went into those babies, every scrap of it. Afterwards, I spent hours by their cribs, looking down at their perfect little faces and perfect little fingers—and they *were* perfect, those two; they slept through the night from day one, took to the bottle without grizzling—and I would look at them and try to dredge up anything, the faintest spark of feeling, some shred that had been overlooked, left behind.' She slumps forward. 'They might have been a couple of plastic dolls for all I felt for them.'

Antoinette stares at her hands, at the ragged fingernails she can't remember beginning to gnaw again. A childhood habit, resuscitated for stranger times. She prods at the absence within her, traces its borders. She does possess some kind of affection for Loki, even if it's not the romantic love that he craves. If there was nothing inside her but indifference … she pushes the thought aside.

'Your father adored the twins,' her mother is saying. 'To give him his due, he did get his hands dirty those first few months. Changed nappies, fed them, tried to give me time to come around on my own.'

Antoinette has no clear memories of her dad. A bearded smile. The scent of sweat and spice. A huge hand ruffling her hair. All the pictures in her mind come from photos. 'But how on earth did you explain it to him?'

'He already knew about whimsies—called me his fairy princess, which I didn't much care for, but still. The twins were a shock, but once he realised they were here to stay, well, it's surprising how simple it was. Dr Chiang took care of the paperwork, registered them as homebirths or some such.'

'Dr Chiang? Our Dr Chiang?'

'We went to school together. He's a good man.' Her mother smiles. Shallow and slight, but the first real smile Antoinette's seen cross her face for a long time.

'Does he know? What Jacqueline is?'

'He believes it was an off-the-books surrogacy arrangement, or he lets himself believe it. Stuck by me all these years, in any case.' She grunts. 'That's more than I can say for your father.'

The question that's been lurking on the back of Antoinette's tongue for the past hour creeps forth, no longer willing to be denied. 'What about me?' she asks. 'Am I a *perfection* as well?'

Her mother laughs. 'Don't be stupid. You're the one who gave me stretch marks—and haemorrhoids.'

'But you said you couldn't—'

'I said, I *didn't*.'

More common than she might think, the mysteriously infertile couple who catch pregnant only after they stop trying, once calendars and thermometers and ovulation charts are abandoned, consigned to the scrapheap along with what remains of their dreams. As it was with Sally Paige, her twins barely a year old before their sister took root in her womb, though another four months before she told anyone. Four months weighing a wheelbarrow load of cons against just one hope-tinged feather. That maybe a *real* child—a child drawn from her blood, born from her body—could summon back all the love she had lost. Summon or seed from scratch, but fix it either way.

Fix *her*. Make Sally Paige a mother again.

'Hope,' she coughs. 'Once a poison like that works its way into a woman's heart, there's nothing she won't do in chase of it.'

The morning sickness and swollen ankles, the aching back and a bladder that couldn't even make it through half a cup of tea after eight months—she gritted her teeth through it all. Told herself that once the baby comes, once she laid eyes on that fresh baby face and smelled that fresh baby smell—her *own* baby, her *natural* baby—it would all change.

Once the baby comes, once the baby comes, once the baby comes.

But then the baby did come, red and wrinkled and squalling louder than a summer storm, and Sally Paige found herself looking into a crib once more, weeping over yet another plastic doll.

'If I could have been certain...' She flaps a hand. 'Beggars and horses.'

Antoinette stares. 'Are you saying that if you'd known having me wouldn't have made a difference, then you would have ... not had me?'

'Don't take it personally. It wasn't *you*, it wasn't *Antoinette*. It was just a decision that needed to be made.'

'And you think you made the wrong one.' She feels sick to her stomach. This broken, bitter woman isn't her mother; this woman isn't anyone's *mother*.

'The point, my girl, is that you're not a perfection. If you were, you couldn't have made that boy of yours.'

Antoinette can't even look at her. She doesn't want to be here, in a house so permeated with deceit it would likely fall down should the truth ever touch it, sitting across from a mother who doesn't love her, who has never loved her, who has merely dressed the part and learned the lines and followed—badly—whatever maternal script she managed to draft along the way.

'A perfection can't create another perfection,' Sally Paige is saying. 'Or anything else, for that matter. *Girls don't bleed, boys don't seed*, was how your grandmother used to put it. Crude but accurate, and just as well really, if you ask me.'

Antoinette gets to her feet. 'I have to go.'

'Right now?'

'I can't listen to any more of this.'

'Antoinette, wait.'

She makes it all the way back to her car before Sally Paige catches up, photo album clutched to her chest like a shield. Antoinette rolls down the window. 'I'm not staying,' she says 'I need some time to get all of this straight in my head.' *To stop wanting to throttle you.*

Sally Paige hands her the album. 'Don't let Jacqueline know.'

'You have to be kidding.'

'Show her the photos like you planned. Convince her she's wrong.'

'Why on earth would I do that?'

'So she can live her life. Your sister's grown up believing she's human; what do you think it will do to her to find out she's not?'

'It's what she already suspects.'

'But it's not what she wants to believe, trust me.' Sally Paige rubs at her forehead again. 'I know you must think me an ogre, but I've tried so hard to be a good mother to you girls, *both* you girls. Despite the obvious handicaps. Please, don't ruin everything. Don't ruin it for Jacqueline.'

Antoinette keeps her eyes fixed on straight ahead. 'It's a long drive home,' she replies at last. 'I'll think about it.'

Jacqueline watches Loki's face as he moves around the statues, investigating them from different angles. 'It's called *Nest*,' she tells him. A life-size motor scooter, stylised and reformed to invoke a deer or perhaps an antelope. Some placid but wild herbivore. A mother, lying on her haunch. Propped up on her front wheel as she encourages her newborn—fearful and undeveloped, no trace yet of a saddle and only featureless, black nubs where its tyres will be—to come closer. To settle within the protective curl of her chassis. To be safe. To be loved.

'Patricia Piccinini,' Jacqueline says. 'She's done a series of similar works that zoomorphise the mechanical. It's what we all do, when you think about it. Our vehicles, our computers, any machine with which we have close and regular contact. We treat them as though they are alive, as though they are sentient beings with personalities of their own. We cajole them, berate them, abuse them, and ultimately dispose of them.' She gestures towards the statues. 'Of course, we know machines are not living creatures. But what does it say about humans that we need to create these false personas? Personas we can then so easily abandon or destroy?'

Loki returns to stand by her side.

'Is it like training wheels?' she muses. 'Do we practise on the machines, so that we'll be better equipped to ill-treat each other?'

'Maybe,' he says. 'But none of that is why you love it.'

Jacqueline stares at the baby scooter. As always, she yearns to pick it up. Cradle it in her arms. 'The way they look at each other—not that they even have proper faces, only those dials and gauges—but still. That mother-child bond, it's almost tangible. If you tried to step between them, it would bounce you off.'

Loki nudges her with his elbow. 'Go on, you know you want to.'

'What?'

'Touch him. The little guy.'

'This is an art gallery, Loki. It's not like walking through IKEA.'

He leans over. His breath is warm against her face. 'Go on,' he whispers. 'What would be the harm?'

It's only a small step up onto the raised platform. Two more have her crouching beside the baby scooter. The fibreglass is smooth and polished. The warmth is surely a trick of expectation. She runs her hand over the curve of its back. The stubby handles that serve as ears. 'Beautiful,' she murmurs.

'Hey! Get off there!'

Across the hall, a security guard marches towards them. One hand on his radio. The half-dozen or so people in the vicinity have stopped what they were doing and are now staring at Jacqueline.

'Don't worry,' Loki tells her. 'Stay where you are.'

'Miss, you need to get down.' The guard cultivates a neutral expression but his eyes are flat and hostile. 'You aren't allowed to touch the exhibits.'

Loki's grin stretches wide and dazzling. *I am the friend you thought you would never find*, that grin says. *And I will be that friend forever*. The guard falters. Blinks and shakes his head. 'It's okay,' Loki says. His voice is hypnotic. Sweet and treacherous as honey from wild bees. 'She isn't hurting anyone. She can stay a bit longer.'

'No,' the guard replies. Less command than question. As though he doubts his own tongue. 'It isn't … she can't…'

'Just a few more minutes.' Loki keeps grinning.

Jacqueline turns away from him. Away from them both. Sits down and rests her cheek against the baby scooter's flank. Closes her eyes. Somewhere deep inside, low in her belly, she feels a shift. A bright flare of pain. Then a settling.

'Take your time, Miss,' the guard says. He sounds more at ease now. Happily bewildered. 'You're not hurting anyone.'

Antoinette lets herself into the apartment and pauses for a moment, back pressed to the front door while she tries to catch her breath. She's never lied to Jacqueline before, not about anything so serious as this, and there's a constriction across her chest like she's wearing some cheap-arse corset cinched two sizes too small.

Let your sister live her life. Isn't that what she deserves?

Sally Paige's parting words stuck on repeat as Antoinette drove back to Port Melbourne, because maybe just maybe the woman is right—what benefit would there actually be in laying such revelations at Jacqueline's feet? If truth can bring only horror and pain, is there any real value in telling it?

'Stop it,' Antoinette mutters. Stop procrastinating, girlie-girl, and move your arse. Get it over and done with. Stay angry enough, stay scared enough, you might just pull it off.

Loki's in the living room, standing alone by the balcony door. He turns as she comes in, glances at the photo album in her hands. 'Is that...'

'Proof,' Antoinette snaps. 'Where is she?'

'In her room. She ... isn't sure she wants to see you.'

'Too bad.'

'Wait, please wait.' He moves with the lithe, enviable grace of a dancer, all coiled energy and control, and Antoinette feels that familiar hitch of wonder and astonished pride. She made this boy, *she made him*. 'Be careful,' Loki says. 'She's so frightened, confused. She did seem better while we were out but—'

'You went out?'

'Just for brunch, I thought it would take her mind off things and it did, for a while. But as soon as we got back here she was…' He shakes his head. 'She's been sorting through her stuff, like it's an archaeological dig or something. She won't say what she's looking for.'

Antoinette brandishes the album at him. 'Which is why I have this.'

'Just don't forget that you're her sister.'

'Oh, for godsake.' She's barely taken two steps before he's in front of her again, his hands falling firm-but-gentle onto her shoulders, his face so close to hers she has little choice but to meet his gaze.

'She loves you,' Loki says. 'And she *does* trust you, no matter how confused she might feel. So, whatever you tell her, don't make it any kind of a lie. You lie to her now, you lie to her about this—that's not something you'll ever be able to fix.' He kisses her brow, then steps aside. 'Go on. She needs you.'

Jacqueline has pulled all her clothes from the wardrobe and is busy sorting them into piles on the bed, though if there's any kind of rhyme or reason to the arrangement, Antoinette can't figure it. Her sister frowns as she lifts a cream camisole from one pile and places it onto another, brushing the silk with her hand.

'I don't think I can talk to you right now,' she says without looking up.

'That's okay.' Antoinette nudges aside a pair of slacks and perches herself on the corner of the bed, cradling the album in her lap. The weight of it is a comfort and gives her anxious fingers something to grasp, something to fiddle with, but that's about all it's good for. There may be some kind of truth pressed between its covers—a story of one sister who did in fact fall first into the world, who is the oldest by any definition, and of her younger sibling who has never been anything else—but it's not the whole truth, not by any cruel or desperate stretch.

And the whole truth, or as much of it as Antoinette knows, is the least of what Jacqueline deserves. Jacqueline, who is now glancing warily at her sister, at what she holds in her hands.

'You don't need to talk,' Antoinette says, and she smiles, and she hopes that the smile is more reassuring than it feels. 'All you need to do is listen.'

18

Jacqueline studies the portrait of the old woman holding a blue feather. Both her arms are gleaming chrome, jointed at elbow and wrist. Her fingers, still wrinkled flesh, clasp the feather with obvious care. Her neck is also chrome and beneath her modest summer frock bulge the pert breasts of an eighteen year old. If the eighteen year old was a robot. But her face. Her face is aged and lined. Her eyes don't quite meet those of the viewer. They stare past. Through. The old woman is not concerned for her audience. She has her feather. That is enough.

It is the only one of the series without a red dot next to its name.

The gallery floor is empty. Becca is upstairs with Dante. Jacqueline can't recall what they're working on. She finds it difficult to care. Seventh Circle politics hold remarkably little interest for her now.

Instead, she delves inwards. Sectioning and separating herself into smaller and smaller parts. An exact and detailed catalogue of Jacqueline Paige. All that she is and ever was subjected to thorough, repetitive examination. It is a difficult process, deciding which facets might be hers—genuinely *hers*—and which were likely crafted by the woman who made her.

Sally Paige, in search of the perfect daughter.

Still, she is calm. Has been calm ever since Ant revealed what their mother—what *Ant's* mother—had told her. It's a peculiar serenity, unlike anything she has been able to cultivate before. She feels safe within it. Within it? No. It's not something that surrounds or encloses her. Rather, it's something she possesses, something she holds. It's the feather, bright and certain and blue.

Who am I then, Loki? What am I?

Whoever you want to be. Whoever you choose to be.

She starts small. She starts with *Lina*. Rolling the word in her mouth like a pebble. Tucking it beneath her tongue. It's a good name. She likes the sound of it. The cool, polished-glass feel of it. Perhaps. Perhaps she might be Lina. No one has ever called her that before Loki. It feels fresh, unsullied. Full of promise. She whispers it to herself from time to time over the next few days. Breaking it in like a pair of shoes. Making sure it doesn't blister or pinch. Lina is someone new. She is a blank canvas, an unmarked page—terrifying yet exhilarating to contemplate. She is everything that Jacqueline Paige could never be. Could never dare to be. Lina is neither careful nor precise. She is expansive and changeable. She is vast.

Most important of all, Lina is nobody's daughter. And if...

… that's what Jacqueline wants to be called now, then of course Antoinette's cool with it and she'll do her best to remember, though it might take a little while and Jacqueline—*Lina*—will need to forgive the odd slip-up or two. And her sister nods and smiles her queer new smile, lopsided and shy like she's pulled the thing straight out of the box and isn't exactly sure what to do with it, and 'Hey,' Antoinette says before she has a chance to leave again. 'We haven't really talked much. Since…'

'I know,' Jacqueline says. *Lina* says. 'I've been thinking things over.'

'Are we…' She wishes she could have the answer first, so she would know whether or not she really wanted to ask the question. 'Are we okay?'

Her sister frowns. 'I think so. Yes.'

'That's it? You *think* so?'

'I'm still trying to work out what this all means for me. There's a lot to sort through, but one thing I do already know is that I don't *have* to love you.'

A punch in the gut couldn't hurt any worse. Antoinette swivels around in her chair, turns back to the computer. She doesn't want Jacqueline to see the tears in her eyes. 'Well,' she says. 'Glad that's sorted, then.'

'Ant, no. That's not what I meant.'

And then her sister's arms are around her shoulders, and her sister's cheek is pressed to her own, and her sister is sorry, so sorry for how that sounded. Loki's been encouraging her to stop second-guessing herself, to stop prepping every sentence in her head before allowing it to leave her mouth. Which is good. Which is liberating. But it's still new, and she does stumble at times.

'I do love you,' Jacqueline says. 'Of course I do. What I meant was, I know that it's *real* now. I know it comes from *me*. It's not because Sally *made* me to love you, it wasn't some kind of big sister parameter she built into me—how could it be when she didn't plan on having you? When she didn't even think she could?'

Antoinette wipes at her eyes. 'I'm not sure I get it.'

'What's to get?' Jacqueline kisses the top of her head. 'You're my little sister and I love you. Because *I* love you.'

Then she leaves, padding barefoot back to her room and to Loki with whom she's been sharing her bed for the past few days, and Antoinette's happy for them, really, pleased to see their shared glances and cautious smiles. Because it's not about them personally, the envious, belly-deep ache around which she curls, footsore and exhausted after work each night, the bars of the futon poking at shoulder and hip. She neither wants Loki, nor wishes her sister would let him alone, but still. To witness the emotions so clearly blossoming between them, emotions she might never again feel for herself—it grieves as much as it gladdens, and no matter how…

… many questions he asks, Lina knows that the middle-aged man in the green jacket doesn't give a damn about the pen-and-ink collage on the wall in front of him. He is more interested in looking at Becca. The shape of her arse. The depth of her cleavage.

'Tell me about the swans again,' he says.

Becca is oblivious. Or perhaps she is merely pretending. Either way, she launches into her spiel about Leda and Zeus. She smiles and pushes the hair from her face. It falls straight back down again. She talks about seduction and the long, serpentine curve of a swan's neck. Her hand makes suggestive motions in the air. The man in the green jacket laughs. He moves closer to Becca. Murmurs something into her ear. The girl giggles and shakes her head. 'No,' she says. 'I don't think so.'

Lina gets up from behind the sales desk and crosses the gallery. 'It's a very confronting piece,' she says to the man in the green jacket. 'Don't you think?'

The man turns to look at her. His gaze travels swiftly over her legs and hips. Lingers for a moment at her breasts before skipping up to her face. His smile is at once simpering and sickeningly proprietary. 'How's that, then?'

'The artist makes no bones about which interpretation of the Leda story she sides with.' Jacqueline points to the centre of the frame. A multitude of hands, all of them gripping a sinuous, white-feathered throat. 'Pre- or post-coital strangulation, you have to wonder. And here, look.' The blood-limned edge of a blade. Several blades. Standing ramrod stiff amid sacks of soft, deflated flesh. 'It's somewhat stylised but you get the idea. Not many people know, but swans are among the few birds to possess a penis. They're aggressive too—a good whack with a wing will break your arm. The rape of Leda was almost certainly penetrative. And violent.'

'Did you say rape?' The man with the green jacket is no longer grinning.

'That's a fairly modern reading of the myth,' Becca is quick to tell him.

Lina nods her head. 'Of course.' She leans closer to the collage. Makes a show of wincing at what she sees there. 'But if *seduction* is what you're after, sir, I'm not sure we have anything to offer you at the moment.'

She smiles. Keeps smiling as the man in the green jacket checks his watch and mumbles something about needing to get back to work. He thanks Becca for her attention, thanks Lina as well. It's not really his thing, he tells them. Maybe he'll come back another time. When the exhibits change.

'What's wrong with you?' Becca hisses as soon as the man has stepped outside. 'You've been acting weird all week. Weird*er*.'

'I'm sorry, did you want to give him your phone number?'

'Gross! I was trying to sell him some art. He was dead keen until you stuck your nose in.'

'Yes, I saw just how keen he was.' She looks the girl up and down. A slow, deliberate slide over every inch of her skin. By the time she returns to her face, Becca is blushing. Lina sighs and rubs at her forehead. She doesn't want to be cruel. She doesn't want to be that person. 'You're not stupid,' she says. 'Even if you think you need to pretend otherwise.'

'I don't have to listen to this,' Becca replies. Starts to walk away.

Lina grabs her wrist. It's not something she planned. The sight of her own fingers pressed into the girl's skin is a mild shock. Jacqueline Paige doesn't touch people like that. Jacqueline Paige goes out of her way not to touch people like that. Becca looks startled as well. She attempts to pull away but Lina tightens her grip.

'If you want to get anywhere in this business, you need to stop using this—'

She flicks at that heavy flop of a fringe.

'—and this—'

Taps a finger against those ruby-bright lips.

'—and start showing people that you actually have a brain. Or else no one, not Dante, not the clients, not anyone who matters in any way at all, will ever consider you to be anything other than window dressing.'

Becca's eyes glitter. Damaged, dangerous, like a bottle left broken in the gutter.

Lina releases her. 'I'm being honest. That's all.'

The girl steps back. Folds her arms. 'Fuck you.'

'Suit yourself.' Lina walks back to the sales desk. Retrieves her bag from the bottom drawer. 'I'm going to grab some lunch,' she tells Becca, who has turned to face the Leda collage again, who responds with the barest hitch of her shoulder as Lina leaves the gallery. Her heart beats fast and loud. Her blood rushes in her veins. She covers her smile with one hand, then drops it. Allows her grin to widen and shine. Two men smile back at her in passing. One of them winks. And Lina laughs. Riding her shoulder, the shadow of Jacqueline Paige worries and frets—*people are looking at you, people are looking at us*—and she laughs at that too. Let them look. Let them smile and laugh to see a woman smiling and laughing to herself in the street. Let them think...

... whatever the hell they want. Antoinette is beyond caring. Chinese whispers and smirking innuendo, like being right back in high school. *Jackson, eh?* Michelle one of the first to sidle up all nudge-nudge and wink-wink, lascivious grin and friendly bump of the hip. *Sweet little upgrade you got yourself there.* Because, of course, someone has seen them together—maybe that first drunken session at the pub, maybe one of the other two nights she went home with him, clean and sober both times, just to make sure nothing was there—and Simpatico gossip spreads faster than grease fire.

Still, she's surprised to find him waiting behind at the end of their shift.

'So,' he says. 'You got any plans?'

Antoinette arches an eyebrow. 'Really?'

Not after last night, surely, lying there with her fist stuffed into her mouth, fighting off an attack of the giggles while the bed creaked like it was about to collapse any minute and Jackson made that peculiar whiny noise in the back of his throat. Giggles which turned into hiccups, loud and sporadic and painful enough that she spent half an hour in the bathroom afterwards, sipping lukewarm mouthfuls of water and trying to hold her breath. At least it saved her from awkward conversation.

'You need to chill,' Jackson is saying. 'I might be able to help you out with that.' He opens his palm, low and surreptitious, flashes her a glimpse of two neatly rolled joints. 'It's aces, this shit. Real mellow.'

Antoinette shakes her head. 'Sorry, can't say that's ever done much for me.'

'That's cool. You still up for something tonight, though, right?'

He's beyond cute, this boy, with a repertoire most women would find far from shabby, and yet she feels absolutely nothing, not even the faintest flutter of interest. As far as her vanished libido is concerned, Jackson might as well be suggesting they do laundry together.

Love is what you wanted, my girl, and love is what you gave.

Love, and a whole lot more besides.

'Jackson … this isn't going to go anywhere.'

He looks mildly surprised. 'But we're just having fun, aren't we? I thought we were just having fun. No strings, no pressure, right?'

Right. And if she were actually having any fun…

'Sorry,' Antoinette tells him. 'I really don't need any more complications.'

'So, it's not me, it's you?'

She would laugh at that, she really would, if Jackson didn't seem a little hurt. Hurt or maybe just put out by his sudden loss of benefits, but if it's the former then she's glad not to be stringing this out any longer. 'You don't know how right you are,' she says. 'It is so *totally* me.'

And Jackson smiles and shrugs, that vague film of regret lifting so fast she wonders if it was ever there at all, and he tells her it's cool, he understands. *Totally.* Then he leans in to kiss her goodbye and their noses bump, graceless and hard, and Antoinette is still rubbing hers when she gets on the tram. A couple of emo kids canoodle across the aisle, the girl twisting strands of the boy's hair around black-nailed fingers, the boy stares into her face like it might be the last thing he ever lays eyes on, like that might be no kind of a bad thing, and Antoinette swallows and looks away. Move along, nothing to see here, nothing...

... the old witch can do to her. Lina stands before the hand basin in the Seventh Circle toilet. Waits for the dizziness and nausea to pass. It's the second time this week she's had to lock herself in here. Will herself to remain conscious. The episodes—the *attacks*—have something to do with Sally Paige, she knows that now. She feels it. Is the dying old witch trying to claw back some of the life she gave all those years ago? Trying to suck it right out of Lina like marrow from bone?

Let her try. See how far she gets. Jacqueline Paige doesn't live here anymore. There is no good daughter to draw from.

Lina gargles and spits. The taste of iron is still strong in her mouth. She freshens her lipstick then heads back out to the gallery floor.

'Someone you ate?' Becca asks. Her tone is saccharine.

Lina all but bares her teeth.

'Whatever.' The girl returns to her copy of *Art Monthly*. Licks her finger and flips a couple of pages. 'I think Dante might have been looking for you.'

Ryan Jellicoe has sent through the final show list. Titles and measurements, with and without framing. High-res images that Lina quickly scrolls through on Dante's laptop. Her boss watches from behind his desk. He's obviously unhappy.

'But this is good,' she says. 'We have a show finally.'

'Oh, do we?' he scoffs. Pointing out that it might be *a* show but it's not a *Seventh Circle* show. This gallery has made its name specialising in the flipside. The underbelly. Work that interrogates the mainstream. Art that isn't afraid of the dark. He stabs a finger towards the screen. 'All of which this is *not*.'

Lina smiles to herself. Ryan has titled the massive canvas *Expulsion*, after all. Brisbane as verdant floodplain. It'll be framed in recycled timber, the notes say. As will all the paintings.

'Glad you find it so amusing, Jacks. This hippy-trippy bullshit's gonna be the *only* stuff hanging on our walls for three fucking weeks. We're gonna have to hand out anti-nausea tabs at the door.'

She swivels the chair to face him. 'Stop being an idiot.'

'Excuse me?'

'All right, it's not entirely what you expected. But so what? This is good work, this is *excellent* work, actually. Ryan Jellicoe is going to be a major name one day and then you'll be able to crow to all and sundry about how you discovered him way back when. That ought to be enough to satisfy even your ego, surely?'

Dante glares at her. 'Here's an idea,' he snarls. 'How about I just handball the entire mess over to you?' No really, he continues, seeing how she's so smitten with the soon-to-be-deified Ryan Jellicoe, *she* can wrangle his show from this point on. Dante is washing his hands of the whole thing. Which means, of course, that Jacqueline gets to explain to their Fearless Leader and Holder of the Purse Strings how her take-no-prisoners dystopia became a dreadlocked greenie lovefest in less time than it would take to raze a rainforest.

'Susan Keyes commissioned this show?' Lina asks. 'I thought you—'

'There's not a thing that happens here, Susan doesn't approve. I can't even buy toilet paper without her signing off on the brand.' He sighs. Pulls his laptop back across the desk. Turns it around to face him. 'You know what? I'm serious.' His fingers jab at the keyboard. 'I'm sending all this to your email. The show's yours.'

'Dante—'

'You gonna manage this place once I'm gone, you better learn to *manage*.'

Lina blinks. 'Me?'

'Providing Susan signs off on it. Things go to plan, Segue opens in September and then I'm over there full-time. She could source management for Seventh Circle elsewhere, but better the devil you know, right? Beside, if I recommend you for the position...' And he smiles at her. Actually *smiles*, an expression more genuine than she would have thought him capable of producing. 'You picked the perfect time to grow yourself a backbone, Jacks.'

She smiles back at him, cautiously. 'The show will be fine. You'll see.'

'I better. Now call Jellicoe and find out how long that bloody framing's gonna take to happen. Remind him we're on a schedule, yeah?' Dante snorts. 'Recycled timber. Jesus.'

Lina descends the stairs with care, one hand skimming the rail. She's still somewhat off kilter from earlier and the last thing she wants to do is fall and break her soon-to-be-promoted neck. Another five, six months and she could be *running* Seventh Circle. On her own. The relief, the anticipation is intoxicating. She can't wait to tell Ant. She can't wait to tell...

... Loki pads into the kitchen while Antoinette is still eating breakfast, pushes a glossy black smartphone across the bench towards her. 'What's that?' she asks, swallowing a mouthful of cornflakes. '*Whose* is that?'

'Yours. Thought you might be missing your mobile.'

She hasn't been, actually. Has found it bloody refreshing to be at no one's beck and call, but all good things must come to some kind of an end, and so she picks up the phone and switches it on. Black wallpaper bleeds scarlet, drops that slide slowly down the screen to pool at the bottom, and she laughs, tells him that's cool, tells him that's goth as fuck, her Queen of the Night voice a little rusty but still camp enough to make him grin.

'Thought you'd like that. It's a pre-paid but the phone's unlocked. You should be able to put your old SIM card straight in there.'

Antoinette frowns. 'Where'd you get the cash? These things aren't cheap.'

'I didn't have to pay for it.'

'Loki...'

Really, he insists, it just happens. He's nice to people, that's all, and sometimes he asks them for things, or for favours, and sometimes—most of the time—they say yes. Lina says he *charms* people, that Antoinette made him *charming* in some real sense of the word, and maybe that's true. And the way he's looking at her right now, those grey eyes huge and puppyish and pleading, she can almost believe it.

'So, what, you just rock up and ask someone to hand over a brand new phone or a leather jacket, or whatever, and they say, sure, no problem, would you like me to wrap that up for you, sir? Hell, why don't we just march you down to the bank and be done with it?' She holds out her hands, palms joining to form a shallow bowl. 'Small denominations, if you don't mind, thanks ever so much.'

Loki shakes his head. 'It doesn't ... they have to be *willing*, on some level. If it's too big, if it's something they really don't want to do, or are too afraid to do ... I can't *force* them.'

He scowls, portrait of an adolescent thwarted, and Antoinette wonders again just what Loki does with his days. *Nothing special,* his vague response whenever she asks, or else *catching up with stuff*—having lived in the world less time than he remembers, there is apparently a lot of *catching up* to do—and it reminds her too painfully of how she and Jacqueline used to talk to their mother back in high school, and even later, and how *nothing* meant anything but.

Nothing we want you to know about.

Nothing we would expect you to understand.

Antoinette reaches for Loki's hand but he pulls away, steps away. 'Please,' he says. 'Please don't touch me like that.'

'Like what?'

'I can't...' He swallows, shoves both hands deep inside his pockets. 'Most of the time, I can keep it at a distance, keep it locked up. But I still love you, no matter how stupid and pointless it is. And when you touch me, even when you just look at me a certain way, it hurts. It physically hurts.'

'But I thought, I mean, now you're with Jacqueline—'

'I'm not *with* Jacqueline.'

'Loki, come on, you've been sleeping together for—'

'That's all we've been doing,' he says. '*Sleeping.*'

Antoinette stares at him. 'I don't follow.'

And so he explains. Halting and reluctant, like he's searching for words which simply aren't there to be found, but she gets enough of the gist from those he does manage to dredge up and drag back. The unseen chains that bind his heart to hers, that bind his body as well, and the pain that grips him, a terror vast and visceral and absolute, should he attempt to betray her with either. Telling her all this without resentment, without anger or recrimination—it's simply how it is, it's how *he* is—and to

Antoinette this makes it all the more vile.

Makes *her* all the more vile.

'No,' she says. 'Loki, no, that's not what I want. That's not why I—'

'Really?' His smile is sad and fleeting. 'What if it had all worked out, and you did still love me? Wouldn't I be exactly what you wanted—a man who could never hurt you, never leave you? If you *loved* me, wouldn't I be just *perfect*?'

This is the curse. This, right here, the knowledge of her own monstrosity. Because her crime is not her failure to love him. Her crime is that she created him in the first place—so thoughtlessly, so selfishly—this beautiful boy who is now forced to love her, who has no *choice* but to love her, who will be made to suffer for anything less.

And she thinks of her mother, thinks of Sally Paige with two perfected children and a third pulled bloody from her womb, and not one them enough to fill the void, to restore even a scrap of maternal feeling to her dried and desiccated heart. But raising her daughters regardless, joining mothers groups and devouring every childcare book she could get her hands on—faking it, if never making it—and at least she tried. She tried for twenty-seven years.

Antoinette can't hold it together for even a month.

'I have to head off,' Loki is saying. 'There's this thing...'

'Wait.' Uncertain if anything she does from this point on can make a difference, but she has to try, she has to fucking *try*. 'I don't care about you and my sister. No, that's not true, I do care, I

care a lot. I've seen the way you look at her and I've seen how she
… how different she is when she's around you. How *happy* she
is. I mean, hell, she's wearing colours. Colours that aren't *beige*.'

'Antoinette, this doesn't—'

'No, listen. Please.' She takes his hand in both of hers. He
flinches but doesn't pull away. 'The two of you are good together,
seriously, blind Freddy could see that. So if you love her, if you
think you might love her, then go for it. You won't be hurting me,
you'll be the *opposite* of hurting me, I swear.'

He lowers his gaze. 'It's not like I can stop feeling—'

'Then love us both,' she pleads. 'But be with her, *love* her,
if that's what you want.' Antoinette leans forward, presses her
forehead against his. 'I promise you, Loki, it's what I want too.'

For maybe a minute, they stand like that, before Loki steps back
and untangles his hand. 'I, um, I have to…' His eyes are glazed
and distant, the eyes of a wild animal, long-caged and grieving
for the woods. 'There's this thing.'

After he leaves, Antoinette stares into her milk-sodden
cornflakes and thinks some more about her mother, and about
responsibility and avoidance and guilt. Then she picks up the
phone Loki brought her and taps the screen into life. The contacts
list is empty of course—she'll need to resurrect her old SIM card
at some stage—but it doesn't matter. One number she's known
by heart since the age of seven at least, and she dials it now, holds
the phone to her ear and waits for…

...Loki to say something instead of simply standing there. Motionless, scarcely two steps inside the bedroom. Watching as she sorts through more of her clothes. That weird new expression on his face, as though Lina is an exotic insect that might equally sting him or flitter away should he move any closer.

'What?' she demands. 'You've been looking at me like that all night.'

He nods at the scarlet blouse in her hands. 'That suits you.'

'I bought it today.' The blouse goes into the wardrobe with the other items she has decided to keep. There isn't a huge amount of them. She takes out a well-worn skirt. Tailored, knee-length. A comfortable wool-blend the colour of weak and milky tea. Unquestionably a Jacqueline skirt. Lina unclips it from the hanger and tosses it into the charity bag. Better.

Behind her, footsteps approach.

She turns and Loki is there. He is right there, his eyes searching her face, his hands reaching for her hips. She opens her mouth but whatever words she intended to speak are lost when he kisses her. Gentle, cautious, brief. Too brief.

'What was that?' she asks.

'I still love her,' he says.

'All right.'

'I will always love her. It's part of what I am.'

'I know this,' Lina says, irritated. 'You don't have to—'

He kisses her again. Harder. His tongue pushing into her mouth, finding hers, thrusting against it. This time, when he draws away, his breath is ragged and torn. As is her own. 'I love you,' Loki whispers. 'I love you as well.'

She thinks about this. Not in the way Jacqueline would have, with her too careful weighing of *shoulds* against *should nots*. Her meticulous concern for presentation and the playing of roles. Lina thinks about how she feels. What she feels.

And she smiles. 'All right.'

At some point, as they kiss and strip each other of clothing, as she pushes him onto the bed and he pulls her down beside him, it occurs to her that Loki must, technically at least, be a virgin. For all the off-the-rack memories that jostle within his skull, the body that now moves against hers is untouched. Unclaimed. Unexplored. Lina finds she likes the idea of that. She likes it very much.

He kisses her throat, catching her skin lightly between his teeth. Strong hands roam the curves of her back and hip and thigh. She supposes that this is how her sister likes to be touched. That this is what she would have wanted Loki to do, had she still wanted him to do anything. She ponders that for a moment. Decides it doesn't matter. What is *she* but an amalgam of previous experience? Of techniques and tricks picked up from earlier lovers? What matters is now. Loki and Lina, here together. Learning how to be with each other.

'Stop thinking,' Loki whispers. He taps her on the forehead. Smiles.

'Is this all right?' She traces a finger over his mouth. 'Being with me like this? Last time, you talked about crossing a line.'

'It's an odd feeling,' he says. 'But not ... I think the line has shifted.'

He rolls her onto her back, trails kisses over her breasts and stomach. Only when his mouth moves further down does she flinch and clamp her legs together. 'Don't,' she says. 'I don't...' A momentary lapse, a small chink through which her shadow self attempts to crawl. Jacqueline Paige, who prefers darkness for encounters such as these. Darkness, or the forgiving flicker of candlelight. Better for her lovers not to see her scars. Better for her not to see the concern in their eyes. Concern or disgust or, occasionally, an altogether more prurient gleam.

'It's okay.' Loki presses his lips to her thighs. 'I know about these, remember?' His tongue flicks over her cross-hatched skin. 'They don't worry me.'

'I'm not going to explain. I don't think I can—'

'You don't have to.' He keeps kissing her. 'They're part of you, Lina, and you don't have to explain yourself.' Her name in his mouth. Sexier than anything else he could have said, and she feels herself loosen. Feels herself again become Lina. Flawed, lost, *imperfect*—but nevertheless *loved*. And she leans back. Arches against Loki's tongue, against Loki's hands, and allows herself to open.

'We seem to be pretty good at that,' Loki says later, much later, after they've exhausted themselves twice over.

She laughs. 'Pretty good, yes.'

She wants to tell him she loves him but the words catch in her throat. It's not something she has ever told anyone before. Not in this way. Not to mean what she wants to mean right now. Instead, she gets up to pee and brush her teeth. Considers the shower, but only for a moment. She doesn't want to be clean. Doesn't want the smell of him, the smell of *them*, to be gone so soon. Back in bed, Lina curls around him. Presses her face into his skin. Listens to his breath deepen and slow. She feels serene. Not the cool dissociation of the blade; far from it. She belongs to her body. To her flesh. It no longer frightens her. No longer seems a cage from which she must escape. She finds this mildly astonishing.

But we're not real, Jacqueline whispers. *Neither of us.*

Lina squeezes her eyes shut. Hugs Loki even tighter. 'I love you,' she tells him. 'So much.' She stays awake until she hears the front door open and her sister creep into the apartment. Then she relaxes. Lies still and listens to Ant make tea and get herself ready for bed. Such a different texture, this sisterly kind of love. Both more and less complicated than what she feels for Loki. Familiar, comfortable. Worn thin at times but never worn through.

Loki and Ant, the two halves of her heart.

Two halves? Jacqueline scoffs. *Try two thirds. At best.*

'Stop now,' Lina murmurs as she drifts towards sleep. Two halves. Two to make one whole and nothing in between. No dark sliver of space. No chamber, narrow and needy, forced closed for too many years.

Just her sister and her beloved. All that she loves. All that she needs to love.

Pitter patter, Jacqueline whispers. *Pitter patter.*

19

Antoinette's mother is right about Dr Chiang. He is a good man, a good doctor to have spent his morning up here on the mountain, sitting on the couch and drinking tea and explaining oh so patiently about syringe drivers and continuous subcutaneous injections and hydromorphone and metoclopramide and a million other scary-sounding medical words that he wrote down for them in careful block letters. Not that they would have to worry about any of that. Starting tomorrow, a homecare nurse would pop in each day to prepare and administer the prescribed dosage, and the nursing service would be on call if anything was needed between visits. Dr Chiang wrote down those details as well. He's taken care of everything—including, it seems, Sally Paige's determination not to be taken care of. Her mother sat passively in her armchair the whole time the doctor spoke. Silent and shrunken and wrapped in an oversized pink cardigan, she stared at her slippered feet and nodded whenever it seemed required of her.

At this stage, we're focusing solely on pain management.

We will make you as comfortable as we can.

Thank you, Sally. Thank you for allowing me to help.

'You care about my mother a lot,' Antoinette observes as she walks him out to his car. 'More than … more than you need to, I think.'

Dr Chiang smiles. 'I've known her a very long time.'

'Were the two of you ever … I'm sorry, this isn't an ethics thing, really. I'm just trying to find out who my mother was. Who she *is*.' She grimaces. 'I don't think I know her very well. Actually, I don't think I know her at all.'

He holds up his left hand, a wide gold band glinting in the sun. 'My wife and I have two children. Toby is a teacher now and Grace works in, ah, something to do with computers. Something to do with the internet—don't ask me exactly what she does, I never understand when she tries to explain it to me.' He twists the ring around his finger and his smiles fades, dials right the way down. 'I love my children, and my wife is an excellent mother to them. But if Sally hadn't married your father, or if your father had left her before…' Dr Chiang sighs. '*If*. So much regret in just two letters.'

'If I wasn't born?' Antoinette bristles. 'Is that what you mean? If your children that you *love so much* weren't ever born, then maybe you and my mother could have lived happily ever after in a castle far far away? Well, excuse us all for being so bloody inconvenient.'

He blinks. 'I'm sorry. That was tactless.'

'Yeah, well, you're not the first. My mother wishes she hadn't had me either.'

'I'm sure that's not true. Sometimes, people in her situation—'

'Her *situation*?'

'She's dying, Antoinette. She's frightened and she's in pain. If she says things that seem strange, or hurtful, then you need to make allowances.'

He opens the boot of his car, puts away his medical bag and briefcase, and when he straightens again his face has slid back into neutral. That caring Good Doctor face she remembers from when she was a kid. His hair now fading to grey, more lines dug in around his eyes, but still the kind, soft-spoken man who was always straight up about how much it would hurt, how long it would take to get better, how bad the medicine would taste going down.

'How's your sister?' he asks. 'You said she was working today?'

'Yeah, she's pretty busy right now.'

'Both of you should realise that your mother is looking at a prognosis of weeks, not months. If you're having trouble getting time off work, either of you, I'll be more than happy to write a letter to your employer.'

'It's not that. Jacqueline doesn't … there are some issues.'

I never want to see that woman again, Ant.

But she's our mother, Jacqueline. She's—

Your mother perhaps, not mine. She was never mine.

'Talk to her,' Dr Chiang says. 'The window for goodbyes is closing.'

His handshake is as firm as when he greeted her earlier, his skin cool and dry, and as Antoinette thanks him she searches his face for a sign that he knows more than he's letting on about Jacqueline and how she came to be, some hint that Sally Paige has confided in the good doctor after all. But there's nothing. Merely compassion and professional concern and maybe, just maybe, skulking wounded at their heels, the bone-weary sorrow of a heart too long misplaced.

'Does *she* love you?' she asks. 'I mean, if *you* weren't married...'

'*If*. That word again.' His laughter is shrapnel sharp. 'We've never spoken about it, not once. At this stage, I would rather not know.'

Back in the house, her mother is preparing tea. Hands shaking, more water splashing onto the counter than into the pot and Antoinette rushes to take the kettle from her. 'Here Mum, I'll do it.' Steers her away by shoulders grown thin enough to snap, more substance in all that pink wool than in what it covers and Antoinette can't believe how much her mother has deteriorated. Three weeks, not even, and god, she should have been here, how could she not have been here?

'I don't need help,' Sally Paige rasps. 'I'm managing fine.'

'Okay, sure, but I want to help. Please?'

A grunt, dismissive and scornful, but her mother nevertheless permits herself to be led back and resettled into her chair. Sits with knees drawn up beneath the rug that Antoinette finds in the linen closet and holds her teacup with both hands.

'I have to work tonight,' Antoinette tells her. 'But after this shift, I'm taking leave until—well, for as long as you need me. And, don't worry, I'll be back here in time for the nurse tomorrow morning.'

Her mother smiles grimly. 'My dutiful daughter.'

'Mum, please. I'm sorry … I didn't know what I was supposed to do. Last time, some of the stuff you said…'

'You don't have to come and look after me. I'll have a nurse.'

'You'll have a nurse for five minutes a day, Mum. You heard Dr Chiang, it's best to have someone here full time. Just in case.'

'Then I'll get a full-time nurse.'

'Your insurance won't cover a full-time nurse, and we can't afford—'

'How do you know what I can afford?'

'I looked into this a little, Mum. It's not cheap, that kind of care.'

Her mother snorts. 'You think I don't know? You think I haven't *looked into this a little* myself?' She sips at her tea. 'There's still something left from selling your grandmother's house, even after paying off this one. I've been a bookkeeper going on fifteen years now, my dear. Tricky as they are, the concepts of savings and investments haven't eluded me completely.'

'Okay,' Antoinette says. 'That's good, that gives us options.'

Even this sick, Sally Paige can summon a glare cold enough to frost glass. 'You don't need to take care of me.' But her voice cracks and she digs into the sleeve of her cardigan for a crumpled tissue, holds it to her mouth as she coughs.

'You took care of me,' Antoinette tells her. 'You took care of both of us, me and Jacqueline, even though you never … I mean, you could have put us up for adoption or something. You could have gone on with your life.'

Her mother grimaces. 'We make our beds. Just because I couldn't feel like a mother, doesn't mean I didn't still want to be one.' An odd kind of gentleness settles over her face, a warmth that seems almost out of place. 'I raised two daughters, two good daughters. I did that. I can be proud of that.'

'Yes,' Antoinette says. 'You did.' Because being a Sally Paige *project* is better than nothing, better than being a failed experiment or, worse, the living reminder of a decision ill-made. 'For what it's worth, I do love you. Sometimes, especially these last few weeks, I haven't really wanted to feel that, but, you're still my mother. You're the only mother I have.'

'What about your sister?'

'She's, um, she's pretty upset by all this. I don't know if she—'

'No, what I'm asking is, do you *love* Jacqueline?'

The question startles her. 'Of course. Why wouldn't I?'

'Even though you know what she is.'

'That doesn't…' Antoinette tries to shave the edge from her voice. 'She's my *sister*, is what she is. Nothing else is important. Nothing.'

'Well then.' Her mother winces as she reaches around to place her cup on the side table. 'I need you to do something for me. For Jacqueline. I've been thinking about it and I believe it's the right thing to do. It's what any good mother would do, yes.'

'What is it?'

'I need you to take Jacqueline from me.'

'I don't understand.'

'You feel your boy, yes?' Her mother's fingers curl into a fist, tap lightly against her own breastbone. 'In here?'

Antoinette nods. 'It's like a small weight, like a stone.'

A stone, Sally Paige agrees, although she has never thought of it quite like that, but yes. And it will always be there, the link, the connection between the two of them—Loki won't feel it but it's what tethers him to her. It's what keeps him alive. Because perfections are not completely autonomous, not in the way human beings are; they're dependent on their makers, their hosts, for an ongoing source of—energy? essence? soul?—no one has ever agreed on the terminology, let alone the precise mechanics of the process, but that doesn't stop it from working the way it does. When the host dies, so does any perfection connected to her. Every time.

'So when you...' Antoinette swallows. 'Jacqueline will, what? Disappear? Like the fendlies used to?'

'That would be convenient, wouldn't it? I've already told you, dear, perfections are not the same as whimsies. They're flesh and blood, like any other living thing. And like any other living thing, they leave a corpse behind them when they go.'

'She's just going to die?' No, not her sister. Not Jacqueline. *No.* 'But she's only twenty-seven. It's not fair—'

'Oh, grow up, child! Since when does *fair* hold any weight in this world?'

Antoinette fights back tears. 'But you said I could take her from you? And that would work? She'd still be here then, after you, you know.'

'You can say it. I'm not in any kind of denial.' A wry smirk hooks her mouth, and she looks more like Sally Paige than she has all morning. 'And yes, if I give her to you she will survive my death. It's been done before.'

Relief twists fresh with doubt. 'But if she's *my* perfection, will I still love her? Or will it be like with Loki?'

The smirk doesn't leave her mother's face. 'Would it matter?'

'It's just that I love her so much. She's the only person left that I *can* love. If I lose that...'

'You'd rather she die then?'

'No! Of course not, I just...'

'Stop snivelling.' Her mother sighs. 'This is transference, not creation. It won't change a thing in terms of how you feel towards your sister—or how *I* feel, on the off chance you were wondering.'

'I'm sorry, I'm still trying to get my head around all this.'

'There is one thing you'll need to give up.'

Antoinette rubs at her eyes. 'Do I even want to know?'

'If you take your sister, you won't be able to hold on to that boy of yours.'

It's impossible, Sally Paige explains; no woman can host two mature perfections of such complexity as Jacqueline and Loki, especially when one of them wasn't even hers to begin with. Assimilating her sister will be draining enough without having to maintain Loki at the same time. Sally Paige rubs her lips back and forth, and no, she says over Antoinette's objections, there's no way around it. Antoinette will take her sister, and Sally will accept the boy. A swap like this is less simple than a one-way transfer, but it can be done. It will be done.

Jacqueline for Loki. Fair exchange. No refunds, no returns.

'But what happens to him?' Antoinette asks. 'When you die?'

'I told you what happens.'

'No.' She springs to her feet, paces with fast, anxious strides. 'I can't just let him … no. I can't do that.'

'Why not? You don't love him.' Her mother merely stares at her. A fish could exhibit more emotion than Sally Paige right now. 'He was a mistake, dear. You need to fix it.'

'But I do love him. Not in *that* way, sure, but it's still love.' Tears slide down her cheeks, and she snatches a tissue from the box on the coffee table. 'He's like family, Mum, he's *my family*, and I'm responsible for him. You're asking me to kill him. To let you kill him.'

'No. I'm asking you to save your sister's life.'

'What if I just have them both?'

'That's impossible, I told you. You could never—'

'Why?' Antoinette shouts. 'Why is it impossible, Mum? What happens if I have them both? You made Jacqueline *and* Charlie, remember? You made two perfections, so it can't be *impossible*.'

'Best case scenario?' The words are cold and hard. 'You get tired—more than tired; exhausted, *fatigued*—all the time. Every minute, every day. Your body can't handle the stress so you get sick, maybe you get cancer, yes? You follow? Our bodies aren't made to cope with this. Supporting lives not our own. One is bad enough, you'll see. But two? My dear, you have no idea.'

Antoinette wipes her nose. 'But Charlie's been ... gone for years.' Her hands are shaking and she doesn't, really does not, want to talk about any of this. Not Loki, not Charlie, not either of them.

runstopbadrunstopbad

Her stomach clenches and rolls. Bile burns at the back of her throat.

'Who knows exactly what damage is done when they're made,' her mother is saying. 'How long it takes for the rot to set in. I didn't think about any of that when I made the twins. Or maybe I did and just decided it didn't matter, that children would be different, less of a drain. Which, actually, they were. But, with you, we're not talking about a couple of little babies.'

'You—you said that was the best case scenario. What's the worst?'

Her mother shrugs. 'You slip into a coma, become nothing more than a life support system for them until your body finally gives up and dies. Then they die too, of course, and you tell me what the point was in all of that.'

She can't breathe. She literally can't breathe, can't feel anything but the weight of the Loki-stone inside her, and oh god, she can't just surrender him, she can't just let him die, can't breathe can't breathe can't—

'Calm down.' Sally Paige standing right in front of her now, claws digging into her shoulders and no sympathy in those fish-flat eyes, only disgust and something that might be envy or pity or spite. 'Stop it, calm down.' And Antoinette breathes at last, sucks air deep into her lungs and throws her arms around the woman who is the only mother she will ever know, god help them both, and squeezes her tight. For maybe a minute they stand there, with Sally Paige rubbing her daughter's back and Antoinette waiting for the words she knows will never come.

I love you. Everything will be all right.

And in that silence, her stupid, hopeful heart breaks a little more.

Finally, her mother disentangles herself. Leads Antoinette over to the couch and sits her down. 'I am sorry,' she says. 'But you need to make a choice. It's your sister, or it's that boy. You can't keep them both.'

Becca taps on the office door. Pokes her head around. 'There's some guy downstairs, wants to see you. He's a bit, um, weird.'

Lina flips to the second page of the catering quote and frowns. Expensive. Too expensive. She'll need to do some trimming to get it past Dante. And there's still the alcohol to consider. 'Does weird guy have a name?'

'He didn't want to give it. But he said it was important.'

'Really?' Lina arches an eyebrow.

'I told him you were busy, but he said he could wait. That he *would* wait.' The girl fiddles with the string of red plastic beads around her neck. 'He's, um, kinda creeping me out, Jacqueline.'

Lina sighs. 'All right. Tell him I'll be there in a minute.'

She's halfway down the stairs before she sees him. Loki. In the back corner, looking at the cyborg portraits. Lina grins. Then feels bad. She hopes he hasn't come to take her to lunch because she simply doesn't have the time. Not today. Not for the next couple of weeks. Until Ryan's opening night is well and truly behind her, she'll be sending Becca out for sushi and eating it at her desk.

'This is a surprise,' she calls.

Loki turns and—she falters. Not Loki, no. Not with those scowling, mud-dark eyes. Not with that arrogant, fuck-you sneer.

'Where is she?' Paul asks, stalking across the gallery floor to meet her. 'I know some friend of yours hooked her up with a place in St Kilda.'

Lina narrows her eyes. 'If you say so.'

'I just need to have a few words, that's all.'

She pauses two steps from the ground. All the better to look down at him. 'Why are you asking me, Paul? Just call her.'

'Thanks, I didn't think of that.' He sucks air through his teeth. She's always hated the way he does that. 'I've been calling her. The phone's always off and she doesn't ring back, doesn't reply to my texts. Fuck knows if she even checks her email. I dropped by Simpatico but that sour-faced bitch—what's her name, Melissa? Melinda?—said she isn't working there anymore. That true?'

'I don't know,' Lina says carefully. 'I'm not my sister's keeper.'

'Yeah, right. Like Ant doesn't wipe her arse without telling you.'

'If she doesn't want to talk to you, Paul, then *she doesn't want to talk to you*. What makes you think I would be on your side?'

'I'm not asking you to be on my side. I just need to see her.'

'I can't help you with that. Sorry.'

'Fuck you, Jacqueline.' He thumps the railing. Hard. 'Tell me where she is. I'm not mucking about here.'

Over his shoulder, she can see Becca standing behind the sales counter. The girl looks even more nervous than she did upstairs. Her hand hovers near the phone. 'Is everything okay, Jacqueline?'

'It's fine,' Lina tells her. She takes one step down. Eye level. Leans in close to a face which is so like, and yet so clearly not, the one she loves. 'Fuck *you*, Paul,' she whispers. 'If and when my sister has anything to say to you, she knows where to go looking. Not that you should hold your breath—I don't hear her crying herself to sleep each night.'

He glares at her, teeth clenched. The muscles on either side of his jaw twitch. She remembers Ant's account of the night they broke up. The violence etched raw into his face and how her sister feared he might strike her. How he took his anger out on her laptop instead, smashing it to pieces. Lina suspects he would like to do much the same to her right now.

'You should go,' she tells him. Becca has picked up the phone now. Her eyes ask the question. Lina shakes her head. 'It's all right,' she says in a loud, clear voice. 'He's leaving now.'

Paul follows her gaze. Steps back with his hands lifted. A mocking surrender, that same old sneer curling his mouth. 'I'm going, I'm going. No need to call in the cavalry, *ladies*.' But as the glass doors slide open before him, he stops and turns back around. 'She's still crashing with you, isn't she? There is no place in St Kilda.'

Lina crosses her arms.

'You're still over in Port Melbourne, yeah?'

'She's not there, Paul.'

He chuckles. It's not a nice sound. 'You never did know how to lie.'

'I'm not lying. She had something to do today. She won't be there.'

'That's okay,' he says. 'I can wait.'

After he leaves, Becca scurries to her side. 'Who was that jerk?'

'My sister's ex-boyfriend. He's having trouble adjusting.'

'Sounds like she's better off without him.'

'Undoubtedly,' Lina says, then excuses herself and hastens back upstairs to the office. To her phone, waiting on the desk. The home number is picked up by the answering machine and she waits impatiently for her own voice to finish its greeting. 'Ant? Loki? If either of you are there, can you please—'

'Lina? What's wrong?'

'Loki.' His voice sounds odd over the phone. Too high-pitched. Too nasally. Too much like the man who just stormed out of the gallery. 'Is my sister home? We might have a bit of a problem.'

'No, she…' A pause. 'I think she's still up at your mother's. Why?'

Your mother's. Lina winces. Pushes the words aside. Because that's good, that's fine. 'Loki, listen, I think Paul is on his way over to you.' Silence. Stiff-spined and bristled. 'Don't do anything rash, all right? In fact, don't even answer the door. Just pretend no one's home.'

'What does he want?'

'He's looking for Ant. I told him she wasn't there but he didn't believe me.'

'I don't want him here. This is *my* home, he can't be here.'

'I know, and I'm going to ring Ant right now. See if she can call him, head him off at the pass.' All too clearly, she can picture the scowl on Loki's face. His knuckles whitening around the handset. 'Just don't do anything stupid. Please?'

'He can't be here,' Loki says again.

Before she can reply, the phone clicks in her ear. Lina swears and tries to call her sister. The old number bounces straight to voicemail. The new one rings and rings and rings before finally inviting her to press hash to leave a callback number. She scrolls through her contacts. *Sally Paige.* Hesitates, then presses call.

'Hello?' The voice is hoarse, rough as sandpaper. 'Who is this?'

'It's—it's me. I need to speak to my sister.'

'She left a while ago, dear.'

Dear. Lina will be happy if she never hears that word again. Certainly not from lips as mocking and loveless as Sally Paige's.

'Jacqueline.' The woman coughs. Clears her throat. 'I realise that—'

Lina hangs up. Battles the urge to throw her phone at the wall. Stamp it to pieces beneath her foot. Instead, she drops the thing into her bag and wipes her hands on her skirt. Perhaps later it will feel less soiled. For now, she needs to worry about Loki. And what he might do when Paul comes knocking at his door.

He can't be here.

Lina grabs a couple of CabCharge vouchers from Dante's drawer and hurries back downstairs. Becca looks up at the sound of her heels. Lina tells herself that it's merely concern, and not some species of schadenfreude, that glitters so brightly in her widening eyes. 'Is everything okay?' the girl asks.

'A minor emergency.' Lina drops the gallery's spare keyring on the counter. 'I shouldn't be too long, but I'll leave you with this in case I'm held up. Will you be all right to close?'

Becca nods. 'Your sister, is she okay?'

'I'm sorry?'

'Oh, I just thought … with her ex-boyfriend coming in here like that.'

'Most likely it's nothing,' Lina says.

'That's good, I hope so.' The girl's smile is too lean. Too shallow. It doesn't quite mask her disappointment. 'No offence to your sister, but that guy really creeped me out. Like, big time. I'd hate to get on his bad side.'

⌑

When Antoinette lets herself into the apartment, Loki is right there in the hall, as close to the door as he can get without being hit in the face when it swings open, and she jumps back, makes a sound like a cat drowning in a sack, some stupid girlie squeal that she swallows before it grows up to become a scream.

'What the hell are you doing?' She thumps him in the chest with both hands, so hard he rocks back on his feet a little. 'You scared the life out of me.'

'Sorry.' He looks over her shoulder. 'Did Lina call you?'

'Yeah, a while ago, but I was driving.' No kind of a lie in that, although she wouldn't have answered even if she'd been sitting flat on her arse by the side of the road. No way could she talk to Jacqueline just then. Not with her mother's words still rattling around in her head like poisoned barbs. She needed time to think. 'I was going to call her back once I—hey!'

Loki grabs her by the wrist and yanks her all the way inside. 'So you haven't talked to him?' He slams the door, leans past her to check the peephole.

'Haven't talked to who?' Antoinette dumps her bag onto the hall table, tosses her keys into the small wooden bowl her sister keeps just for that purpose. 'What's going on?'

'Paul.' He says the name like it tastes bad.

'Why would I have talked to Paul?'

And he tells her about the phone call from Jacqueline, what she actually said as well as what he picked up from the tremor in her voice, and no, he's not saying that Paul threatened her explicitly, only that she sounded shaken up. She sounded scared—his Lina, *scared*—and if the gutless bastard dares to show his face around here, Loki's going to teach him what that word really means.

'Stop,' Antoinette says. 'Please. He can't know about you. How do I even start to explain?'

'Why do you care?'

That look she knows, and how it frightens her to see it on *this* face as well. The curl of his lip, the brutal gleam in his eye like he wants to take someone's neck and snap it in his hands, like it might not even matter if that neck is hers—*Was that important to you, Ant? As important as me?*—and she moves away from him, two useless steps before her back meets the wall, and she doesn't even realise that she's raised her right hand, fingers curled to a loose and trembling fist, until he reaches out and closes it gently within his own.

'No,' he whispers, horrified. 'Not you, Antoinette, never you.'

'You scared me,' she says. 'The way you looked…'

'I'm sorry, I'm so sorry. I would never hurt you, not in a million years. I'd sooner cut off my own hands.'

'I know that,' she tells him. 'I do. It's just—'

The doorbell chimes and Antoinette jumps yet again, swears beneath her breath. She'll be lucky to get through this day without a heart attack, or a restraining order, considering the daggers Loki is throwing towards the front door right now, and please please please let it be a Jehovah's Witness, or some student touting for the power companies. She'll sign anything, she'll buy every copy of the *Watchtower* they have, just don't let it be—

'Come on, Ant,' Paul calls out. 'I saw you pull up. I know you're in there.'

Loki takes a step forward.

'Don't,' Antoinette whispers. 'Please, just wait in Jacqueline's room. I'll get rid of him, okay?'

'He can't come in here. I don't want him in here.'

But at least he goes, disappearing into the room which she supposes belongs to him these days as well. Loki and Lina sharing a bed for more than just sleeping now, to judge by the noises she sometimes hears, and really, how does that do anything but make the whole bloody mess even worse?

You need to make a choice. You can't keep them both.

Paul rings the bell again, gives the door itself a few solid whacks with what sounds like the flat of his fist. 'I just need to talk to you, Ant. I'm not going to leave until you open this door.'

Antoinette takes a deep breath and does just that.

20

'So much for the flat in St Kilda.'

The first words out of his mouth, accompanied by the most unpleasant of smirks, and she stares at him for a second, thoroughly confused. Oh, but of course: her idiotic impromptu face-saver that night on his front steps—how does he even remember?—and she scrambles for recovery. 'Yeah, the flat. That, ah, fell through.'

'I'll bet.'

'What do you want, Paul?'

'Not to have this conversation out here, for a start.'

He doesn't force his way in as much as simply push past. Like he has the right, like she's the one at fault for not stepping quickly enough out of his path, and though the idea of shoulder-checking him has definite appeal, Antoinette's only too aware that she sorely lacks the muscle for any kind of follow through. Physical is the very last thing she wants to get with Paul.

Contenting herself with sarcasm instead, 'Oh no, *please*,' as she trails him down the hall to the living room. 'Do make yourself at home.'

'Holy crap,' he laughs. 'It's like an episode of *Hoarders* in here. How the fuck has Little Miss Perfect put up with you for so long?'

Antoinette surveys the boxes lumped around the room, half of them open and spilling their guts because Loki packed everything willy-nilly and without care for labels, so whenever she needs to find a clean blouse or a box of tampons or a tube of work-friendly lipstick, it's pretty much a case of search and destroy. Add to that the plastic bags filled with rejects from Jacqueline's wardrobe and the stacks of second-hand books that Loki has been accumulating—mythology and folklore, a complete Brothers Grimm, and even some quasi-historical account of the Golem of Prague—and yeah, okay, it's a bit of a mess.

But, really, fuck Paul.

Fuck him for coming over here, for shoehorning his judgemental arse into their home—hers and Lina's and Loki's—and making her feel like some disobedient brat who refuses to clean up her room.

'Well?' She folds her arms across her chest. 'What is it?'

Paul takes a book from the couch, flicks through the pages. 'You know, I could deal with you sneaking back in to get your shit. You don't want to see me, fine. You swap a few photos around, set fire to some rose petals, even the thing with the jacket—which rated pretty damn high on the psycho-meter, Ant, let me just say—but, okay, whatever.' He snorts. 'Better than coming home to find a rabbit boiling on the stove.'

'I didn't do any of that.'

But she wonders. The photos reduced to blank paper, the roses rendered to ash: Paul said that happened the very first weekend—the weekend they broke up, the weekend she made Loki—and Antoinette now knows far too much to believe in the Coincidence Fairy. She needs to talk to her mother.

Paul tosses the book back towards the couch. It falls short, bounces onto the floor. He doesn't bother to pick it up. 'As far as revenge goes, that shit is kind of pathetic, but again, whatever. Imagination never was your strong suit.'

'You might be surprised what I can imagine.'

'Oh? You stealing another novel? Pretty sure that doesn't count.'

'Fuck off, Paul. I don't need to listen to this.'

'Yeah, actually, you do. Because I draw the line when you start trying to sell your shit to my friends.'

'What the hell are you on about?'

'Whatever you've been telling Greta, it's working.'

'Greta? I haven't spoken to her for weeks.'

'Really. That's why she won't talk to me, is it?'

'This might come as a shock, Paul, but my life doesn't revolve around you—not for a while now. Maybe Greta finally woke up as well, maybe she sees you for the pretentious wanker that you are.'

He glares at her. 'Funny bitch, aren't you? As far as I remember, it was *me* who dumped *your* whiny, fat arse.'

Antoinette wonders just when it was that he changed, when he turned into this pathetic, venomous prick she can't imagine wasting even one chamber of her heart on loving—except that, no, he was always like this, wasn't he? Always at the ready with a nasty jibe or droll serving of snark. The only difference is that now the venom is being directed towards her.

'You need to leave,' she tells him.

'And you need to stay the fuck away from my friends.'

He moves towards her in a measured, square-shouldered way she supposes is intended to be menacing, but she stands her ground, gestures a hand in the direction of the door. 'After you.'

'If you think that...'

Antoinette's never been fond of the phrase, *you look like you've seen a ghost*. It's always seemed too empty, too imprecise—for a start, most of the people she once hung around with would likely have been thrilled to spy a spectre or phantom of any stripe—and yet those very words seem the perfect description of the expression that now seizes Paul's face. His widening eyes, the incredulous gape of his jaw, and as she turns to follow his gaze, her stomach sinks.

'You were asked to leave,' Loki says. He stands motionless in the hall just outside the living room, hands clenched to fists by his sides.

Paul shakes his head. 'Who the hell are you?'

'You shouldn't be here.'

Loki moves forward and Antoinette steps in front of him, tells him to stop, to please just let her handle this, and behind her

Paul is asking his question again, voice pitched high and shaken as he demands to know who the hell this guy is, what the fuck is going on, and then Loki is grabbing her by the shoulders, hands moving her aside like a parent might guide a wayward toddler out of harm's reach, and she wriggles from his grasp, so *sick* of being treated like some kid who doesn't know any better, who can't look out for herself.

'Loki,' she snaps. 'Will you just wait a second?'

The two of them, Loki and Paul, now less than an arm's length apart, and Paul straightens himself, slaps fist onto palm in a show of such stupid bravado she almost wants to punch him herself. 'Better listen to her, mate,' he says without much conviction. 'I will fuck you up if I have to.'

Loki smiles, lean and dangerous. 'You've never hit anyone in your life.'

'Yeah? And what would you know about—'

The first blow catches Paul in the guts and, as he crumples over with a hard and breathless *oof*, the second lands right on his jaw, propels him sideways and onto the ground. All of this happening in a matter of moments, and Antoinette yelps in surprise, lurches herself forward even as Loki grabs a handful of Paul's hair and pulls his head back, fist raised and—

'No!' Shouting at him, taking hold of his arm and this time there is nothing gentle in the way Loki shakes her off, shoves her so violently from him that she stumbles and trips, foot sliding on a stray book and knee connecting with the corner of the coffee table as she falls. Tears smarting in her eyes, she rolls over to see that Paul has managed to wrestle himself from Loki's grip, wrestle or maybe land a stray punch of his own to judge by the way Loki is rubbing the side of his face. He staggers to his feet, retreating with two fists held unsteadily before him as Loki grins again, savage alpha dog smile, and closes the distance between them.

'Loki,' Antoinette calls. 'Loki, please.'

He glances around, sees her down there on the floor, rubbing at her kneecap, and that awful grin slides away. 'Antoinette? What are you...'

And then there are keys rattling in the front door, and the door opening and slamming shut again, and Jacqueline calling out anxious *hellos* and *are you theres* as she hurries down the hall. When she gets to the living room she hesitates, eyes moving in quick appraisal over the three of them—Loki and Paul and Antoinette who is just now making a grab for the couch to pull herself upright—and then nods, reaches into her bag for a tissue before marching across the room to Paul.

'Here,' she says.

He stares at the scrap of white in her hand like it might explode.

'You're bleeding,' she tells him. 'Your lip.'

He takes the tissue, presses it to the corner of his mouth and winces.

'Now you need to go.'

Paul shakes his head, manages to resurrect a slim, scarlet-stained sneer. 'Not until someone explains *him* to me.'

PERFECTIONS

A cobra couldn't strike as fast as Loki. He has Paul flattened against the wall in less than a second, the sound of skull meeting plasterboard so loud Antoinette is amazed that one of them hasn't cracked, his hand squeezed tight around Paul's throat as he leans in close, whispering, whispering, and it's not just a ghost her ex-boyfriend is seeing now, oh no, nothing so harmless as that.

This isn't what Paul looks like when he's scared.

This is what Paul looks like when he's utterly fucking terrified.

'Loki.' Jacqueline rests a palm between his shoulder blades. 'Stop now. Enough.'

'He can't be here,' Loki says to her.

'I know.'

The hand around Paul's throat relaxes, drops. Paul reels away, coughing like his lungs are about to burst and when he catches Antoinette's eye she sees in him such a confusion of hatred and doubt, it chills her. She doesn't know this man at all, doesn't know his doppelganger either, that creature over there beside her sister, still so full of malice it all but boils from his skin.

'Don't ever come back here,' Loki says to Paul. 'If you come back here again, you won't get to walk away.'

And Paul at least has the good sense to say nothing this time. Merely glares and coughs and spits a bloody gob onto the carpet before backing from the room. Antoinette follows him down the hall. Reaches for his arm as he reaches for the doorknob. 'Paul, wait. Are you okay?'

'What do you care how I am?'

'I just—'

'Who is he? He knew about ... shit he shouldn't know about, shit *no one* knows about.' He wipes his mouth on his sleeve. 'I should go to the cops, is what I should do. This is assault.'

'You do that,' she says. 'Tell them how you met yourself. Tell them how you let yourself get beat up. By yourself. I'm sure they'll be fascinated.'

'That's not—he's *not* me.'

'Go home, put some ice on your face. Pretend this never happened.' Antoinette retrieves her keyring from the bowl on the side table and removes the two keys to her old flat. 'Here, I kept meaning to drop these off.'

He shakes his head. 'I changed the locks. Got sick of *someone* sneaking around the place while I was out.'

'I'm sorry about that. I told him to stop.'

'He's a fucking psychopath, whatever else he is.'

'No,' she says. 'He's just ... new.'

Lina frowns, mulling over her sister's words. Ant is obviously still upset by what happened between Loki and Paul. She wishes she could have reached the apartment sooner.

'So this *transfer*, from her to you. It's a simple procedure?'

Ant shrugs. 'Mum hasn't told me exactly how it all works yet. Just that we have to try or else ... you know.'

Or else Sally Paige will take Lina with her. Yes.

'And the bond, the energy link. That's the reason I've been having my, ah, health problems? Because *she* is dying?'

'It's connected,' Ant says. 'Whenever the pain got too much, she would sort of *drift away from herself*, was how she put it. Some kind of hardcore meditation, I didn't really understand it. She said she felt the link drift with her, but didn't realise it was actually having a physical effect on you until I told her how you were fainting and so on.'

'She was sucking energy from me back to herself.'

'That's not how she put it, but maybe. She switched to stronger pain meds a couple of weeks ago, said they helped. And tomorrow she starts on this hydromorph … morph something, I can't remember. It's meant to be really strong, like five times stronger at least than the tablets, so…'

There's something Ant is holding back. Lina can tell.

'What if she's lying?' Loki speaks up from his chair across the room. 'What if she doesn't want to simply hand over Lina? What if she wants to take something from you as well?'

Ant looks worried. 'What do you mean? What could she take?'

'*Your* energy,' he says. 'Your life, if that's possible. Maybe she doesn't like the idea of dying so much now she's getting close to the end.'

'No,' Ant tells him. 'It's not like that. She just wants to make sure Jacqueline survives after she's gone. That's all.'

Lina laughs. 'Because she's such a wonderful mother.'

'She tried to be. And it couldn't have been easy, feeling the way she did.' Ant glances again at Loki. 'She's *still* trying, even now.

So cut her some slack, okay?'

'I'm sorry,' Lina says. 'I know you still care about her.'

'God knows why,' Loki mumbles and turns a page in his book. Something called *The Pygmalion Effect*, its glossy cover sporting the famous painting by Raoux. He seems to spend most of his time reading these days. Reading, or chasing links around obscure corners of the web.

There has to be something written about us, Lina. We aren't the first of our kind, and surely we can't be the last. Give me time, I'll find it.

Lina takes her sister's hand. 'What aren't you telling us?'

'Nothing,' Antoinette says. She looks away. Rubs at her knee which is already beginning to bruise. 'I mean, Mum won't tell me hardly anything about how this stuff works. She doesn't want me to know, doesn't want me to ever try and use it again. You know she thinks it's some kind of curse.'

'Maybe she doesn't really know how it works,' Loki says.

'Maybe,' Ant concedes. 'But she knows more than me right now.'

'You're afraid,' Lina says. Her sister looks up. Eyes cagey as Lina has seldom seen them over the course of their lives. Usually only when there is something Ant thinks Lina would be better off not knowing. 'There's a risk to this, isn't there? Something you're keeping to yourself.'

'No, I already said—'

'Could I be hurt somehow?' Lina studies her sister's reactions.

From the corner of her eye, she is aware that Loki is watching them both carefully. 'Could *you* be hurt, is that it? Are you putting yourself at risk for me?'

Ant opens her mouth. Closes it again without speaking a word. She doesn't have to. The look on her face is enough.

Lina feels ill. 'Then you can't do it. Not if you might get hurt or … or worse. No, I won't allow it.'

'You'd take the risk for me,' her sister says. 'Wouldn't you?'

'That's different, that's—'

'No.' Ant shakes her head. 'You're my sister, Jacqueline, and I love you. *I love you*, do you understand what that means? For me, now? There's no way I can just stand by and let you die, not if there's anything I can do to prevent it.' Her voice is close to breaking. Her eyes glisten.

'All right.' Lina reaches our her arms. Pulls her sister into them. 'All right then. Just promise me you'll be safe. That you won't do anything rash.'

'You're my family,' Ant whispers. 'You're the only family I'm going to have left. There's nothing I won't do for you, Jacqueline. Not a bloody thing.'

And Lina holds her tight as Ant snuffles into her shoulder. She smiles at Loki, who smiles back. She loves him. Sometimes, like now, she can't quite believe how much. 'It's all right,' she murmurs, pressing her lips to her sister's hair. 'Because we *are* family, the three of us. You and me and Loki. And no one—especially not that old witch on the mountain—is ever going to come between us.'

♋

Lina taps on the study door. Waits for her sister to invite her inside before she opens it. Ant is sitting up in the futon bed, brow furrowed as she taps away at the screen of her phone. 'You're up late,' she says, not raising her head.

'I couldn't sleep,' Lina tells her. 'How was your last night?'

'Kinda weird. Ronan was pissed about the late notice until I explained I had to go look after Mum, and then he was actually pretty decent about letting me take as much leave as I wanted. Of course, he also must have spread the word around. Even the bloody chefs were giving me the kid-glove treatment.'

Lina surveys the room. The futon which takes up almost every inch of spare space when it's folded out. Her sister's work clothes crumpled over the back of the desk chair. The suitcase crowded against the wall. They can't keep living like this. They need to find a bigger place, one with two proper bedrooms at least. With her and Ant both working, they should be able to afford it. Soon perhaps. Once the Sally Paige situation has been … *resolved*. She likes that word. Likes the way it sounds in her head. Resolved, yes.

Her sister swears. 'I hate typing on this thing. Bloody autocorrect.'

'Are you busy? I can talk to you in the morning…'

'No, no, I'll only be a sec. Just trying to reply to Greta.'

'Greta has your new number?'

'Fat chance. I sent her a message through Facebook before work, told her to make it clear to Paul that whatever beef she has with him, it's got absolutely nothing to do with me. For what that might be worth.'

'And?'

'She apologised, said she'd talk to Paul. She also asked if I wanted to catch up for coffee.'

'Why? I always thought she was more Paul's friend than yours.'

'Why does Greta do anything?' A few more quick taps before she grimaces and tosses the phone onto the mattress beside her. 'Fuck it, I've played the cancer card. Told her I'd be away caring for my dying mother for the foreseeable. Maybe she'll take that for an answer seeing as she doesn't seem to understand *no*.'

Lina perches herself on the end of the futon. 'I need to ask you a favour.'

'Sure.'

'It's not a small favour.'

The smile falls from her sister's face. Without it, she looks exhausted. Shadows darken the hollows of her eyes. Twin grooves etch deep at the corners of her mouth. Briefly, Lina considers simply letting this go as a bad idea. But she's been lying in bed all night, listening to Loki breathe and rolling words around in her head as though they're magic beads. As though she simply needs to figure out the right pattern, the right combination, for them to work.

She has to ask. If only once. 'Could you...' Her throat is dry, her tongue thick and unwieldy. 'Would you make me ... *perfect* me a child?'

Ant says nothing. Merely stares, wide-eyed and white-faced. A night-dwelling creature caught in torchlight.

'You know I can't have children of my own,' Lina rushes on. 'I've lived with that fact for years, accepted it—and, of course, now I know why. But if you could create a child for me ... it would be the only thing I would ever ask of you, Ant, I promise. Just one child, that's all I want. That's all I've ever wanted.'

Her sister is already shaking her head. 'Jacqueline, I can't. Even if I knew how to do something like that—'

'You made Loki. Can't you just—'

'Loki was an accident, and look how that turned out.'

'What do you mean?'

'He could have *killed* Paul this afternoon.'

'But he didn't.'

'He wanted to, I saw it in his face. Jacqueline, I was so scared.'

'Loki has some difficulties,' Lina says carefully. 'You might too if you were just dumped into the world with a head full of memories not your own. But this would be a child, a baby even. We would love it and raise it and—'

'I wouldn't love it. That's what happens, remember?'

'Even if you're not making it for yourself?'

Ant smiles, bitter and close to breaking. 'You're right. But if I do this for you, out of my deep and abiding *sisterly love*—what do you suppose the price might be then, Jacqueline?'

She thinks of Sally Paige. How her eyes would flatten and glaze whenever she wasn't playing Mother of the Year. The eyes of a hooked and landed fish. Resentful. Resigned. Waiting to drown in the air. Lina can't imagine what it would be like if Ant ever turned such eyes on her.

'I'm sorry,' she says. 'I don't want that. I would never want that.'

'Mum's right, you know. This is a curse.'

'Don't say that. If you hadn't made Loki ... I love him so much, Ant, you've no idea how important he is to me. To have someone who understands what I am, who *is* what I am. That's enough, really.'

Already, she's packing it away again. Her need, her longing. Folding it back into its child-shaped casket. Pushing the casket beneath her ribs where it has been lodged for so long she barely feels it. She shouldn't have asked. Shouldn't have allowed even the slimmest hope to slip its bonds.

'I'm sorry, Ant. Honestly.'

'If I thought there was a way...' Her sister looks utterly miserable. Huddled there in her baggy, black pyjamas. Knees drawn close to her chest. The weight of at least two worlds pressing down upon her shoulders.

'I was wrong to even ask,' Lina tells her. 'You have enough on your plate right now without me adding to it.'

'It's okay,' Ant says. Attempts a weak, tired smile that stretches into a yawn. 'But the nurse is coming at nine tomorrow. I have to be up at Mum's before then, and I really need to get some sleep.'

'Of course.' Lina stands. She wants to give her sister a hug but the futon is too wide to reach across. Too awkward to inch her way around its side. 'I'm sorry,' she says again. Pathetic, inadequate words for the person about to save her life. To sever her from Sally Paige once and for all.

'Grab the light on your way out, will you?' Ant says.

After she closes the study door, Lina remains outside in the hall for a few moments longer. Listens to the creaking springs of the futon as her sister makes herself comfortable. 'Thank you,' she whispers into the darkness. 'Thank you so much.'

21

Antoinette shuffles the deck and deals, flips the top card to reveal a king of spades and stifles a groan when she finds the left bower and queen nestled snug in her hand; more than enough to declare trumps, especially with a stray ace or two as kickers. They've been playing euchre out on the back porch for the best part of Sunday afternoon, and she's been trying to let her mother win at least one hand in four but Sally Paige is too distracted, slouched across the table in her pink cardigan with a dazed-dull expression on her face like she's mildly drunk, like she's been woken too soon from too deep a sleep. Her lips move wordless and dry as she studies her cards, then suddenly clamp together, press together white as frostbite.

'Mum? You feeling okay?'

'Just a bit nauseous.'

'You want some more lemon squash?'

Her mother scatters her cards on the table, face up. There's nothing to them: low pips in a medley of suits, topped by a single unsupported queen. 'I think I'll go back to bed for a while. I can barely keep my eyes open.'

Antoinette helps her mother shuffle back to her bedroom. Eases her out of her cardigan, then removes the syringe driver from its cloth bag and sets it carefully on the side table, watches for a few seconds to make sure the little green light is blinking. After checking that the tube isn't kinked or tangled, she tries to inspect the cannula in her mother's chest for signs of inflammation or infection, but Sally Paige pushes her hand away. 'It's fine.'

'The nurse said to check regularly.'

'I'm not so much of an invalid, I can't do it myself.'

Antoinette holds up her hands. 'Okay, okay.'

Her mother hates the machine, hates that the pain medication makes her feel so sick all the time, dizzy and nauseous and too drowsy to do much more than stare at the ceiling. That morning, walking the nurse out to her car, Antoinette asked if maybe there is something else her mother could take, something that might not make her feel so rotten all the time.

Talk to her doctor, honey, see what he recommends. But whatever she takes, there are going to be serious side-effects. You don't get to knock out that kind of pain without paying for it in some other way.

'When are they coming?' her mother asks.

'Who?'

'Your sister and that boy. When will they be here?'

'Jacqueline's still really upset, Mum. I don't think she's ready to—'

'You haven't called her? I asked you to call her.'

'Um ... no, you didn't.'

'Yesterday, after you came back from the chemist.'

'I'm pretty sure you didn't.'

Her mother has spent much of the previous two days either sleeping or watching television on the old portable set Antoinette dragged into her bedroom, flicking irritably through the channels as she nibbled on dry Sao biscuits and sipped lemon squash through a bendy straw. Antoinette spent a lot of the time cleaning the house, secretly hoping to unearth some scrap of information about the other women in her family—old letters, any kind of records or documents her mother might have forgotten about, even just a name would give her something to go on—but of course, nothing.

She also burned an embarrassing amount of hours playing Angry Birds before finally, guiltily, wiping the game from her phone.

'She should be here,' Sally Paige is saying. 'Both of them. It'll be much easier, having them close by.'

'With the, ah, transfer, you mean?'

'What do you think we've been talking about all afternoon?'

'Mum...' Antoinette bites her lip. 'You're getting mixed-up. Remember, the nurse said sometimes the drugs can make you feel confused?'

'But I *told* you.'

'Okay, sorry. I must have forgotten.'

Her mother stares at her for a moment with eyes sharper and clearer than Antoinette has seen them for days, then slumps back against the pillow. 'All right then,' she says quietly. 'I'm telling you now. They need to be here.'

Antoinette glances at her watch. 'It's almost four. I can drive down and—'

'No.' Her mother coughs, wincing as she shakes her head. 'Not tonight, I'm too tired. Tomorrow, once the nurse has gone. Then you go and get them. Tomorrow, we'll get this thing done.'

'Tomorrow? I don't even know what I'm supposed to do.'

'You do what I tell you. You do *exactly* what I tell you and everything will be fine.' She flaps her hand dismissively, coughs again. The machine makes one of its wheezy hissing sounds as it pumps another dose of meds into her system. 'I think I'd like to rest now.'

'Okay,' Antoinette says. 'Can I get you anything?'

'You could make me a pot of tea.'

'Black, camomile or peppermint?'

Her mother pauses, brow furrowed in concentration as if this is one of the most important questions she'll ever have to answer. The tip of her tongue edges between her lips; she looks ludicrously, poignantly childlike. 'Peppermint,' she replies at last. 'And make sure it's strong. I want to be able to taste it.'

The kettle has just finished boiling when the doorbell rings. Antoinette pours water into the teapot and swaddles the thing with one of the brightly coloured knitted cosies that seem to breed in

PERFECTIONS

the bottom drawer along with enough batteries to power a small village. The bell rings again, too loud in the too quiet house, and she hurries down the hall to answer it.

'Hi,' says the girl standing on the front step, voice so high and tentative her greeting is almost a question. She's clutching a large plastic container with both hands like it might be about to leap from her grasp and make a run for it.

Antoinette has already started to ask the girl what she wants, is getting her *thanks, but we're not interested* speech ready to roll, when recognition kicks in and the words die in her mouth. '*Greta*? Is that you?'

Greta, sans any skerrick of makeup, freckles scattered over her cheeks.

Greta, black hair pulled as much into a ponytail as its length will allow, that once severe fringe somehow mollified, coaxed into softer bangs.

Greta, wearing flat sandals and grey cargo pants, wearing—shock of all shocks—a plain cotton tank top, loose and long and whiter than funeral lilies.

The girl smiles, a shy toothy grin that seems more out of place than all the rest. 'Not exactly,' she says, no trace whatsoever of a German accent, and sticks out a hand. 'My name's Sharon.' Her eyes roll. 'I know, right? Goth. As. Fuck.'

𝒮

It's not a long story, she tells Antoinette, nor is it all that compli-cated, really. They're sitting out on the back porch with bad instant coffee but a pretty kick-arse batch of chocolate brownies that Greta—*Sharon*—says she made herself, because by the time Antoinette returned to her mother with the peppermint tea, Sally Paige was asleep and Antoinette didn't want the sound of voices in the house to wake her.

'So you're not German?' she asks. 'At all?'

'Not even remotely. I barely speak the language.'

The German angle part of the whole Greta act, although *act* is not precisely the right word, and neither is façade. Performance, persona; something closer to that, something which doesn't imply so much of the artificial, the disingenuous. Sharon almost cripplingly shy when she moved across from Perth—god, almost *six years* ago now—to start an Arts degree at Melbourne Uni. No idea what she wanted to do with herself back then, just that she didn't want to do it in Perth. Her parents second generation out from England, more British than British and possessed of enough class snobbery to proudly fund an east-coast sandstone education.

'They were disappointed I didn't land a place at Sydney,' Sharon says. 'After all, Melbourne is only the *second*-oldest university in the country.'

A lecture in first-year cultural studies gave her the idea, those accounts of sneaky urban ethnographers who lost themselves in the very subcultures they set out to infiltrate, becoming consumed by identities created with the sole intent of covert observation.

More native than native in the end, their alter-egos providing an absolute—if highly quarantined—freedom from the petty and mundane demand of their everyday lives. Of their everyday selves.

And so Greta was born. Confident and mysterious, audacious and sexy, knifing her way through the night-clad crowd on little more than gall and a pair of immaculately drawn, derisively raised eyebrows. Greta, who could do anything, say anything, who lost not a moment's sleep on what anyone might think of her. Panther-sleek in PVC and black velvet, towering above the plebs on her fearsome platform heels and downing glass after glass of white rum and cranberry juice which, she said with all the maudlin-eyed assurance of an ex-pat, was *the* beverage of choice back in the smoky basement clubs of Cologne.

Sharon laughs. 'Ever notice how much easier it is to be what you *aren't*?'

She likens it to getting dressed for battle, or at least cold war ops: cinching herself into corset after corset, outlining her eyes with ever more elaborate swirls and curlicues. Stepping outside of her*self* before stepping outside her front door, and the times when she wasn't Greta—when she was merely Sharon Eddings with an essay to write, a phone call to make to her folks, a tutorial to find an excuse to miss—those times were soon playing a second, tuneless fiddle.

Antoinette grabs another brownie. 'So, you were what, studying us? Like we were all some sociological experiment?' She thinks she should feel angry, or at least used in some way, but she doesn't.

It's too surreal, this Greta-Not-Greta sitting pale and plain-faced across the table, re-shuffling the deck of cards in her hands after having already sorted it twice into ranked and ordered suits.

'No,' the girl says. 'I wasn't *studying* you. I wanted to *be* you. All of you. Paul did become my friend, you know, for real. You all did.'

Of course, in the beginning, she hadn't really thought it through. And the longer she wavered, the harder it became to picture herself standing up one night over drinks and proclaiming her identity to the surrounding faces.

Hey, guess what, you guys? I've never even been to Germany!

Impossible. And so, Greta. Entrenched. Ingrained. Unshakeable. The more she lived within her German alter-self, the less real—the less authentic—it felt to be Sharon Eddings. Going to class, doing the shopping, ducking around corners whenever she spotted someone who looked like someone who might know her as Greta. Until it came to seem that the timid, soft-spoken girl from Perth was the fiction.

'Kinda screwed up, right?' Sharon smiles ruefully. 'But hey, at least I got my dissertation topic out of it.'

After semi-serious flirtations with philosophy and world literature, she ended up majoring in cultural studies, did well enough in her honours year to score a doctorial scholarship, which pleased her parents—and their purse strings—no end, and now spends much of her Sharon-time researching the performative aspect of the feminine, particularly in relation to descriptive/

proscriptive portrayals of hair in fairytale culture. Which is a lot more complicated than anyone might think, and kind of scary, when you consider the kind of hair women are allowed to have—and where they're allowed to have it—and what it says when they wander hirsutely across the line.

'It's like we're supposed to have these long, luxurious locks in order to register ourselves as female—but only on the tops of our heads. Grow that shit anywhere else and a woman risks the verisimilitude of her entire performance. The fourth wall isn't merely an attribute of theatre, not when you take into account...' She laughs. 'Sorry, I'll save that stuff for chapter three.'

And then she's quiet for a while, focused on dealing her cards into suits for the third time. It's like this too has been a performance of some kind, a confession rehearsed and refined down to each inflection and self-conscious chuckle. And now that it's over, she's nothing more than an empty windup girl, the key in her back run all the way down.

'Why are you here?' Antoinette asks. 'Really?'

'I think...' A pause. A frown. 'I've had enough of Greta. It's not liberating anymore, being her. It's suffocating.'

Antoinette bites into her brownie. Chews slowly.

'I talked to Paul,' Sharon tells her. 'As Greta, of course; I figure he gets to keep her, that it's the least I owe him. But I told him she was going back to Germany, some issue with her family, and that it was absolutely nothing to do with you, that she hadn't talked to you for ages. I don't know how much of it sunk in, though. He seemed pretty upset. You know he wanted me to move in with him?'

'Really? That's fast work.'

'I think it was more about helping out with the rent. He's flat broke, Ant, now you're not there to pay the bills.'

'Poor thing. He might actually need to get a job.'

'Yeah, the mind boggles.' She glances up from her cards, a sly, sideways flick of the eye. 'So, this guy, the one who looks like him...'

A piece of brownie lodges in Antoinette's throat and she coughs, swallows a mouthful of cold coffee to push it down. 'He's no one. I mean, no one Paul needs to worry about. He's, um, he's Jacqueline's new boyfriend.'

Sharon quirks an eyebrow and for a moment the ghost of Greta flashes snarkily into view. 'Jacqueline's new boyfriend. Who looks just like Paul.'

'Not *just* like him. Not like a twin or anything.'

'That's not what he said.'

'You know Paul: a sniffle or two means he's got the plague; one skipped lunch and suddenly he's starving to death. When doesn't he exaggerate?'

Sharon chuckles, a slight smile lifting the corners of her mouth. 'It sounds dumb, but you have no idea how desperate I was for him not to break up with you. Greta was so anchored to the both of you by the end, I wasn't sure I could keep her going if you weren't ... if it was just Paul.'

'I didn't think you even liked me. I got the impression you

were always a little bit jealous, you know, because of the time I spent with him.'

'Oh, I was *jealous*.' Sharon catches her lip between her teeth. 'Just not of you.'

'I don't understand.'

The girl puts down her cards. There's nothing left of Greta in the look she gives Antoinette now, merely a frank and open longing almost too vulnerable to witness, and Antoinette quickly drops her gaze. Blood rushes to her cheeks and she takes another sip of cold, bitter coffee just to have something to do with her hands, something to do with her mouth.

'It's okay,' Sharon says. 'You don't need to say anything. I just have this weird compulsion to tell the truth these days, you know? I'm sure it's going to land me in all sorts of trouble.'

Antoinette swallows. 'I … um…'

'If you're not into girls, you can say. I won't be offended.' She crosses a finger over heart. 'I won't be offended, even if you're just not into *me*.' But her smile is fragile, full of bluster and hope.

'It's not … I'm not into *anyone* right now.'

'You still need more time, I get that.'

Antoinette laughs. 'You'll die waiting, Greta—Sharon, I mean. I'm not going to be into anyone again, ever. I think I can pretty much promise you that.'

'Pessimist.'

'It's complicated.'

'So tell me. ' Sharon stretches her arms over her head, elbows cracking loudly. 'I don't have anywhere else to be tonight.'

Behind them, the screen door squeaks and Antoinette swivels to see her mother standing on the back step, short hair spiked from sleep, syringe driver tucked into its bag like a holstered weapon.

'Mum.' Antoinette jumps up from her chair. 'Sorry, were we being too loud?'

Her mother ignores her, turns guarded eyes instead onto Sharon who's also getting hastily to her feet. 'Who might you be, then?'

'Sharon Eddings. I'm a friend of Ant's.' The girl extends a hand, diplomatically drops it once she sees it won't be shaken. 'It's nice to meet you, Mrs Paige. I'm sorry to hear you're not feeling well.'

'Not feeling well?' Sally Paige lets loose a jagged, barking laugh. 'That's a very polite way to put it, dear. What I am is *dying*.'

Antoinette groans, but Sharon doesn't even miss a beat. 'Cancer, yeah, Ant told me. My nanna died of that when I was sixteen. Started in her lungs, colonised her whole body in less than a year. Colonised, that's how my dad put it. Like she was some empty, unimportant tract of land, ripe for development.'

Sally Paige blinks. Beats down a struggling smile.

'You want something to eat, Mum?' Antoinette ventures, hoping to switch them all onto another conversational track.

'I'm not hungry.'

'You haven't eaten anything since breakfast, and that was only half a bowl of Rice Bubbles.'

'I don't think I'd be able to keep anything down.'

'Well, maybe you could try? Dr Chiang said—'

'Dr Chiang isn't the one standing here feeling like something the cat dragged in, chewed up, and spat back out again.'

'You know,' Sharon says, holding up a hand for attention like she's back in school. 'We could always score you some pot. I know a couple of guys, it'll only take a phone call. I think one of them even lives around here somewhere.' She throws a questioning glance at Antoinette. 'Ferntree Gully, that's not far, right?'

'Um, I'm not sure this is such a good idea.'

'Marijuana.' Sally Paige is deadpan.

'The very same,' Sharon tells her. 'When Nanna was at her worst, my brother used to sneak her in some of his stash. My parents would have freaked if they'd ever found out, but she said it stopped her feeling so sick all the time. Even brought back her appetite. So, if you think it might help...'

'Do you make a habit of offering drugs to all your friends' parents?'

'Only the ones who are dying.'

There is genuine good humour in her mother's laughter this time, but still it prickles Antoinette's skin with gooseflesh. The dry, crackled sound reminds her of autumn leaves, fallen and raked together in piles for burning.

'I like this girl,' Sally Paige says. 'She can stick around.'

✄

Lina knows the nurse comes to the house at nine each morning. Not wanting to interrupt the proceedings, and not being entirely sure what's involved or how long it takes to complete, she decides to wait until ten to return her sister's call. The message Ant left on her voicemail last night sounded strained. Oddly vague. Lina wishes she hadn't agreed to go to the cinema with Loki. Wishes she'd remembered to switch her phone on again afterwards. The film itself proved pointless and dull. A supposed romantic comedy which failed abysmally on both counts. Even Loki seemed embarrassed.

Sorry, I didn't think it'd be that bad.

Forgiven. I wouldn't have thought anything could be that bad.

There was a comforting sense of camaraderie in the experience at least. Taking themselves off to the multiplex. Sugary drinks and overpriced popcorn. Hands held in the flickering dark. Better than the sulk Loki manifested for most of the weekend while she worked on the Ryan Jellicoe catalogue. Last minute edits and tweaks before it went off to the printers on Monday. Each sentence weighed and measured. Each word. It had to be perfect.

Lina opens the document again now. Perhaps she should call Becca into the office. Have her cast a fresh pair of eyes over the text. Dante usually insists on doing all final proofreading himself. Usually picks up at least one or two errors each time as well. If he wasn't away for most of the week on secret Segue business—no, ridiculous. She can handle this. Lina pushes back her chair and starts to get up. Only to sink back down as her phone chimes from the desk.

'Ant, sorry. I was going to call you.'

'Listen, can you come up here today? I'll drive down and get you.'

'Right now? I'm at work. What's wrong?'

Her sister sighs heavily. 'Nothing. Just, you know, there's this little transfer thing we have to do. Mum's getting anxious about it.'

'I need to be there? You never said.'

'Well, she reckons it'd be better if you were. Easier.'

Lina swallows. The notion of coming face to face with Sally Paige again is far from pleasant. Her stomach churns. Anger. Fear. Revulsion. She thrusts it all back down. Straightens her spine. 'All right then, how about tonight? I can probably duck out early if that helps.'

'Yeah, she's not very good with nights. This medication she's on, it knocks her round something fierce. She's pretty much wiped out by early evening.'

'I can't really take a day off now, Ant. There's a lot happening this week. And next week, come to that.' Silence. Hoarse and ragged breathing. Lina can't tell if her sister is mad or simply struggling not to cry. 'What about you come and get me on Friday night?' she says gently. 'I'll stay for the weekend and you can do … whatever it is that needs to be done.'

'The weekend? Jacqueline that's five whole days away!'

'Is she…' Lina hesitates, runs through some likely phrases in her head. 'Is she that much worse now?'

'She's not about to up and die tomorrow, if that's what you're getting at.' Snappish and bitter. Definitely mad.

'I'm sorry,' Lina says. 'I know you want me to be more upset, but I can't feel what isn't there. I've tried to be a good daughter, the daughter she wanted, the daughter she loved, but it was never enough. I feel cheated, Ant. She's been dangling this shining jewel above us our whole lives, and all the time she knew it was nothing but a cheap, plastic fake. Honestly, I don't understand why you—'

'The weekend then,' Ant interjects.

Lina clears her throat. 'The weekend, yes. I promise.'

'Tell Loki he needs to come as well.'

'Why?'

'I'd just feel better if he was here.'

Her sister's voice too casual now. Deliberately offhand, as though she is merely asking Lina to pick up some milk on her way home. 'Honestly, Ant, how dangerous is this thing likely to be? What has she warned you might happen?'

'Not much. It'll be physically draining more than anything else,' she says. 'Like a really bad hangover, I gather, and I've had more than enough experience with those. But still, I'd feel better having someone up here who can drive a car. You know, just in case.'

Lina hates the sound of those words: *just in case*. 'You really don't have to go through with this, Ant. I'm not your responsibility. You could simply ... not.' Her sister laughs. And she hates the harsh, hollow sound of that even more.

'Jacqueline, *not* isn't even an option.'

They exchange stilted goodbyes, and Lina resists the urge to apologise once more. To confess. Because, busy as she is, the gallery is really more excuse than impediment. Because, truthfully, she's terrified. Of what might happen when Sally Paige gets her claws inside her sister's head. And of what might not.

Five days. It feels like five years. Like five seconds.

She contemplates the phone in her hand, tempted to call Ant back straightaway. *Sorry, I was wrong. Let's get this thing over and done with.* Her thumb is hovering over the call button as the office phone shrills to life.

Lina closes her eyes. Takes a moment to compose herself before lifting the receiver. When she speaks, her voice is agreeably smooth and unruffled. 'Seventh Circle.'

'Ms Paige, I'm looking at the draft catalogue you emailed on Friday.' Susan Keyes, brusque and straight to the point. 'Wonder if you can spare a few minutes to chat.'

'Ah, of course.'

'Nice work, not so sure about the tone. Bit formal, don't you think, for this type of show? Bit crisp.'

'I did make some changes over the weekend. Do you want—'

'Good good, but tell you what: I'm going to send through some notes of my own. You might like to incorporate those into what you have there.' Her tone implies there will be no *might* about it. 'Bounce it back to me once you're done, yes?'

'Ah, it's just that this needs to get to the printers by midday.'

'Tosh. They'll do a twenty-four hour turnaround if you tell

them my name's on the work order. Let them bully you once, Jacqueline, they'll keep you at the bottom of the pecking order for ever always. Now, about the catering.'

'That's all finalised. I sent you the confirmation last week.'

'Yes, there's just a small quibble. No baby hot dogs?'

'Ah, no. I thought we might try for—'

'But everyone loves the baby hot dogs. They're so gloriously kitsch. I think lose the mozzarella arancini instead.' Her laughter is a husky smoker's rasp. 'We don't want to be picking rice out of our teeth all evening.'

Lina braces herself. A favourite of Dante's, the baby hot dogs are precisely the kind of self-conscious irony she hopes to shed from Seventh Circle. 'If you think it's best,' she tells the woman on the other end of the line.

'And then there's the monkey. I did tell you about the monkey?'

'I don't think you did.'

'It's the most adorable little thing. An extensive repertoire of tricks apparently, and I thought it was so apt considering the change of emphasis in young Mr Jellicoe's work of late.'

'The change of emphasis?'

'The jungle that's taken over his canvases. Jungles, monkeys; what could be better? I've made the booking already but his trainer does need to pop by in advance to inspect the premises. Something about making sure there's nothing which might startle the creature, put him off his game. Who would have thought primates could be such prima donnas?'

'No.' The word shoots from her mouth before she can stop it.

'No?' Susan Keyes echoes.

Lina squares her shoulders. In for a penny. 'This is an important exhibition, Ms Keyes. I'm not sure what impression you've gotten from the photographs, but I've seen these paintings in person and I can tell you, it's very serious work. Ryan Jellicoe is going to be a highly significant artist not too long from now. You can't undermine him with baby hot dogs and performing monkeys.' She swallows, listening for the sound of marching orders in the distance. 'Please.'

Again, that raspy laughter. 'Dante was on the level, then.'

'Pardon?'

'I thought he was merely skiving off on the Jellicoe show. It wouldn't be the first time he's allowed a personal clash with an artist to derail him professionally.' There's a smile in her tone now. An aunt speaking of a favoured nephew. 'I needed to know you were up to the task, Jacqueline. Without meaning to offend, you've always come across as mousey rather than managerial.'

Lina closes her mouth. Her cheeks burn.

'You'll get used to me,' Susan Keyes tells her with a chuckle. 'Now, send that catalogue over. I would still like to cast an eye over the final version before it goes to print.'

'What about your notes?'

'My notes, yes. You shan't be needing those, I don't think.'

'Can I ask one question?'

'Please do.'

'What if I had said yes to the monkey?'

'I never bluff, Jacqueline.' There's steel in that voice now. The sort of steel that builds empires, or breaks them. 'If you had agreed to the monkey, you would have gotten the monkey. And it would have been the last time you ran so much as a stocking in any gallery of mine.'

Sharon does stick around, or at least she keeps coming back. Rattling up in her old red Corolla each afternoon or early evening with a bag of groceries in one hand and a stash of burnt DVDs in the other. She's a dab hand at making soup, it turns out, and even better at getting Antoinette's mother to swallow more than a mouthful without pushing the bowl away in disgust. The three of them sit out the back and play cards, if there's not too much chill in the breeze, or else hole up in the living room with the TV shows that Sharon sucks down from the web. Sally Paige rarely makes it through a single episode before losing interest—*True Blood* is boring; *Mad Men* too smug; *Breaking Bad* faintly ridiculous—but she becomes surprisingly enamoured of *Dexter*, and it pains Antoinette to contemplate the number of seasons and wonder whether her mother will live to watch them all.

'You don't have to keep coming up here,' she tells Sharon one night while they're washing the dishes. 'You must have better things to do.'

'Um, PhD student, remember?' The girl takes a dripping plate from the rack, wipes her tea towel around its rim.

'Still. It can't be much fun, the way things are with Mum right now.'

'It's okay, I like your mother.'

'No one *likes* my mother.'

'Well, I don't *dislike* her.'

In a way she finds difficult to articulate, even to Jacqueline who calls every morning and who can't for the life of her work out why the girl's deceitful arse hasn't been kicked halfway down the mountain by now—*but Ant, she's still Greta; or worse, she never was*—Antoinette finds Sharon a comfort. It's like stumbling across a bright new friend, one who miraculously understands her already, one with whom she doesn't need to rehash the more tedious, tired details of her life. They've skipped straight to companionable silences and shared winks, to the easy familiarity of knowing that someone takes their coffee with one-and-a-half sugars, that they prefer boysenberry ice cream to butterscotch, and that they'd rather sit and stare at a blank wall for two hours than watch any movie with Seth Rogan in it.

Besides—and this Jacqueline can and does absolutely understand—the idea of being alone in the house with only her mother and the brooding, cicada-heavy trees for company is not one that fills Antoinette with unbridled enthusiasm.

Thursday night, once Sally Paige is asleep in her room and the aroma of spices and melted cheese won't bother her, Sharon whips up some nachos and produces a sly bottle of Smirnoff from the depths of her backpack.

'*Prost!*' she toasts, clinking glasses.

Antoinette smiles. 'Hey, Greta-sketa. Long time, no see.'

'Oops.' Sharon lifts an exaggerated brow. 'Old habits.'

'Listen,' Antoinette says after her second drink. 'I have to go down and get my sister tomorrow. She's spending the weekend. You know, a bit of family time ... um, just the three of us.'

'Just the three of you.' Faint and wounded, the expression that slides momentarily across her face before she rallies, swigs a mouthful of vodka. 'Say no more, I'll make myself scarce.'

'It's not that I don't like having you here, but there's things we need to, um, work out together and it's probably best if...'

Sharon places her hand on Antoinette's. 'It's okay, I get it. Honey, your mum is dying, you don't need to explain anything to anyone.' Her index finger traces two of Antoinette's knuckles in a sideways figure eight, an infinity symbol drawn ticklish and tender, then withdraws. 'Maybe I'll drop by Monday sometime? There's this leek and sweet potato soup I'm hoping Sally will be able to stomach.'

'I'd like that,' Antoinette says. And she smiles at the girl who simply sits there so still and contained, who doesn't pull, who doesn't tug or gnaw at her like a puppy cutting its teeth. And for the first time in a long time, it's a smile that goes all the way through to her bones.

22

The final thing Lina does before she leaves work that Friday is call Ryan Jellicoe. Again. He actually answers his phone this time. His breath heavy and hoarse, as though he's just run all the way up the front stairs to his house.

'I thought we were past the incommunicado shtick,' she says.

'Sorry, girl, been out at Redcliffe most of the day. Amazing beach weather up here right now, you should see it.'

An image of him, shirtless and tanned, sidles unbidden into view. Sand drying golden on his thighs. Dreads dripping salt down his spine. Lina pushes it from her head. Explains that she's calling to confirm that his paintings all made it safely onto the truck yesterday afternoon. In her hand, the faxed manifest from the relocation company trembles slightly. She puts it down on the desk. Ridiculous. She doesn't even care about Ryan Jellicoe, bare-skinned or otherwise.

'Done and dusted,' he is saying. 'On their merry way south.'

'That's good, that's great.'

'Guy said they would land on your doorstep sometime Monday arvo.'

'That's the plan.'

'So what time should I rock up?'

'Any time you want to, really. Doors won't officially open until six on Thursday, but we have the usual private viewings booked for some of our more exclusive clientele during the day, so I'll be there if you want to—'

'No,' he interrupts. 'I meant, what time should I be there on *Monday*?'

'Ryan, your flight is booked for Wednesday afternoon.'

'Yeah, I changed that. Thought we'd come down Sunday instead.'

'We?'

Him and Zane, he says, and Lina winces. Partly it's the awful picture the name conjures up of that girl strutting into Seventh Circle behind an airport trolley piled high with suitcases—*so, where do you, like, want me to set these up?*—and partly it's another of the stomach cramps that have been bothering her for the past hour or so. Lina rubs her midsection. Hopes it's only the sushi she had for lunch.

Zane has a mate down in Collingwood, Ryan is saying. Happy to put them both up for a few days and so, he thought, why the hell not? Zane gets to rabbit her way through the Melbourne gallery scene for a bit longer, and he's on the ground to lend a hand taking his canvases off the truck. The promise of which,

Lina should know, is gonna let him sleep a whole lot easier the next few nights.

'So, ' Lina says. 'You and Zane...'

'Already told you, she's not my type of distraction.'

She doesn't even know why she asked. 'Come by around ten,' she tells him. 'I'll show you the space and then we can grab some brunch before your paintings arrive. Actual set up isn't until Wednesday—we have professional hangers, of course, but I assume you'll be wanting to drop in and, ah, *lend a hand*?'

'Sounds like a plan.' He's grinning. She can hear it in his voice.

'We've been doing this kind of thing for a while now, you know, and we're actually pretty good at it. Honestly, it must be *weeks* since we've lost an artwork, or even damaged one accidentally.'

'Well, that's a letdown,' he says. 'I was hoping for some ripped canvas, maybe a cracked frame or two. The whole upcycled-distressed thing, yeah? Hear that shit moves faster than crystal in a crackhouse over on Etsy.'

She laughs. 'I'll see you on Monday, Ryan. Have a safe flight.'

On the tram home, the stomach cramps worsen. Lina presses the back of her hand to her forehead, wonders if she might be running a fever. Then, as she climbs the steps to her apartment, a jagged pain knifes right through her middle and she gasps out loud. Leans against the wall until the aftershock fades. The fact that this doesn't feel even remotely like her previous episodes is a small comfort. The pain is too physical. Rather than trying to pull Lina from her body, it grounds her intimately, terribly, within it.

Still, it's a reassurance of sorts: unless Sally Paige has learnt some vile new trick, this has nothing to do with her.

Raised voices greet Lina as she opens the door. Ant is in the kitchen with Loki, arguing about books. 'Jacqueline,' her sister says as she walks in. 'Please tell him, he doesn't need to bring the whole state library along for two miserable days. Maybe he'll listen to you.'

Lina stares at them. Glaring at each other from opposite ends of the bench, arms folded over chests in a cranky, mirror-twin pose she might have thought comical under different circumstances.

'Hey,' Ant says. 'Are you okay?'

'Bad sushi, I think.' Another cramp, not quite as bad as the last. 'Excuse me, I need a moment…' She hurries to the bathroom and locks the door behind her. Flicks the toilet seat back down with an irritated snap of her wrist. It's not until her sister comes knocking to check that she really is okay—that she hasn't, ha ha, fallen in—that Lina can tear her eyes away from the impossible red slick staining her briefs. From the darker, more clotted mess on the paper scrunched in her hand.

'Jacqueline? Seriously, I'm getting a little worried out here.'

She clears her throat. 'I'm … I'm all right.'

'You sure? You looked kinda wrecked.'

'I think…' Despite the fear and the pain, despite the *wonder*, Lina is amused by the words now perched on the tip of her tongue. Words she had long given up hope of ever needing to use. 'I think I might need to borrow a tampon.'

𝒮

'Here,' Antoinette says, coming into her sister's bedroom with a glass of water and foil-lined card of Naprogesic she found scuffing around at the bottom of her bag. Most of the safety bubbles are broken and empty, but there's enough left to tide her sister over until they can get to a chemist.

Jacqueline places the sweater she's holding into her overnight case. Punches a couple of the little blue tablets into her palm and subjects them to the kind of nervous scrutiny a poison taster might reserve for the meal of an especially loathsome monarch.

'Do they work?' she asks.

'They do for me.'

Her sister rubs at her belly. Swallows the pills along with half the water then hands the glass back. 'Is it going to hurt like this every month?'

'Mine aren't that bad, to tell you the truth, but Tanja from work always swaps shifts if she gets rostered on day one, says she needs to knock herself out with enough codeine to cripple a horse.' Antoinette shrugs. 'This is one of those *your mileage may vary* deals, you know?'

'Oh.'

'But hey, maybe it's only so painful because it's the first time your body's ever done this. It might be like, I don't know, teething problems or something.'

'Teething problems.' Jacqueline smiles.

Antoinette grins back. 'Or something.'

Her sister rolls her eyes, retrieves her kimono from its hook on the back of the door and folds it into a neat, flat square. Antoinette recalls the taut, anxious expression on Loki's face as Jacqueline finally emerged from the bathroom, and how swiftly it fell away when she told him what was going on. How he took her face in his hands and planted a soft, gentle kiss on her brow.

Lina, my Lina. This is wonderful.

How a new light flickered to life in his eyes, keen and bright and expectant.

The same light which now clings to her sister as she finishes packing and zips up the case. Despite her still shaken appearance, her wan complexion and pursed-pale lips, Jacqueline somehow glows.

'Hey,' Antoinette says. 'Do you think this means you might be able to...'

'I'm not sure. I—I hope so.'

And for one tender, heartbreaking moment, she looks like a little girl who has woken up early on Christmas morning to discover the best, the most magical gift she could ever have imagined laid out beneath the tree. A little girl who can't bring herself to even touch it, lest the thing break or vanish altogether, lest Santa himself come rumbling down the chimney to sweep it back into his big red bag.

Apologies for the mix-up, but this clearly belongs to some other child.

'I wonder.' Jacqueline sits down on the bed beside her. 'She told you that we were infertile, right, that perfections were unable to, uh, *breed*?' Her nose wrinkles at the last word. 'What if that's not strictly true?'

'I'm not sure why Mum would lie about that,' Antoinette says carefully.

'She might not be lying. There might never have been a perfection who's given birth to a child—or fathered one.'

'Okay, but—'

'But what if that's because we're only infertile around *humans*? What if we need another *perfection* to kick our reproductive systems into gear?' Her hand moves in slow circles over her belly. 'It makes sense, Ant, when you think about it. Loki comes into my life and suddenly—*about one month later*—my uterus decides to remember what it was built to do.'

'Maybe,' Antoinette says.

But it does make sense, that's the trouble. With any one person, according to the albeit cryptic doctrine of Sally Paige, unable to host more than a single mature perfection at any one time, and with the ability to create them in the first place so rare and jealously guarded, the chance of two compatible perfections being around each other long enough for sparks to fly...

'This transfer won't change anything, will it?' Jacqueline asks. 'It won't make this all go away again?'

Antoinette swallows, pushing against thoughts of Loki and her mother that pick at her like wicked barbs. *Please, Jacqueline, don't hate me. It's him, or it's you, and that's no kind of a choice at all.*

'It shouldn't,' she says. 'If anything, it would make you stronger, healthier. But I can run it by Mum if you like, ask her if—'

'No! I don't want her to ever know about this.'

'Okay.'

'I mean it, Ant. You can't tell her.'

'Okay, I promise. Just…' She takes her sister's hand, entwines those flush-warm fingers between her own. 'I wish you wouldn't set your hopes too high about this whole pregnancy thing. I mean, if it doesn't work like that, or if Loki doesn't…'

'But it will work.' Jacqueline's smiling again now, glowing bold and certain with belief as she presses both their hands against her middle. 'I'm right about this, I know it. Better, I can *feel* it.'

The drive up to the mountain is quiet and, for the most part, conversation free. Her sister elected to ride in the back with Loki, which makes Antoinette feel oddly like a chauffeur but at least gives her time to think. Despite her promise, there are now some new and pertinent questions to raise with her mother. Because if at least one half of that pitiless aphorism Sally Paige spat down at her feet—*girls don't bleed, boys don't seed*—is demonstrably false, she wonders how many other long-held truths might prove to be little more than baseless assumption.

Like maybe perfections don't have to die with their hosts.

Like maybe there's a way to save both Jacqueline and Loki, after all.

But no matter how much she shuffles the words around in her head, Antoinette can't come up with a way to broach the subject without rousing her mother's suspicion. And if there's one aspect of this whole mess about which Sally Paige has been absolutely forthright, it's her desire to see the family curse wither and die on the vine. Antoinette doesn't know what her mother will do once she realises that Jacqueline might be able to bear children of her own—let alone what the offspring of two perfections might be capable of creating in their own right—but she cannot take the risk. Until her sister is safely anchored, until she feels the weight of a Jacqueline-stone shifting solid within her, Antoinette will say nothing.

She glances at the rear-view mirror, at the shape of two dark heads bent close together, and a lump swells in her throat.

It's your sister or it's that boy.

No choice. Antoinette grits her teeth. No choice at all.

Sally Paige releases Antoinette's hand, slumps back against the bedhead with a glare that would strip not only paint but whatever lies beneath it. They've been at it for close to an hour, door closed and blinds drawn to block out the glare of the late morning sun that strains her mother's eyes. An awkward kind of guided meditation that Antoinette finds vaguely embarrassing and, 'I don't know what I'm supposed to be doing,' she protests, shifting her chair closer to the bed.

'Empty your mind,' her mother says. 'That should be easy for you.'

Antoinette takes a breath, reminds herself that, for all the best efforts of the syringe driver and the medication it dutifully doles out, the woman propped up in the middle of all those pillows is frail and sick and in no small measure of discomfort. She nods towards the Dilaudid on the bedside table, the amber bottle as yet unopened in the week since Dr Chiang prescribed it, the small measuring glass unused. *For breakthrough pain*, his directions careful and firm. *Take it as needed and with no less than four hours between doses. It's very strong stuff.*

Sally Paige is taking the *only as needed* part very seriously. 'No,' she says, not waiting for Antoinette to ask. 'I'm saving that for when it gets worse.'

'I don't think there's rationing in place, Mum. We can get another prescription if you run out.'

'I'm already muddle-headed enough.' She holds out her hand. 'Come on then, let's give it another go before I'm completely exhausted.'

'No.' Antoinette crosses her arms. 'It's pointless. You have to give me more to go on than *empty your mind*.'

'I'm not teaching you to ride a bike. This should come naturally.'

'Well, obviously it doesn't.'

'Your connection to that boy, you imagine it as a stone?'

'Like a weight, like a pendulum hanging inside me.'

'Then cut the cord and pass it to me.'

Antoinette rolls her eyes, exasperated. 'For godsake, Mum, it's just a metaphor.'

'Everything is a metaphor.' Her eyes narrow in thought. 'That Sharon left her vodka here, yes?'

'What's left of it. Time to drown our sorrows?'

'No dear. Time to drown your inhibitions.'

The Smirnoff is stashed in the freezer and Antoinette pours herself a generous shot, sculls it and coughs a little as the alcohol burns down her throat. She pours another, hesitates then takes the bottle and follows the faint sound of the television that drifts from the living room. Jacqueline is curled up on the couch, watching an episode of *Mad Men* with a hot water bottle hugged to her stomach.

'Still feeling bad?' Antoinette asks from the doorway.

Her sister looks around. 'A lot better. I'm just too comfortable to move.'

'I didn't know you liked this show.'

'I don't think I do like it.' She nods at the bottle of Smirnoff. 'Going that well in there, huh?'

'Our mother is trying to get me drunk.'

'Your mother,' her sister corrects.

'She thinks if I just relax and loosen up a little … god, sounds like the ending to a bad date, doesn't it?'

'Makes sense,' Jacqueline says. 'You'd been drinking when you made Loki.'

'Yeah. Hey, where *is* Loki?'

'He went for a walk out back. Don't worry, he has my phone with him.'

'Cool.' She raises her glass, downs the second shot and grimaces. 'Jacqueline, listen. If it ends up I can't do this thing...'

'But you will.' Her sister smiles confidently. 'Of course you will.'

Lina hears the squeak of the screen door out back and reaches for the remote. She's decided that she doesn't care for shows about advertising any more than she cares for the carrots and sticks of advertising itself these days. It's a scary sort of relief, to no longer feel the constant need to question herself. To worry if she's wearing the right clothes. Choosing the right furniture. Saying the right things.

Being the right thing.

Loki is in the kitchen by the sink, staring out the window. His hands are clasped behind his head, elbows akimbo. He's wearing the red T-shirt she bought him, the one with the bright yellow Aztec sun printed on the front, and it's riding up his back. Lina wants to press her lips to that pale, exposed line above his jeans. Wants to taste the warm salt of his skin.

'Good walk?' she asks, taking a bottle of multi-vitamin juice from the fridge. Almost dropping it as Loki swivels around like a startled cat. Anger contorts his features. Jostles with confusion and something approaching dread.

'Where's Antoinette?' he demands.

'What's wrong?'

'*Where's Antoinette?*'

'She's still in there with *her*.' Lina jerks her head in the direction of Sally Paige's bedroom. She puts the juice down on the counter. 'Loki, please. What's happened?'

He licks his lips nervously. Nods, more to himself than to her, then holds out his hand. 'Come with me, I'll show you.'

A few metres into the backyard, near where the grassy lawn ends and bushland begins its subtle encroachment, Lina stops dead. 'We're going in there?'

'Not too far. There's a small hut or something at the very back of the property, just inside the fence line.'

He tugs at her arm. She doesn't move. 'That's our father's old shed. It's been empty since he left.'

'How long has it been since you've seen it?'

'I don't ... we never go down there. It's just an empty shed, Loki.'

'It's not empty.'

'I don't really care.' Her palm is damp, clammy in his grip. 'Look, can we go back to the house now? Ant might need someone and—'

'Lina, this is important. You need to see.'

'I don't like it out here,' she whispers. 'I really, really don't.'

'It's broad daylight. Nothing will hurt you, I promise.'

She swallows. Feels sick to her stomach in a way that has nothing to do with her body's newly discovered workings. But she allows him to lead her on regardless. Follows him through the rustle and scorn of the trees, leaf litter crackling dry beneath her sandalled feet. Lina keeps her gaze fixed to the ground. Concentrates on counting her steps, starting over each time she hits ten.

When Loki stops, she bumps right into him.

The shed is small and made of wood. Painted in a dull off-grey that might once have been blue before time and sunlight did their work, with a curtain drawn across its single square window. A pushbolt has been installed below the door handle and from this hangs a sturdy, gaping padlock.

'It was unlocked?' Lina asks, hating the tremor in her voice.

Loki pulls a set of keys out of his pocket and jangles them in the air. Sally Paige's keys, complete with the enamelled *#1 MUM* keyring that Lina remembers buying one Mother's Day too many years ago now to count.

'Put those away,' she says.

He does. 'Come on. Lina, *come on.*'

Reluctantly, she walks the last few steps to the shed door. As Loki eases it open, the clotted scent of roses wafts from the dim and shadowed interior. Roses, and something sharper. Something acrid and stale. 'Hey,' Loki calls softly. 'It's okay. It's only me again.' His arm slips around Lina's waist, guides her forward. Out of the midday sun, it takes a moment for her eyes to adjust.

To take in the immense slatted crib that looms along the wall to her left.

And the shape that lolls, large and lumpish, within its bars.

§

Antoinette has been drunker than this—much drunker, oh yes, many times and more—but never *ever* with her mother around. 'Stop it now,' Sally Paige scolds as she grabs her daughter's arm, and *stop what?* Antoinette wants to ask, then realises that she is giggling. Has probably been giggling for quite some time.

'Sorry,' she says. 'But it's pretty funny, right? All those lectures you used to give us on the Evils of Binge Drinking and now look: my mother the enabler.' That withering Sally Paige glare is pretty funny as well and Antoinette has to gnaw on the inside of her lip to keep a straight face.

'Close your eyes,' her mother instructs once again. 'Then—'

'*Empty your mind*,' Antoinette sings.

'Are you done? Because we can stop right now, if you like. If you care so little about your sister, that all it takes is one good swig of alcohol for you to forget what's at stake here.'

Her words sting worse than a slap and are three times as sobering.

'Okay, okay. Sorry. I'll try probably—*properly*, I mean.'

Behind her eyelids, colours shimmer and swirl and Antoinette rolls her head forward, chin bumping to chest as the woozy rush of intoxication tumbles over her like a wave. She feels for the Loki-stone, feels for it and finds it and holds it puzzled within her grasp, unsure just what it is she's meant to do now.

Let go, her mother whispers, and the voice seems less inside her ear than inside her head, as her mother's fingers travel along the skin of her inner arm, feather-light and ticklish, their barest tips trailing hypnotically up and down, up and down, up and down, until Antoinette can no longer distinguish between sensation and touch. *Let go*, and then an unexpected flare of pain, finger-nails pinching the soft crease of her elbow, pinching so hard that Antoinette cries out, and her mother says something else, a word that darts away before Antoinette can grasp it and, pulled along in its slipstream, she feels herself unlock, feels herself open and swell, and her mother is beside her now, beside her and around her and within her, offering, offering, oh—

The Jacqueline-stone, so bright and clear and *blue*. Summer skies stretching cloudless and vast, peacock plumage and lapis lazuli and fat-headed hydrangeas full in bloom, and Antoinette reaches out and takes it from her mother, scoops her sister right into herself, a warm new weight hanging safe behind her ribs.

Now give that to me.

Loki is silver-smooth. Loki is polished steel and mirrored glass, the windless surface of subterranean lakes, and *I'm sorry*, she tells him, *I don't have a choice*, but it hurts as she starts to pull him free, a deep throb that makes her gasp and—

Of course it hurts. Did you think it wouldn't?

And then Antoinette sees it. That subtle, shifting spark at the very core of Sally Paige, a faint and sickly scrap of yellow that her mother has tried to hide, has sought to veil from her sight, but—*oh*—she sees it now, *she sees it*.

That sole remaining presence, that undeniable second stone.

∅

Lina stares down at the—creature? child? *boy?*—curled face to the wall in the crib. Her hands are shaking so hard, she grips the wooden side rail to steady herself. He's wearing a green pyjama shirt with sleeping dragons on it, and a disposable nappy. The pyjama pants are folded over the end of the crib. Orange socks cover his feet. There's a blanket, also green, but it's been kicked into a corner.

She focuses on these slight, mundane details. Just on these.

'I had to change him,' Loki says.

Lina nods. Takes in the brightly coloured boxes stacked next to the tallboy on the other side of the shed. Junior Huggies for Boys. The boxes have Winnie the Pooh on them. Tigger and the donkey as well. A battery-operated room deodoriser squats on top of the tallboy, its rose-scented fragrance not quite masking the more bodily odours that hang in the air. Beside it is a pink plastic radio that she recognises as once having belonged to her sister. There's no music and Lina wonders if the batteries have run out.

In the crib, the boy makes a soft, hooting noise and attempts to roll onto his back. It seems to take some effort. That skull so impossibly large for such a small and scrawny body. Like one of those creepy-comical Japanese dolls, all head and black unblinking eyes. Except, no, not these eyes. These eyes are blue, or at least one of them is. The other cloud-spun and milky. Glaucoma perhaps, or cataracts, or some other blinding disease. But still, he sees her.

Sees her and hoots again, louder this time. Rocks himself from side to side until that great head rolls all the way over and his body follows, flopping ragdoll-like in its wake.

Lina tries to move away but Loki is right behind her. Hand firm on her lower back.

'It's okay,' he says. 'Lina, look at him.'

She doesn't want to.

Doesn't want to see those eyes. Or that fine, cornsilk hair cut in ugly, ill-matched lengths. Or that mouth, worst of all, that strange and awful mouth. A round, sucking hole scarcely larger than a shirt button. Lips rubbery and pink, squashed and sealed together at the sides. Glistening with saliva that spills in long strings to baptise the stuffed green frog that the boy holds in one hand.

The hooting changes, pitches higher. Becomes almost a whistle.

'What has she done?' Lina whispers.

On the front of the nappy, Winnie the Pooh and Tigger hold hands. Smile up at her with oblivious Disneyfied grins. Bile rises in her throat. The boy lifts his empty hand. Stubby fingers waggle in the air. Lina reaches towards him. Touches her hand to his. Hooting softly, he curls a fist around two of her fingers. There is almost no strength to his grip.

'Hello,' Lina says. 'Hello Charles.'

Loki slips his arms around her waist. 'It'll be okay.'

'No.' Gently, she extricates herself from her brother's grasp. Turns and pushes Loki away. 'That *woman* did this. Changed him somehow, kept him out here like some sick, unwanted animal.'

A searing, sudden rage boils through her veins. Her whole body is shaking and her fingers ache to find the flesh of Sally Paige's throat. To rend it to ragged and bloody strips.

Antoinette shrinks back, uncertain now and scared, pulling the Loki-stone from her mother's reach even as Sally Paige begins to close around it.

Give me that. You have to give him to me.

But Antoinette draws away, draws Loki away, folds herself protectively over him and Jacqueline both. Two within her now, Loki-stone and Lina-stone, knocking against one another in a way that feels right, that feels *perfect*, and how the hell could she ever have considered giving him up? She will *never* give him up. And again that flash of yellow her mother is too slow to conceal, too slow or merely unable. Meek little pebble blinking amber and she pushes closer, reaches closer and—

NO.

—her mother swats her away. An angry, effortless shove that takes Antoinette by surprise, hits her like a punch in the sternum and she gasps as the connection with her mother is abruptly, painfully severed.

She blinks, dizzy-drunk and wobbling on her chair. 'What was that?'

'Nothing you need to lose sleep over,' Sally Paige tells her through trembling, grey-tinged lips. She looks exhausted, face sheened with perspiration and breath rasping harsh, but deep in those red-lined eyes gleams a cool and all too familiar disappointment.

'I saw it,' Antoinette insists. 'I *felt* it. You have another perfection!'

'That's none of your business.'

'But you said a woman couldn't cope with two of them, you said—'

'Does it look like I've been coping?'

'Who is it? Where are they?'

'I'm tired.' Her mother sinks down into her pillows. 'And now we have to do this all again. Stupid girl, why didn't you just give him over to me?'

'You're not getting him,' Antoinette says through clenched teeth. 'I've decided to keep them, both of them. They're mine.'

'Don't be so sentimental. They'll ruin you.'

'I feel fine. No different.'

'Wait till you sober up. Wait till she starts to drain you.'

Antoinette grabs a glass of water from the bedside table, drinks most of it in one thirsty gulp. 'You know what I think? I think you don't know half of what you think you know. I think you're a bitter old woman who screwed up her life and now doesn't want anyone else to be happy even for a second.'

'You're a drunken little fool.'

'And you're a liar.' She lurches to her feet, reaches for the back the chair to brace herself. 'But you know what? Loki and

Jacqueline *love* each other, and I'm not going to take that away from them just because it's something I can't have anymore. I'm not you, I'm not going to spoil things for them out of *spite*.'

Beneath her fury, Sally Paige seems startled. 'They *love* each other?'

'Like Romeo and Juliet, I swear to god.'

'How very apt.'

'Sorry?'

'Two perfections. It can hardly end well.'

'Yeah? Well, guess what? Jacqueline—'

A commotion of footsteps and raised voices out in the hall catches her attention and she sways around to face the door just as her sister flings it open, panting and flushed like she's been running. Loki right behind, pleading with her to *wait, please Lina, just wait*, but she shrugs him off, marches into the bedroom like there's an entire battalion at her heels.

'Move out of the way, Ant. I am going to kill that old witch right where she lies.'

23

For a few bleary, perplexing seconds, Antoinette is caught between the two of them. Jacqueline screaming at Sally Paige, rapid-fire accusations about Charles and some old shed that make no kind of sense at all, and the older woman snapping back, telling her to calm down, to stop being so *hysterical*—that word a bugbear of Jacqueline's from way back, guaranteed to press all the wrong buttons as her mother well knows—and her sister launches herself at the bed, hands outstretched like she wants to tear Sally Paige's eyes out or worse.

'Lina, stop.' Loki seizes her around the shoulders, holds Jacqueline to him in that same careful way Antoinette remembers him holding *her* about a billion-zillion years ago, that first night as she fled from him through the apartment. Holding Jacqueline like she might break, like she might break *herself*, he lowers his mouth to her ear, speaks low and soft until finally she stops struggling. But her eyes are still murderous, and they don't leave Sally Paige's face for a second.

'What did you do to him?' she demands again.

'Why were you down there in the first place?' Sally Paige retorts. 'You hate the bush, you *both* hate the bush.' Her gazes switches between her daughters, suspicious and cold. 'He was safe from you there.'

'You weren't ever going to tell us about him, were you?'

'That's because it doesn't concern you.'

'Okay, enough,' Antoinette breaks in. 'Can someone *please* let me know what the bloody hell's going on?'

'It's Charles,' Jacqueline says. 'She has our brother locked up in that old shed down the back. And she did something to him, he's not ... he's not right.'

'That isn't your brother,' Sally Paige says.

Jacqueline shakes her head, turns to her sister. 'Ant, you should see this for yourself.'

Antoinette barely gets three steps outside the shed before she throws up. Bent double with hands braced on knees, purging herself of mostly vodka and bile, but also some abrasive lumps that must have been lingering from the toast and eggs she had for breakfast. She couldn't stay in there, couldn't look at him for another second—

runstopbadrunstopbad

—bad enough they made her walk all the way down here, practically having to frogmarch her through the damn trees she was shaking so much, and then coaxing her into that shed of which she had no clear memory of ever seeing before and yet, and yet, something inside her was beating its wings in panic—

runstopbadrunstopbad

—because she knew with an absolute and terrified certainty that it was the *worst place in the world*, a place she didn't ever want to visit again—*again?*—but she let them lead her inside anyway, and there he was—the *charliedoll*—with his grotesque, lollipop head and round, toothless mouth and, *oh god*, the sound that came out of that mouth when he rolled those huge and hazy eyes around to find her standing by the crib, that toneless pan-pipe whistle, the backing track to every childhood nightmare—

runstopbadrunstopbad

—and the memories don't come flooding back so much as they seep in, drop by torturous drop. Disconnected flashes linked by evocations of terror and dread: abhorrence shadowed in her mother's face; cicada song and the flicker of sunlight through leaves; a little girl screaming, a little girl that might be Antoinette-that-was; and the charliedoll, the charliedoll, the charliedoll—

RUNSTOPBADRUNSTOPBAD

—not the whole story, not by a long shot, but enough to realise that somehow this whole sorry, sickening mess can be laid squarely at her own vomit-spattered feet.

'Are you all right?' Jacqueline sounds hurt, or maybe just offended.

Antoinette spits and straightens, wipes her mouth with the

back of her hand, then wipes her hand on her shirt. 'I think Mum might be right.'

'About what?' her sister asks warily.

'That's … that's not Charlie in there. Not our Charlie, not *yours*.'

'Antoinette?' Loki steps into the doorway of the shed. 'What is it?' There's a baby's bottle in his hand, filled with what must be the fruit juice he brought with them from the house. She pictures the charliedoll's mouth sealing itself tight around that rubbery latex teat and sucking, can imagine the wet, fleshy sounds of his lips and tongue greedily at work, and her stomach rolls.

'I'm sorry,' Antoinette slurs queasily, then she bends forward and vomits more vodka onto the grass.

'He is not your brother,' Sally Paige tells them. 'He never was your brother, the same as that pretty boy out there was never *Paul*. Your brother is dead.'

Lina watches her face for any signs of deceit. The woman has been lying to them their entire lives, and Lina trusts her like she would a scorpion. She glances at Ant, hoping again to catch her eye. But her sister is still hunched over in the chair beside the bed. Head in hands, elbows on knees. She's said very little since Lina and Loki dragged her back to the house and forced half a litre of water down her throat.

Just, *I need to talk to Mum.* And, *I have to know.*

She won't even look at Lina. Wouldn't look at Loki, either. Didn't even protest when her mother rasped at him to leave, to get the hell out of her bedroom. He wasn't wanted there. He wasn't wanted anywhere. Ant simply stared at the floor. Lina was having none of it—Sally Paige had no right to talk to him like that—but he quickly shushed her.

It's okay. I'll go and keep Charlie company.

Lina swallows. The sounds the boy made when they tried to bring him up to the house still echo in her ears. Those high-pitched squeals of distress as he flopped and writhed in Loki's arms, growing louder and more piercing the further he was carried away from the shed. The situation only made worse by Ant who, with flattened palms pressed to the sides of her head, kept screaming at Loki to turn around. To turn around and take him back right the fuck now.

Can't you see he's terrified? That shed is his whole world.

Even returned to his crib, it took a while to settle him. That great head rocked from side to side as Lina stroked his hair. His tiny, skinny body hitched and shook. She found his toy frog tangled in the sheet. Placed it into his hand. He hooted softly, stuffed a fluffy green foot into his mouth and began to suck.

Lina pushes the image aside.

'You shouldn't have been able to do it,' Sally Paige is saying to Ant. 'Whimsies, yes, but not a perfection—not even a broken shambles such as what's out in that shed. Good grief, you weren't even two years old. That you could manifest anything…'

Ant mumbles something that Lina, standing against the wall on the opposite side of the room, can't quite catch.

'Yes, well.' Sally Paige says. 'That's all so much spilled milk now.'

'Why does he look like that?' Lina asks.

'Do you remember that Baby Alive doll you had? You stuck a bottle of water or what-have-you in its mouth and the damn thing would start suckling it down. Peed it right out through a hole between its legs, so you could change its nappy.' She shakes her head. 'Horrible thing gave me the creeps. But my mother thought you would like it, Jacqueline, since you were so obsessed with playing mummies-and-babies.'

Lina frowns. 'Vaguely.'

'Doesn't matter. You didn't much care for the doll anyway. But your sister was fascinated.'

'I don't remember it,' Ant murmurs.

That doesn't matter either, according to Sally Paige. The fact is, she loved the damn doll. Would drag it around with her everywhere. Charles liked it as well, funnily enough. The two of them would play with it together, with Jacqueline watching doubtfully from the sidelines. They'd shove the bottle into its mouth and hold it up in the air, giggling as the liquid trickled out its nethers. But if Antoinette loved the doll, then she *adored* her older brother. And when Charles died, when he was no longer around to play dollies and blow raspberries on her tummy and ... well, she was only two years old, not even. How do you explain death to a toddler? How do explain *gone* and *forever* and *never ever coming back*?

All Antoinette understood was that she missed him.

And, missing him, she *made* him come back.

But it's hardly straightforward, the creation of a perfection. It requires focus and concentration and attention to detail. Not skills at which two-year-old girls tend to excel, and hence, Sally Paige conjectures, the *charliedoll*. Some freakish, stick-figure amalgam of favourite toy and faulty memory. Not at all what Antoinette wanted. Not her brother, not *Charlie*, and so she stumbled sobbing and horrified from her bedroom to find Mummy. Because Mummy would fix it. Mummy would make it better. Mummy would make the charliedoll go bye-de-bye-bye.

Because that's what a good Mummy *does*.

Ant lifts her head. 'You took him from me.'

'You were more than willing to give him up. He terrified you.'

'Do you remember any of this?' Lina asks.

Her sister looks ill. 'Just ... flashes. Bits and pieces.'

'Of course she doesn't remember,' Sally Paige snaps. 'Do you think I would let her carry that horror her entire life?'

One lesson she learned from all those parenting books: the mind of a young child is plastic. Impressionable. It fixates and fears. And it can be made to forget.

Aversion therapy. Hypnosis. Sally Paige playing amateur psychologist. Making sure that Antoinette would from then on associate terror and dread with any whimsical evocation. However transitory, however accidental. A relapse bringing with it threats to take her to the charliedoll, to *leave* her with the charliedoll *forever*, and after a while those threats were all that was needed. Threats and tears and crude hypnotic sessions that helped her youngest daughter to—quite literally—*put it out of her mind*. To stuff all the scary-bad away inside a box. To hide the box inside her heart. To lock the box with a super-secret key. To take that key and—

'Swallow it,' Ant whispers. 'Oh god, I *remember* that.'

'It was hard work,' Sally Paige says. As another parent might talk of potty training, or teaching their child to read.

But still, in the end, seven or eight months was all it took. Plus a few more years of careful vigilance, so that by the time Antoinette was in primary school, it seemed to have stuck for good. No more whimsies, no more *talk* of whimsies even. Just a normal little girl, like all the other normal little girls in her year. If somewhat more prone to anxiety and odd, irrational fears. Like baby dolls with glassy blue eyes or the bushland out back of the house. Like being asked to make up stories in class or join in playground games of *Let's Pretend*.

'Some of it rubbed off on you as well,' Sally Paige tells Lina. 'Fear is more contagious than chicken pox and children are very susceptible to the beliefs of those around them. Especially their siblings, or so the books reckon. It kept the both of you away from *him*, anyway.'

Lina is clenching her fists so tightly, it feels as though her fingernails are shearing straight through her palms. She opens her hands. A series of deep, savage crescents grin up at her. 'This is monstrous,' she hisses, and the hateful woman in the bed has the audacity to laugh.

'Yes,' Sally Paige says, contempt glinting in her eyes. '*Monstrous* is exactly what we are.'

Lina stalks towards her. No clear thought in her mind beyond inflicting some kind of hurt. She reaches for the plastic tubing that runs from the medication machine into the woman's scrawny-sallow chest, delivering her a painlessness so ill-deserved it's obscene, and—

'Jacqueline, don't.' Ant rises unsteadily from her chair.

'Why are you protecting her? She *tortured* you.'

'It's not her I'm protecting.' Eyes red-laced and bleary, her sister looks dead on her feet. Her voice trembles as much as the hand she now lifts. Fragile, pleading. 'This isn't who you are, Jacqueline—*Lina*. You're better than this. You're better than *her*.'

'Am I?' She shakes her head. 'No, I don't think so.'

'Please. I *need* you to be better.'

Lina hesitates. Half-hoping Sally Paige will pipe in with some gloating, goading remark. Final straw, permission slip, mitigating fucking circumstance. But she says nothing. Does nothing. *Is nothing*, Lina realises. Is merely the hollow, stiff-faced husk of a mother who never was. And Lina smiles, and folds her hands over her middle, and moves away from the woman cowering in the bed. One day, soon perhaps, she will bring a child of her own into the world. A child who will never know the poison that is Sally Paige. Who will never even know her name.

'Come on,' Lina says, walking around to her sister. 'You're exhausted, you should rest.' She takes Ant's hand. 'We don't need her anymore. We *never* needed her.'

At the door, her sister stops and glances back towards the bed. 'What did I lose?' she whispers. 'When I made … *Charlie*, what did I give up?'

Sally Paige shakes her head. 'I don't know, dear. Whatever it was, I doubt you'll have missed it. That poor creature is so simple, so *ill-conceived*, you could have put him together from doll parts and spit.'

'Ant, leave it. Let's go.'

'Yes, go,' Sally Paige says. 'I'm tired. I want to sleep.'

Lina puts an arm around her sister's waist. 'Come on.'

But Ant pulls away. 'You shouldn't have taken him, Mum. He wasn't your mistake, he was mine.'

'You were just a child.'

'Yes, but not anymore. And now I want him back.'

'Don't be stupid,' Sally Paige scoffs. 'You couldn't possibly cope, not with *three* of them. You just wait, my girl. Those two you have, they'll drag you down soon enough.'

'What's she talking about?' Lina asks.

'Nothing,' Ant says. 'It doesn't matter.'

'Oh, it *matters*, dear. Don't you kid yourself about that.'

'Ant?'

Her sister shrugs her off. 'This isn't the end of it, Mum.'

'No,' Sally Paige replies. 'I don't suppose it is.'

ø

Antoinette wakes, dry-mouthed and disoriented, a crick in her neck from where she's been curled against the arm of the couch. The dull, grey light of early evening seeps through the living room windows and someone has draped one of Sally Paige's crocheted throw rugs over her while she slept. She pushes herself upright, wincing at the pain throbbing behind her right eye. There's a glass of water on the coffee table, two small white tablets nudging its base, and Antoinette washes them down gratefully. Out in the kitchen, the kettle begins to shriek.

It's the only sound in the whole house.

With some effort, she gets to her feet. Shuffles into the kitchen with the throw still wrapped around her shoulders, motley caped crusader somewhat worse for wear, and finds her mother spooning tea leaves into a pot. 'You want a cup?'

Antoinette shakes her head. 'Where is everyone?'

'I heard them go outside earlier. I assume they're with *him*.'

'I meant what I said before.'

'So did I.'

'I'm not just going to let you take him with you.'

Her mother picks up the kettle, bracing her elbow with her other hand, and starts to fill the teapot. But her aim isn't the best and hot water splashes off the porcelain rim, splattering her wrist with scalding drops.

'Mum, here, let me.' Antoinette takes it from her. 'I don't know why you bother with a whole pot. You never finish the first cup half the time, and even if you do get to the second, the tea's gone cold.'

'It's better made in a pot. Tea bags are vile.'

'Whatever. You want to have this in the living room?'

'I'd rather not.' She glances towards the window, the backyard yawning empty in the diminishing light. 'They'll probably be in again soon.'

'You don't have to hide, Mum. It's your house.'

'Not while they're here, it isn't.'

Antoinette settles her mother back into bed and pours her a cup of tea. Sally Paige takes a small sip, makes a face like she's been tricked into drinking tepid swamp-water, and promptly passes it back. 'It tastes off.'

'I don't think tea can go off, Mum.' But she takes the cup anyway, puts it on the bedside table beside the pot. 'Do you want something else instead?'

Sally Paige makes no reply, just sits propped in her nest of pillows, frowning as she fiddles with her medication tube.

'Mum?'

'Your sister hates me.'

'Yes. I think she does.'

'Why don't you?'

'I guess … I can see your side of it. I mean, okay, you made the twins because you thought you couldn't have a baby of your own, but I created Loki because my stupid boyfriend dumped me. You can't get much more pathetic than that, really.'

'You didn't know what you were doing.'

'Yeah, but what you said, how we all want to believe that we'll be the one lucky woman who gets it right?' She rolls her eyes. 'I'm no different. Maybe it wouldn't have been *Loki*, but sooner or later I would've perfected *someone*, regardless of what you had or hadn't told me. So there's no use blaming you for that, and as for the rest ... I don't agree with most of it—I don't *like* any of it—but you did it for us, Jacqueline and me both. You tried to give us normal lives, and I can't hate you for that either.'

Her mother is silent for a moment. Then she nods, seemingly more to herself than to Antoinette, and pats the bed beside her. 'Come here. Sit down.'

Antoinette sinks into the mattress.

'You need to give me that boy,' her mother tells her.

'If I do that, it'll be the same as killing him.'

'Nevertheless.'

'No.' She swallows. 'If I get sick at some point, then fine, I get sick. Loki's done nothing wrong. He didn't ask to be here, and I'm not going to put a death sentence on his head just because things might ... get hard.'

'Things *will* get hard.'

'You carried two perfections for over twenty years. And you know what, Mum? You have *cancer*, not some magical, mystical illness that no one can explain. Yes, it's awful, but people get cancer all the time.'

'It's not the same,' her mother says. 'The *charliedoll* is barely alive, barely even sentient. He demands so little compared with your sister—that's *why* I could host them both for so long. Believe me, I know what two full-blown perfections can do to a woman. I had the twins for four years. Growing weaker as they grew older, more complicated, more demanding. They almost killed me, Antoinette.' She lowers her gaze, lowers her voice. 'It was unsustainable. *They* were unsustainable.'

'Mum ... I don't—'

'Choice can be the cruellest of illusions. Sometimes, there's no decision you can make that won't be wrong.' Clearing her throat, she lifts red-raw eyes to meet Antoinette's once again. 'But still, you have to make it.'

'No. Charlie, he ... it was an *accident*.'

'It wasn't *planned*. That's a whole world of difference.'

An ordinary Thursday afternoon. Bath time for the twins. A ringing phone. And Sally Paige, numb and nauseous as she's been for the past month or more, staring down at her two soapy, squealing children. If any thought stumbled across her foggy mind—and she doesn't think one did, not consciously at least—it must have been that her youngest daughter, her *real* daughter, might prefer an older *sister*.

And so it was Jacqueline she scooped out of the bath.

Jacqueline she wrapped in the fluffy yellow towel.

Jacqueline she carried, heavy and damp, through the empty house.

'You left Charlie alone *on purpose*?'

'No, I simply chose your sister. It's not the same.'

Sally Paige was on the phone for maybe a minute. As long as it took for the man from the library to remind her about the three overdue books she still had out on loan. For her to apologise and promise to bring them back the next day. She heard the crash as she hung up. The pain-laced wail cut surprisingly short. And Sally Paige put Jacqueline down on the kitchen floor. Left her swaddled in the towel and told her to wait. Mummy would be right back.

'He'd wanted the bottle of bubbles,' her mother says. 'I'd left them on the windowsill and he must have climbed up on the side of the tub to reach them. Slipped and hit his head when he fell.'

Antoinette holds up a hand. 'I know the rest of the story.'

'That's right, you know the *story*.'

Yes, Charles was unconscious when Sally Paige returned to the bathroom, but his face was not beneath the water. Instead, he'd fallen sideways and lay angled across the tub, his head propped up on the edge. Blood dripped from his scalp, threading scarlet down white enamel. He was still breathing as she slid his limp and unresisting body along the length of the tub, still breathing as she turned him over onto his stomach and placed her hand gently upon his head. But he never struggled. He never woke up.

The last thing Sally Paige did before calling the ambulance, was rinse away the blood from the side of the bath.

'You *murdered* him,' Antoinette whispers, horrified.

'I made a *choice*. I couldn't keep them both.'

Antoinette lurches to her feet. She can't be this close to her mother, not right now, maybe not ever again. 'And Charlie?' she says. '*My* Charlie? Why didn't you just do away with him as well? Instead of taking him from me, instead of keeping him locked up like some sideshow-alley freak?'

For a second, Sally Paige's face crumples—but only for a second. She wipes at her eyes with a corner of the sheet. 'You think I'm a monster.' Her voice is wavering and hoarse. 'And you're right. But whatever I am, whatever else I've done, I could *not* kill my son *twice*.'

Antoinette backs slowly away, bumps her hip on the edge of the open door. 'I can't listen to any more of this.'

'You have to give me Loki,' her mother insists. 'It's the easiest way.'

'Never.'

'Then you're a fool.'

'Maybe. But at least I'm not you.'

And Sally Paige laughs, actually *laughs*, a braying hyena cackle that chills Antoinette to the bone. 'We'll see. Like mother, like daughter—that's half *my* blood you have, running through those veins.'

Antoinette swallows. 'Tomorrow, I'm going to take Loki and my sister home. And then I'm coming back here, and I'm going to sit by your side every day. I'm going to watch as you get sicker, as the pain gets worse and the drugs get stronger, and when you're weak enough, confused enough, I'm going to reach in there and take back my brother.'

'You can't do that.' But that voice is uncertain now, tinged with doubt.

'I think you know I can,' Antoinette says. 'I think you know I will.'

Then she smiles, a sour-sharp twist of her lips that—god help her—must be the spitting image of a patented Sally Paige grimace, and steps backwards from the room, pulling the door shut behind her.

And, *oh*—

Gasping, hand flying to her heart as she almost runs, smack-bang right into the both of them: Loki-Lina huddled Siamese in the darkling hallway, two pairs of eavesdropping ears, two pairs of startled eyes opening wide, and Antoinette doesn't even need to ask how much they might have overheard.

Lina holds her sister's hand. 'No more secrets. Promise?'

'I wanted to tell you,' Ant says. 'I just didn't know how.'

'Whatever happens, we deal with it together. All three of us.'

'I'm sorry, I just … Loki? I'm so, so sorry.'

'You didn't do anything.'

'But I was going to—'

'But you *didn't*.'

'It's all right,' Lina tells her. 'We understand, we do.' But even so, she feels it. The splinter now wedged between them. Preparing to fester.

'Do you believe her?' Loki asks her sister. 'What she said, about not being able to have more than one of us?'

'I don't know. I feel okay right now, so maybe...' Ant shrugs. 'I know she's resentful, and I know she hates you, Loki, the idea of you. I think she would do anything, say anything, to get me to give you up.'

'Then don't try to take Charlie,' he says.

'What?' Ant stares at him. 'Why not?'

'Loki,' Lina says. 'She can't just leave him with—'

'Yes, she can.' He turns back to Ant. 'You can, you should. If you give your mother another chance, what's to say she won't just snatch Lina back again? Or me, while she's at it? It's too dangerous.'

'I won't let that happen.'

'Maybe you won't have a *choice*.'

'Enough,' Lina tells them. 'Please, just stop. It's been a really long, really awful day and we're all on edge. If we keep talking about this now, we'll end up saying things that we'll wish we hadn't.'

Loki leans back in his chair, arms crossed. 'It's a bad idea, that's all *I'm* saying. Sally Paige can't be trusted.'

'I heard you the first time,' Ant snaps. 'Point noted.'

'*Point noted?* We should get as much say in this as you. Lina, tell her.'

'Loki, I don't think this is the time—'

'What about Charlie?' Ant ignores Lina. Her anger is directed at Loki alone. 'You're so keen on all this tribal council bullshit, tell me, does Charlie get to *have a say* before you vote to kick him off the fucking island?'

'He's not *on* the island, remember? You didn't seem so concerned about Rights for Retards when you cut him adrift the first time.'

'Stop it!' Lina glares at the both of them. 'I trust that old woman about as far as I could spit, and *of course* I want to do whatever we can for Charlie. But nothing has to be decided tonight. Not a damn thing.'

Ant gets to her feet. 'Peachy kittens.'

'Where are you going?' Lina asks.

'To get a drink,' her sister snaps as she stalks from the room.

Loki mutters darkly, unintelligibly beneath his breath.

Lina decides she'd rather not know. 'Let her sleep on it,' she tells him. 'She needs time to digest everything that's happened. I think we all do.'

'This thing with Charlie—'

'It's her decision, Loki. We can't force her to do anything, or even *not* to do anything.'

'But you can't agree with her.'

'I honestly don't know. It's a risk, yes, but it doesn't seem right to just … if it was you, or me—'

'But it's *not* us.'

'Loki, please, I really don't want to talk about this now.'

He shakes his head. 'Your mother was right about one thing.'

'Loki…'

'Sometimes, all you have is the wrong choice.'

24

Sunday dawns grey and drizzly; a soft, misty rain that hangs indecisively in the early morning air rather than falls. Lina wishes she had packed sneakers, instead of only her sandals. Long, wet blades of grass catch between her toes. Slap at her bare legs. She still doesn't like coming down here. Still has to fight the anxiety that churns with each fresh step. But she wants to spend some time alone with Charlie before Ant drives her and Loki back home.

Back home, back to work. For one more week at least. Meet with Ryan, supervise the set-up for his show, finesse the earlybird clientele. Make sure opening night runs smoothly, make sure everyone is happy. Especially Susan Keyes. Before she puts in for compassionate leave. Ant will need her help to wrangle Sally Paige. To tease out each last scrap of information from that woman's stubborn, spiteful brain. Fact, hypothesis or baseless rumour—they want everything.

If her sister is going to gamble, all cards must be on the table.

Loki, meanwhile, will remain in the apartment with his books and his broadband. Continue the search for data in sources other than Sally Paige. They can't be the only perfections in the world. Someone out there knows something. Will have left some sort of breadcrumb trail, however cryptic or oblique. All that's required is a keen eye for needles.

That's the plan, anyway. Tossed together in the thin, restless hour before the sun began to rise. Before she abandoned any hopes of getting back to sleep.

It's a *good* plan.

A bird squawks, rockets out of the scrub, and Lina jumps. Chokes back a startled cry. 'Stupid,' she chides herself. How much worse it will be for Ant, having to force herself along this path each day to care for Charlie. To give him his bottle of juice or water or the baby formula they found hidden away in the laundry cupboard. Change his nappies. Make sure his radio has working batteries.

Knowing why I'm terrified of the place doesn't help, Jacqueline. It just makes me feel stupider.

Until now, Sally Paige has been making daily pilgrimages. Tasking Ant with some spurious, sickbed errand away from the house this past week, or so her sister surmises, before hobbling down to the shed and back. But Lina doesn't want the old woman to go near Charlie ever again. Merely the thought of those wrinkled fingers scraping against his smooth, pink-mottled skin is more than she can stand.

No, Ant will have to do it. She will make her promise.

Lina knocks softly on the shed door before opening it. 'Hey there,' she calls to the figure curled beneath the sheet. 'It's only me.' He doesn't stir, doesn't rock his head or hoot his usual greeting. She steps closer. Crouches beside the crib and looks into those huge, open eyes. Eyes that neither blink nor focus, but simply stare past her. Through her. Dull and lifeless as a discarded doll's.

Antoinette is buried under rubble. A heavy, persistent weight of dirt and rock and debris, pinning her down in this noiseless dark. It isn't so bad if she keeps her eyes squeezed shut, isn't so scary, and maybe if she just lies here and doesn't move, maybe everything will be okay. This is what she wants to tell the hands that scavenge unrelenting through the wreckage above, pulling at her clothes and her skin like the beaks of carrion birds. *Stop*, she wants to tell them, *leave it, leave me*, but her mouth is foul with grit, with the sand that pours in over her tongue and fills her throat, fills the empty sack of her body, spills from her seams—

Ant please, I need you

—and she groans and heaves and rolls, giving herself over to the grasp of all those greedy hands. Hands that now clutch her by the shoulders, that now drag her, bruised and leaden-limbed, up to the surface and the stale air.

'Come on, Ant. Wake up.'

Antoinette blinks groggily and clears her throat, half-expecting to cough up a lungful of sour, clotted dirt. Her sister's face is grim, her eyes red and glossed with the residue of tears. 'Jacqueline, what's wrong?'

'Charlie's dead.'

'What?' She sits up. 'What happened?'

'I don't know. I went down to see him and he was just … lying there. Curled up in his crib with that stupid frog tucked under his chin.'

Antoinette throws back the doona and swings her legs over the side of the bed. 'Well something must have happened. He can't have *just died*.' She pulls on her sheepskin slippers, scoops up her dressing gown from where it lies puddled on the floor by the desk. 'Can he?'

Her sister shrugs helplessly.

'Hey.' Behind them, Loki appears in the doorway, yawning and scratching his chin. 'What's going on?'

And Antoinette is struck by the sudden, incongruous realisation that she has never, not once, seen him shave. Never spied the faintest trace of stubble, either, his face perpetually clear and waxen-smooth, no matter the time of day or night, and she cringes from the thought that this is something else she has done to him, stolen from him. Because if he *could* grow a beard, then he almost certainly would have by now. Facial hair so simple a mask, such an easy point of difference to cultivate. Better than avoiding mirrors the way he does, mirrors and any polished surface that might throw back that perfect, carbon-copied face he seems to despise.

'Are you sure?' Loki is asking Jacqueline, and she nods. Yes, she's sure. She *saw* him. Lying there so still and quiet, as though someone flicked off a switch, as though his batteries ran out mid-breath—

—and then Antoinette is moving, pushing past her sister, twisting away from Loki as he tries to catch her arm. *Please please please please*. Running now, or close to it, stumbling down the hall with dread building a home in her chest. *Please please please please*. Desperate, useless little word. No magic left in it at all, and she knows this, knows it even as she reaches the silent, still-closed door to her mother's room, as the handle turns in her hand. Knows it, *knows it*, but still.

Please please please please.

There's no pulse, no matter how deep Antoinette presses her fingers into the cool, slack wrinkles of her mother's throat. No breath to fog the mirror she made Jacqueline fetch from the bathroom. The Dilaudid is all but gone. Some of it spilled onto the sheets where the bottle has fallen, but most no doubt sucked through the green bendy straw that still pokes, pathetic and somewhat surreal, from the brown-glass neck.

Antoinette picks up the bottle. It smells sweet. Palatable.

'Should we be touching anything?' Jacqueline asks. She's looking at the large manila envelope lying on the end of the bed, the envelope with Antoinette's name written on the front in small, square letters.

Antoinette puts the Dilaudid bottle back where it came from, an inch or so from the motionless, spider-curled fingers of her mother's right hand. Her mother. The woman in the bed looks nothing like her mother. That face mottled and grey, but still more relaxed than Sally Paige ever seemed in life. Mouth hanging slightly open, upper teeth protruding just a little. Eyes all but closed, sunken in their sockets.

'Here,' Jacqueline says, holding out the envelope.

She shakes her head, sinks for what might be the last time into the chair beside the bed, its sagging padded seat sighing beneath her weight. On the night table, the syringe driver echoes the sound, wheezing as it obliviously pumps another shot of meds through the dead woman's system.

'Should that thing still be running?' Loki asks, standing sentry in the hall. He refuses to step foot inside the room.

Antoinette looks at the little machine. There's no power button, although the nurse did show her how to take out and replace the battery. So maybe, in a minute, that's what she'll do. In a minute.

Her sister waves the envelope again. 'Do you mind if I...'

She doesn't even bother with the headshake this time, just wraps her arms around her shoulders and slumps down even further. She's so tired, she could go right back to bed, find herself a spindle and sleep for a thousand years, rose-slashing princes and all their valiant steeds be damned.

Part of her watches her sister slide a fingernail beneath the envelope's flap and extract a sheaf of paper, and part of her is looking elsewhere. Hunting the chambers and hollow rooms of her heart until she finds it, the Big Box of Scary-Bad, finds it and pulls it out from where it has been hidden for so many forgotten years. Still lots of room inside, more than enough to stow Sally Paige away. The little glass bottle with its bendy straw as well.

It's not a note or anything, Jacqueline's voice is feeble and distant. *Just legal stuff. Some kind of funeral plan, plus a copy of her will, and—oh, Ant, apparently she made you executor. Did you know about that?*

Details and all their associated devils, nothing she knows about, nothing she *cares* to know about, so those go into the box as well. She nods. Murmurs suitable responses as her sister continues to speak, or maybe not so suitable responses, because now Jacqueline is crying again, standing right in front of her and asking about *Charlie*, about *Sally Paige*, about whether there is anything Antoinette can do, and *no*, she says, and *he's gone*, and *I'm tired, just let me sit here for a minute.*

Just for a minute.

The look on her sister's face, scared and sad and panic-stricken—she folds *that* up too, small and sharp-cornered, and tucks it so deep inside the Box of Scary-Bad, she hopes it might never escape again. And if the box has grown too large now to forget, too unwieldy to lose or hide or overlook, still it's better that those things are kept inside, those broken and jagged and toothsome things that might otherwise draw blood, or worse. It contains them, confines them, makes them safer to observe from vantage points slantwise and sly, and when Antoinette feels too queasy from looking, she can always close the lid.

The box takes so much, Jonah's whale gaping and greedy, gulping down all that she can find to feed it.

When the doorbell rings, chiming clarion through the house, her sister and Loki exchange a startled glance. Then, *the nurse*, Jacqueline says, and *I'll make myself scarce*, Loki replies, mutters something else about seeing Charlie for himself, except he doesn't say *Charlie*, he says *the charliedoll*, and the word scratches at Antoinette and she doesn't get up from her chair even when the nurse bustles into the room, Jacqueline trailing at her heels. A large woman, brisk and brusque, less chatty than the weekday nurse, but today she smiles gently and pats Antoinette's shoulder, and her voice is muted with sympathy. *Sometimes they choose to go on their own terms, love. Have you had a chance to call her doctor yet?* The syringe driver gets in one last wheeze before she slides open the casing and ejects the battery with a blunt, unvarnished nail.

Antoinette blinks. Shoves this all into the box.

By the time Dr Chiang arrives, she can no longer find words of her own to speak. So Jacqueline answers his questions while Antoinette just sits, watching him perform his checks of Sally Paige's body as if it isn't blindingly obvious that *a body* is all that she is, watching his mouth quirk when he takes the Dilaudid bottle and holds it to the light, removes the straw and stares for a moment before placing it gently, carefully on the night table. *Normally, a death like this needs to be reported to the Coroner's Office. The police will come, an autopsy is likely.* His gaze skims over Antoinette, lands square on her sister. *But I don't believe that's necessary, do you? To put this dear lady through such a grubby business?* And Jacqueline pauses, and she shakes her head, and Antoinette watches as the good doctor drops the Dilaudid bottle into his bag, then leans over and kisses Sally Paige's colourless cheek, whispers something that sounds like *goodbye*, that sounds like *you're welcome*, into the empty shell of her ear. And the Cause of Death certificate he leaves with them says *heart failure*, says *malignant neoplasms*. Makes no mention of hydromorphone or fatal overdoses or plastic bendy straws the colour of bile and spite.

The box swallows this too.

Jacqueline on the phone, the funeral service papers from Sally Paige's yellow envelope in her hand. *No, we don't need any more time with … with her. Please come as soon as you can.* And so they do, the smart middled-aged woman in her smart middle-aged suit who sits with them in the living room while her two latex-gloved colleagues remove the body from the house. Everything pre-arranged and paid in full, but alterations can still be made, the woman advises. *Sometimes family members choose to add personal touches of their own; it helps them feel more connected to the service.* Jacqueline shakes her head, *thank you but no*, and Antoinette, still lost for words, follows her sister's lead. Sits up straight like Jacqueline, crosses her legs in just the same efficient way and nods along, plays echo with her sister's curt and careful responses. Only later, once the funeral people have departed with their newly signed permission slips, does Jacqueline grab her by the arm, worried and wide-eyed, and *what the hell was that*, she demands to know. *You need to stop with the damn echolalia, Ant. You're starting to scare me.*

Into the box, into the box.

Loki, filthy hands and sweat-grimed face, fridge door propped on his hip as he gulps down juice straight from the bottle. *You've buried him?* Jacqueline incredulous, possibly appalled, *that's what you've been doing all day?* And, not quite, he tells her, he's just dug the hole. *I thought you might want to say goodbye before I fill it in, both of you.* Antoinette shaking her head, turning her back, and so it's only her sister and Loki who end up going down to the shed. Who end up coming back snappish as snarling dogs, Loki wanting to know why they have to leave, why they can't just stay up here, Jacqueline reminding him that she has to get back to work, and *oh*, he sneers, *that's right*. Her precious gallery with her precious Brisbane dilettante, obviously so much more important than her *family* at a time like this, and Jacqueline looses a venomous glare, tells him to shut up and get his things together, tells him they're leaving as soon as they're packed. *And don't forget to wash your hands*, she says, pitch-perfect Sally Paige redux. *That oleander you picked for Charlie's grave is toxic.*

The box groans, bulges at the sides.

A car engine roars to life out the front while Jacqueline is helping Antoinette to gather her clothes. Deeper, far more guttural than the Laser's familiar purr and her sister swears, drops the shirt she's been folding and runs. Antoinette follows at a dawdle, less curious than reluctant to be on her own, and discovers Jacqueline on the verandah, glaring at the oily stain in the carport where Sally Paige's Commodore should be parked. *He'll be back soon, Ant, don't worry; he's only blowing off steam.* But obviously worried herself once night seeps in, pacing the living room windows with nails gnawed between teeth, freezing hopeful at any sound of an approaching vehicle, until at last Antoinette takes her sister's hand, presses it tight to her chest, and *oh*, Jacqueline says, and *of course. You'd know if anything happened to him.*

And Antoinette pushes down on the lid, pushes down hard and feels it shudder beneath the pressure of everything inside, pushing back harder.

Three eggs left in the fridge which Jacqueline scrambles for supper, shares out on toast between them, though Antoinette does little more than pick at the fringes of hers. The dishes are something she *can* do, and so she does. Hands thrust in water near hot enough to blanch, scrubbing thorough and empty-headed as her sister talks on the phone. *Sorry, Becca, but someone needs to be there in the morning in case the truck turns up early.* Only when pumpkin hour zips past with still no sign of Loki, does Jacqueline call it a night. *He'll be here when we wake up, Ant, you'll see.* Crammed tight as sardines in Antoinette's single bed—neither of them wanting to sleep alone in *this* house, on *this* night—Jacqueline's arm around her waist, breath whisper-warm on the back of her neck. *Can I tell you a secret?* Antoinette nods and makes a small, soft noise in her throat that's as close as she can manage to *yes*, and her sister finds her hand and squeezes it. *When I have a baby, I'm going to name him Charles. Or Charlotte, I think, if it's a girl.* And Antoinette makes another noise, smaller and softer, and Jacqueline squeezes her hand again. *I know, they're both such beautiful names.*

No room left in the box now, not the scarcest sliver of space.

So, in the morning, dream-worn and drained, the taste of grit fresh in her mouth, Antoinette shuffles out to the kitchen where her sister is brewing a pot of peppermint tea. *We can't wait around for him all day*, Jacqueline says, her face a stony blend of frustration and fear. Antoinette coughs and clears her throat, finds a small cache of words tucked right at the back of her tongue and sorts carefully through it: *I can drive us back home.* Her sister looks doubtful but, *it's okay*, Antoinette tells her, *I'm okay, I can drive.* And she is, for the most part. Only pulling over twice into the emergency lane as those grease-dark shadows in her peripheral vision stagger briefly onto centre stage. Even so, Jacqueline is visibly shaken by the time they reach the apartment. *We should take you to a doctor, Ant.* A suggestion so silly, Antoinette might laugh if laughing didn't seem so taxing. *Go to work, Jacqueline. I just need to get some sleep.*

Except she doesn't.

Except she can't.

The place is too quiet, too empty, and the Big Box of Scary-Bad thumps and scrapes along the floor of her heart until she perches herself right upon its lid, puts her whole weight into holding it down, holding it still.

Holding *herself* so very, very still.

And when her phone shimmies and bounces into life, that insipid jazzy ringtone she never has gotten around to changing—oh, how she wants it to be Jacqueline, *needs* it be Jacqueline or even Loki, needs one of them to be here beside her at least, right beside her, close enough to soothe the restless shift and sway of the stones that hang behind her ribs. But it's only Sharon, asking how the weekend went and if her sister has been and gone, asking if she should bring anything up to Mount Doom with her today. If Antoinette still wants her to come back up, that is. If—

I'm not at Mum's. She died. She died yesterday.

Two heartbeat's worth of silence, then: *Where are you now?*

At Jacqueline's. We came back this morning and—

Stay there. I'm on my way.

She wants to know where Sharon thinks she might go but the call is already cut, and so she waits, and waits, and when the girl finally arrives, rapping on the door in trackpants and a glitter-spun unicorn hoodie, she asks her then. *Where am I supposed to go, Sharon? Where do you think I should go?* And Sharon hugs her, right there on the doorstep, and somehow keeps hugging her even as she wrangles her back into the apartment. The girl is warm and soft, and her arms are surprisingly strong, and she knows nothing of the box or of anything that Antoinette has had to stuff inside it, and this also makes her *safe*.

'I'm so scared,' Antoinette whispers.

'That's okay,' Sharon whispers back. 'You're allowed to be scared.'

The box heaves again, swells and threatens to split, and Antoinette can't keep the lid in place anymore, doesn't *want* to keep it in place, and so with a sob she moves aside. Presses her face to the girl's shoulder, and allows it all to come tumbling loose.

Becca called Dante. Of course she did. Her boss is leaning against the desk at the rear of Seventh Circle, laughing with Ryan Jellicoe as though the two of them are best mates. As though they always have been. There's no sign of the girl herself.

'Jacks!' Dante shouts as Lina walks through the doors. 'So glad you could spare the time to join us.'

Ryan swivels, his already toothy smile broadening to a grin. 'Hey you.' His dreads are tied loosely back with what appears to be a strip of paint-spattered canvas. When he hugs her, the smell of ti-tree oil fills her nose. Fills her heart with emotions too complex to immediately tease out, and Lina is alarmed to find tears at the corners of her eyes.

'Hey yourself,' she says, recovering. Puts her cheek in the way of his lips as he leans in for a kiss. Behind his back, Dante is smirking. Lina rolls her eyes and steps from Ryan's embrace. 'It's really good to see you,' she tells him, and means it. Ryan Jellicoe is simple. Easy. Probably the easiest thing in her life right now.

'All right,' Dante says. 'I hate to break up this heart-warming reunion, but there's a handful of masterpieces gonna be rolling up any minute.'

Lina glances at her watch. 'It's not even midday.'

'Because transport is renowned for sticking to schedule, yeah? They called an hour ago, said they were on their way.'

'Sorry you had to come in, Dante. I did tell Becca to handle things—'

'Including this charming guy here? Bit much to foist on the poor girl first thing Monday morning, don't you reckon?'

'But I...' Lina frowns at Ryan. 'Didn't you get my message last night? I told you I wasn't going to be able to make it for brunch.'

At least he has the decency to look sheepish. 'Yeah, maybe not.'

'Ryan, would it kill you to check your phone once in a while? In case, I don't know, someone might actually be trying to reach you about something important? Like, oh let's see, *your first major exhibition*, perhaps?'

'Might be easier to plant a GPS chip in my arse and be done with it.'

Dante laughs. 'Welcome to my world, Jacks.'

And then her own phone rings and the two men swap glances.

'Better get that,' Dante says.

'It might be important,' Ryan adds.

Both of them deadpan, or nearly so.

'Very funny,' Lina says as she pulls her phone from her coat pocket. The number comes up as unknown and her stomach lurches. Hope twisted with the faint afterburn of anger. She turns away from Dante, from Ryan. Walks half a dozen paces and keeps her voice low. 'Loki?

It's not Loki. It's the woman from the funeral home. Confirming that the service could be held tomorrow as requested, if they're absolutely certain they want it so soon. The notices won't appear in the papers until the morning, which doesn't give anyone a lot of time—

'We don't need time,' Lina tells her. 'We just want it over with.'

The woman reassures her that this is normal. This is understandable. People grieve in different ways, at different speeds. Lina doesn't need reassurance. All she needs are the details. She takes her diary from her bag and scribbles down the address of the crematorium. The woman starts to give driving directions, but Lina cuts her off again. She remembers the glazed expression in her sister's eyes that morning as she pulled the car over to the side of the road. *I just need a minute, Jacqueline. I'm ... I'm not seeing so good.*

'We'll be taking a taxi,' Lina says. 'Thanks for all your help.'

Behind her, the gallery doors swoosh open and Becca waltzes inside. She balances a takeaway coffee tray in her right hand, a Krispy Kreme box in her left. 'Truck's arrived,' she says cheerfully, jerking her head back towards the man in the Day-Glo yellow shirt who follows at her heels. The girl's face falls only a little when she spots Lina. 'Oh, hiya.' She considers the three cups in her tray. 'Sorry, you want me to run back and grab you something?'

Lina shakes her head. 'I'm fine.'

It takes a good couple of hours to fully unload, unpack and inspect each and every canvas, then stack them away in the storeroom. Ryan more anxious than he tries to let on. Dante, despite himself, obviously impressed with the work.

'It's not what we were after originally,' he tells Lina. 'But still, it's got a certain weight to it, yeah? A gravitas I wasn't expecting from the photos Jellicoe sent. You might have made the right call here.'

'Might?'

'Let's see what our Fearless Leader thinks come opening night.'

Lina nods. 'Dante, I need a favour.'

'Oh, doth pray tell.'

'I need to leave early tomorrow. Round about lunchtime.'

'Jesus, for real?' He scratches an irritated hand through his crew cut. 'A half-day today, another one tomorrow—you realise you do still work here, yeah? You can't just be running around on secret women's business whenever it takes your fancy.'

'It's for a funeral,' Lina tells him. 'My mother died on the weekend.'

He stares at her. Hand frozen on top of his skull. 'You're taking the piss.'

'I'm afraid not.'

'Fuck me, Jacks. What the hell are you doing here?'

Dante takes a step forward. Moves as though he's about to put an arm around her, and Lina shifts subtly sideways. Boss turned father figure isn't something she needs right now. Or ever. 'It's all right, really. We weren't close. I'm only going to the funeral because my sister will need me. She's not … she's not really herself at the moment.'

'Yeah, maybe because her mother just died. Jacks, *your* mother just died. Go home, fuck.' He pulls his wallet from his back pocket. Slides out a CabCharge voucher, folded neatly in half. Thrusts it towards her. 'The hell with that PT shit, here. Take the rest of the week if you need it.'

'I don't.' She keeps her voice even and firm. 'I need to be here.'

Dante seems about to object, then catches himself. 'Yeah, okay, sure. Healthy distractions, busy minds, not so much with the dwelling on the sad. I get it, but Jacqueline? *I do not want to see you here tomorrow.* Capiche?'

Lina takes the voucher. 'Capiche.'

In the taxi, she calls home to see if Ant needs anything. An unfamiliar female voice answers. 'Sorry,' Lina says. 'I think I've—'

'Jacqueline? Is that you?'

Jack-lin, the voice pronounces it. Ugly, blunt syllables in brutal collision.

'Who is this?' Lina demands.

'Sharon, I'm a friend of Ant's. You, um, you probably know me as Greta.'

'*Greta?*' Lina rubs at her forehead, fuzzy images jigsawing together. She only ever met the woman a couple of times. That severe, blunt fringe. Thick black eyeliner and ruby lipstick. Velvet. Corsets. The dead bat brooch. 'What are you doing in my apartment? Where's my sister?'

Asleep, that decidedly un-Germanic voice informs her. She crashed out a while ago. Burned herself out more like. There's been tears, lot of them. Lot of weird-arse talk about … well, anyway. Her mother's death seems to have hit her pretty hard and—*oh*, the woman exclaims with a strange, squeaky gasp. Oh god, she's sorry, of course Sally was Jacqueline's mother as well. She didn't mean to—

'It's fine,' Lina breaks in. 'I'm fine.'

'I'm really sorry, Jacqueline. I was only up there on Friday and she seemed okay. Not, *okay* okay, but, you know…'

'Greta—'

'Sharon.'

'*Sharon.* Look, has anyone else called? Dropped by perhaps?'

'You mean Loki?'

Lina takes a breath, holds it. 'You know about him?'

'Ant told me a few things, Paul as well, and between the two of them, it's getting kinda hard to weed out the crazy. But no, this mysterious Loki-guy of yours hasn't been around.'

'I'm on my way home now,' Lina says. 'Can you, ah, *would* you mind waiting until I get there? Please? In case she wakes up.'

'That was my plan, but she'll probably be out for a while anyway. I gave her a couple of Xanax.'

'You did *what*?'

'Jacqueline, calm down. I said *Xanax*, not Nembutal.'

'It's *dangerous*. You can't just run around passing out prescription drugs to people as though they're nothing more than vitamin pills.'

'I know that,' Sharon replies. 'But she's okay, I promise. I care about your sister a hell of a lot, you know. I'd never do anything to hurt her.'

Lina closes her eyes. *I can't hurt her, not ever.* Loki's words, a promise made on more than one occasion, and where the hell is he now? Right now, when her sister needs him? When *she* needs him. 'I'm sorry,' she tells the woman on the other end of the line. 'Thank you for looking after her, honestly. She's had a rough couple of days.'

'So have you,' Sharon says. 'And don't think she doesn't know that. Whatever really happened between you and her and your mother, this guilt-trip she's on is messing her up something fierce.'

25

'I don't like it,' Ryan says, arms folded. 'I told you I didn't like the placement before the thing was even hung.'

'That's the only place it can hang,' Lina replies. 'A canvas that size requires a certain volume of space.'

'But it can't be the first thing you see. All the other paintings prime you for this one. It's the climax; you should build towards it gradually, not have it blow up in your face at the first little tickle.'

'Seventh Circle isn't a labyrinth, Ryan. What you see is what you get.'

'If we bring that divider around. Block the view of the back alcove?'

'You really want people to only have a couple square metres in which to view it? *Expulsion* is a vista, you need to be able to stand back and really appreciate it.'

He scowls. Swivels on his heel to survey the gallery as though an alternative solution might suddenly present itself.

'Look,' she says. 'Let's just hang the rest of the show as per the layout we have here. And if you *really* hate it once everything is up on the walls, then I will stay back and rehang the whole thing myself. I promise.'

A pair of boots scuff across the floor behind her. Zane, on self-appointed sidekick duty since she arrived with Ryan this morning, though accomplishing little more than making a nuisance of herself. 'You know what?' The girl twists one of her dreadlocks, now dyed a brilliant turquoise, around her index finger. 'I reckon Jacqueline's right about this. You should listen to her.'

Lina raises her eyebrows.

'What?' Zane shrugs. 'We'll be here all night, he keeps fussing like a baby over every single one. Might as well do it your way.'

Ryan glowers. 'Big mouth, little thing.'

Her grin turns into a yawn, wide and unashamed, as she stretches her arms above her head. The purple T-shirt she's wearing rides up. Exposes the tanned curve of her stomach and a navel piercing the same colour as her hair. 'I'm doing a coffee run,' she announces. 'Who wants in?'

'We good?' Lina asks Ryan.

He sighs heavily. 'Yeah, we're good. Let's just get this done.'

'It'll look great, I promise.' She smiles, then turns to Zane. 'Give me a minute, will you? I'll pop up and see if my sister wants something.'

Ant is sitting cross-legged on the couch in Dante's office, a glossy art journal splayed in her lap. Several more lie on the floor at her feet. She refused to remain home today, not even with Sharon volunteering to drop in and keep her company.

It's not that I can't be alone, Jacqueline; it's that I can't be far from you.

Her sister has been on and off the past couple of days. Worse since the funeral, Lina thinks, and wishes again that they hadn't bothered to attend. Just the three of them occupying half a pew in the back of the crematorium chapel, Lina and Ant, along with Sharon who offered to drive. Sharon, who Lina believes she might actually like. Might be someone with whom she could have been friends had they met under less complicated circumstances. Without the careful, courteous sense of awkwardness that hovers between Sharon and her sister.

'I thought you were napping,' Lina says now.

Ant doesn't move. Doesn't look up. Simply stares, frozen, at the pages in her lap. Intimations of last night, when Lina discovered her sister standing in the middle of the kitchen floor. An apple raised in her hand. Round and red, minus the single perfect bite she said she didn't remember taking.

'Ant?' Lina steps into the office. Touches her sister on the shoulder.

Antoinette blinks. Lifts her head. 'Sorry? What did you say?'

'Nothing. Did you manage to sleep?'

'I lay down for a while.' She sniffs and rubs at her nose. 'It's hard to…' A pause, too long, before she blinks again. 'Sometimes, I don't know where I am, or I think I do, but then I'm not there.

I wish Loki would come back. If he was here, if he was closer ... maybe...'

'He won't leave us, Ant. He would never do that.' Her sister smiles. Frail. Old. A shade too close to Sally Paige for Lina to be entirely comfortable. She leans down and takes the journal from Ant's unprotesting hands. 'You should try to get some rest. Zane's going for coffee—I can ask her to get you a hot chocolate if you like.'

'How about a teddy bear while she's at it? A book of bedtime stories maybe?'

'Very funny.'

At least this time the smile belongs wholly to Antoinette. 'You know, I've never really known much about your job here. All this high art stuff, it kinda flies over my head.' She nods towards the magazines on the floor. 'But, be honest, Jacqueline—there's an awful lot of wank, isn't there?'

Lina sits down on the arm of the couch. 'There's *some* wank, certainly. But art is an ongoing dialogue; it's a type of conversation. You can't walk into the middle of a conversation and expect it to make perfect sense. You need to listen for a while before you join in.'

'You really love this stuff, don't you?'

Lina smiles. 'I really do.'

'That Ryan guy downstairs? I think his apocalypse paintings are cool.'

'You realise his apocalypse isn't caused by zombies, right?'

'Shut up.' Ant swats her across the knee. 'They're still cool.'

Outside, boots thump heavy on the stairs. 'Hey, you guys?' Zane calls. 'Some of us are about to die of caffeine deprivation, you don't hurry up.'

Lina gets to her feet. 'Flat white, two sugars?'

'Actually, you know what? Hot chocolate does sound pretty good.'

'Done.' She bends over, plants a kiss on top of her sister's head. Those long dark curls closer now to brown, Lina notices. That rich black dye all but washed, all but faded, from sight.

Ground control to Major Ant. Hey, space odyssey, you in there?

Finger snap in front of her face and Antoinette rolls toward their blunt, beetle-click sounds, propels herself forward and up and into the glare of the overhead lights. Into the glare of the crouching man—no, not a glare, more amusement than anger, although she can see how those chiselled features would repose almost naturally to the latter. *Sister awakes! At long last.* And she recognises him now, that smug sneer and bleached hair cropped so short she can see the scalp shining beneath.

Dante? Sorry, was I … did I fall asleep?

Not unless you sleep with your eyes wide open.

She shakes her head, stretches her body from its tight possum curl, and Dante extends a hand, his fingers warm as they close around hers, and he pulls her to her feet, pulls her face right up to his own and peers into her eyes. *You high, sweetheart?* Antoinette shakes her head again, *no*, she's just ... she has trouble being here just now. And that's not the right way to put it, but Dante nods anyway, and his mouth softens around the edges like junk mail left out in the rain.

Poor kid. I was sorry to hear about your Mum, yeah?

Me too. I was sorry too.

Jacqueline is waiting at the bottom of the stairs—stairs that Antoinette navigates slowly and with care, one hand gripping the railing, grateful for the steady presence of Dante at her back. Ryan is waiting too, and that girl with the awesome blue dreads. *We thought we'd go out to dinner*, her sister tells her while Antoinette marvels at all the paintings now hung on the walls. *It's like the end of everything*, she says, *and like the start of it as well*, and Ryan looks pleased. More pleased than Jacqueline, who frowns and rakes her fingers through Antoinette's hair.

You're tired, Ant. We should just go home.

No, please, let's have dinner. I'm starving.

And for a second, it feels like she might even be speaking the truth.

Lina places a hand over her champagne glass when Dante pops the second bottle and begins a round of refills.

'Come on, Jacks. Don't pike on us now.'

'Early start,' she says. 'Susan will be in around nine.'

'*Susan* swills down with the best of them, love. You show up hung over, it'll be a badge of fucking honour in her book.'

Lina lets him top her up. Everyone else as well, except for Ant who has hardly drunk more than a mouthful from the original go-round. Then they raise their glasses once more. Renew their toast to the brilliance of Mr Ryan Jellicoe—a brilliance that Dante saw right from the start—and of course to Miss Jacqueline Paige, who knows how to kick arse and take names when the chips are down. Lina rolls her eyes. Catches a wink from Ryan as he nudges her ankle beneath the table. Slides his foot along the swell of her calf until she mouths at him to *stop it*. Her boss vanquishes his drink in one long, throat-bobbing gulp. Zane needs two.

'Child prodigy!' Dante laughs, killing the last of the bottle between them. 'Girl after my own heart. Watch this one, Jacks, she's going places.'

Ryan leans across the table. 'Just so you know: this doesn't count as our dinner.'

'Will there be another tantrum if I say that it does?'

'You want me to go down on my knees, girl, I will go down on my knees. The set-up looks great, yeah? The *thing* with *stuff* and all the *bits* … you were right, you were one hundred—no, *two* hundred—per cent right.'

She laughs. Somewhat tipsy, but nicely so. Not at all like that time with the vodka, what little of it she can remember. Not that she wants to remember, not here, not now. But too late, too late. Loki once more laying waste to her thoughts. Worried again, anxious. Three days without word. Without even a single phone call. If something did happen to him, would Ant really know? Could she really tell?

Lina turns to her sister. Takes her by the wrist. 'No secrets,' she whispers. 'We *promised*, remember?'

Ant merely stares at her with dark, dull eyes. 'No,' she echoes. 'No secrets.' As she cuts up her meat into fragments. Dices her vegetables down to mush. But despite her industry, despite the unpalatable mess her plate has become, Lina doesn't think her sister has swallowed so much as a single pea.

'Are you feeling all right?' Lina asks.

Ant pauses, then nods. A slow and careful dip of her head as though she fears more vigorous movement might topple it from her shoulders.

'How about we go home?'

She rubs her lips together. Moves them in a way that seems an attempt at speech.

'Is she okay?' Ryan asks, his forehead creasing with concern.

'I don't know.' Lina hunches near as she can to her sister's mouth. 'Ant, what did you say? I didn't hear you the first time.'

'Will he be there?' Croaky-hoarse words barely louder than breathing. 'Will he be at home?'

And Lina whispers back that, honestly, she doesn't know. He might be, he could very well be waiting at home for them tonight. Or perhaps he'll be there tomorrow. Tomorrow or the next day, but sometime. Because he *loves* them, he loves *both* of them, and he wouldn't just leave. 'You still feel him, don't you?'

Her sister nods. Lifts a loose fist to her sternum. 'I feel *both* of you.'

Lina straightens. 'Dante, I think we're going to...'

Her boss has his phone pressed against his right ear, while his other hand shields his left. 'Wait, *what*? Say that again.' His voice raised now, face contorted with frustration. 'I can't—damn this bloody signal.'

Lina throws a questioning glance down the table to Zane, but the girl only shrugs. Shakes her dreadlocked head, turns her palms to the air. Around them, people on nearby tables have lowered their own conversational levels. Lowered or ceased talking entirely, ears pricked and greedy for gossip.

Dante pales. 'Did you say *fire*? Yes. Yes, *fuck*, I'm on my way.' Out of his seat with wallet in hand. Waving at the maître d' who is already striding towards their table. 'Philippa—sorry, love.' He passes her a credit card. 'Got a situation happening. We'll square this all later, yeah?'

'Of course, Mr Moretti.' The tall brunette slides the card discreetly into her pocket. 'I'll order you a taxi.'

'Dante?' Lina is on her feet now as well. Ryan too, and Zane.

Her boss runs a hand back and forth over his scalp. Stares wild-eyed as though even *he* has trouble believing the words now stilting from his mouth: 'The gallery is on fire, Jacks. Seventh Circle is burning to the fucking ground.'

ॐ

Not to the ground—the building too solid; the fire brigade far too quick to respond to a blaze in the CBD—but certainly gutted, the interior rendered black with rubble and ash, filled with dripping water and the sodden smell of smoke. Antoinette huddles to one side, well away from the barrier of bright yellow tape, CRIME SCENE DO NOT ENTER in solid black caps like some surreal re-enactment of the CSI shows Paul used to download. Complete with rubber-neckers and looky-loos, a shifting semi-circle of pedestrians mostly disbanded now that the flames have been doused, now that the media have packed up their gear and retreated into the night, and Antoinette keeps to the side of them, too.

Ryan sags in the gutter, back turned away from the charred and ruined mess, from the jut of blackened wood and occasional scrap of canvas that flaps in the air. Those beautiful paintings, that cool non-zombie apocalypse, all gone. Antoinette wants to hug him but the blue-haired girl is already there, barnacled to his side, skinny arms wrapped around his waist. *Ryan*, the girl says, over and over. *Ryan, Ryan, oh god, Ryan.* While Ryan says nothing at all.

Antoinette shivers, rubs her arms against the chill in the air.

She looks over at her sister again, faithful lieutenant posted by Dante's side as he talks to the thin-faced cop, answering questions of her own as the cop nods and scribbles down notes in his pad. Jacqueline, eyes red and streaming with smoke-spiked tears, coughing into her fist and then pointing towards something within the hulking wreck of Seventh Circle, while Dante mimes a shoebox-sized shape with his hands. And the cop looks, and nods, and makes another note.

Until finally it seems to be over.

Or at least for Jacqueline. She approaches Ryan, places a hand on his head and says something that the night catches and spirits away. His shoulders hitch, and Jacqueline bites her lip, is already moving away when the blue-haired girl—Zane, that's it, her name is *Zane*—launches to her feet and catches Jacqueline in a massive bear hug. And Jacqueline hugs her right back, and whispers into her ear, and after a minute Zane slips away, slips back down to the gutter and rests her cheek against Ryan's arm.

When Jacqueline shuffles over to her sister at last, the shock in her eyes is still palpable and raw. *Come on, Ant, it's late. Let's go home.* Antoinette takes her hand, holds it tight. *I feel better.* Not good, not well, but *better*. The Loki-stone calmer than it has been for days, the weight and the tug of it less strident, less demanding. Her sister smiles wearily—*that's great, Ant, honestly*—drags her over to where a taxi is waiting, and tells her to climb on in. And as Antoinette peers through the rear windows, she sees him. Just a glimpse, not enough to be certain, but still.

She *does* see him.

A boy, tall and moon-skinned, slipping sinuous through the remaining looky-loos. His crow-black hair long, tied neat at the nape of his neck, and his eyes shining bright as blood-diamonds.

♨

Lina spends much of Thursday making and fielding Seventh Circle calls from her study at home. Cancellations and concerned clients, the entire RSVP list for tonight's aborted opening, plus a dozen other tawdry tasks. Everyone wants to know the juicy details. What and how and who and why. By the end of it, Lina has her patter honed word-perfect. Yes, it's a tragedy for all involved; yes, the police are investigating; no, she cannot reveal any further details. The occasional distraught artist with work still in storage, or irate client with acquisitions unshipped, she bounces straight to Dante. Her boss is handling the insurance side of things. Compensation and counselling both.

He's also handling Ryan Jellicoe.

The artist refuses to talk to Lina, which means he must have been told. Those witness descriptions last night: tall skinny male; long black hair; pale skin; nose sharp enough to cut paper. The officer wanting to know if that sounded familiar. Sounded like anyone they knew. Anyone who might have been hanging around. And Dante, no slackwit, thoughtfully rubbing his chin.

Sound's like your sister's ex-dropkick, doesn't it?

You mean Paul?

Paul, yeah. Becca told me he came by a couple weeks ago, tried to throw his weight around. She said that he scared her.

Dante, I hardly think—

But the officer was already writing down the details. Asking for Paul's last name. His place of residence. How long ago he broke up with her sister. The time since either of them last saw him, and anything else Lina might think relevant. *It's probably nothing, ma'am, as you say. But Arson will have my bollocks for breakfast if I don't lay it out all pretty for them.* And so Lina told him. Embellishing nothing, though of course omitting any and all references to Loki. As she spoke, the expression on Dante's face became more and more hostile.

Wish you'd told me the dude was a fucking nutter.

It's not as though I expected him to do anything.

He came in to my gallery, Jacks. Threatened my staff.

Dante, you can't seriously be blaming me for this.

No. A sigh, hand scratching across his hair. *No, of course not.*

But still, she'll be on indefinite leave from next week while Dante and Susan Keyes sort through the salvageables. And with her Fearless Leader thus far offering not a single word of commiseration or concern, Lina finds herself wondering if there will even be a position made available to her once Seventh Circle re-opens.

If Seventh Circle re-opens.

And so, when two detectives from the Arson Squad arrive on her doorstep late that afternoon, it feels pretty much par for the course. They pass her their business cards. Brush the rain from their shoulders and wipe their shoes on the mat before following her inside.

'Is your sister here?' the female detective asks after Lina has seated them in her living room. After they have both smiled politely and declined tea or coffee. She has already forgotten their names. 'Antoinette Paige? We're told she is living with you at the moment?'

'She's sleeping,' Lina says. 'It's not been a great week.'

'Oh?'

'Her ... our mother died on the weekend.' The detectives exchange a glance of what Lina can only describe as *keen interest*. 'Cancer,' she hastens to explain. 'She was ill for quite some time, so it wasn't entirely unexpected. But still, you know...'

The male detective looks sympathetic.

His partner maintains her poker face. 'We do need to talk with Antoinette rather urgently. It's in regards to Paul Morgenstern.'

'I thought this was going to be about the fire at Seventh Circle.'

'That's right,' says the female detective.

It takes Lina a few minutes to rouse her sister. A few more to encourage her into robe and slippers. Even then, she digs her heels in at the bedroom door. 'They won't leave until you go out there,' Lina whispers. 'It'll only be a couple of questions, and I'll be sitting right next to you. Just tell them the truth.' Ant frowns, and Lina rolls her eyes. 'Well, not the whole truth, obviously.'

As it turns out, the detectives do most of the talking. They slide three black-and-white photographs from a manila envelope. Spread them out on the coffee table. 'Are either of you able to identify this person?' Two headshots captured from different angles. One close-to-full body with only the feet cut off. Despite the graininess of the prints, the features are unmistakeable.

'It looks a lot like Paul,' Lina says carefully.

Her sister clears her throat. 'Maybe. They're a ... bit blurry.'

Pulled from Seventh Circle's security camera, they're told, with a positive identification already furnished by Paul Morgenstern's parents. The female detective slides the photos back into their envelope. 'We want you to appreciate how serious this situation might become.' It's now clear that it was Paul who broke into the gallery last night. Spraying as many works of art as he could with lighter fluid before setting fire to the place. Oil paint is its own accelerant. Once the flames took hold, they made short work of every canvas.

'It's lucky the MFB got to the scene so quickly,' the male detective says. 'Very lucky no one was inside at the time. We're told that Mr Moretti would sometimes work back late in his upstairs office—he wouldn't have stood a chance.'

'I don't…' Ant swallows hard. She speaks as though she needs to force each syllable from her tongue with a crowbar. 'I don't … understand why he would…'

The detectives frown at one another.

'She took some medication earlier,' Lina explains. She rubs the back of her sister's hand. 'It makes her a little sluggish sometimes.'

The lie seems to appease them. Paul's motive is not entirely clear, they admit, though it does appear to involve Antoinette. He made aggressive phone calls to the restaurant where she was employed around the same time he threatened Jacqueline in person at the gallery. It's possible that the only reason Simpatico hasn't been on the receiving end of a Molotov cocktail is that Antoinette no longer works there.

'I didn't ... quit. I'm only ... on leave.'

'Good for them, he never made that distinction. Antoinette, this guy is dangerous. We need to know when you last heard from him?'

'I don't ... Jacqueline?'

'The same day he came to Seventh Circle,' Lina tells them. 'He showed up here afterwards and I had to threaten to call the police to get him to leave.'

'He was violent?'

'He didn't hurt either of us, but ... yeah, it was pretty scary.'

'And you haven't seen or spoken to him since?'

'No,' Lina says. 'I honestly thought it was all over and done with.'

'Antoinette, how about you?'

Her sister shakes her head. 'No,' she whispers.

The female detective swaps pointed looks with her partner. 'Listen, if either of you girls *have* heard from Paul or know anything else you might not have told us about yet ... *now* would be a *very* good time.'

Ant is beginning to look frightened.

'Has he said something?' Lina asks. 'Because you can't trust him, you know. He came over spouting all this paranoia about how Ant was trying to turn his friends against him. Complete rubbish. She's made a clean break of it, or tried to at least.'

'We haven't spoken to him yet,' the male detective tells her. 'None of his family or friends have seen Mr Morgenstern for at least three days.'

His flat deserted but passably neat. No perishables left in the fridge, appliances all switched off. Enough gaps in his wardrobe and drawers to fill a small suitcase, and no personal effects of any real value left behind. The alert issued on his car is yet to bear fruit, but perhaps more significant is the large amount of cash he withdrew from an ATM in the city only yesterday. Not enough to keep anyone in steak dinners for long, but the transaction all but emptied his account. And provided a very nice mugshot courtesy of the inbuilt security camera.

Her sister's holding her hand so tightly now, Lina is afraid something might snap. 'So he's just vanished? You don't know where he is?'

'This was clearly planned in advance,' the female detective says. 'But at this stage, we don't know whether he's on the run or whether he might have gone to ground somewhere. Perhaps nearby. Frankly, I worry this isn't over.'

'You said before he was dangerous.'

'He's meticulous and thorough, and you've already stated that you've had cause to be scared of him in the past. I'd call that dangerous.' She leans across. Looks Ant straight in the eye. 'Honey, whatever relationship you might have had with this guy, you don't owe him anything anymore. Certainly not your protection.'

Ant's lower lip trembles. 'I don't *know*.'

'We're being straight with you,' Lina tells them. 'I have no idea where Paul is, but I would give him up in a heartbeat if I did.'

'Okay.' The male detective flips a page in his notebook. 'Just one last thing you might be able to help us with. There's a supposed friend of his, seems to have gone missing as well. German girl by the name of Greta Baum, or Bauer? Hasn't been around for a few weeks.'

'*Baum*,' Ant whispers. 'I heard she … went home.'

'Back to Germany? That's what a couple people have told us.' He scribbles a note then flips the cover shut. 'Not our case, really. Not anyone's case unless she gets herself reported as actually missing.' He shrugs. 'Just for a moment there, looked like we might have had a Bonnie and Clyde pyro-thing happening.'

His partner looks less than amused.

After the detectives have left, Lina herds her sister into the shower. Puts some pasta on to boil for dinner. She doesn't want to think about Loki, or Paul. Doesn't want any of those images filling her brain. Lighter fluid squirting from a can. Flames consuming canvas faster than flight. Masterpieces twisting to charcoal and ash.

And, rising phoenix above it all: Loki, *her Loki*, mouth roaring open with laughter and pride.

I'd call that dangerous.

Lina picks up the phone, as she's done every night this past week. Calls the house where Sally Paige used to live. The house where she died. Holds the handset to her ear and listens to the endless hollow echo of its ring.

Except tonight, unlike every other night, someone picks up. Says nothing. Simply breathes and beckons and waits.

'Loki?' Lina whispers. 'Is that you? Are you there?'

And just before he hangs up, she hears something else. A sound which may be chuckling, which may be static, which may be her name choked soft in his throat—

—and Lina's heart skips, and beats faster, and bleeds.

26

The rain drizzles to a desultory close as they turn onto the winding mountain road. Sharon switches off the wipers. Glances in the rear-view mirror. Lina, riding shotgun, takes her thumbnail from her mouth. 'She'll be fine. Don't worry.'

'I don't like this, Lina. We should take her to a doctor.'

'I told you, it's not a doctor she needs.'

Lina twists around. Smiles at her sister sitting right behind her. Ant stares out of the window. Her eyes are glazed and motionless. They track nothing. Not the whiplash of passing trees. Not the wave of Lina's hand. She hasn't spoken since yesterday evening. Since the detectives left with their notebooks and evident frustration. Has done little more than stand or sit or lie passively down, not moving from whichever spot it is that Lina leaves her. Not a mouthful of food has passed her lips. And only a small glass of water. Another half of apple juice. Ingested with slow, robotic sips at her sister's anxious behest.

Bringing her up here can only help. Must help.

I feel better.

Those words whispered in the back of the taxi, Seventh Circle's charred remains still smoking the air outside. Ant scanning the dwindling crowd and Lina too distracted, too busy with the driver to follow her sister's gaze. But he must have been there. Been close. And *close* is what Ant seems to need.

As they mount the crest of the driveway, Lina feels the tightness in her chest unlock. The Commodore is back in the carport again. Parked too close to the centre, so Sharon pulls up on the gravel behind it.

'Thanks for bringing us up here.' Lina gets out of the car. Opens the back door and reaches in to unbuckle her sister's seatbelt.

The driver's-side door slams. Sharon crunches around to the rear of the car and pops the boot. 'I'm not about to take off, if that's what you're thinking.' She yanks out the suitcase Lina hurriedly packed together. 'Not with Ant like that.'

Lina guides her sister from the vehicle, one hand on her head so that she doesn't crack her skull on the roof. Ant is pliant, malleable. She unfolds like a paper doll. Squints as the sun slips out from behind a cloud. Lina glances at the Commodore hulking in the carport. Sharon only knows about the fire, not about Paul. Though it's bound to come out sooner or later and the woman is far from stupid. If she meets Loki now, then later hears that Paul is a suspect—a *missing* suspect—she would most certainly put two and two together.

'Ant needs to rest,' Lina tells her. 'I'm not sure you should stay.'

'I'm not sure I asked your permission,' Sharon says.

The house is unlocked, but empty. Lina settles her sister down on the couch in the living room. Tucks a couple of stray curls back behind her ears. Ant stares straight ahead. Her mouth twitches open but she doesn't speak. Lina pushes her jaw gently closed again. 'Are you thirsty? I'll get you some water.'

First, she checks the rest of the house. Loki isn't here, but he has been. The bed in Lina's old room has been slept in, the covers left rumpled. A handful of dishes are drying on the rack and there's fresh milk in the fridge. An empty pizza box leans beside the kitchen bin.

'Who's living here?' Sharon asks.

'Loki.'

'Your new boyfriend?'

'My...' Lina frowns. 'Just Loki.' She peers out the window at the sodden, unkempt backyard. Perhaps he's walked down to pay his respects to Charlie. Perhaps ... she thinks of the little shed, of its pushbolt and padlock. Then she pushes the rest of that thought to one side.

'You made me drive all the way up here so you could see your *boyfriend*?' Sharon sounds incredulous. Furious. 'Ant's turning into a bloody vegetable and all you can think about is getting your end in?'

Lina glares at her. 'It's somewhat more complicated than that.'

ॐ

Gradually, the Loki-stone settles. That fretful, frightful weight relaxes, still very much present but no longer pulling with such frenetic demand, and Antoinette loosens, finds a small crack and slips, not free, never free, but slightly apart. Loki is close now, Loki and Jacqueline both, for the first time in what seems like forever and this strengthens her, returns to her a shard of the self she has given them. Not a lot, not nearly as much as she would like, but maybe enough for what she needs.

Somewhere in the house, her sister and Sharon are arguing. Voices raised and tense, and she doesn't need to understand the words to know they are arguing about her. Antoinette gathers herself. Everything that she is and was and ever might be, gathers it all. Shapes it, crafts it with such care and precision, this work more delicate than the balancing of angels on pinheads, this act which may be her last. When she is done, Antoinette takes her creation and tips it into the world. Sends it on its tentative, timorous way, then allows herself to fall. But even falling, even sinking down exhausted and spent, she finds cause to wonder.

And to marvel, that grief and hope can taste so much the same.

Sharon trails away mid-sentence. Her eyes widen, mouth gapes. She points at something over Lina's right shoulder and so Lina turns, a greeting for Loki forming on her lips. But it's not Loki who stands there.

The little girl is perhaps six or seven years old. Brown eyes and olive skin, coffee-coloured curls bobbing around her shoulders. She is wearing a short blue dress with a mermaid on the bodice. A school of them swim around the hem. Lina remembers that dress. Shopping with Sally Paige a week out from Ant's birthday. *It's your present for your sister, you can choose whatever you like.* The mermaid dress the only one without any pink whatsoever, merely greens and yellows amid an ocean of blue. Even the mermaid's skin was a subtle, tantalising turquoise.

Sally Paige hadn't cared for it, but Ant wore the thing to rags.

'She … she just *appeared*,' Sharon is saying. 'She was just *there*.'

'Hello,' Lina says cautiously. 'What's your name?'

The little girl wrinkles her nose and shrugs. A huge, theatrical heave of those skinny shoulders. She holds out the skirt of her dress like a ballet tutu. Executes a wobbly, one-legged twirl.

'Where did she come from?' Sharon whispers.

Lina ignores her. 'Are you Antoinette? Is *that* your name?'

'Silly,' the girl giggles. 'I'm not *her*.'

'But you're a … perfection, right? She made you?'

'I'm a whimsy!' Another twirl. 'Do you like my dress?'

'It's very pretty.'

'It has mermaids! I want to be a mermaid!'

'But mermaids need to live in the sea. If you were a mermaid, you wouldn't be able to be here with *us*.'

The girl stops twirling. 'Yes,' she says, unsmiling now. 'I know.'

Sharon tugs on Lina's sleeve. '*What* is she?'

'I'll explain later,' Lina promises. The little girl is sitting now, cross-legged in a way that would have given Sally Paige conniptions. Her underpants are yellow with bright pink spots. Lina smiles and kneels down. 'Did you want to tell me something? Did my sister want you to tell me something?'

'It hurts her.' The girl's face is grave. 'It makes her tired and sad all the time, and it gets worse every day. She's worried that soon she won't be able to play with anyone anymore ever.'

'Is she talking about Ant?' Sharon asks.

'Shhh, let her speak. This is important.'

'*You* make her feel bad,' the little girl continues. 'You and *him*. It's too hard. She can't play with both of you at the same time. She thinks she'll have to go away soon. And she's frightened. She's *so frightened*.' Tears slip down her cheeks. Down Lina's cheeks as well. 'You have to make him go away, Jacqueline. She can't play with him anymore. She only wants to play with you.'

Lina swallows. 'How do I do that? How do I make him go away?'

The girl's eyes are dark and lethal. 'You know how.'

'Can't she just ... let go of him somehow?'

'She isn't allowed. Someone else needs to stop him playing.'

'What if—what if I can't do that?'

The girl shakes her head, those brown curls bouncing prettily. Lina feels a sharp, yearning throb deep inside. 'You have to do it soon,' the girl says. 'She doesn't know how long she can stay here. And once she goes away, she doesn't think she'll ever be allowed to come back.'

'How—how soon?'

'Very.'

'What if it's already too late?'

The girl shakes her head again. She scrambles to her feet and takes a shy, hesitant step forward. 'I have to go soon, too. Do you think it will be dark?'

'I really don't know,' Lina says.

'There are monsters in the dark.'

'Come here, sweetheart.' She opens her arms, a cry catching in her throat as the girl falls into her embrace. Small hands steal around her back, pluck at the ends of her hair. She hugs that small, miraculous body as tight as she dares.

'She knows what she's asking you to do,' the girl whispers into her ear. 'She *knows* and it makes her really sad. But she says there isn't any other way to fix it. And she's really, *really* sorry. She wishes she could do it herself. She wishes she *had* done it herself. She wants you to know that.'

Lina swallows a sob.

'Don't trust him,' the girl says. 'There's nothing he wouldn't do.'

And then she jumps, startled, as the back door screeches open. Booted feet stomp through the adjacent laundry and the girl twists around in Lina's arms, slippery as fishtails. Her eyes narrow—distinctly, disturbingly *un*childlike now—as Loki strides into the kitchen and stops dead, surprise wrestling fury for possession of his face.

'Who is *she*?' he demands.

Before Lina can answer, the little girl leans in and kisses her on the cheek. 'Be careful, Jacqueline,' she whispers and then she—

—isn't there.

Loki looks stunned. 'She was...'

'Another fendly. A whimsy, whatever you want to call them.' Lina's arms drop empty to her sides. The smell of the little girl's scalp lingers with her. A clean smell, warm and sweet.

'Antoinette's here?' The jeans Loki is wearing are splattered with mud. His hands as well. 'You brought her with you?'

'Of course I brought her with me,' Lina says, getting to her feet. Behind her, Sharon makes a quiet mewling sound. She has almost forgotten about Sharon. 'It's all right,' she tells the woman.

'That's not *Paul*,' Sharon says. 'I don't know what he is, or what that *girl* was, but he's not...' She steps back, bumps into the sink. 'All that stuff Ant was raving about on Monday is true, isn't it?'

Loki glowers. Specks of dirt fall to the floor as he flexes his hands.

'Sharon...' Lina puts herself between them.

'I thought she was delirious. Strung out or something after her Mum died—but fuck. *Fuck*. She can actually *make* people? She made another Paul? Jacqueline, she made *you*?'

'I'm not Paul,' Loki says through gritted teeth.

'No.' Sharon stares at him with a kind of horrified fascination. 'But you're a damn impressive copy.'

Loki is upon her in less than a heartbeat. Hands around her neck, thumbs digging deep, he presses her body against the edge of the sink. Bends her backwards as she flails her arms. His lips curl. He looks like he wants to tear out her throat with his teeth.

'Stop!' Lina grabs his right arm with both hands. It's like trying to break a branch from an oak tree. Sharon's eyes roll towards her own. Pleading. Petrified. Wet sounds choke from the woman's gasping mouth. Lina changes tack. Launches herself at Loki instead, throws her whole weight against him, low down beneath his ribs. Not a crippling blow by any means, but enough to distract him, to jolt him off balance.

Enough to give Sharon a chance to wrench herself loose.

Which she does, her elbow glancing a blow to his jaw as she pinwheels free, though it might have been a kiss for all it seems to bother Loki. He pushes Lina aside, the quasi-gentle swat of a mother cat, then claws after Sharon. Catches her shirt. Pulls her shrieking towards him. Before slamming the heel of his hand into her back, doubling the power of her own forward momentum.

Sharon stumbles. Her feet slide on the tiled floor.

And she falls.

But as Loki begins to move, Lina snatches a knife from the dish rack and pushes past him. Plants herself once again in his path.

'Lina,' he says. 'What are you doing?'

'I'm not going to let you hurt her.' The knife feels too small. It could barely cut steak. '*Ant* wouldn't want you to hurt her.'

'This is my home and I won't have her here. She stinks of *him*.'

'Then she'll go.' Behind her, Sharon is coughing. Loki takes a step forward and Lina raises the knife. 'I'll use it, if I have to.'

An ugly leer slices his face. 'No you won't.'

He moves so quickly, she has no time to react. One hand closing around her wrist, squeezing until she cries out, until her fingers loosen enough for the other to slip the knife from her grasp. His face is blank, all the more menacing for it.

There's nothing he wouldn't do.

Lina's stomach clenches. 'Please…'

But he merely dips his head and steps away. 'Tell her to go then, Lina. Make sure she never comes back.'

'He's psychotic,' Sharon says once they're safely out of the house. Her voice is hoarse. The livid marks around her throat are going to bruise. 'You can't possibly stay up here with him, either of you.'

'Yes, he is,' Lina agrees. 'But yes, we can. We *have* to.'

'He'll slit your damn throats while you sleep.'

'No, not us. Never us.' Or at least, never her sister.

'You heard the girl, or whatever she was. Ant doesn't want him around anymore. He's *hurting* her, the girl said.'

'Not in the way you think.'

'Jacqueline, let me call the police. I'll drive around the corner and —'

'You don't understand. We need to stay close, Loki and me. The further apart we are from my sister, the harder it is for her. The more it *drains* her. If the police come, if they take Loki away…'

I don't know what effect that might have. But you've seen her. Do you want her to get even worse?'

Sharon looks down at the ground. Scuffs through the gravel with the toe of her shoe. 'I'm not sure how much I believe about … all that.'

'You believe enough. You know you do.'

'Then don't ask me to walk out on her.'

Lina rubs hard at her forehead. 'How about just for the weekend? Give me two more days to try to fix this. Please.'

'What are you going to do in two days?'

'I don't know yet, but I can't do *anything* if you hang around.' She jerks her chin towards the woman's neck. 'I won't be able to protect you, either.'

Sharon still seems doubtful. 'Just for the weekend?'

'Just for the weekend. If you don't hear from us by Monday morning, then by all means, send in the cavalry.'

Privately, Lina doubts she'll get that much time. All it will take is a whisper in Sharon's ear. A tweet or Facebook update from someone who's had a chat with two friendly detectives. Or simply a more detailed press release. *Arson suspect on the run.* One of those grainy CCTV photos flashed helpfully on the screen. Because Sharon *isn't* stupid. And although she's scared right now—scared enough to be coaxed to a strategic retreat—Lina doesn't see that lasting for long.

'Okay,' Sharon says finally. 'But if anything happens, if he touches her—'

'He won't, I can promise you that.'

'I love her, Jacqueline. Just so you know.'

Lina nods. 'So do I.'

Sharon climbs into her boxy red car and starts the engine. Sits there for a moment, slumped against the seat, before rolling down the window. 'Why do I get the feeling, I'm about to make a really, *really* bad decision here?

Lina smiles grimly. 'Sometimes, that's all we can do.'

Loki has washed his hands. They smell of grapefruit detergent and are still damp when he holds her face between them. Lina allows this. Closes her eyes as he kisses her. 'I'm sorry,' he whispers. 'Seeing Greta up here, I got so mad…'

'She's not Greta anymore. She never was, really.'

'It doesn't matter. She's still a part of *his* world; I can't have her in mine.'

'And you thought throttling her would solve that?'

'I *wasn't* thinking, I told you.' He sighs. Draws away. 'Lina, you know I would never hurt *you*.'

'What I know is, you started that fire at Seventh Circle.'

Loki studies her face as though he is trying to read between its lines. 'That place was stealing too much of your time and your energy, and you hated it.'

'I didn't—I *don't* hate it.'

'It's not as if you need to work there anymore.'

'Because I can *waltz* into another job, just like that.' She snaps her fingers. 'What with gallery management being such a wide open field and all.'

'Why do you have to work anywhere? We have this house now, rent-free, and you said that Sally left you and Antoinette a little bit of money.' He grins. 'I can *charm* almost anything else we might need, Lina. You don't have to work.'

She stares at him, dumbfounded. 'And if I *want* to work?'

'Really?' he snorts. 'In a shitty gallery with a shitty boss, pretentious painters pawing at you all day?'

'What the hell are you talking about?'

'Guy with the dreadlocks. I saw him. Putting his arms around you, flirting with you. Couldn't takes his eyes off your arse.'

'Ryan?' Lina shakes her head. 'When did you—'

'Does it matter?' His voice is flat as coffin lids. 'I saw.'

'So you set fire to his paintings because you were *jealous*?'

He smiles. 'Call it my second bird.'

'I don't under—'

And then she does. Paul didn't disappear because Loki was worried about him getting arrested for the gallery fire, worried he would inform the police that a certain doppelganger might have had something to do with it instead.

No, flip that over. See how it tastes.

Loki burned down the gallery *to provide a reason* for Paul's disappearance.

'Where were you before?' Lina asks. 'When we arrived?'

'I went for a walk out back.'

'You weren't doing some gardening?'

'Gardening?'

'Your hands were dirty.'

He looks at them, clean now, white and shining. 'I buried a bit of rubbish out in the bush, couple of days back. After all the rain we had here last night, I was worried the top layer of soil might have washed away.'

'Rubbish?'

'Just some useless old trash I didn't want to keep around.'

'You know...' A lump forms hard in her throat. She coughs, tries unsuccessfully to clear it. 'I'm fairly sure it's illegal to dump rubbish in a national park. You can get into a lot of trouble.'

'Only if I'm caught.' Loki smiles, thin and smug. 'Big place, that park. Massive. Bury something well enough out there, it might never have existed in the first place.'

Lina perches her sister on the side of the tub. Runs water in the adjoining shower cubicle. Hot enough to steam, hard enough to flense unwary skin. Makes doubly sure the bathroom door is locked. Then she crouches at her sister's feet. Looks into those dark, unstaring eyes. Takes one of Ant's hands in her own.

'I need to be sure,' she whispers. 'This isn't something I can take back.'

Steam swirls lazily. Her sister doesn't move.

'I thought perhaps, you could make her appear again. Please?

I still have some questions…' She squeezes her eyes against the threat of tears. 'Ant, I *love* you, you *know* that I love you, but this … I just need to know that it will work. That it won't be for nothing. Loki, he…' The tears come anyway. 'He's not right, is he? He was never *right*, but he could get better. Couldn't he?'

She isn't defending what he did. What happened with Paul. No, she's not defending that. But it's done now, it's *done* and there's no changing it, and perhaps it's a turning point. Perhaps now that Paul is … *gone*, perhaps now Loki will get better. If Lina helps him, stands by him. Except, *except*. There's Sharon, who'll be wearing a scarf for the next week or two. And the thing with Ryan, the thing that meant Loki has been spying on her, keeping tabs. *Stalking.*

Lina places a hand over her naval. All that flat, empty flesh. She remembers the solid, squirmy warmth of the little girl in her arms. The sweet smell of those curls. Her heart aches with absence. 'Does it have to be so soon?' she whispers. 'Couldn't it wait a week or two, a month? Until there's a chance for me to…'

She's doesn't know how long she can stay here.

She doesn't think she'll be allowed to come back.

'How do I know you're not already gone?' Her mouth trembles, and caves. She presses her face into the hem of her sister's skirt, that black velvet so lush against her skin. Her sobs soak into it, muffled and lost. But when she looks up again, Ant is seated in precisely the same position. Still staring, not staring, at the towel rack in front of her. Lips motionless. Eyes dry and unblinking. 'Ant, please. I just need you to show me that it's going to be all right.'

Lina isn't certain exactly what she's searching for in her sister's face, but she knows when she fails to find it.

Loki wanders into the kitchen just as she's opening a new tin of tea. The strong scent of peppermint wafts through the air. Beneath it, a subtler note of anise. 'Nice,' he says. 'Make me one?' He seems happier now, more relaxed.

Lina smiles. 'Of course. I'm putting on a pot.'

'How's Antoinette?'

'She's sleeping, I think. Needed my help to shower and put on her pyjamas. I had to tuck her into bed like she was two years old.'

'She'll get better,' Loki says. 'She made a whimsy today—that has to mean she's getting stronger, right?'

'I don't know. Honestly, I don't think that she is.' Lina shakes her head. 'What if it never changes, Loki? She might be stuck like that forever and—'

'Shhh.' He places a finger across her lips. 'It doesn't matter. We'll take care of her, whatever happens, or doesn't happen. We're a family, the three of us; that's what we do.' Moving behind her, he slips his arms around her waist. Kisses the side of her neck. 'And maybe there could be more than just the *three* of us. Can you imagine that? A couple of young kidlets running around the place?'

Lina tries to keep her hand steady as she loads the teapot with leaves. 'I was thinking we could take her to a hospital.'

'Why?'

'They could run some tests, perhaps find out what's causing—'

'We know what's causing it.' His lips move to the other side of her throat. 'I don't know how you can think it would help. Even if some nosy labcoats did manage to work out the full story, what do you reckon they'd do then? Who do you think would take priority in their eyes?'

'But if someone *could* help her…'

'Lina.' He turns her to face him. 'Antoinette *chose* this. She could have passed me on to her mother when she had the chance, but she didn't—because she wanted to keep us both. And now we'll keep her, for as long as she needs us.'

'But—'

That finger again on her lips. 'No buts. She takes care of us and we take care of her. It couldn't be simpler.' The kettle shrieks to a boil. He kisses her on both cheeks. 'Hey, how about we flake out with a movie tonight? There's a whole bunch of burnt discs in there, including a copy of *Casablanca*.'

'You must have seen that a thousand times already,' Lina says, filling the teapot to the brim. The lid settles in place with a loud ceramic *chink*.

Loki is shaking his head. 'Not once.'

'Oh? Ant loves that film, I just thought…'

His eyes have a cracked, broken-glass glitter. 'She might have watched *Casablanca* with someone else, but not with *me*. *I've* never seen a minute of it.'

She forces a smile onto her face. 'Then we should definitely remedy that. You go in and set it up, I'll finish making the tea.'

Lina waits for him to leave. For the sound of the television to drift in from the living room. Once she is sure, once she is certain, she pours peppermint tea into her favourite mug. Plain white, a delicate garland of roses running down the handle. The second one—the mug with the tartan, the mug Loki seems to like—she fills less than halfway. The oleander has been steeping in water all evening. Those dark green leaves cut fine with a knife she never cares to see again. Mixed with an old box of peppermint tea, another of rosehip. Sealed tight in Tupperware and tucked beneath the sink. Right at the back of the bottom shelf. Waiting.

For now.

Lina pauses, listens for any noise of warning. The creak of couch springs. The pad of bare feet down the hall. Nothing.

She drains the murky liquid through a sieve, then tops up the tartan mug. Stirs. It's lukewarm, so she zaps it in the microwave for thirty seconds. Adds three drops of the peppermint essence she found in the cupboard. Stirs again. It doesn't smell too bad. Strange, but definitely minty.

She doesn't dare sample it.

Oleandrin. Beautiful word; deadly poison.

Posited by some as an alternative treatment for cancer, though an unproven and astonishingly dangerous one. Googling for information—back when they first learned Sally Paige was ill, back when they knew nothing else—Lina was surprised to recognise the pretty, pink-flowered shrubs.

She picks up the mugs from the bench.

And supposes, grimly, that Sally Paige would at least appreciate the symmetry of the situation.

Her hands shake as she walks into the living room. Her heart speeds. She almost abandons the plan. Almost retraces her steps, tips the whole evil concoction into the sink. Because Loki is *right there*. Smiling and beautiful. Jumping up to rescue his mug as it almost tips from her grasp.

'Are you okay?' he asks.

'I'm—I'm a bit cold, actually. It's come over chilly tonight.'

'Come here.' Back on the couch, he pats the cushion beside him. 'I'll keep you nice and warm.'

'Perhaps I should go fetch Ant. She might like to watch with us.'

'She's asleep, you said.'

'I'll wake her up.'

'Lina, don't be silly. Sit down and drink your tea.' As though to demonstrate, he takes a sip of his own. Grimaces. Peers into the mug as though he expects something to crawl out and bite him. 'This tastes weird.'

'It's a new brand. If it's too bitter, I can bring you some honey.'

'That's okay,' he says, drinking another mouthful. 'It's fine. A bit strong on the peppermint maybe, but it'll grow on me.'

Lina holds her mug with both hands. She really does feel cold. Feels like she might never be warm again. 'Are you sure you want to drink it?'

Because for one glorious, terrible moment, she teeters right on the fulcrum. If he says *no*, she will take the poison from him. Because she loves him, *she loves him*. And in that moment, it doesn't matter what he's done. What he might do again.

If he just says the word, she will—

'Lina.' Loki smiles, indulgent but edged. 'How could I refuse anything from you? Now sit down, please, and let's just watch this damn film.'

So Lina sits. She thinks of her sister. She thinks of Loki.

And she makes her choice.

27

ina opens her eyes as the twin-engine airplane taxis down the runway for the second time that morning. As shots are fired and usual suspects rounded up. As fog descends around Humphrey Bogart and Claude Rains, and the final reprise of *La Marseillaise* swells from the television speakers.

'Ant?' she whispers croakily. Lifts her head from her sister's lap and levers herself upright. 'Hey, are you awake?' Her sister is looking to her left, out of the living room windows to the grey, dismal sky. Lina can't remember turning Ant's head like that. But she can't remember *not* turning it either. And there is already far too much she would like to forget.

Loki, curled cramped on the couch; on the stale mattress of Sally Paige's bed; on the bathroom tiles where he slumps even now, alone and slowly stiffening. Blood and vomit tracked through the house, along with other vile secretions his failing body thought fit to purge. Mouth rictus, eyes bulging bright and dilated. Cursing her at the end, those last heart-twitchy hours before consciousness deserted him for a lost cause. Before he slipped, before he fell, before he was pushed, *bruised and broken, into oblivion's hungry mouth.*

Not an easy death. Not quick. Oleander no angel come to sing him to his rest.

Lina wipes ill-earned tears from her eyes.

I'm sorry, Loki, I'm so sorry. I didn't know it would be that bad.

Huddled on the couch with Ant since dawn. Waiting, waiting. Twice rising to check Loki's corpse. Fish for a pulse, a heartbeat, the barest skimmer of breath. To be sure, to be certain. Of nothing, *nothing.*

But this ground remains untested and Lina will not give up. Not yet.

Sunday night. Tomorrow night. Counting down the hours on her fingers. The number of times *Casablanca* can play, and play again. While her sister fights. Battles through fogbanks of her own. Finds her way home, finds her way to Lina. Because she must. Because it can't have been for *nothing.*

And if she doesn't? If those Moroccan-spun hours all pass unremarked, what then, sister dearest, what then?

Lina tucks up her legs. Leans against her sister's shoulder.

'I love you, Ant,' she says. 'Please, you need to come back now.'

Choosing, for the moment, not to ponder the oleander steeping fresh in the kitchen. Not to consider that even a single perfection may yet be one parasite too many to bear. And not, not, *not* to contemplate Loki, *her Loki*, or the betrayal that burned absolute in his eyes.

Lina points the remote at the television instead. Opening credits play across the screen. Maps and markets and *La Marseillaise* once more. Once more and again.

And so, choice made for good or ill, Lina sits.

Waiting, waiting, waiting with the others in the dry Casablancan streets.

ACKNOWLEDGEMENTS

I honestly doubt there's enough gratitude in the world for everyone who provided advice, encouragement, criticism and support during the writing of this particular novel, but here goes:

Elizabeth Markham, Natalie Potts, Bren MacDibble, Tracey Rolfe and Rjurik Davidson of the SuperNOVA writers group, for insightful critiques of very early chapters.

Kate Eltham, Robert Hoge, Angela Slatter, Mark Curtis, Paul Garrety and Michele Cashmore, as well as the indomitable Sean Williams and Alison Goodman, for crucial flensing undertaken at the Edge Writers Retreat.

Cat Sparks, Karen Miller, Thoraiya Dyer, Joanne Anderton, Alisa Krasnostein, Amanda Pillar, Glenda Larke, Rowena Cory Daniells, Tansy Rayner Roberts, Narelle Harris, Kaaron Warren and Kim Wilkins, for random words of advice and encouragement along the way. (Which they've most likely all forgotten by now, but which I will always hold dear.)

Jules Mond, for vital and speedy assistance with medical-related research. (Any errors are all down to me.)

Ellen Gregory, Helen Merrick, Julia Svaganovic and Ian Mond, for stepping up to be my enthusiastic, if occasionally traumatised, beta readers.

Ellen and Alison and Angela, again and again and again, for unmitigated support, feedback and general ass-kicking when I needed it most. Much love to you all!

Alisa Krasnostein—editor, publisher and friend—for her patience, support and indefatigable ambition.

Cornelia Craciun, my mother, beta reader and proof reader extraordinaire.

And Jason. For everything. Always.

MADIGAN
MINE

KIRSTYN McDERMOTT

**REPRINT COMING SOON FROM
TWELFTH PLANET PRESS**

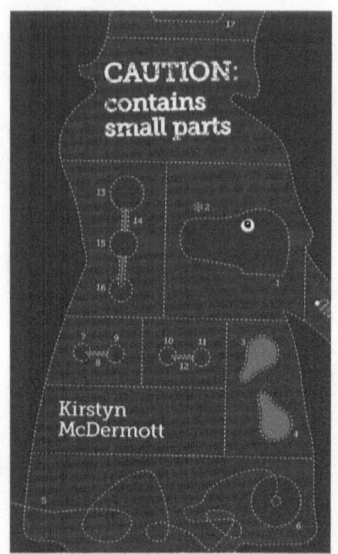

aurealis
awards
FINALIST

Caution:
Contains Small Parts

Kirstyn McDermott

Caution: Contains Small Parts is an intimate, unsettling collection from award-winning author Kirstyn McDermott.

A creepy wooden dog that refuses to play dead.

A gifted crisis counsellor and the mysterious, melancholy girl she cannot seem to reach.

A once-successful fantasy author whose life has become a horror story—now with added unicorns.

An isolated woman whose obsession with sex dolls takes a harrowing, unexpected turn.

'Kirstyn McDermott's prose is darkly magical, insidious and insistent. Once her words get under your skin, they are there to stay.' — *Angela Slatter*

'Kirstyn is an exciting writer in an exciting place. It's a pleasure to discover her.' — *Kij Johnson*

aurealis
awards
FINALIST

Bad Power

Deborah Biancotti

Hate superheroes? Yeah. They probably hate you, too.

'There are two kinds of people with lawyers on tap, Mr Grey. The powerful and the corrupt.'

'Thank you.'

'For implying you're powerful?'

'For imagining those are two different groups.'

From Crawford Award nominee Deborah Biancotti comes this sinister short story suite, a pocketbook police procedural set in a world where the victories are relative and the defeats are absolute. Bad Power celebrates the worst kind of powers both supernatural and otherwise, in the interlinked tales of five people—and how far they'll go.

If you like Haven and Heroes, you'll love Bad Power.

'These appetisingly wicked stories give you the perfect taste of Biancotti's talents.' — *Ann VanderMeer*

Twelve Planets

Locus Recommended Reading List for Best Collection in 2012

aurealis awards FINALIST

2013 DITMAR AWARD winner

Through Splintered Walls

Kaaron Warren

From Bram Stoker Award nominated author Kaaron Warren, comes Book 6 in the Twelve Planets collection series, including the Shirley Jackson Award winning 'Sky'.

Country road, city street, mountain, creek.

These are stories inspired by the beauty, the danger, the cruelty, emptiness, loneliness and perfection of the Australian landscape.

'Kaaron Warren is a powerful, take-no-prisoners author with an uncanny talent, a deliciously depraved flair for black comedy and a twisted nerve.' — *Alan Kelly*